7/16

W9-APM-189

COMPASS SOUTH

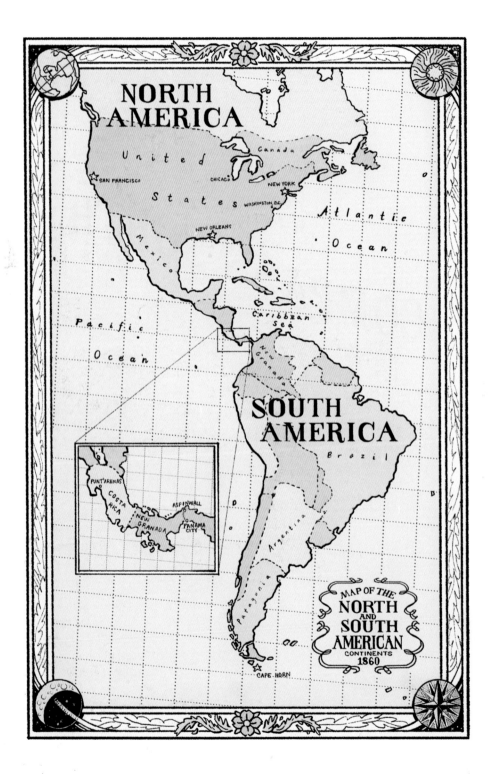

NORTH AMERICA

United States

SAN FRANCISCO

CHICAGO

NEW YORK

WASHINGTON D.C.

Canada

Atlantic

Ocean

NEW ORLEANS

Mexico

Pacific

Ocean

Caribbean Sea

New Granada

SOUTH AMERICA

Brazil

Argentina

Patagonia

PUNTARENAS

COSTA RICA

ASPINWALL

NEW GRANADA

PANAMA CITY

CAPE HORN

MAP OF THE
NORTH
AND
SOUTH
AMERICAN
CONTINENTS
1860

HOPE LARSON

COMPASS SOUTH
FOUR POINTS
BOOK 1

Illustrations by
REBECCA MOCK

MARGARET FERGUSON BOOKS
FARRAR STRAUS GIROUX
New York

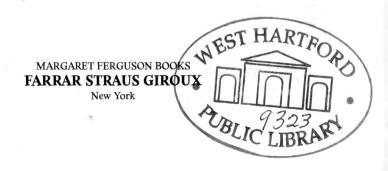

WEST HARTFORD
PUBLIC LIBRARY
9323

To Will, the original red-haired brother
—H.L.

To John and Kelly, my Alex and Cleo
—R.M.

Farrar Straus Giroux Books for Young Readers
175 Fifth Avenue, New York 10010

Text copyright © 2016 by Hope Larson
Art copyright © 2016 by Rebecca Mock
All rights reserved
Printed in China by Toppan Leefung Printing Ltd.,
Dongguan City, Guangdong Province
Designed by Andrew Arnold
First edition, 2016
1 3 5 7 9 10 8 6 4 2

mackids.com

Library of Congress Control Number: 2015039907

ISBN: 978-0-374-30043-2

Our books may be purchased in bulk for promotional, educational,
or business use. Please contact your local bookseller or the Macmillan
Corporate and Premium Sales Department at (800) 221-7945 ext. 5442
or by e-mail at MacmillanSpecialMarkets@macmillan.com.

J
GRAPHIC 9.21
NOVEL
LARSON
HOPE

TABLE OF CONTENTS

Prologue 7

1 The Black Hook Gang 11

2 Imposters 37

3 To Sea 65

4 The Breaker and the Boiler 81

5 The Pocketknife 99

6 Cape Horn 123

7 Tooth and Nail 153

8 *El Caleuche* 181

9 City in a Cloud 203

PROLOGUE

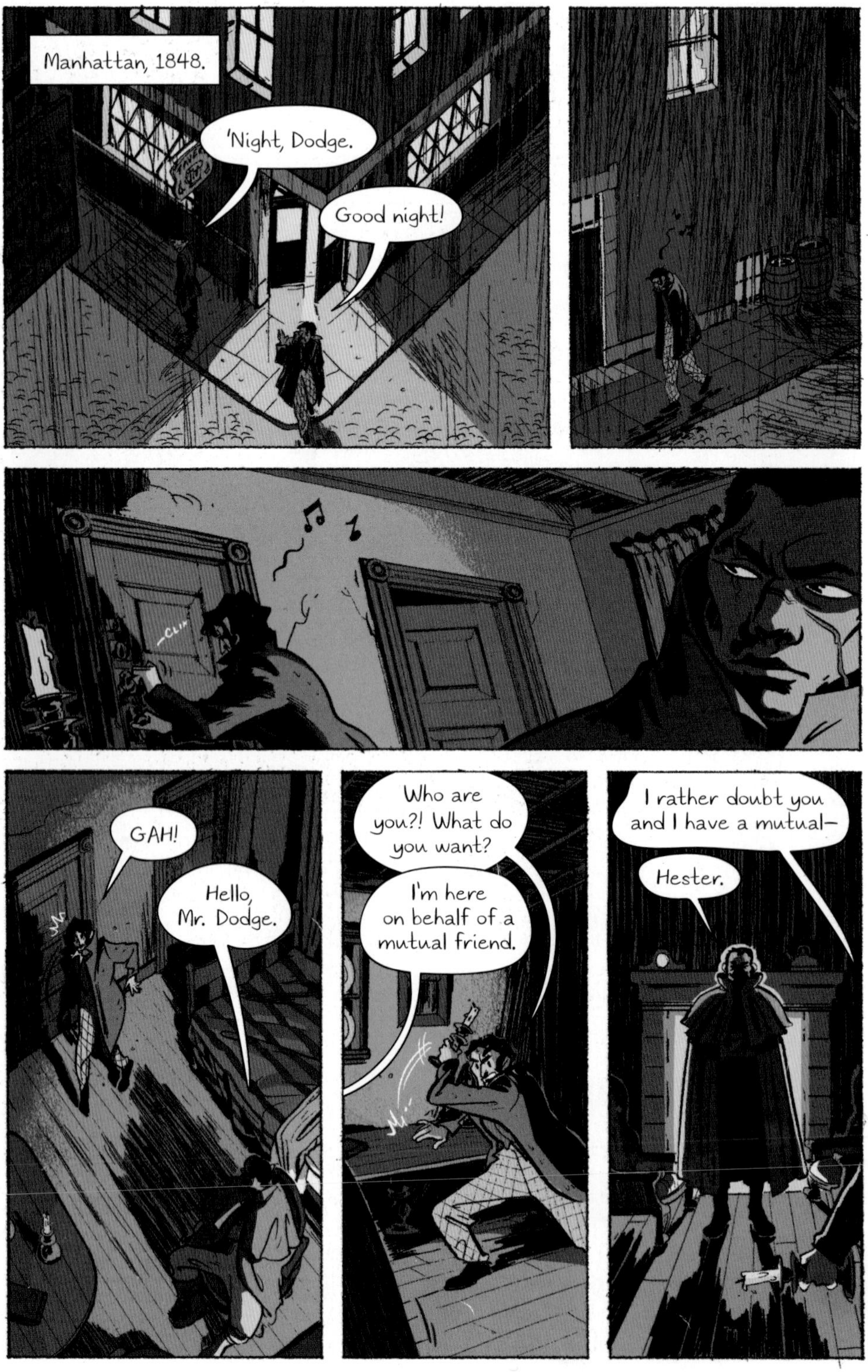
Manhattan, 1848.
'Night, Dodge.
Good night!
GAH!
Hello, Mr. Dodge.
Who are you?! What do you want?
I'm here on behalf of a mutual friend.
I rather doubt you and I have a mutual—
Hester.

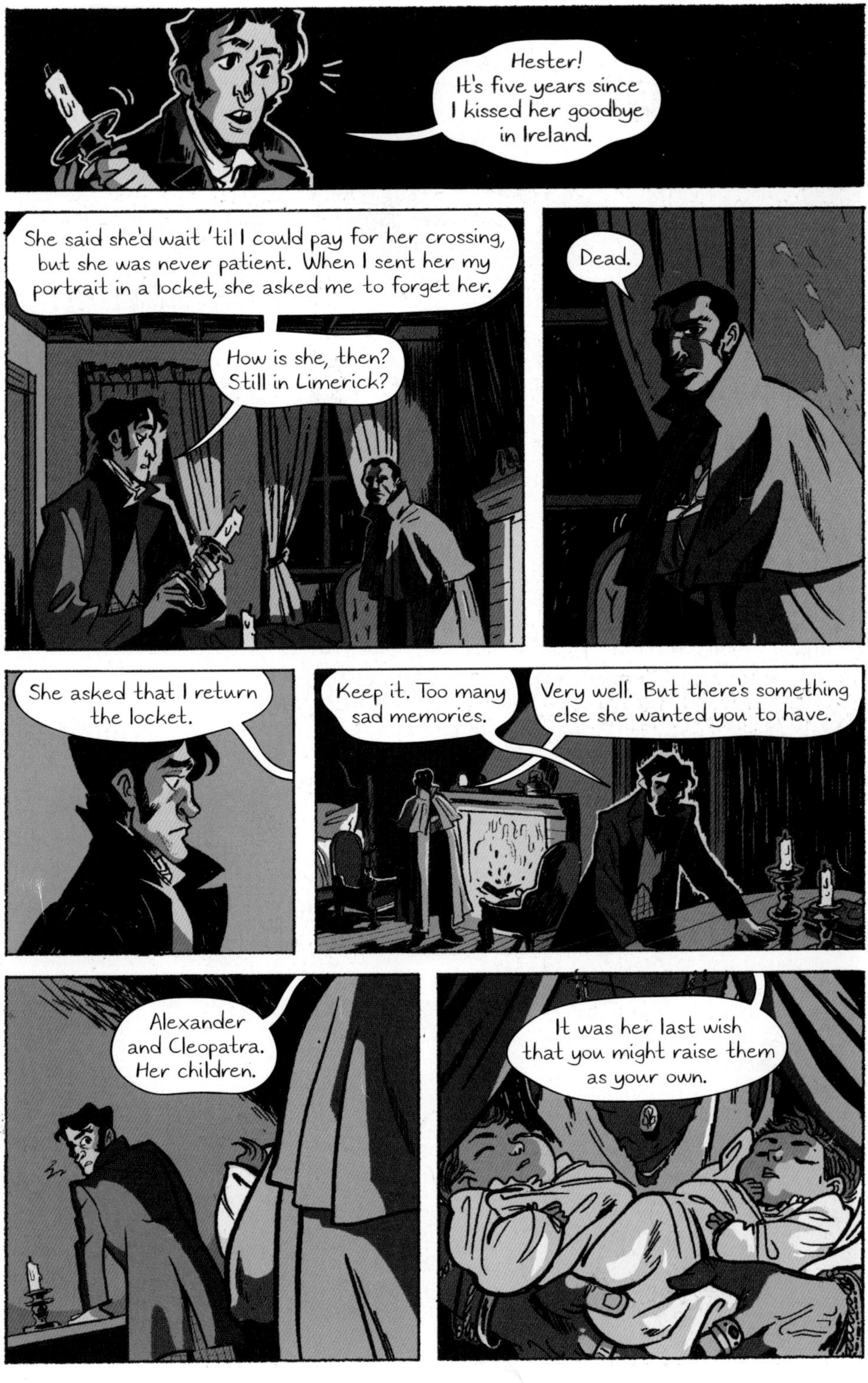
Hester!
It's five years since I kissed her goodbye in Ireland.
She said she'd wait 'til I could pay for her crossing, but she was never patient. When I sent her my portrait in a locket, she asked me to forget her.
How is she, then? Still in Limerick?
Dead.
She asked that I return the locket.
Keep it. Too many sad memories.
Very well. But there's something else she wanted you to have.
Alexander and Cleopatra. Her children.
It was her last wish that you might raise them as your own.

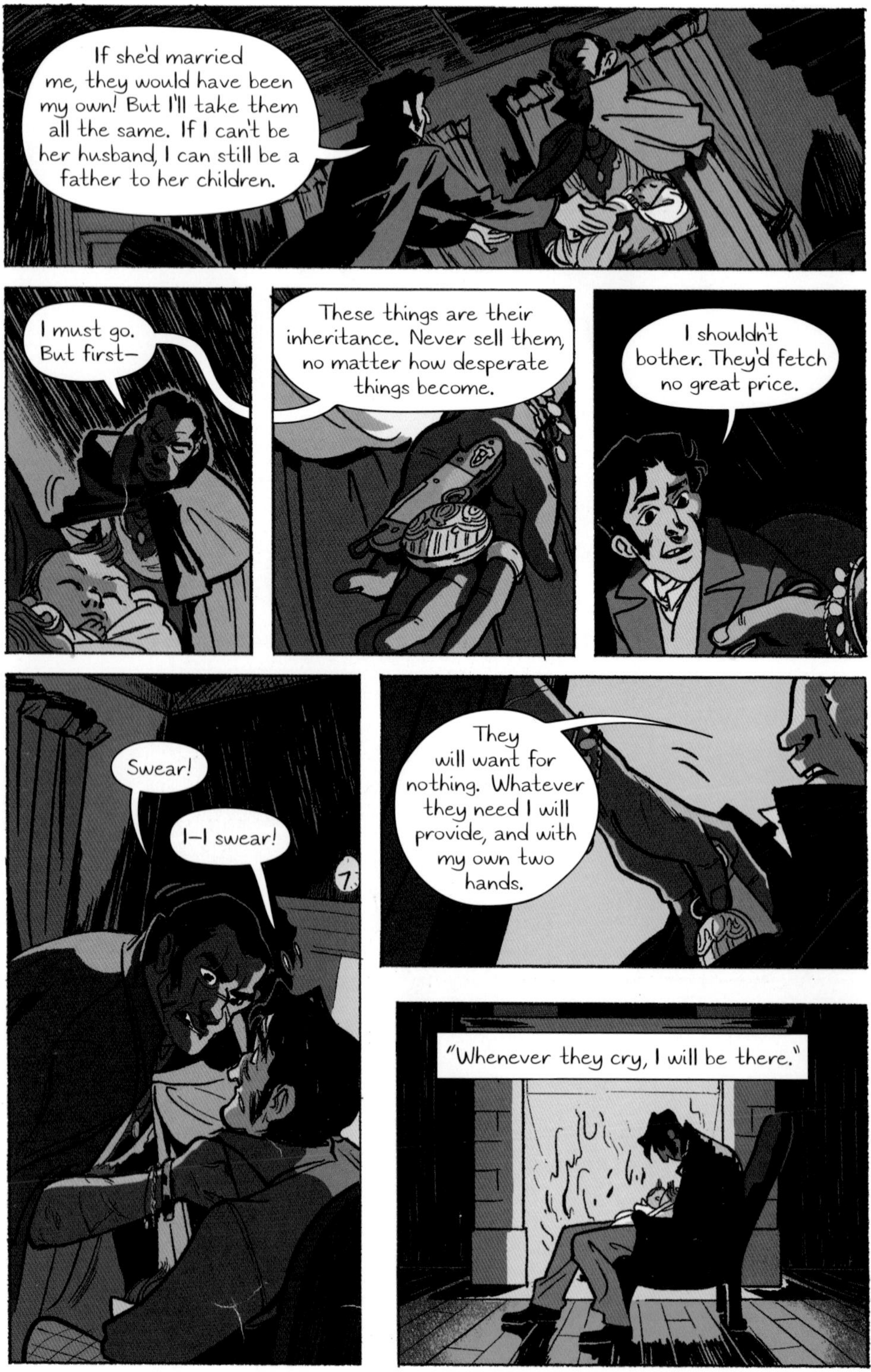
If she'd married me, they would have been my own! But I'll take them all the same. If I can't be her husband, I can still be a father to her children.
I must go. But first—
These things are their inheritance. Never sell them, no matter how desperate things become.
I shouldn't bother. They'd fetch no great price.
Swear!
I—I swear!
They will want for nothing. Whatever they need I will provide, and with my own two hands.
"Whenever they cry, I will be there."

CHAPTER ONE
THE BLACK HOOK GANG

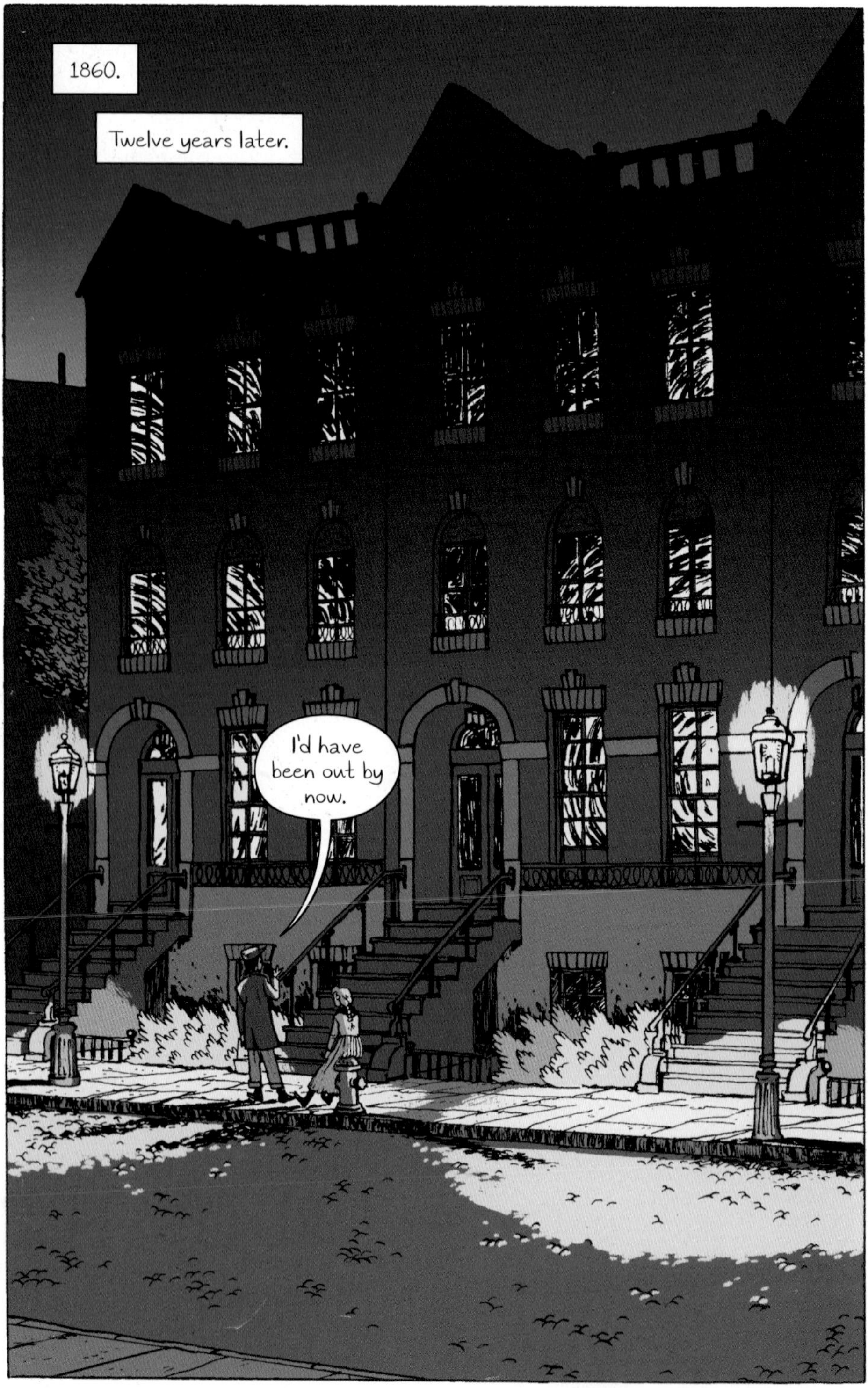
1860.
Twelve years later.
I'd have been out by now.

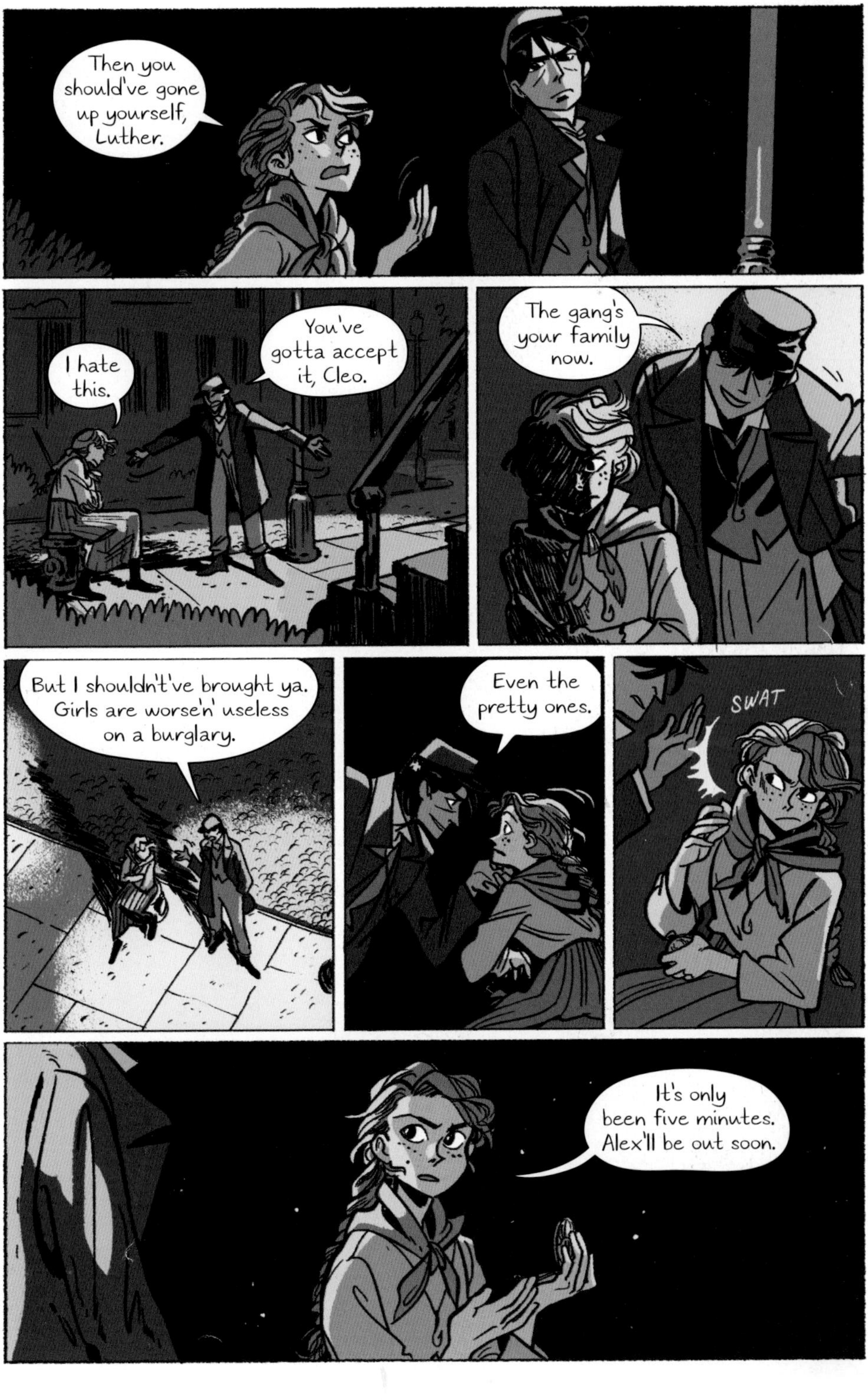

Then you should've gone up yourself, Luther.
I hate this.
You've gotta accept it, Cleo.
The gang's your family now.
But I shouldn't've brought ya. Girls are worse'n' useless on a burglary.
Even the pretty ones.
SWAT
It's only been five minutes. Alex'll be out soon.

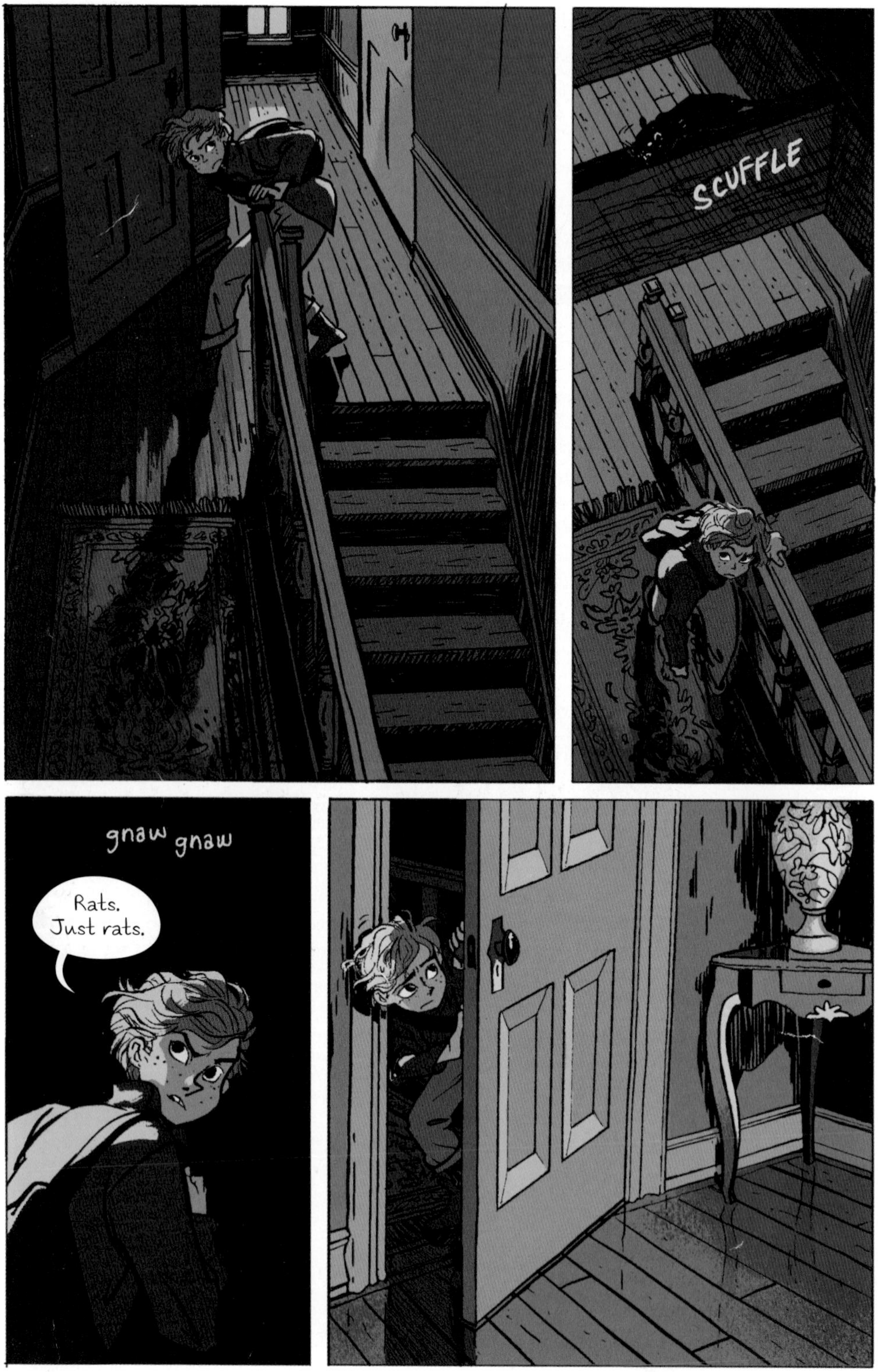
SCUFFLE
gnaw gnaw
Rats.
Just rats.

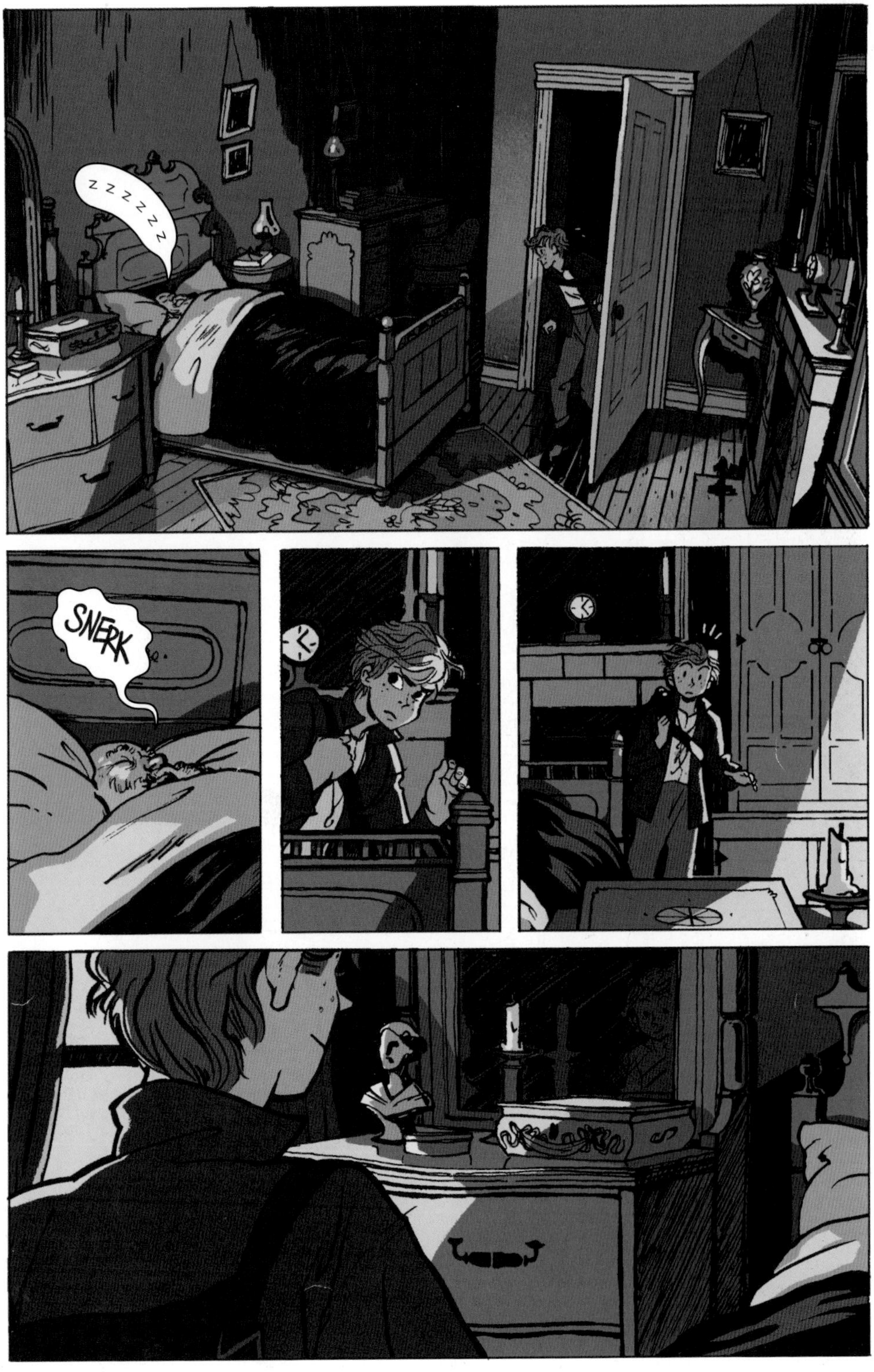
ZZZZZZZ
SNERK

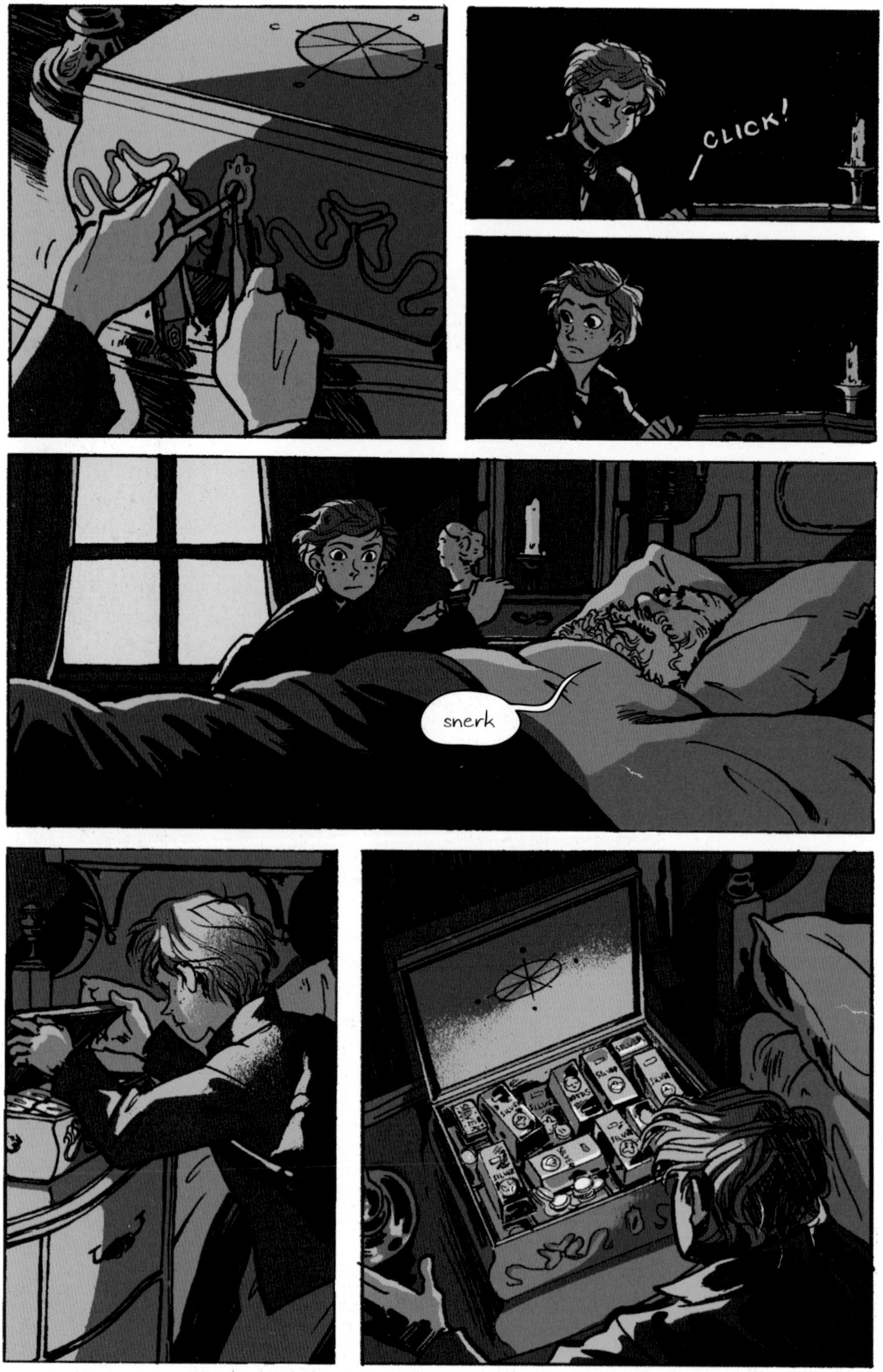
CLICK!
snerk

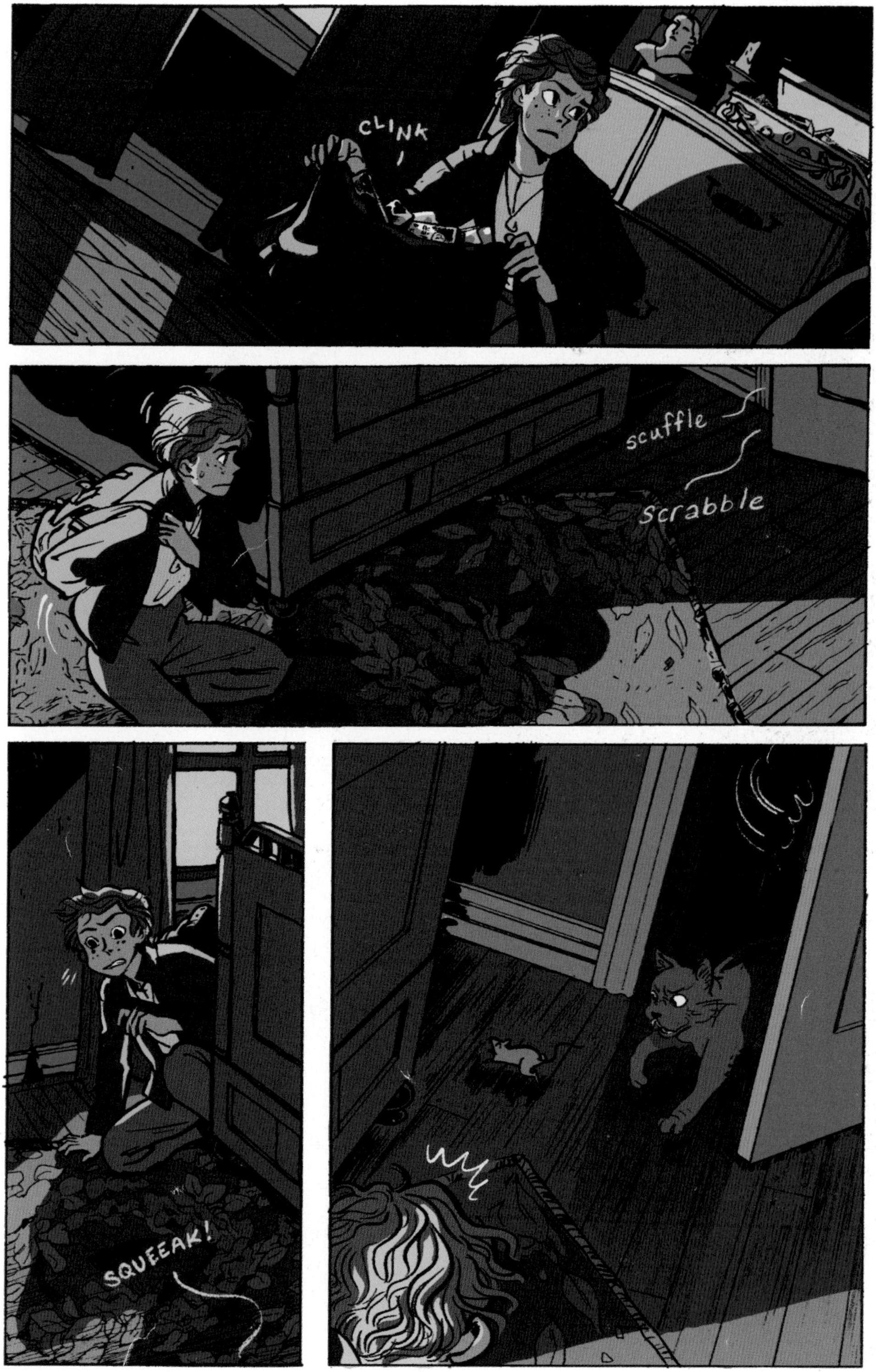
CLINK
scuffle
scrabble
SQUEEEAK!

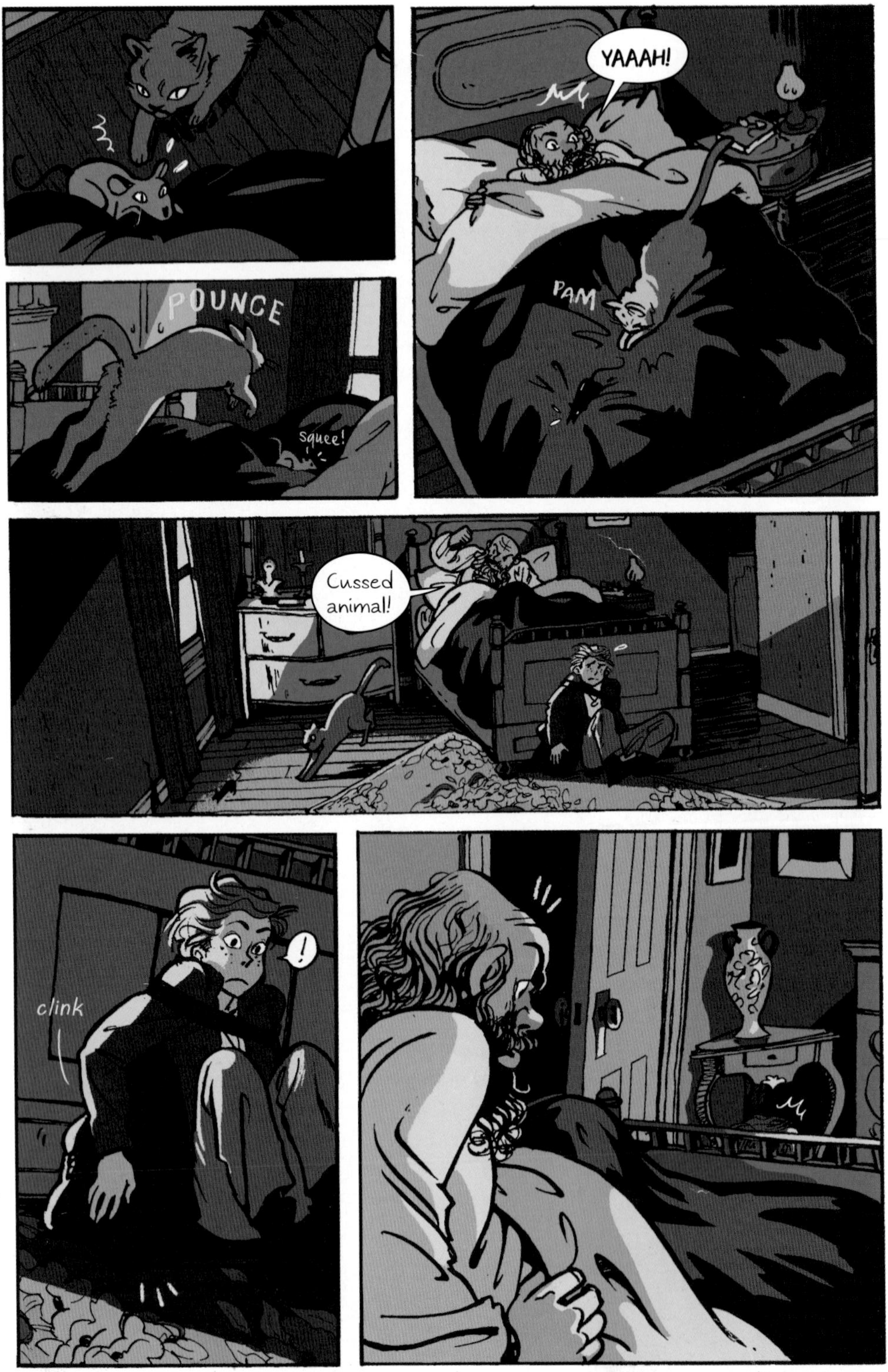
YAAAH!
POUNCE
squee!
PAM
Cussed animal!
!
clink

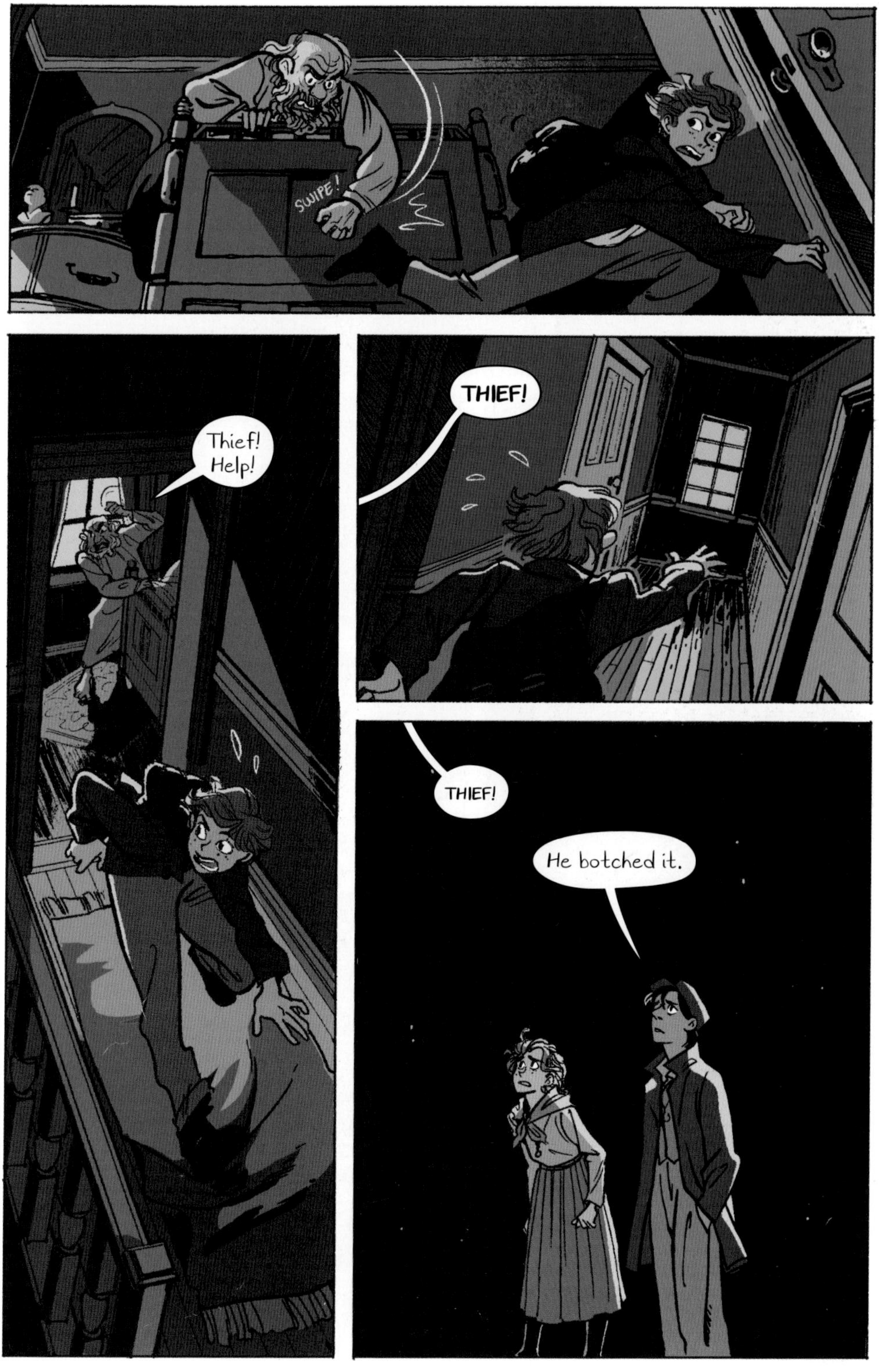
SWIPE!
Thief! Help!
THIEF!
THIEF!
He botched it.

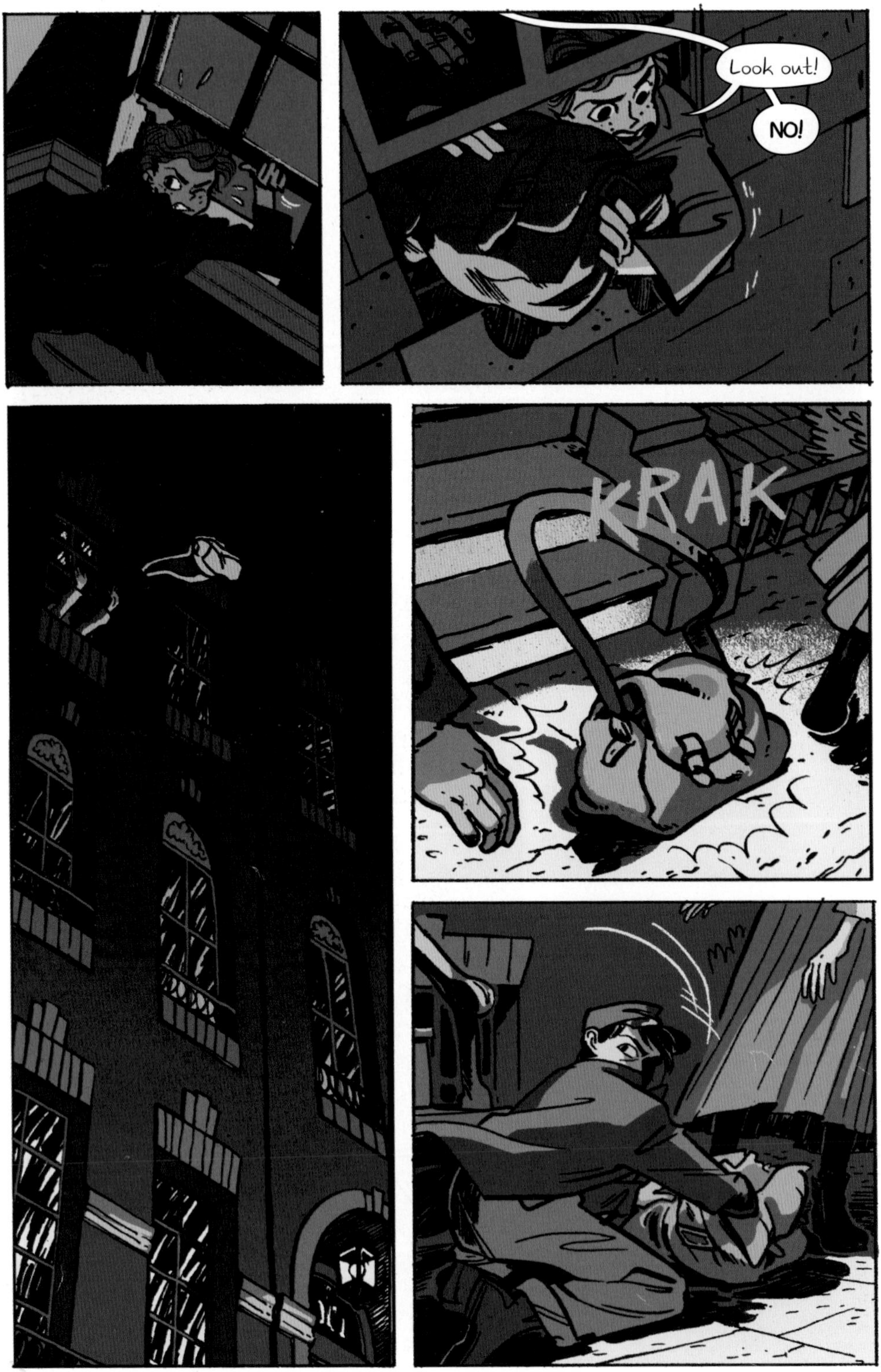
Look out!
NO!
KRAK

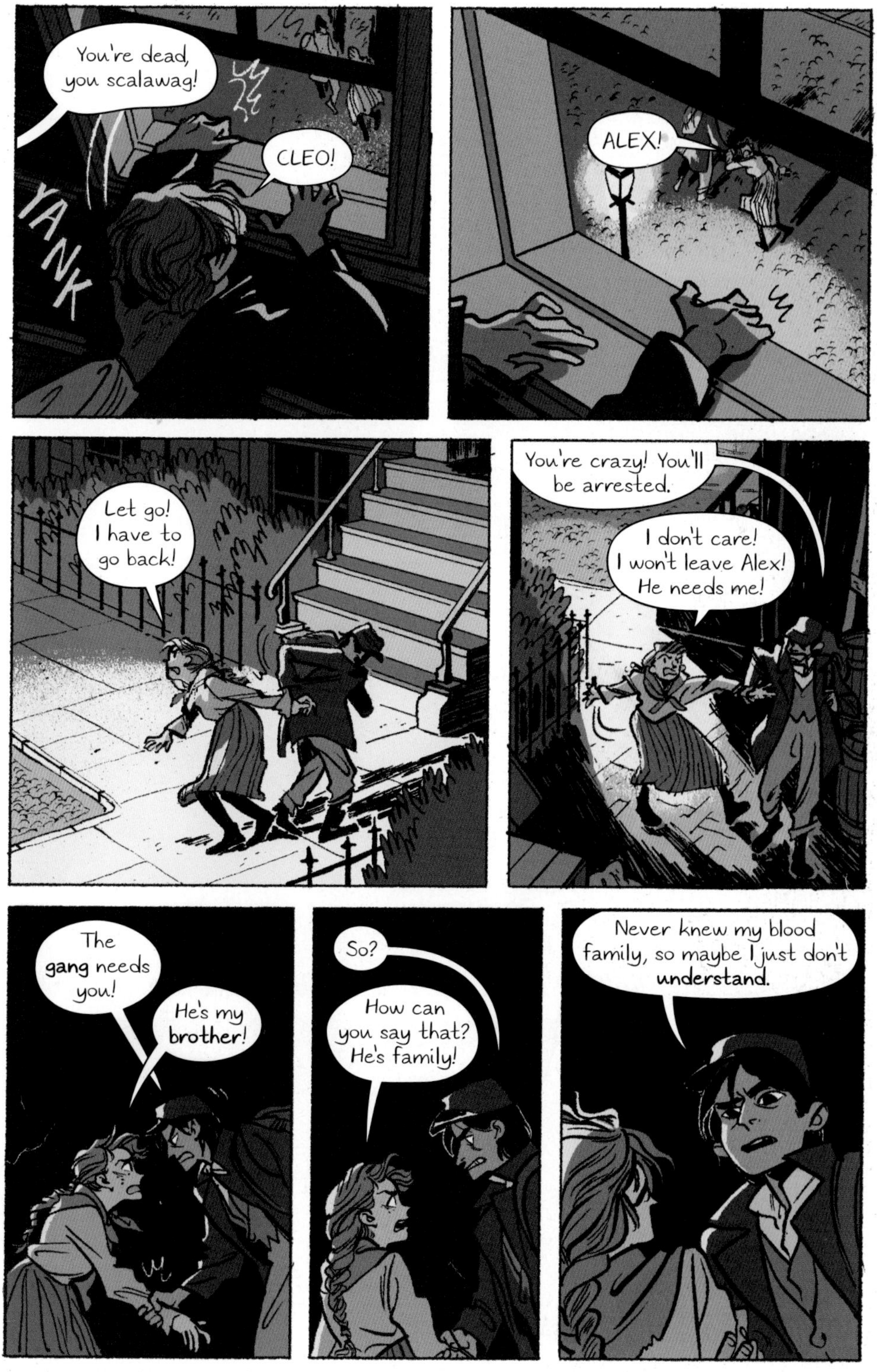
You're dead, you scalawag!
CLEO!
YANK
ALEX!
Let go! I have to go back!
You're crazy! You'll be arrested.
I don't care! I won't leave Alex! He needs me!
The **gang** needs you!
He's my **brother**!
So?
How can you say that? He's family!
Never knew my blood family, so maybe I just don't **understand**.

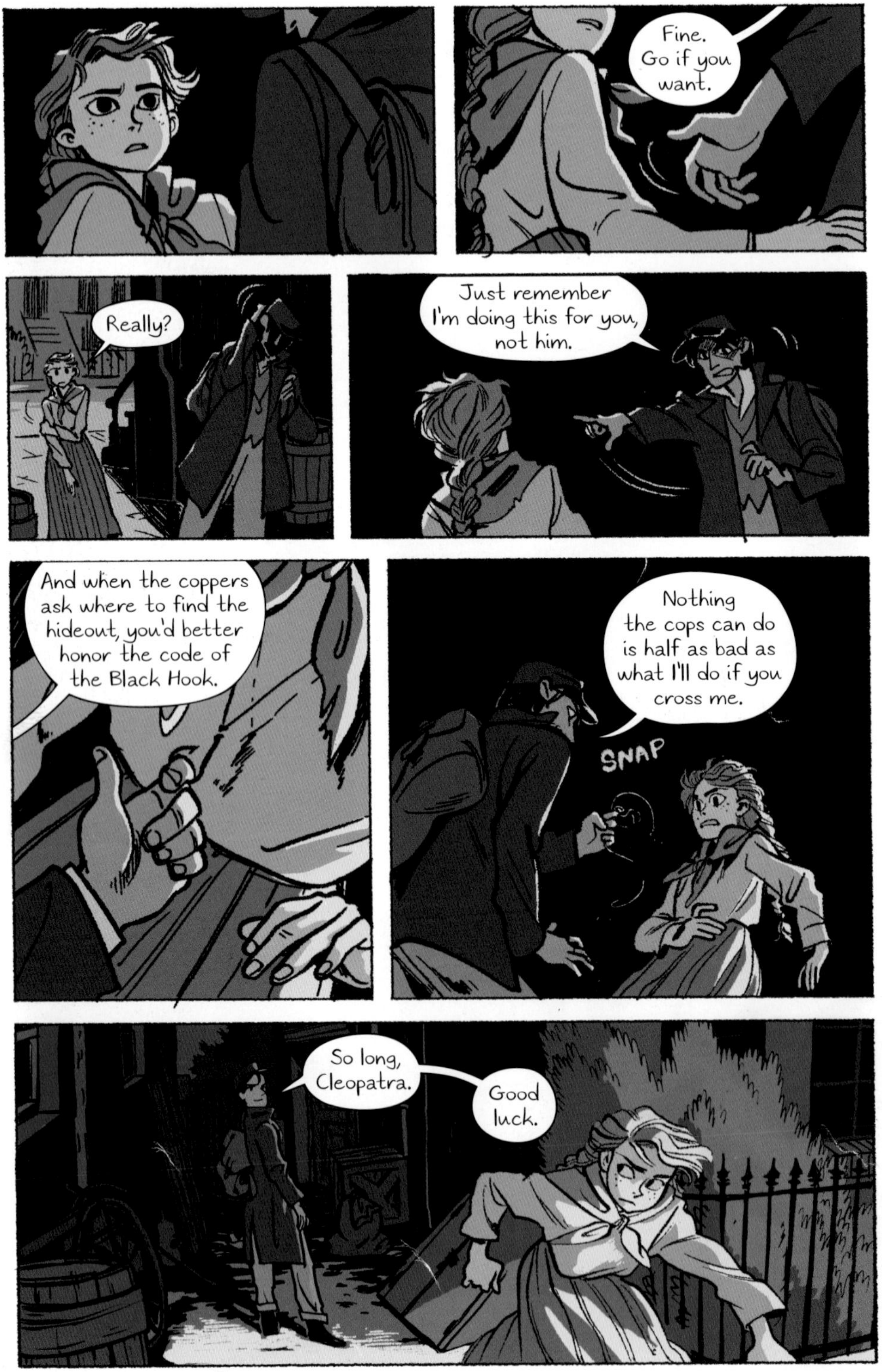

Fine.
Go if you want.
Really?
Just remember I'm doing this for you, not him.
And when the coppers ask where to find the hideout, you'd better honor the code of the Black Hook.
Nothing the cops can do is half as bad as what I'll do if you cross me.
SNAP
So long, Cleopatra.
Good luck.

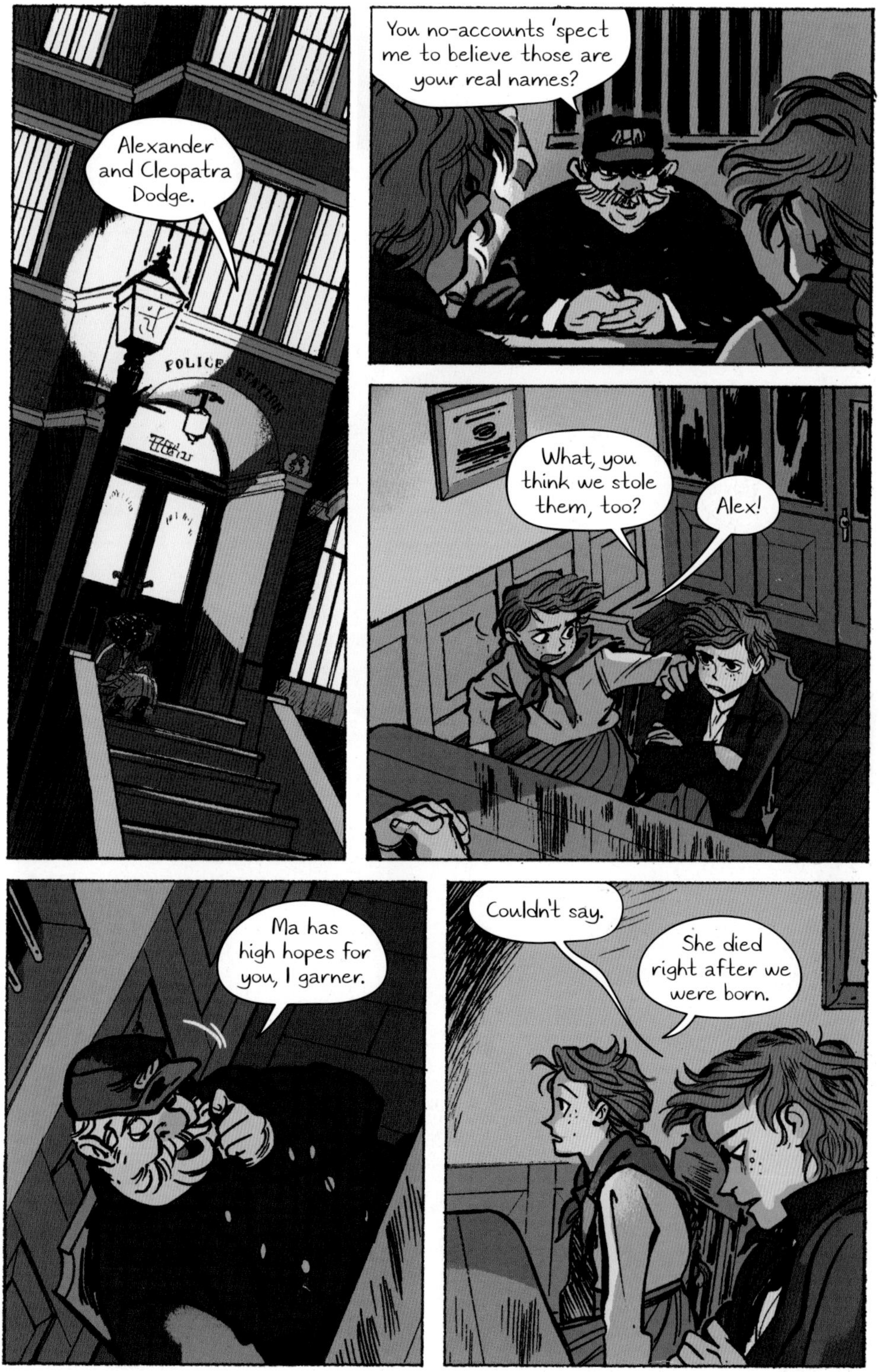
Alexander and Cleopatra Dodge.
POLICE STATION
You no-accounts 'spect me to believe those are your real names?
What, you think we stole them, too?
Alex!
Ma has high hopes for you, I garner.
Couldn't say.
She died right after we were born.

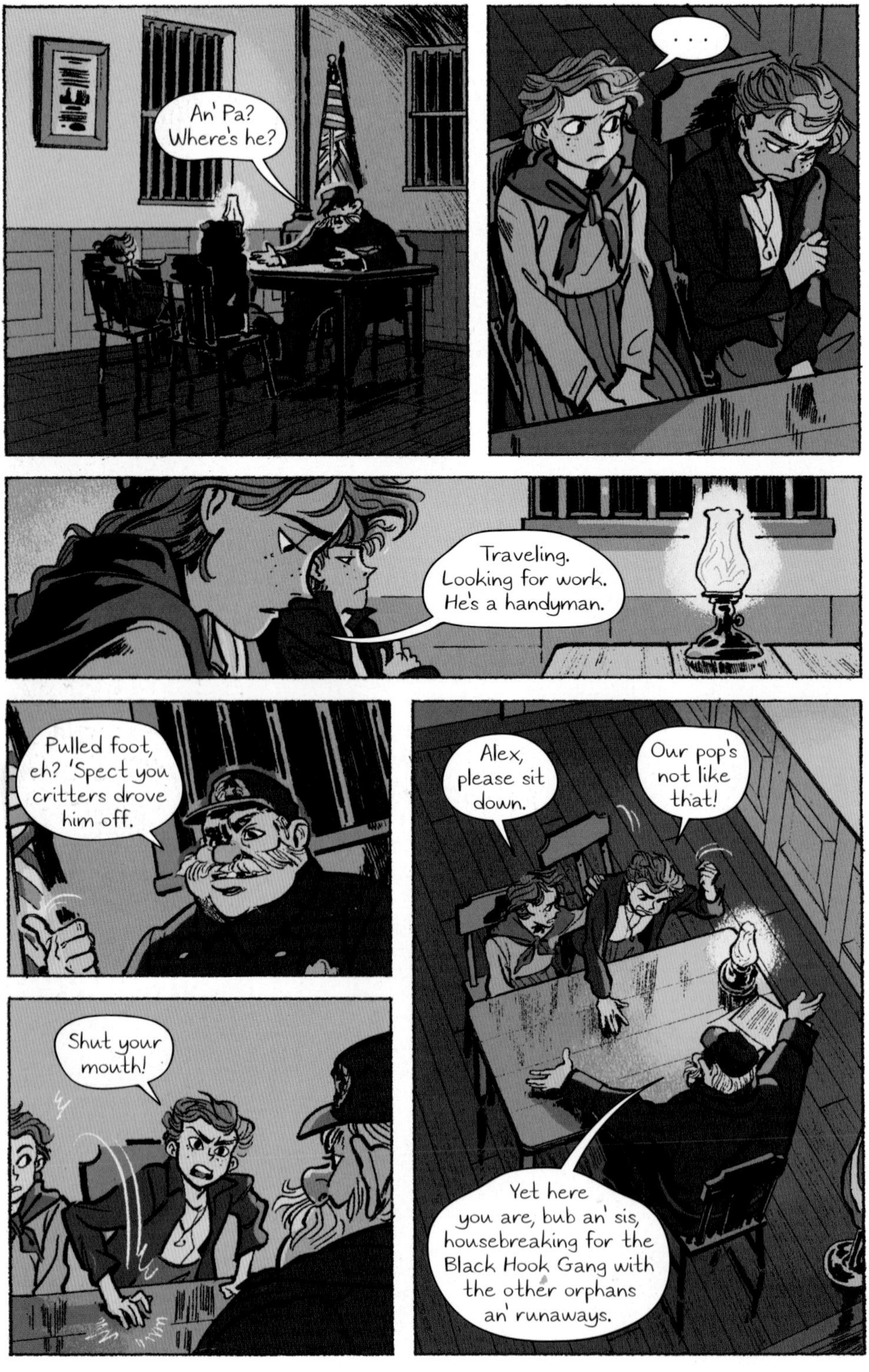
An' Pa? Where's he?
...
Traveling. Looking for work. He's a handyman.
Pulled foot, eh? 'Spect you critters drove him off.
Alex, please sit down.
Our pop's not like that!
Yet here you are, bub an' sis, housebreaking for the Black Hook Gang with the other orphans an' runaways.
Shut your mouth!

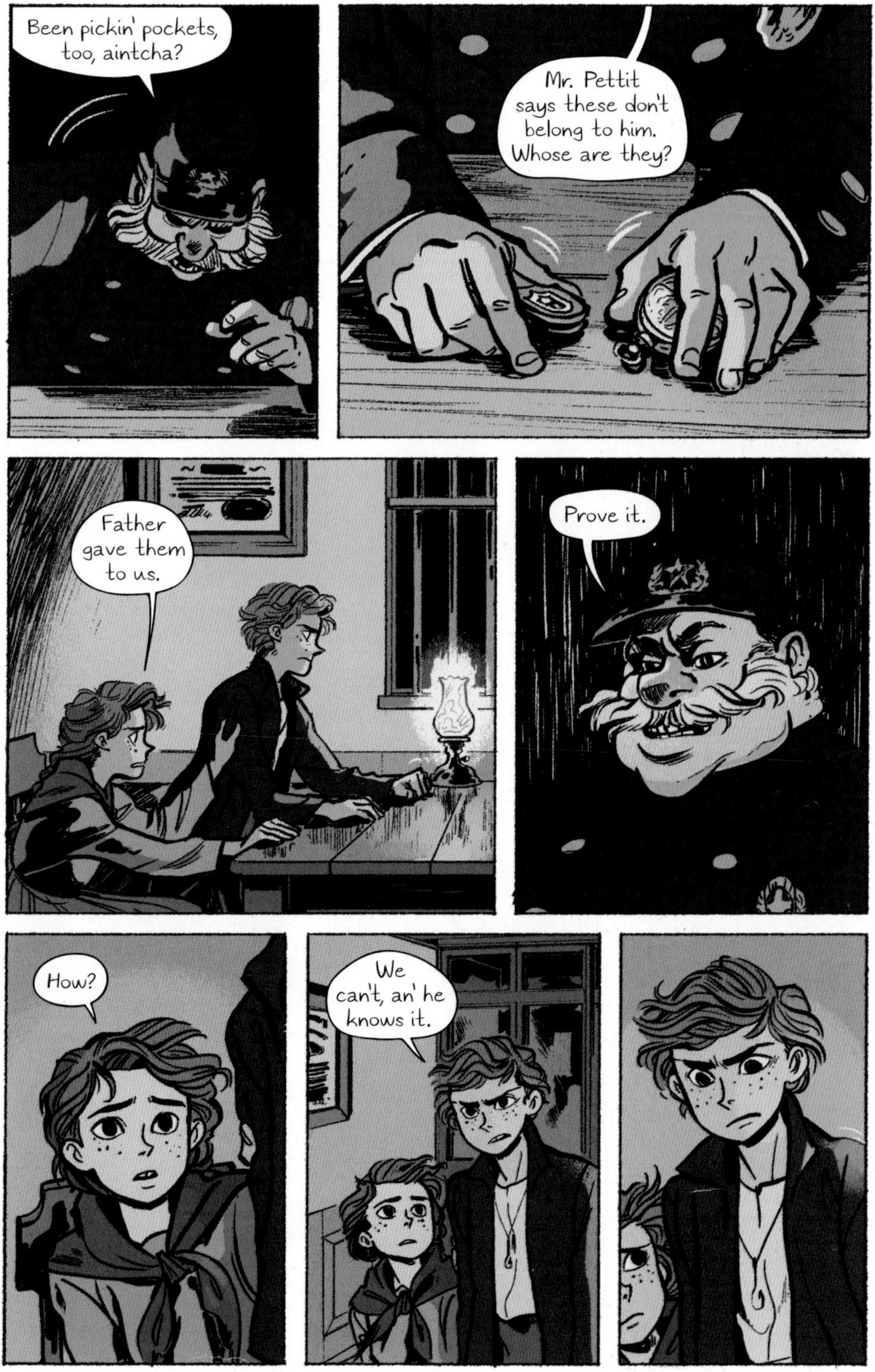
Been pickin' pockets, too, aintcha?
Mr. Pettit says these don't belong to him. Whose are they?
Father gave them to us.
Prove it.
How?
We can't, an' he knows it.

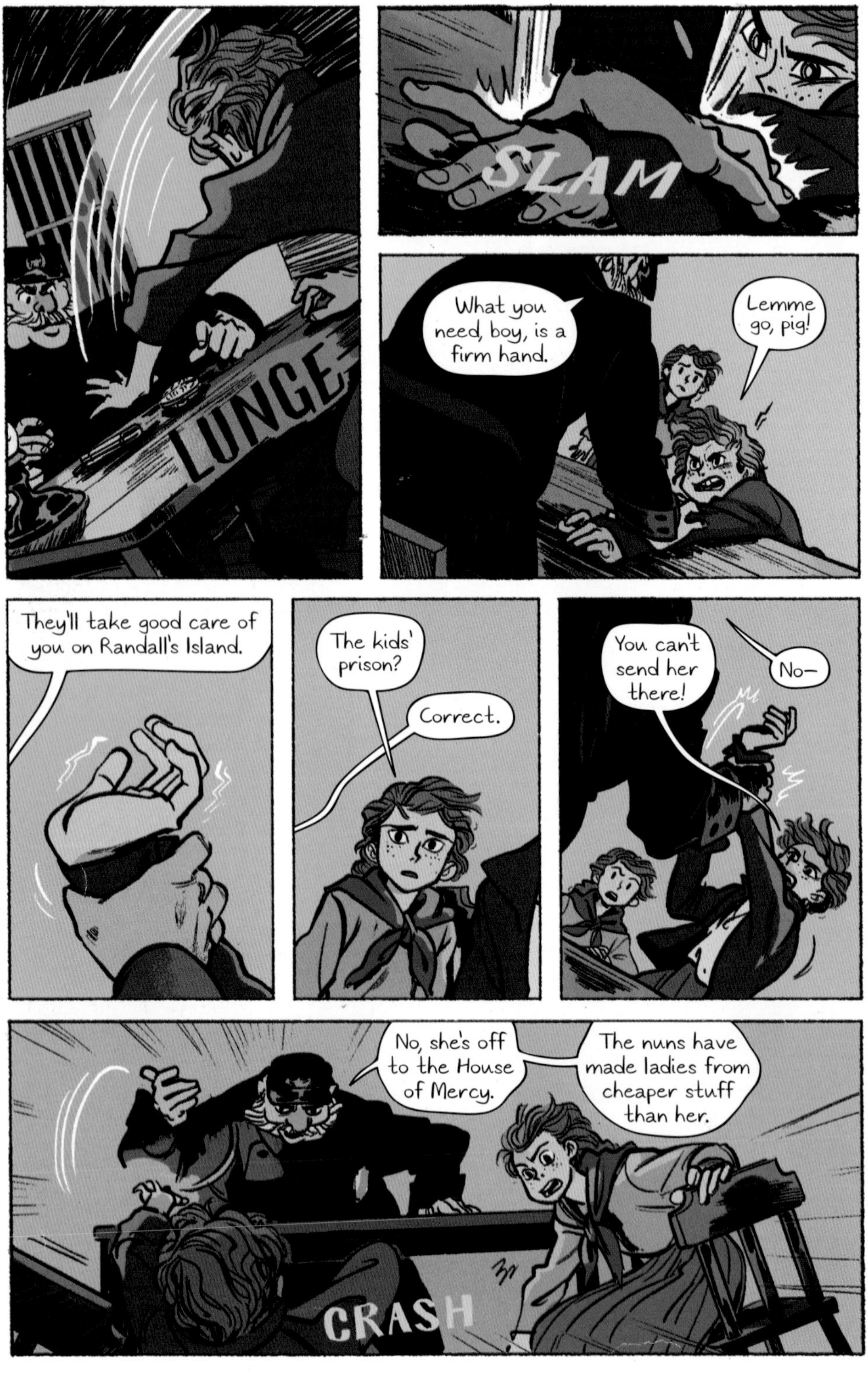
LUNGE
SLAM
What you need, boy, is a firm hand.
Lemme go, pig!
They'll take good care of you on Randall's Island.
The kids' prison?
Correct.
You can't send her there!
No—
No, she's off to the House of Mercy.
The nuns have made ladies from cheaper stuff than her.
CRASH

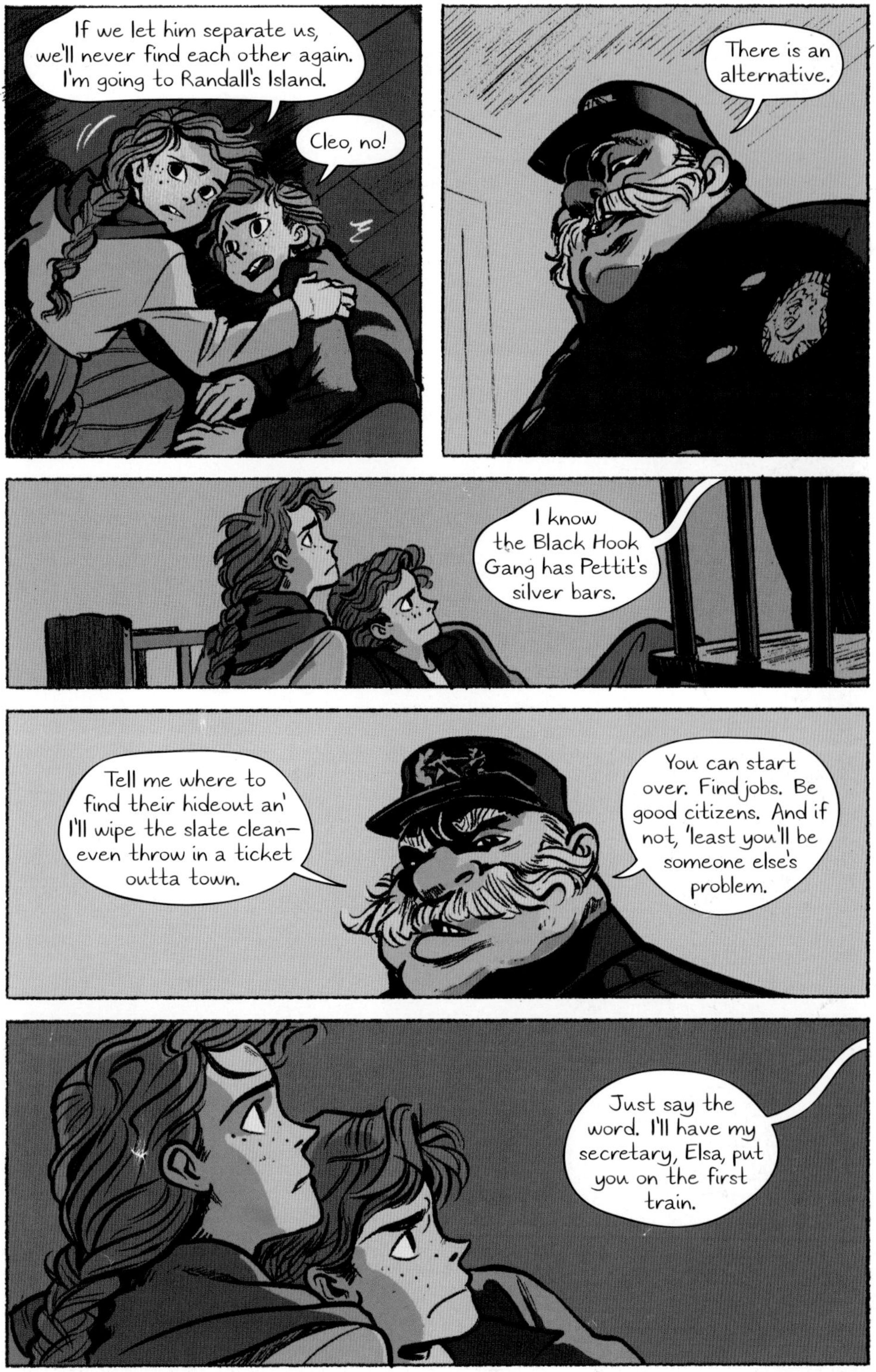
If we let him separate us, we'll never find each other again. I'm going to Randall's Island.
Cleo, no!
There is an alternative.
I know the Black Hook Gang has Pettit's silver bars.
Tell me where to find their hideout an' I'll wipe the slate clean—even throw in a ticket outta town.
You can start over. Find jobs. Be good citizens. And if not, 'least you'll be someone else's problem.
Just say the word. I'll have my secretary, Elsa, put you on the first train.

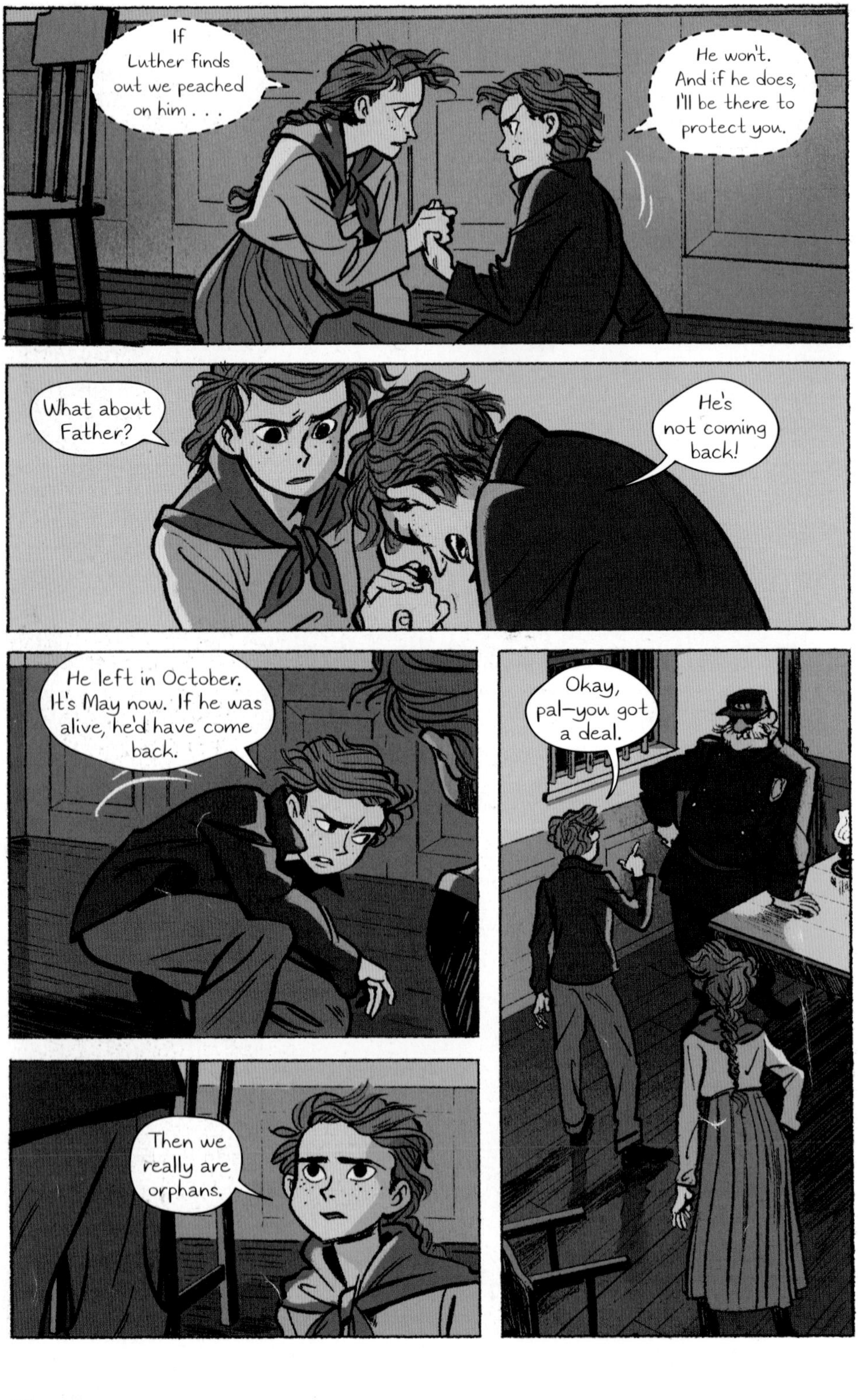
If Luther finds out we peached on him . . .
He won't. And if he does, I'll be there to protect you.
What about Father?
He's not coming back!
He left in October. It's May now. If he was alive, he'd have come back.
Then we really are orphans.
Okay, pal—you got a deal.

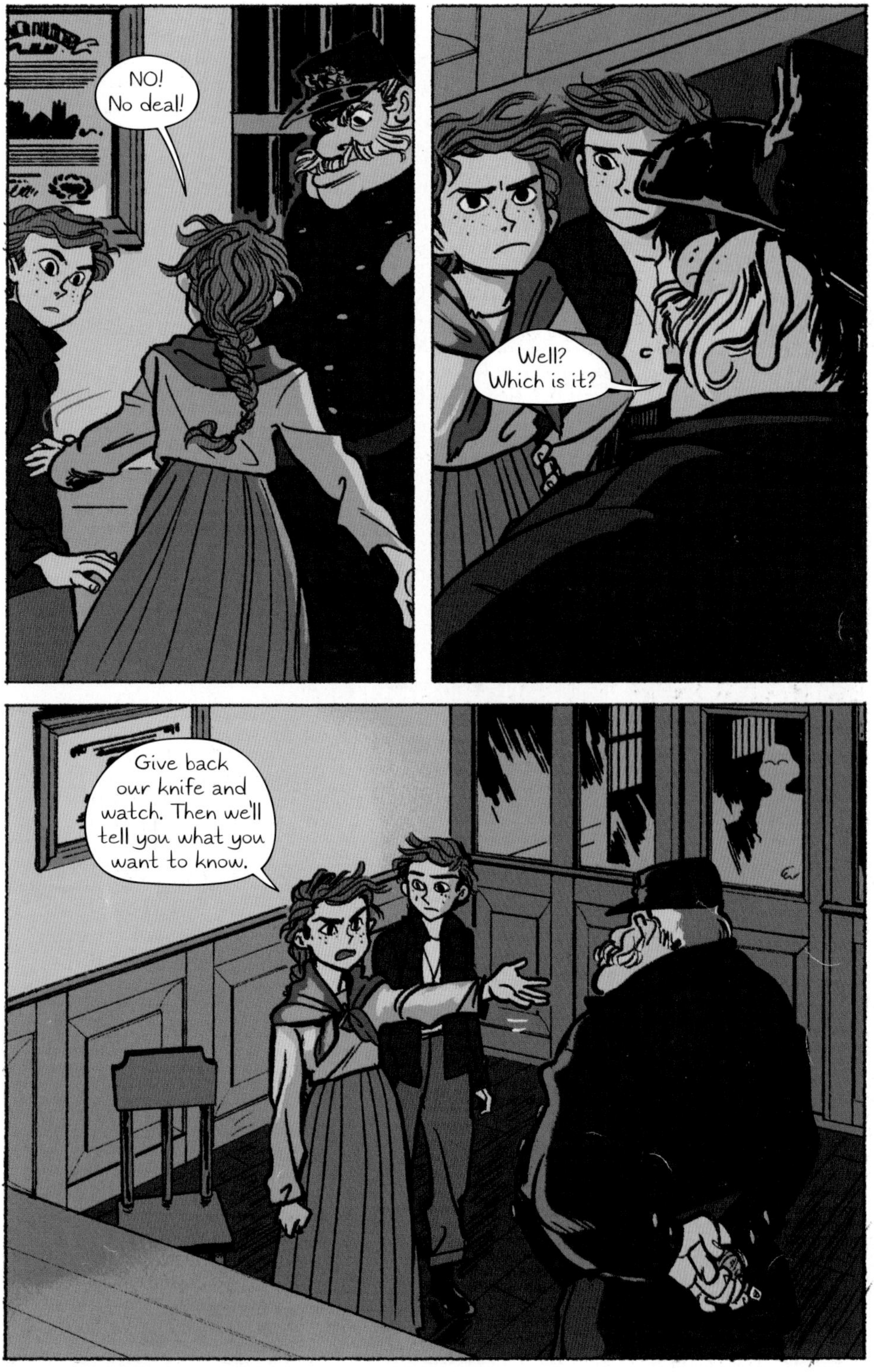
NO! No deal!
Well? Which is it?
Give back our knife and watch. Then we'll tell you what you want to know.

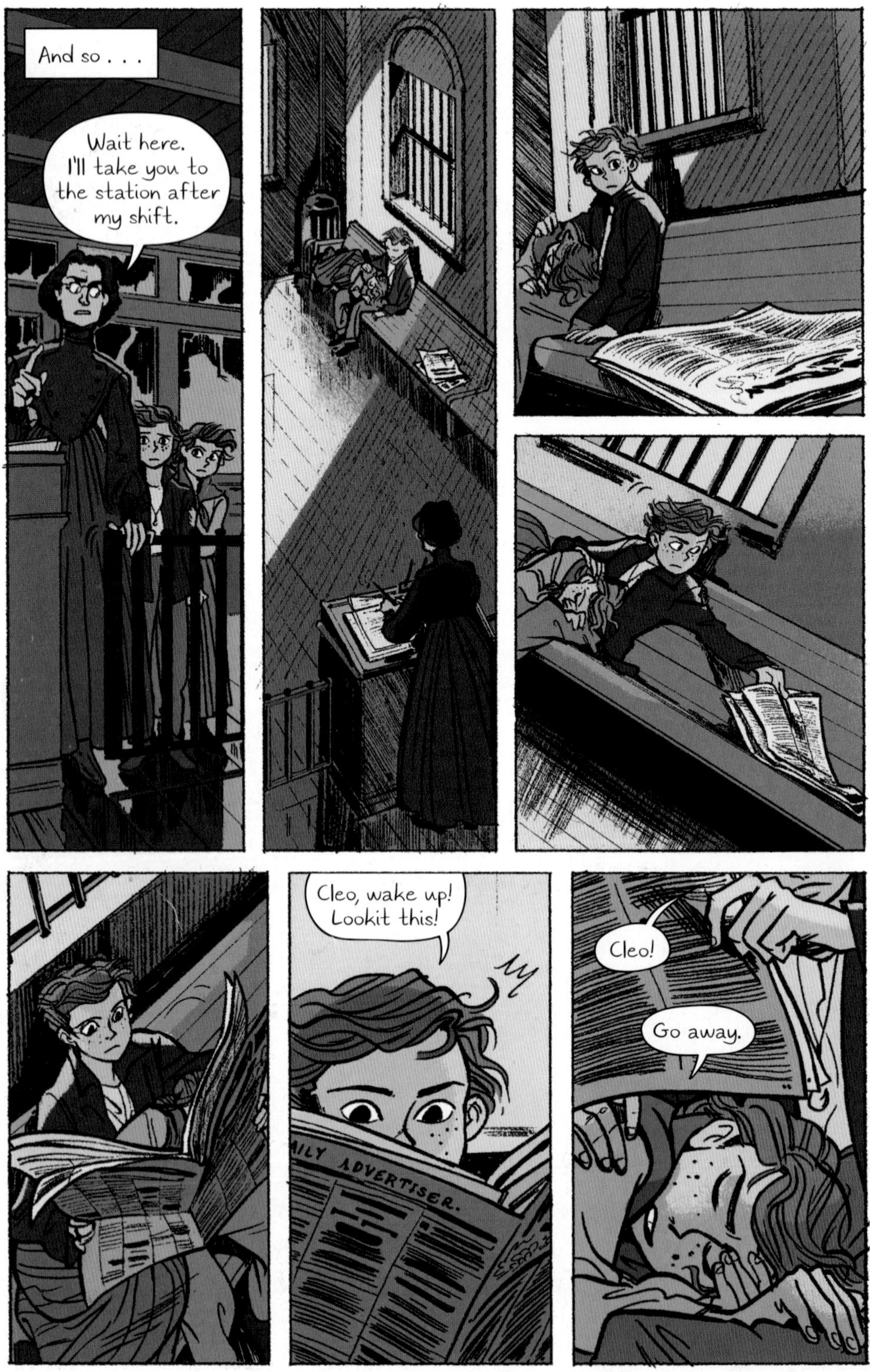
And so . . .
Wait here. I'll take you to the station after my shift.
Cleo, wake up! Lookit this!
ADVERTISER.
Cleo!
Go away.

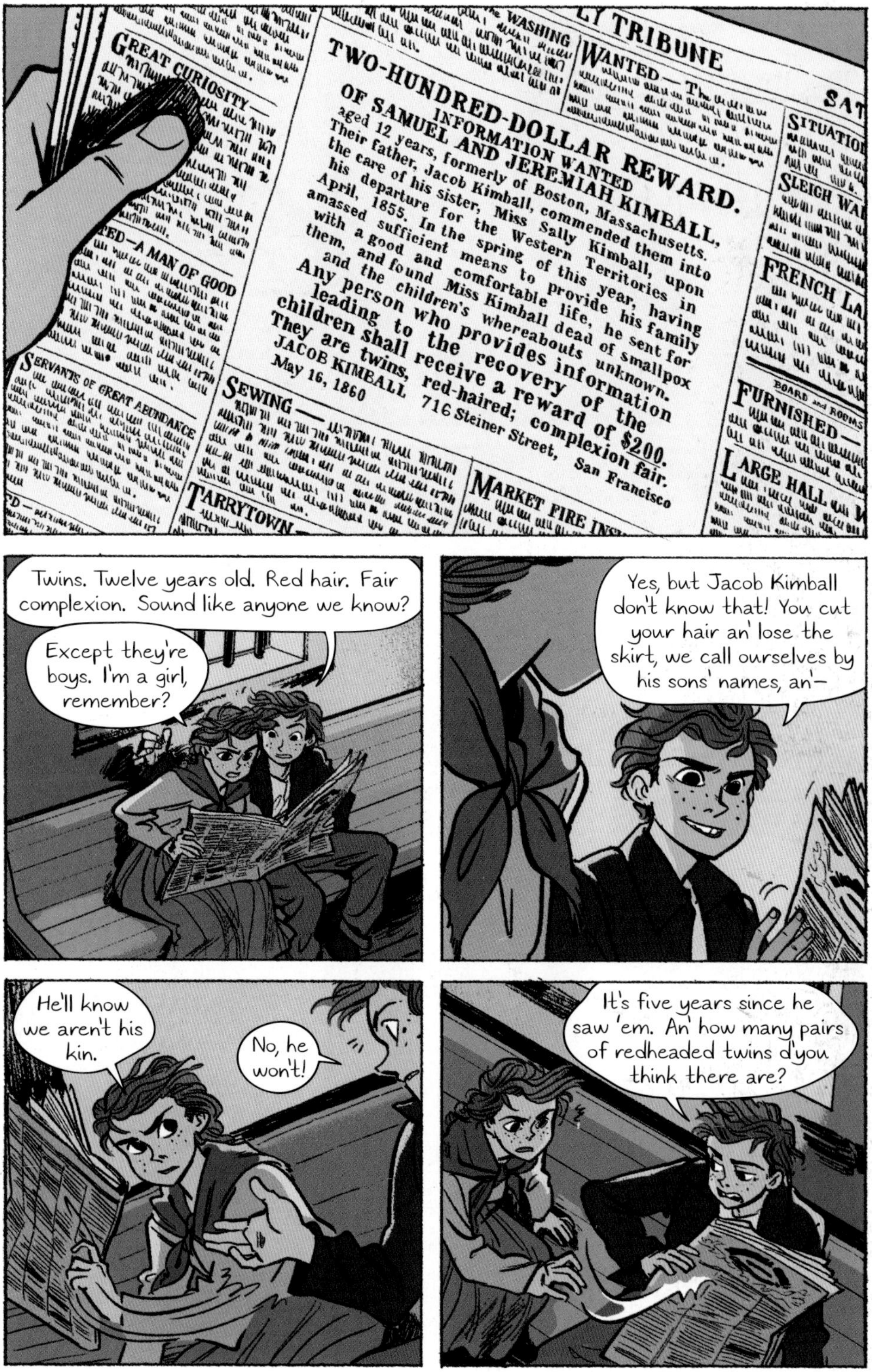

TRIBUNE
TWO-HUNDRED-DOLLAR REWARD.
INFORMATION WANTED
OF SAMUEL AND JEREMIAH KIMBALL,
aged 12 years, formerly of Boston, Massachusetts.
Their father, Jacob Kimball, commended them into the care of his sister, Miss Sally Kimball, upon his departure for the Western Territories in April, 1855. In the spring of this year, having amassed sufficient means to provide his family with a good and comfortable life, he sent for them, and found Miss Kimball dead of smallpox and the children's whereabouts unknown.
Any person who provides information leading to the recovery of the children shall receive a reward of $200.
They are twins, red-haired; complexion fair.
JACOB KIMBALL 716 Steiner Street, San Francisco
May 16, 1860
GREAT CURIOSITY
SERVANTS OF GREAT ABUNDANCE
SEWING
TARRYTOWN
WASHING
WANTED
MARKET FIRE INS
SITUATION
SLEIGH WA
FRENCH LA
BOARD and ROOMS
FURNISHED
LARGE HALL
Twins. Twelve years old. Red hair. Fair complexion. Sound like anyone we know?
Except they're boys. I'm a girl, remember?
Yes, but Jacob Kimball don't know that! You cut your hair an' lose the skirt, we call ourselves by his sons' names, an'—
He'll know we aren't his kin.
No, he won't!
It's five years since he saw 'em. An' how many pairs of redheaded twins d'you think there are?

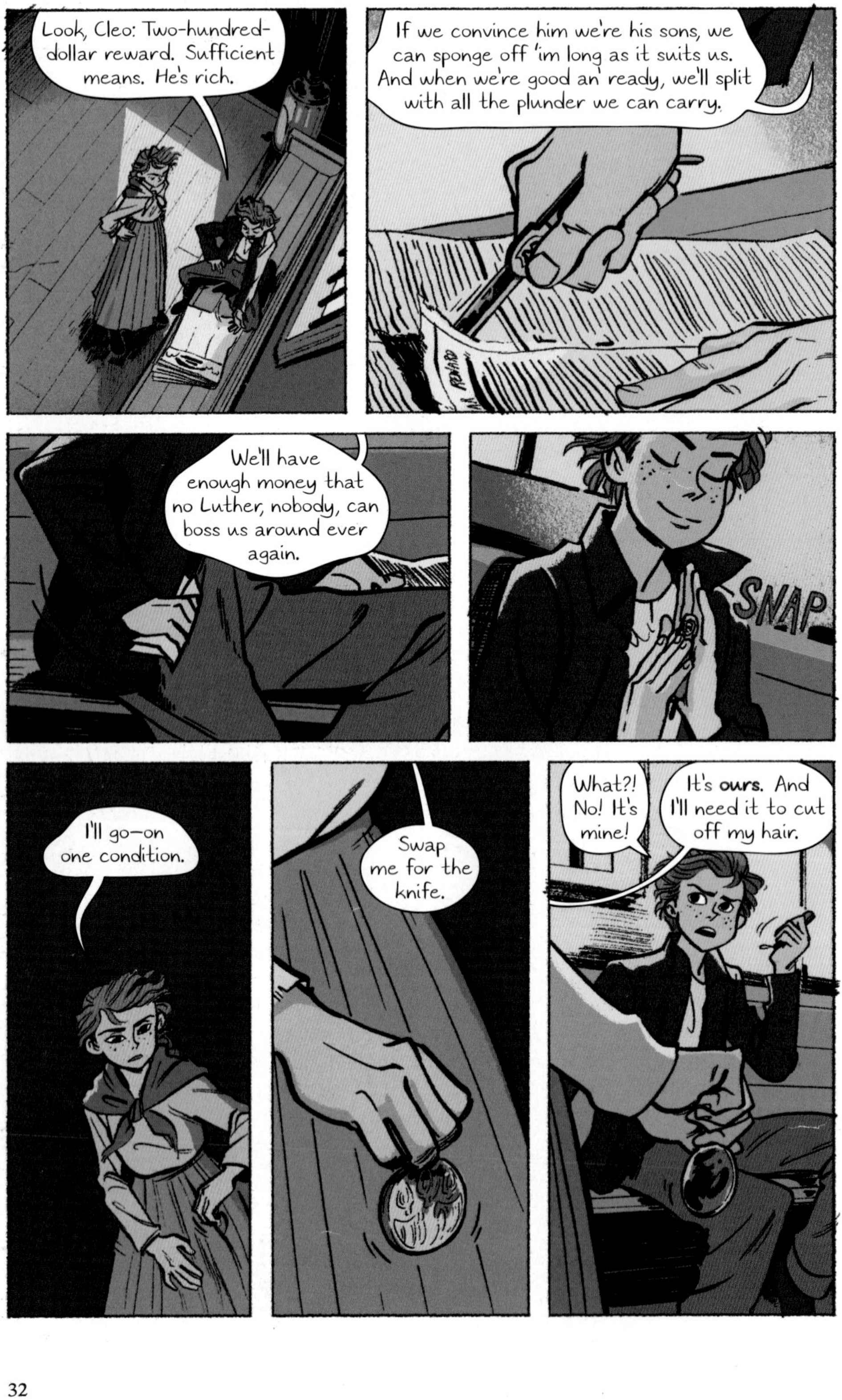

Look, Cleo: Two-hundred-dollar reward. Sufficient means. He's rich.
If we convince him we're his sons, we can sponge off 'im long as it suits us. And when we're good an' ready, we'll split with all the plunder we can carry.
We'll have enough money that no Luther, nobody, can boss us around ever again.
SNAP
I'll go—on one condition.
Swap me for the knife.
What?! No! It's mine!
It's **ours.** And I'll need it to cut off my hair.

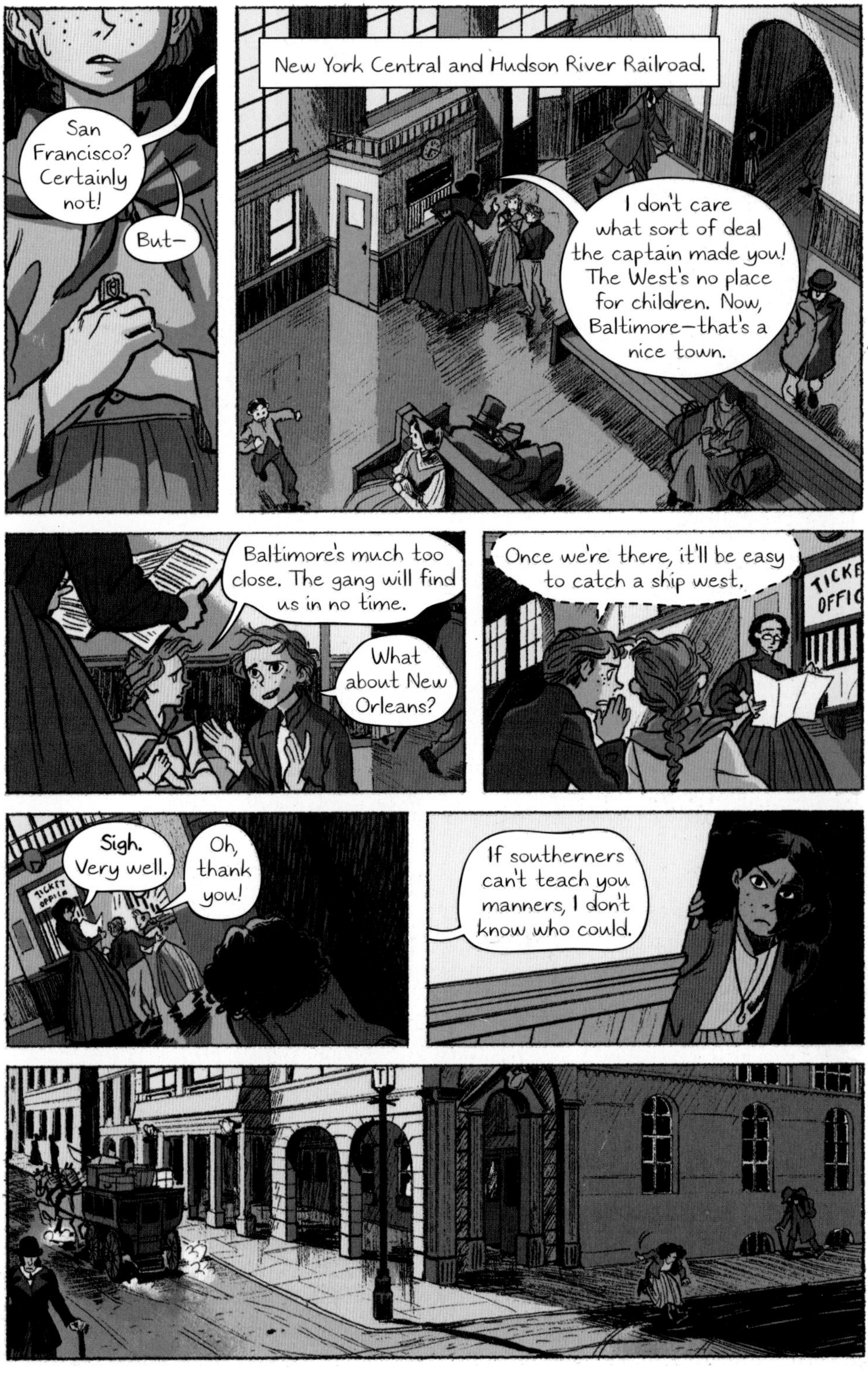
San Francisco? Certainly not!
But–
New York Central and Hudson River Railroad.
I don't care what sort of deal the captain made you! The West's no place for children. Now, Baltimore—that's a nice town.
Baltimore's much too close. The gang will find us in no time.
What about New Orleans?
Once we're there, it'll be easy to catch a ship west.
TICKE OFFIC
Sigh. Very well.
Oh, thank you!
TICKET OFFICE
If southerners can't teach you manners, I don't know who could.

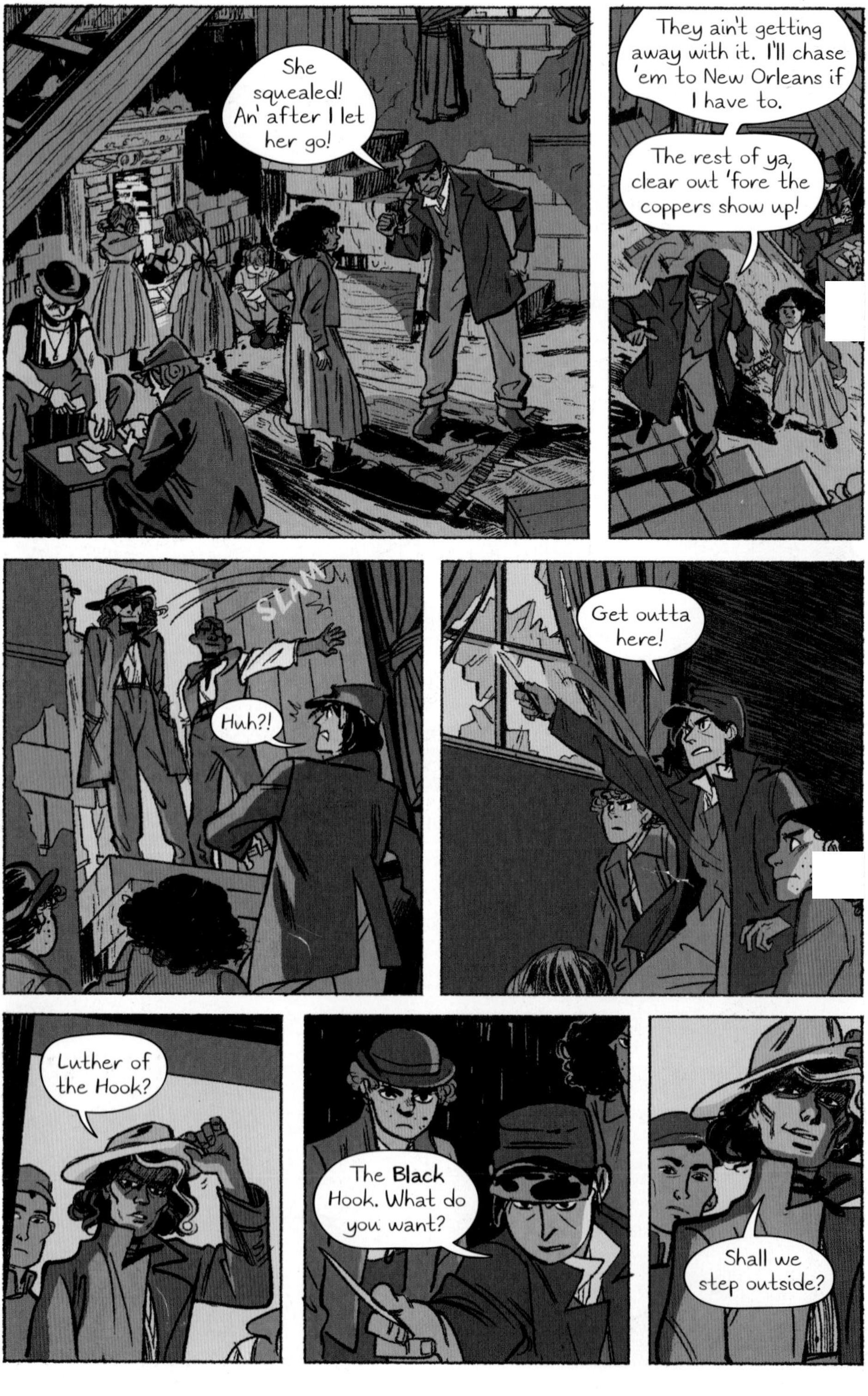

She squealed! An' after I let her go!
They ain't getting away with it. I'll chase 'em to New Orleans if I have to.
The rest of ya, clear out 'fore the coppers show up!
SLAM
Huh?!
Get outta here!
Luther of the Hook?
The **Black** Hook. What do you want?
Shall we step outside?

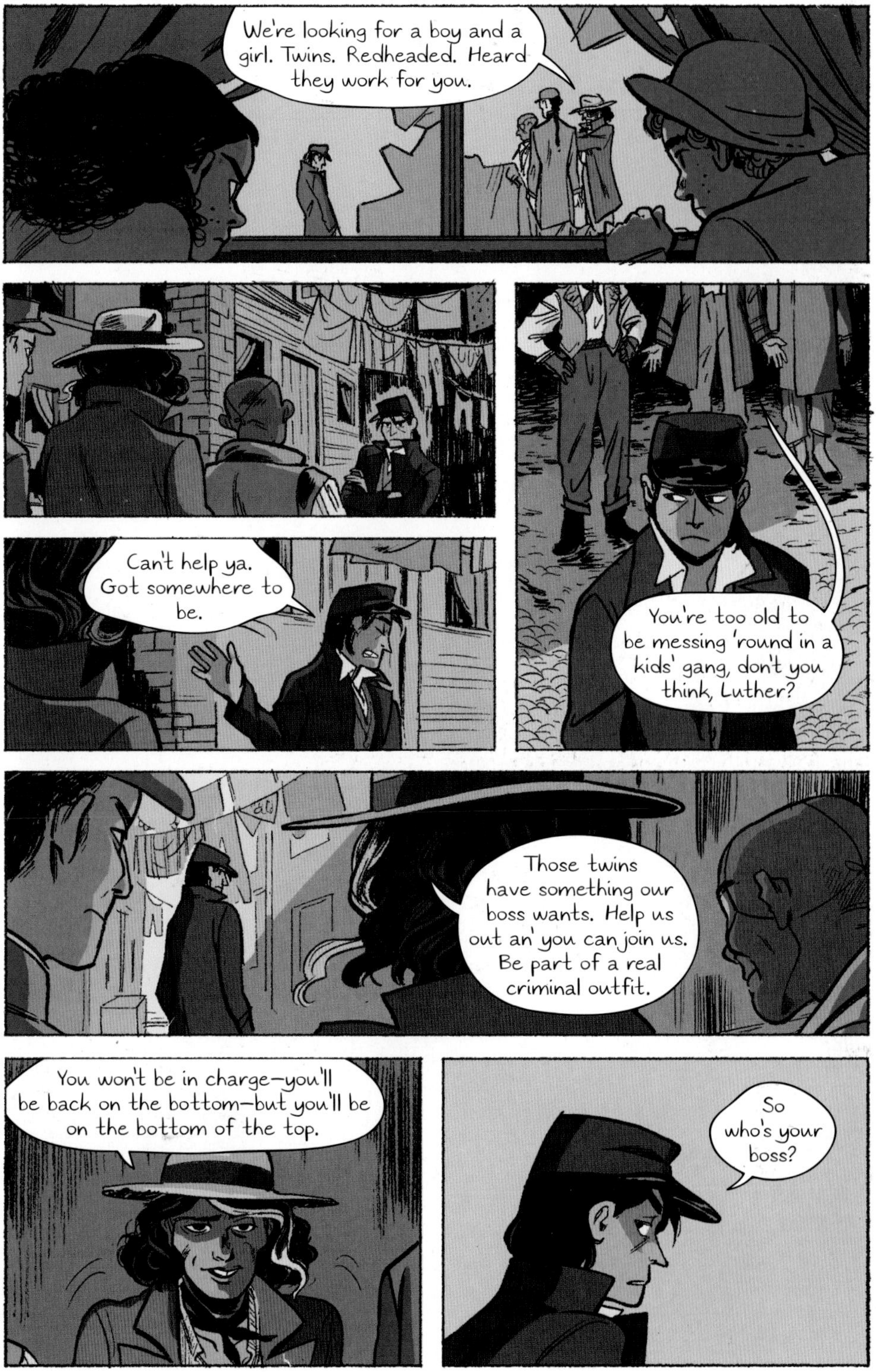
We're looking for a boy and a girl. Twins. Redheaded. Heard they work for you.
Can't help ya. Got somewhere to be.
You're too old to be messing 'round in a kids' gang, don't you think, Luther?
Those twins have something our boss wants. Help us out an' you can join us. Be part of a real criminal outfit.
You won't be in charge—you'll be back on the bottom—but you'll be on the bottom of the top.
So who's your boss?

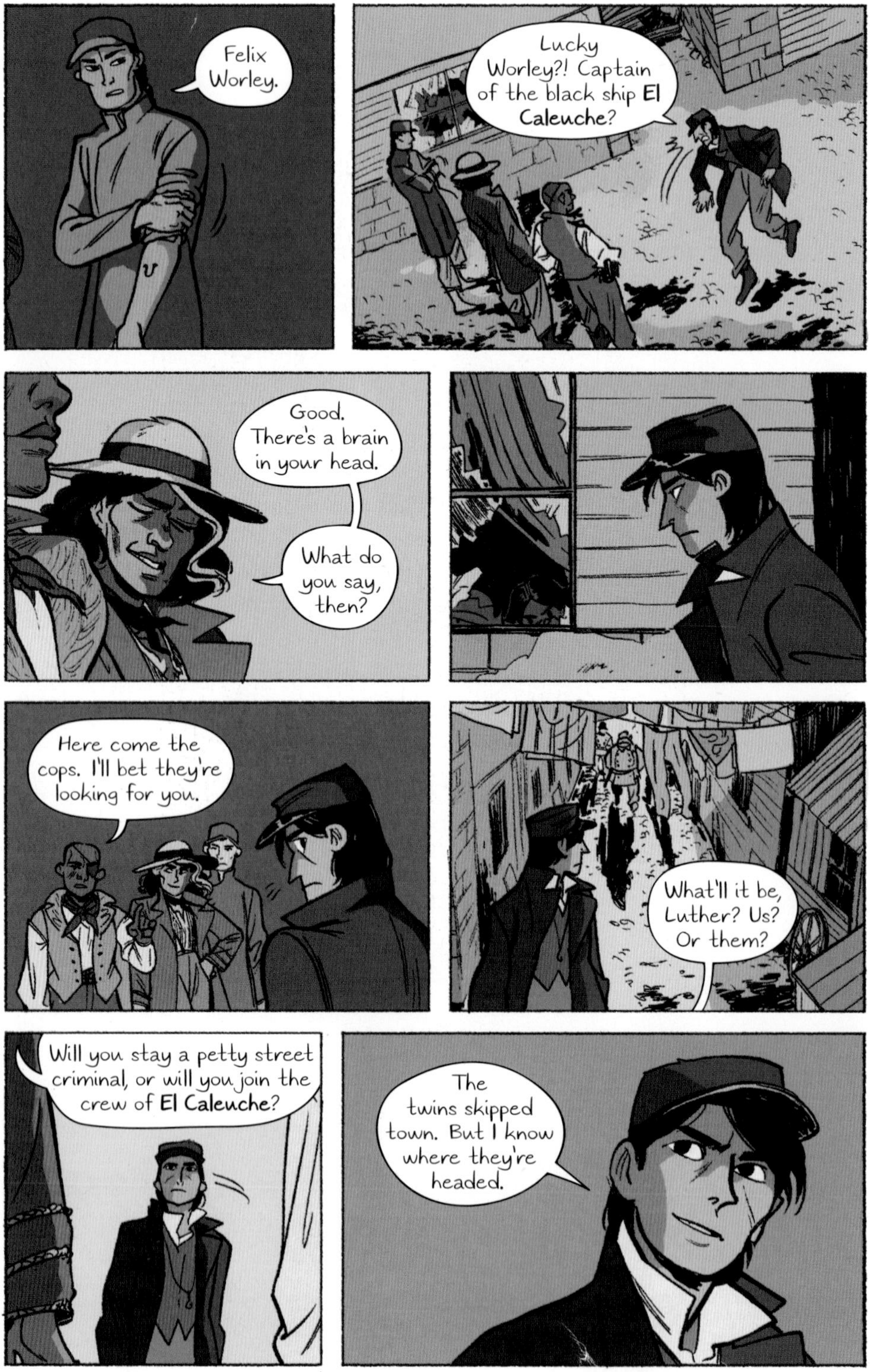
Felix Worley.
Lucky Worley?! Captain of the black ship El Caleuche?
Good. There's a brain in your head.
What do you say, then?
Here come the cops. I'll bet they're looking for you.
What'll it be, Luther? Us? Or them?
Will you stay a petty street criminal, or will you join the crew of El Caleuche?
The twins skipped town. But I know where they're headed.

CHAPTER TWO
IMPOSTERS

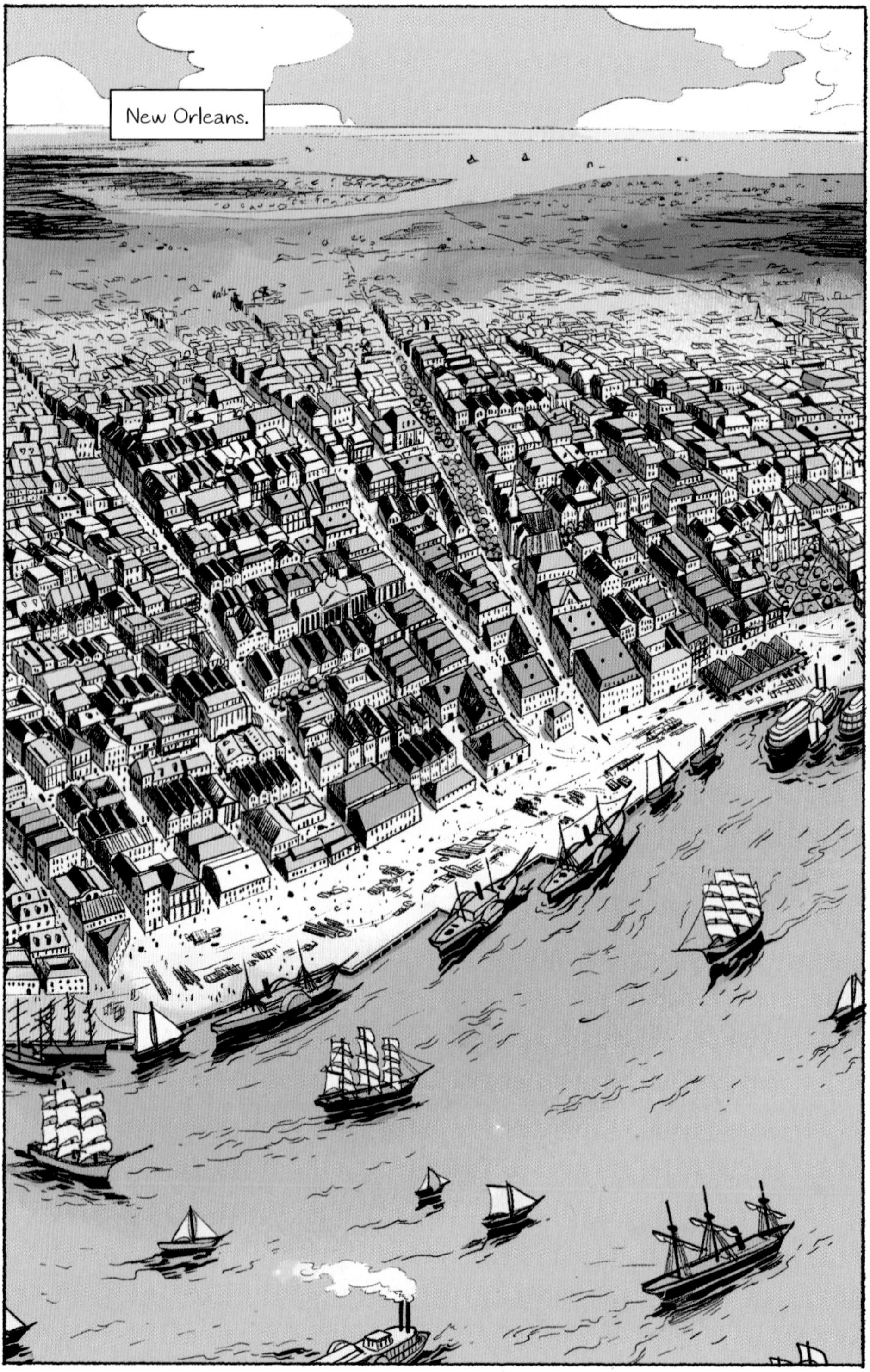
New Orleans.

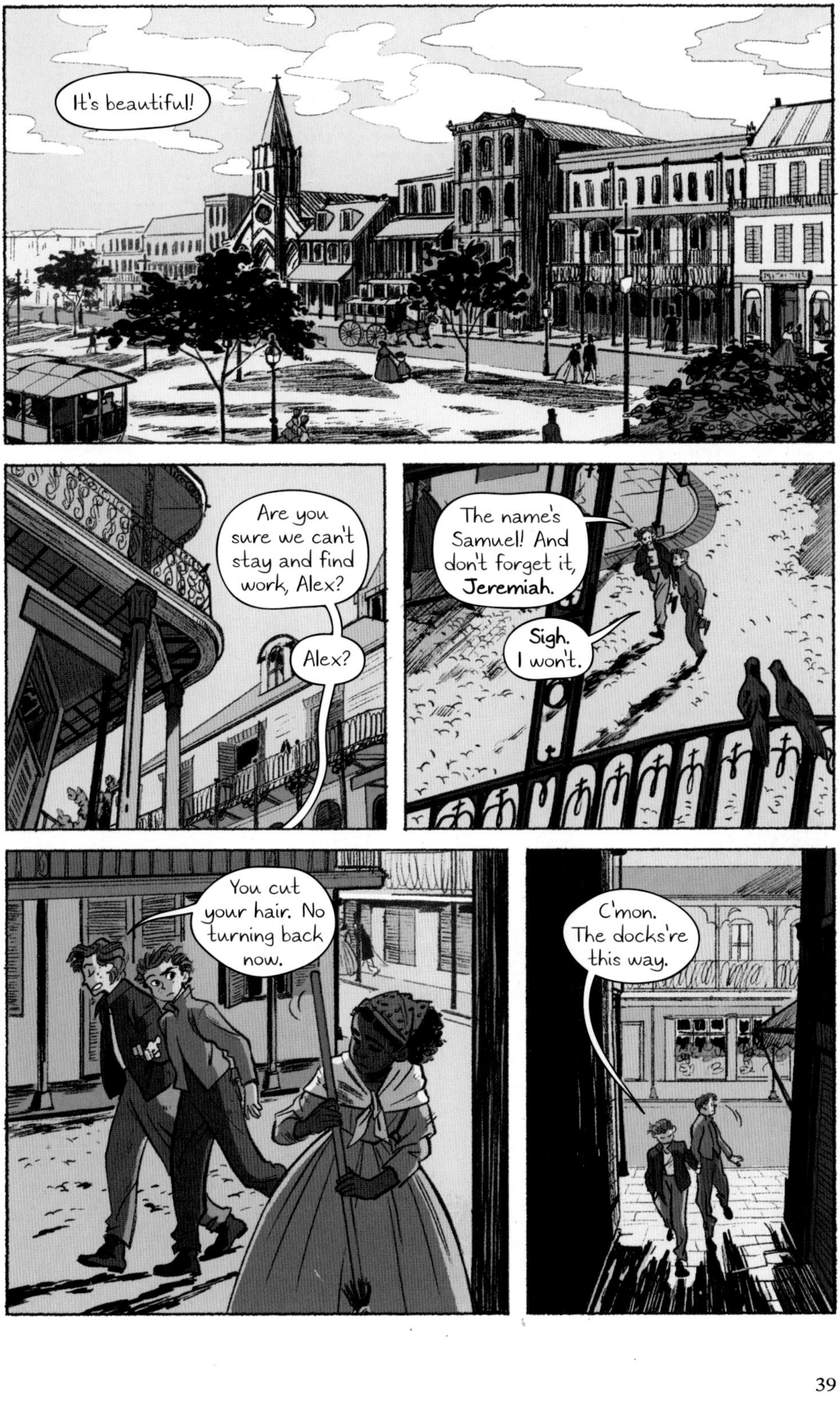

It's beautiful!
Are you sure we can't stay and find work, Alex?
Alex?
The name's Samuel! And don't forget it, **Jeremiah.**
Sigh. I won't.
You cut your hair. No turning back now.
C'mon. The docks're this way.

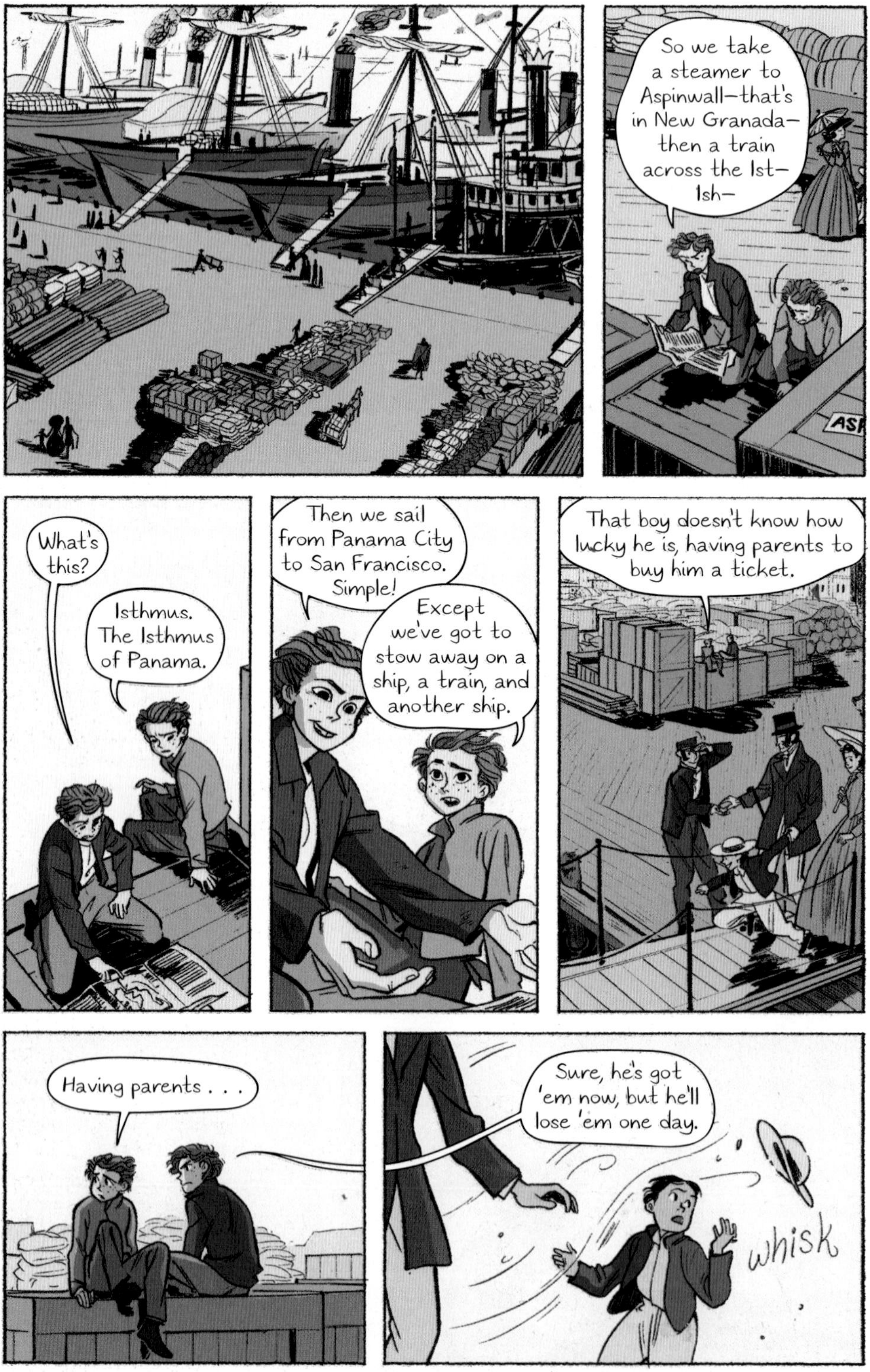
So we take a steamer to Aspinwall—that's in New Granada—then a train across the Ist—Ish—
ASP
What's this?
Isthmus. The Isthmus of Panama.
Then we sail from Panama City to San Francisco. Simple!
Except we've got to stow away on a ship, a train, and another ship.
That boy doesn't know how lucky he is, having parents to buy him a ticket.
Having parents . . .
Sure, he's got 'em now, but he'll lose 'em one day.
whisk

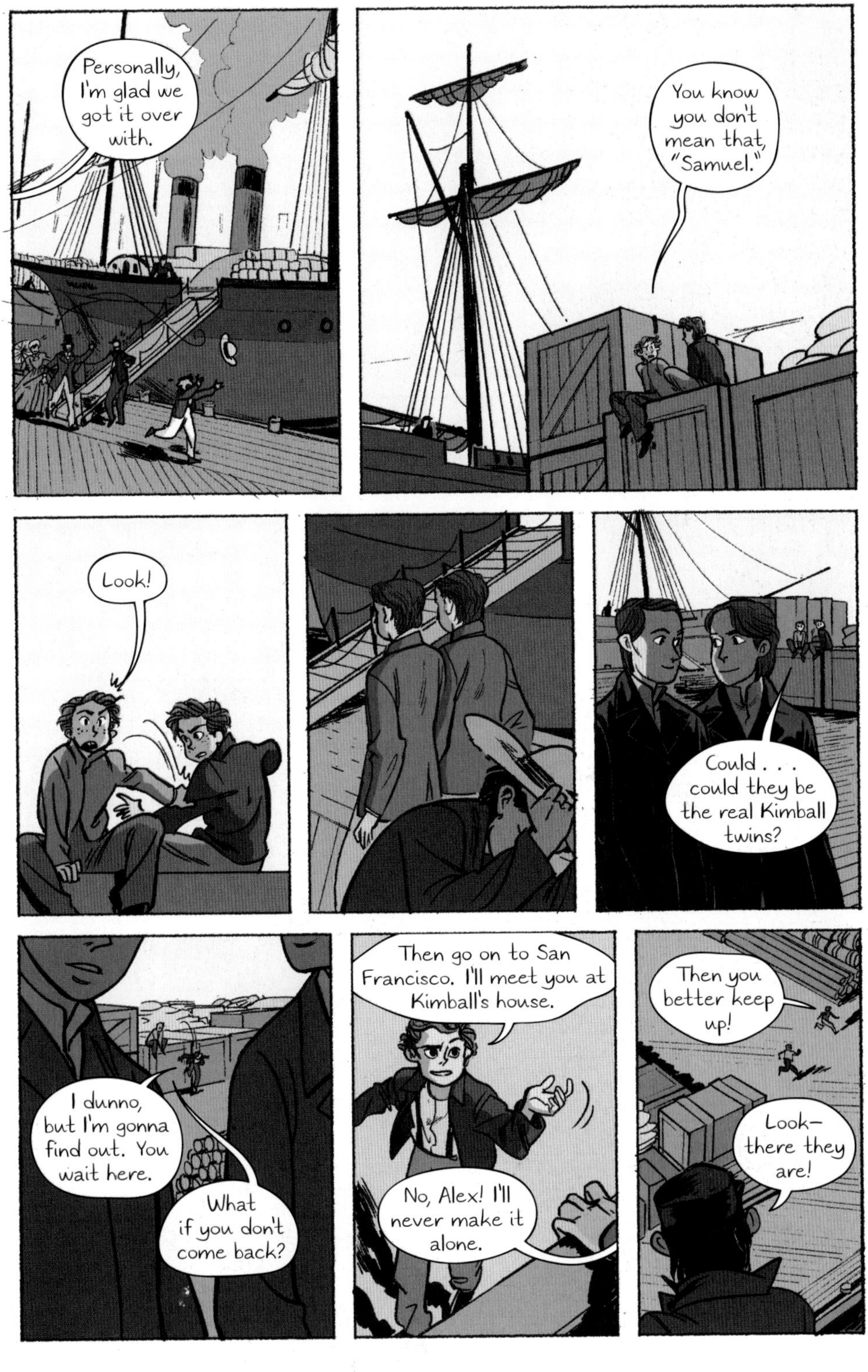

Personally, I'm glad we got it over with.
You know you don't mean that, "Samuel."
Look!
Could . . . could they be the real Kimball twins?
I dunno, but I'm gonna find out. You wait here.
What if you don't come back?
Then go on to San Francisco. I'll meet you at Kimball's house.
No, Alex! I'll never make it alone.
Then you better keep up!
Look—there they are!

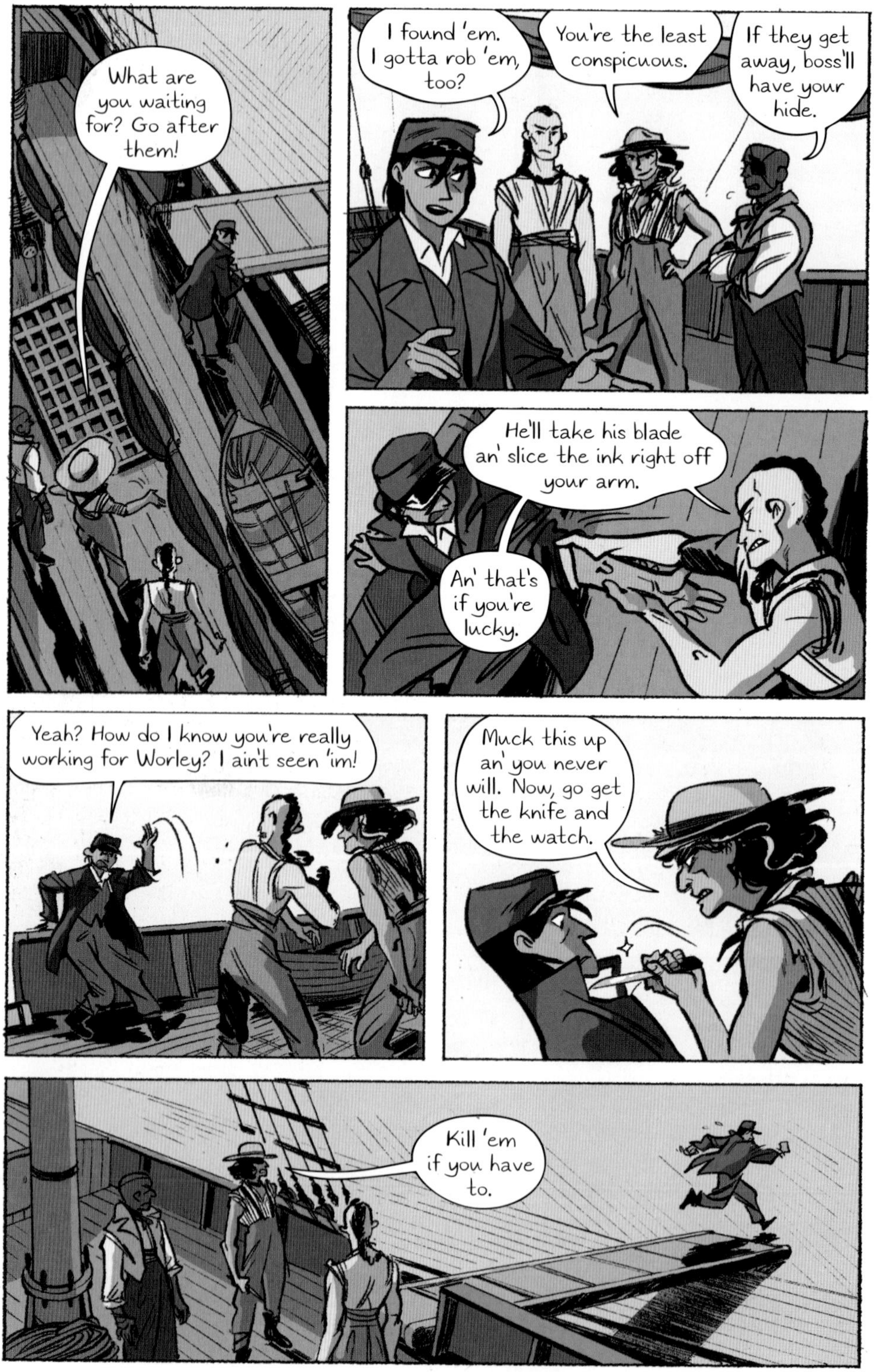
What are you waiting for? Go after them!
I found 'em. I gotta rob 'em, too?
You're the least conspicuous.
If they get away, boss'll have your hide.
He'll take his blade an' slice the ink right off your arm.
An' that's if you're lucky.
Yeah? How do I know you're really working for Worley? I ain't seen 'im!
Muck this up an' you never will. Now, go get the knife and the watch.
Kill 'em if you have to.

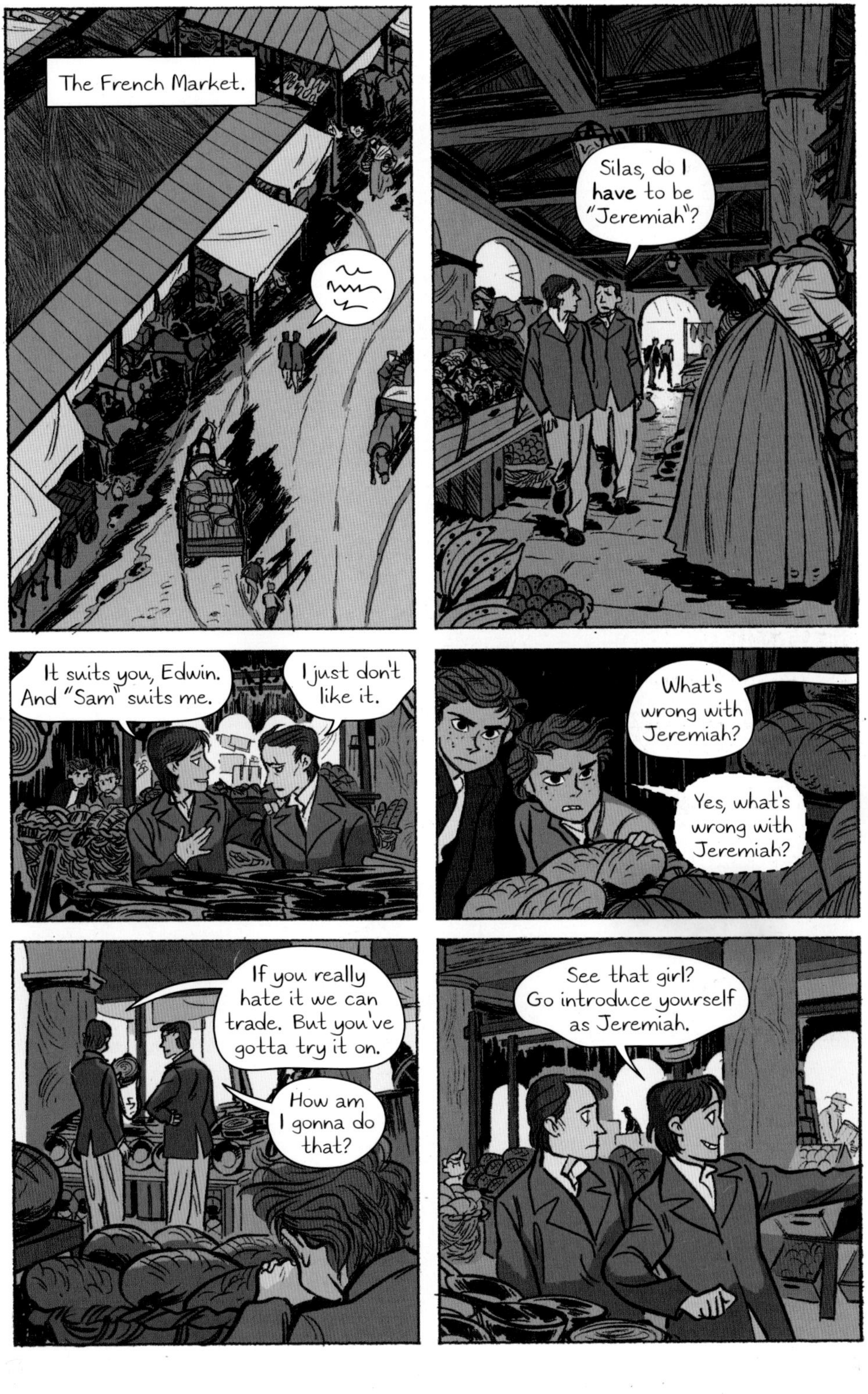

The French Market.
Silas, do I **have** to be "Jeremiah"?
It suits you, Edwin. And "Sam" suits me.
I just don't like it.
What's wrong with Jeremiah?
Yes, what's wrong with Jeremiah?
If you really hate it we can trade. But you've gotta try it on.
How am I gonna do that?
See that girl? Go introduce yourself as Jeremiah.

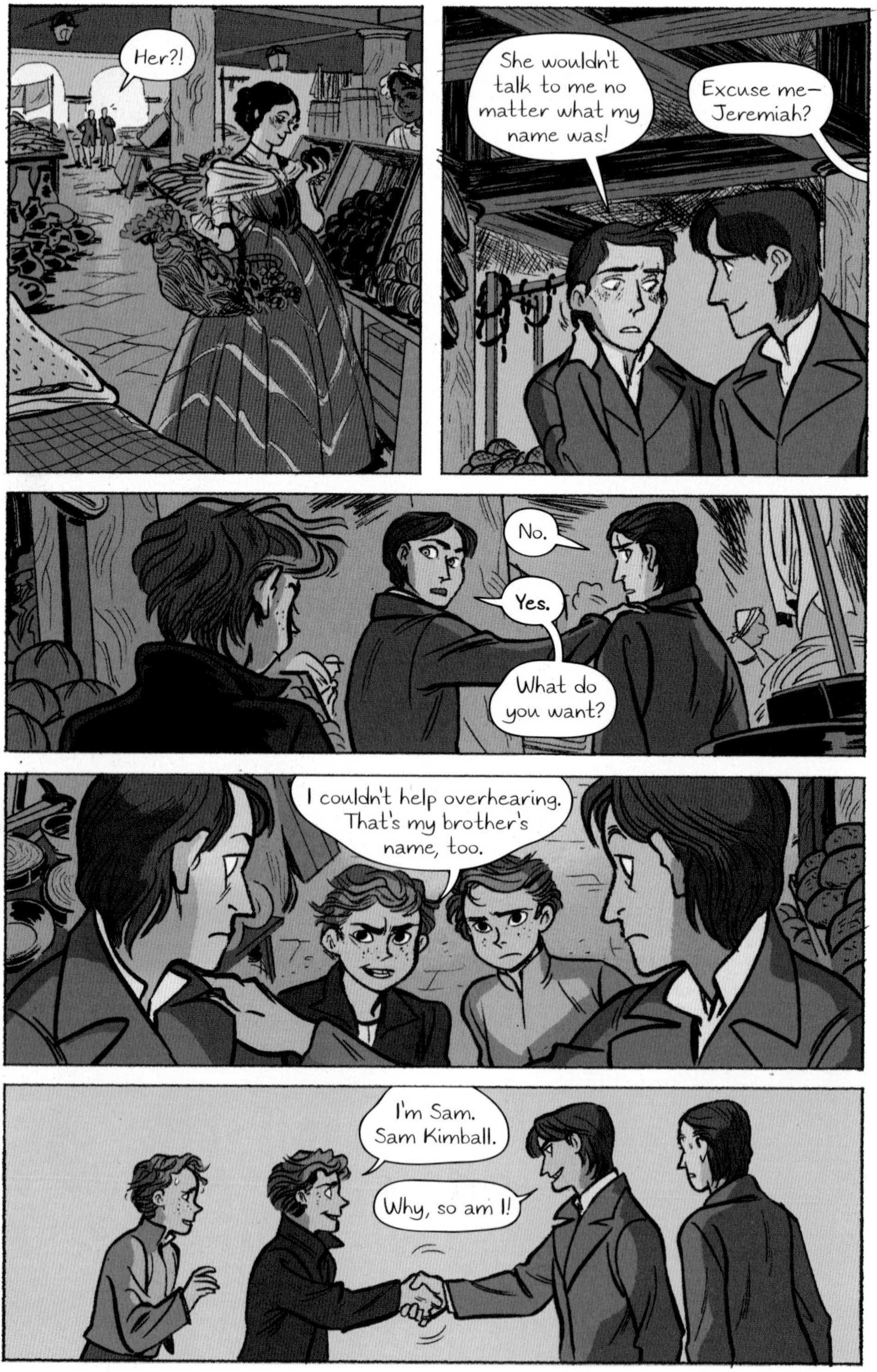

Her?!
She wouldn't talk to me no matter what my name was!
Excuse me— Jeremiah?
No.
Yes.
What do you want?
I couldn't help overhearing. That's my brother's name, too.
I'm Sam. Sam Kimball.
Why, so am I!

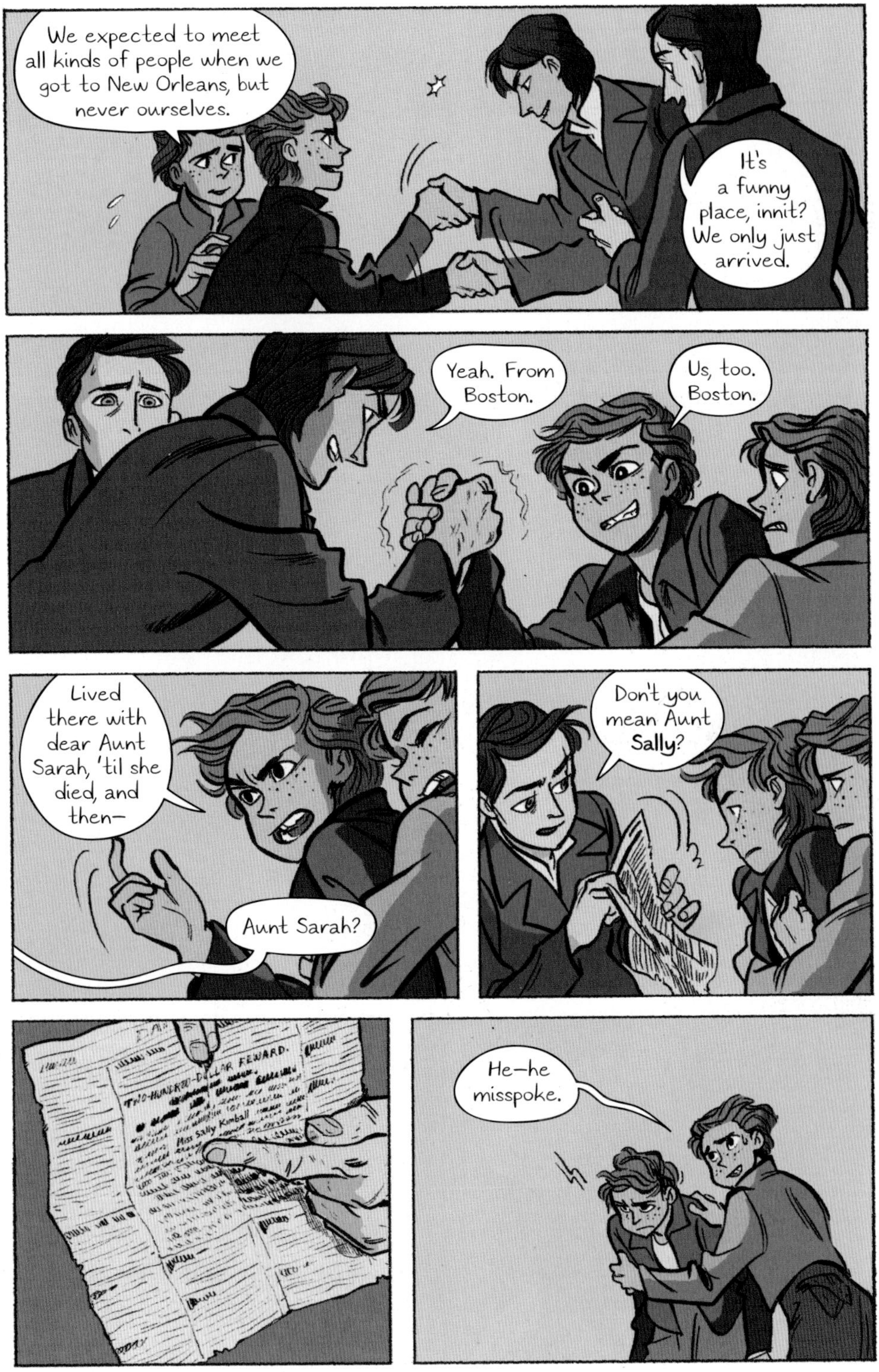

We expected to meet all kinds of people when we got to New Orleans, but never ourselves.
It's a funny place, innit? We only just arrived.
Yeah. From Boston.
Us, too. Boston.
Lived there with dear Aunt Sarah, 'til she died, and then—
Aunt Sarah?
Don't you mean Aunt Sally?
Miss Sally Kimball
He—he misspoke.

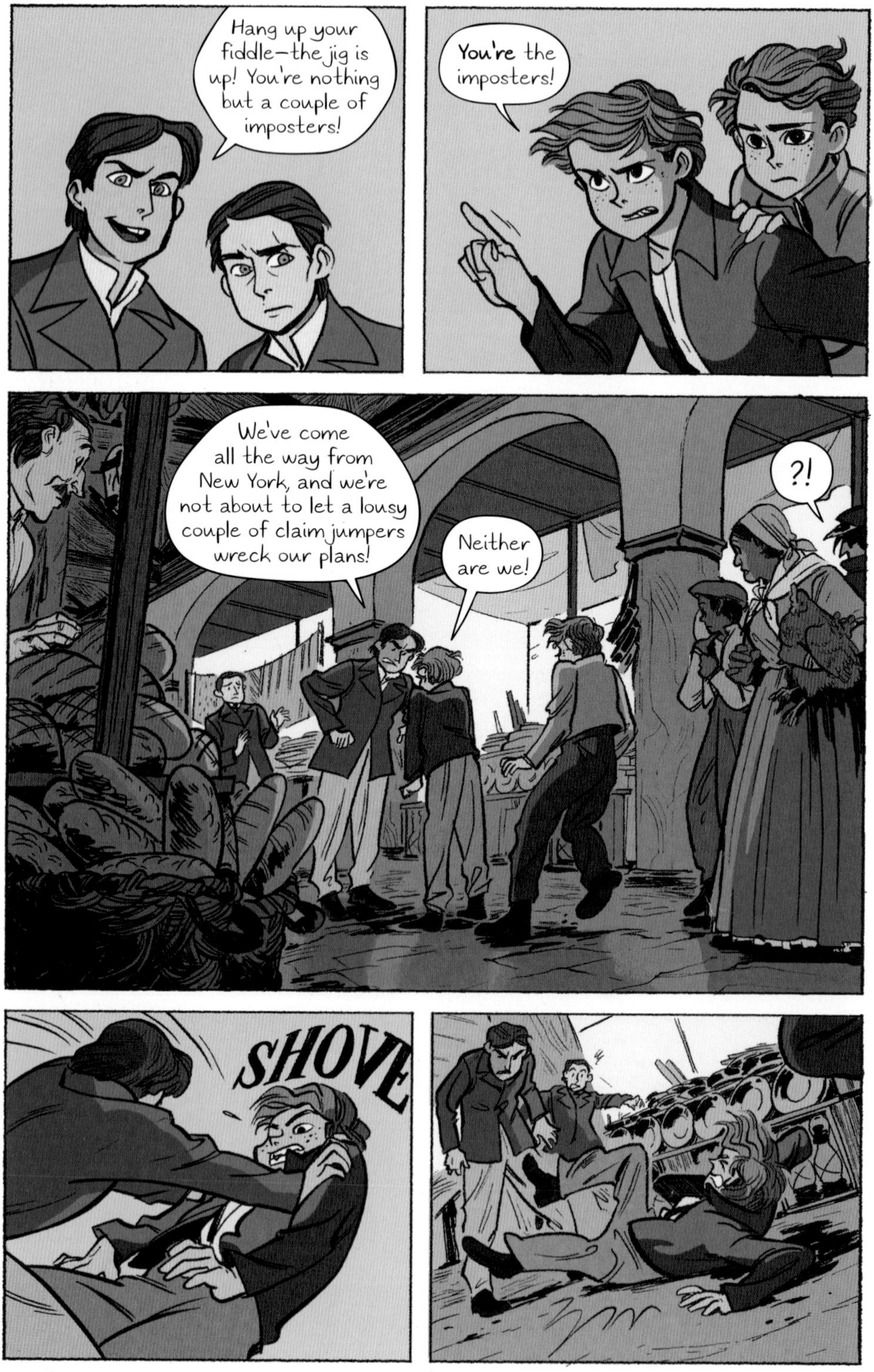
Hang up your fiddle—the jig is up! You're nothing but a couple of imposters!
You're the imposters!
We've come all the way from New York, and we're not about to let a lousy couple of claim jumpers wreck our plans!
Neither are we!
?!
SHOVE

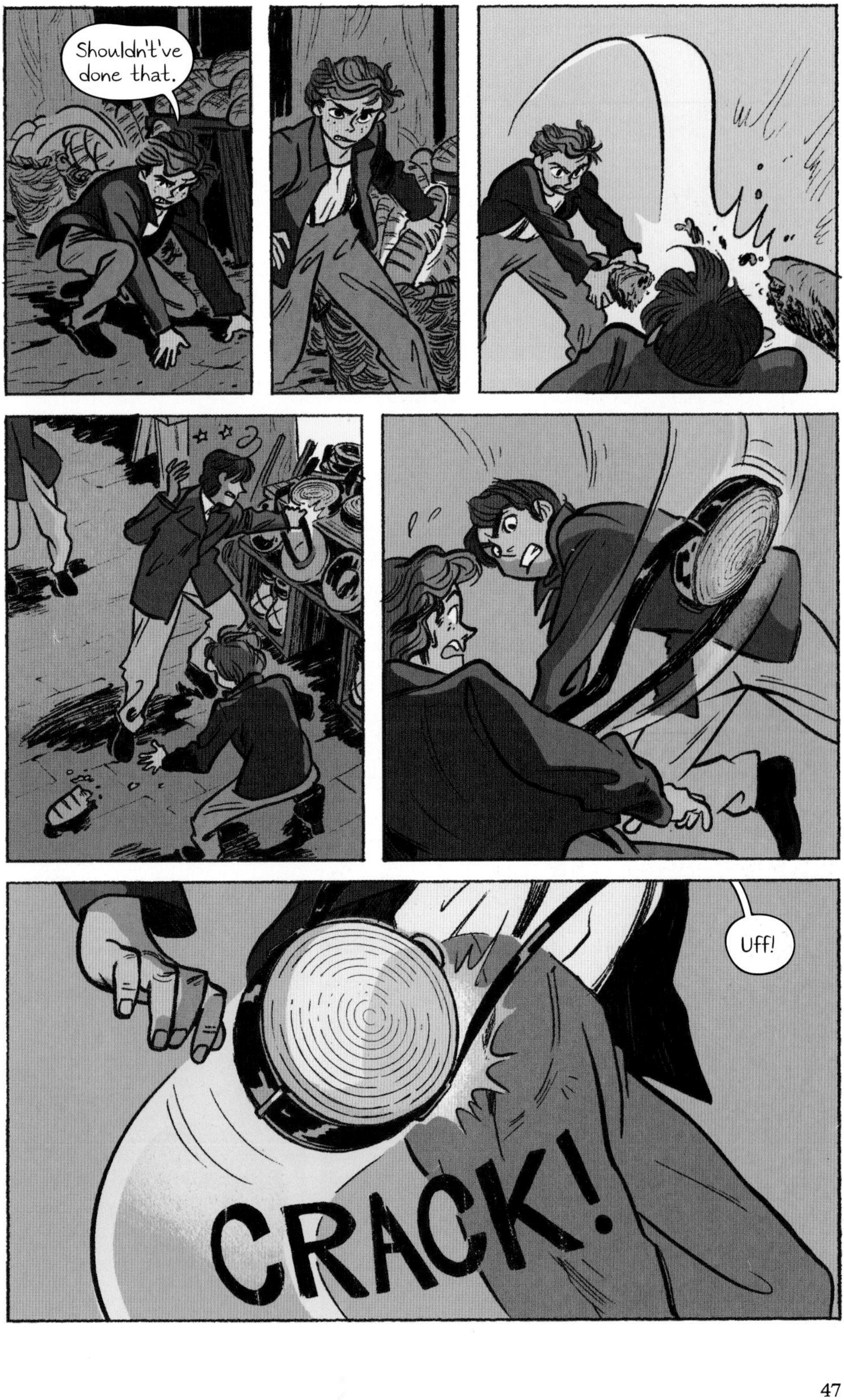
Shouldn't've done that.
Uff!
CRACK!

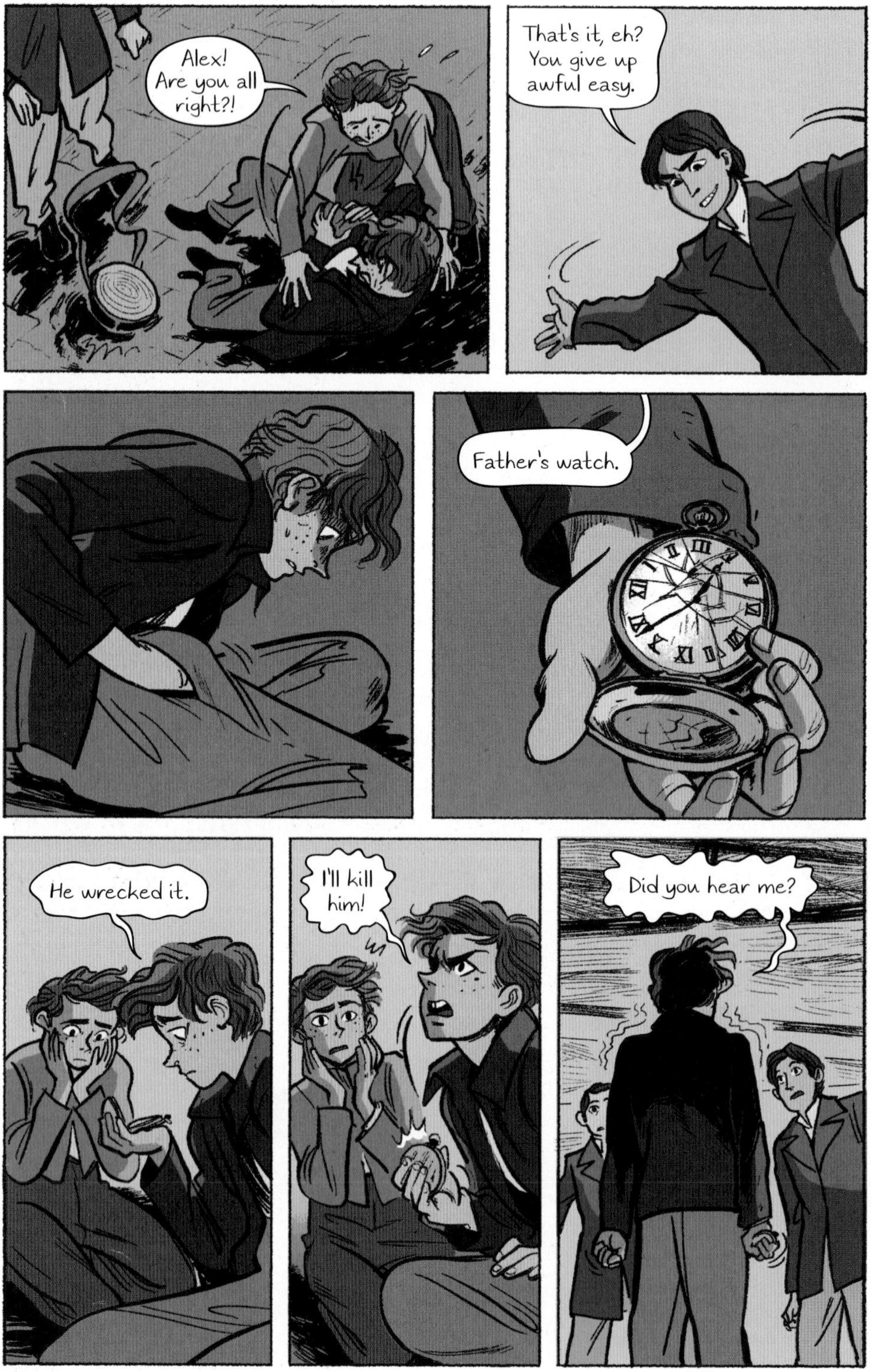
Alex! Are you all right?!
That's it, eh? You give up awful easy.
Father's watch.
He wrecked it.
I'll kill him!
Did you hear me?

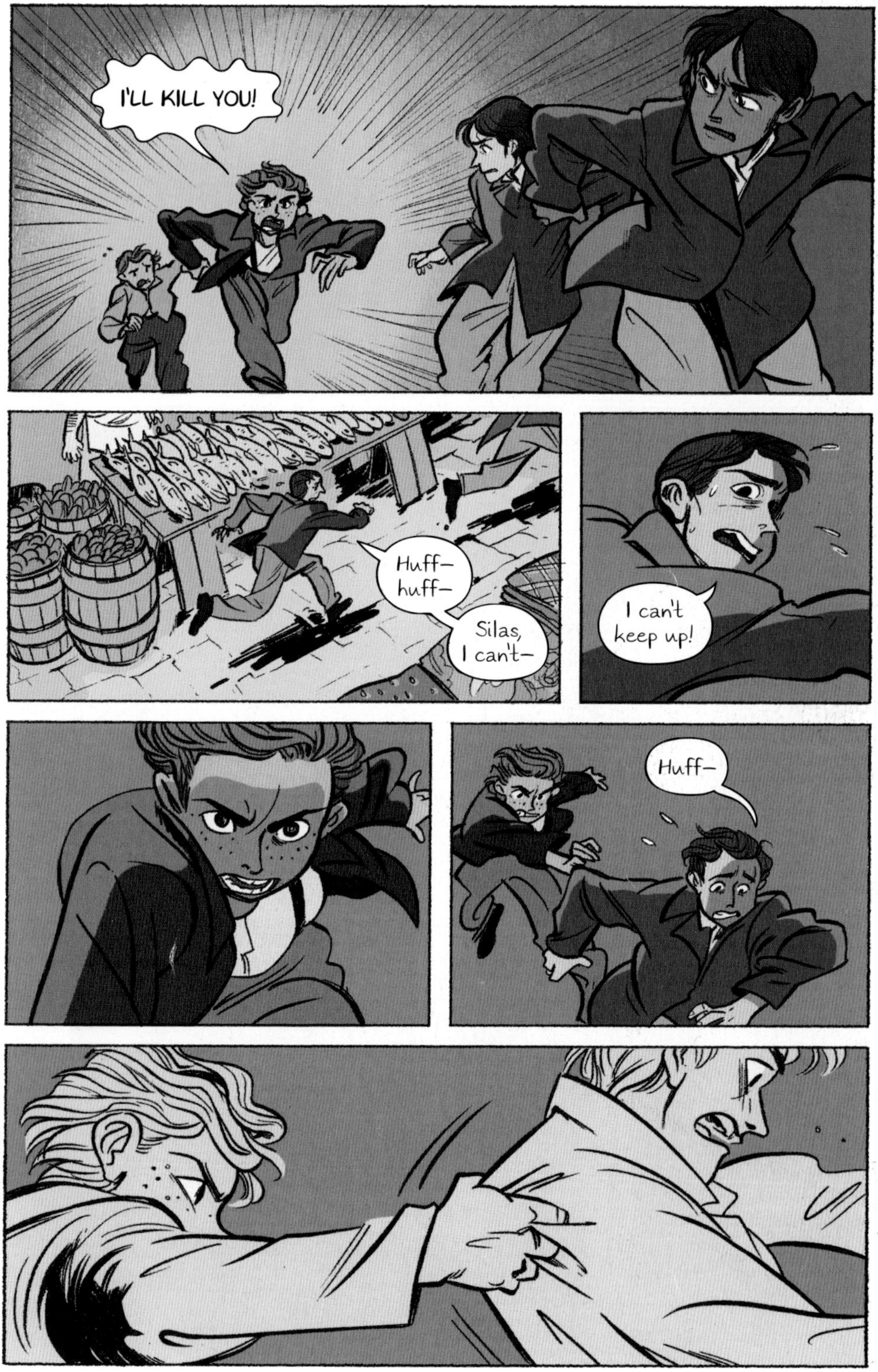
I'LL KILL YOU!
Huff—
huff—
Silas,
I can't—
I can't
keep up!
Huff—

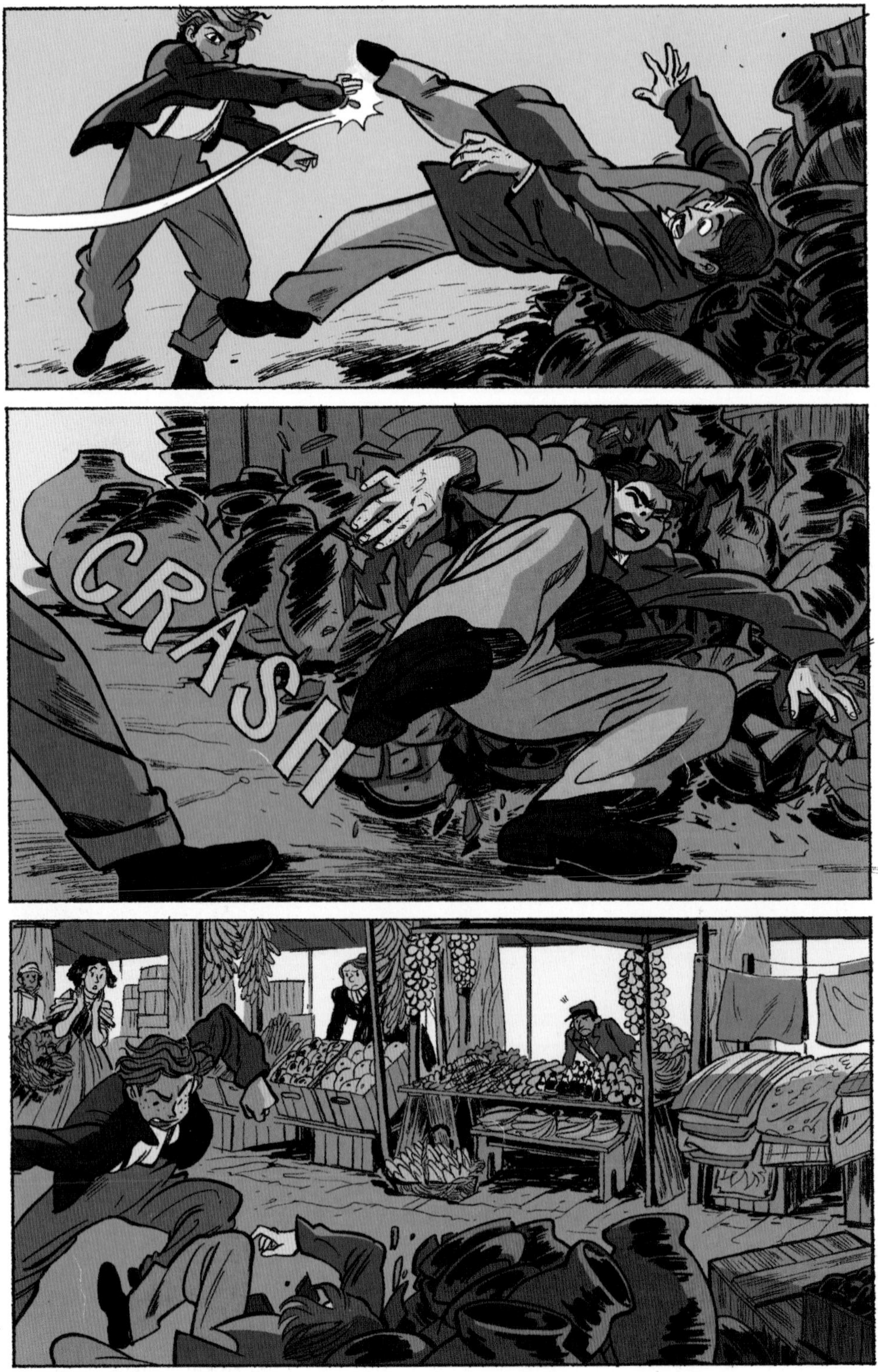
CRASH

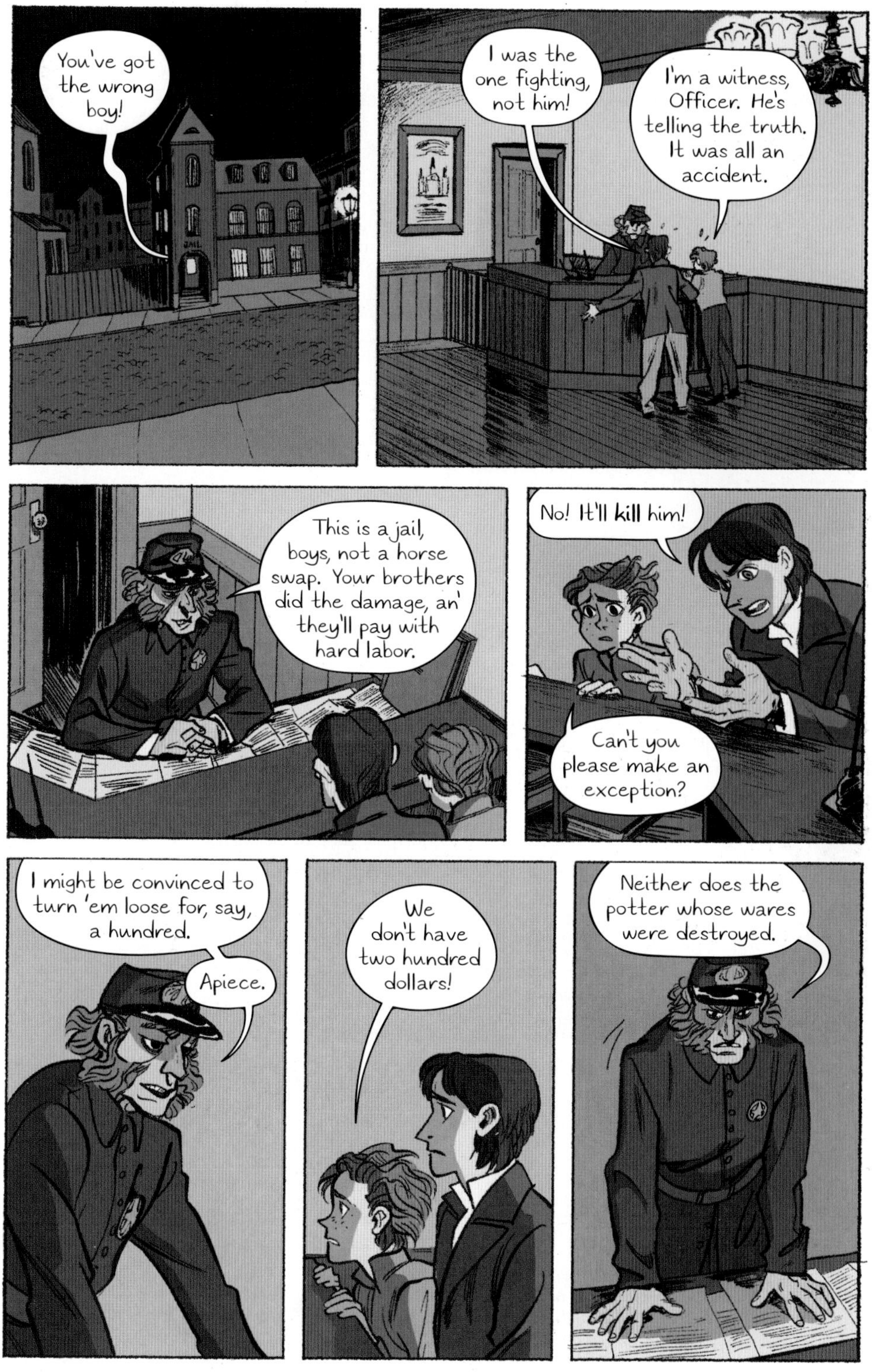
You've got the wrong boy!
JAIL
I was the one fighting, not him!
I'm a witness, Officer. He's telling the truth. It was all an accident.
This is a jail, boys, not a horse swap. Your brothers did the damage, an' they'll pay with hard labor.
No! It'll **kill** him!
Can't you please make an exception?
I might be convinced to turn 'em loose for, say, a hundred.
Apiece.
We don't have two hundred dollars!
Neither does the potter whose wares were destroyed.

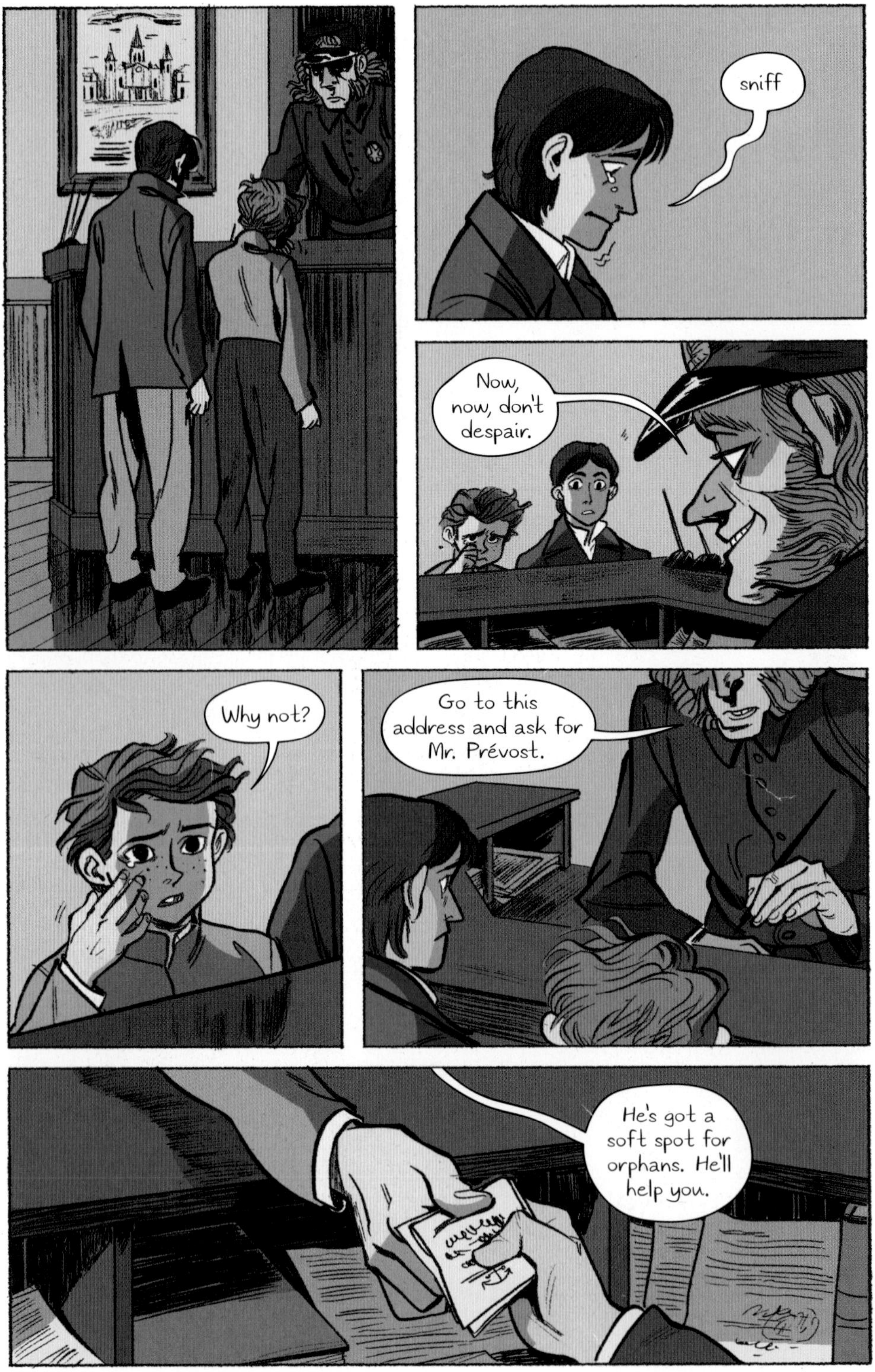
sniff
Now, now, don't despair.
Why not?
Go to this address and ask for Mr. Prévost.
He's got a soft spot for orphans. He'll help you.

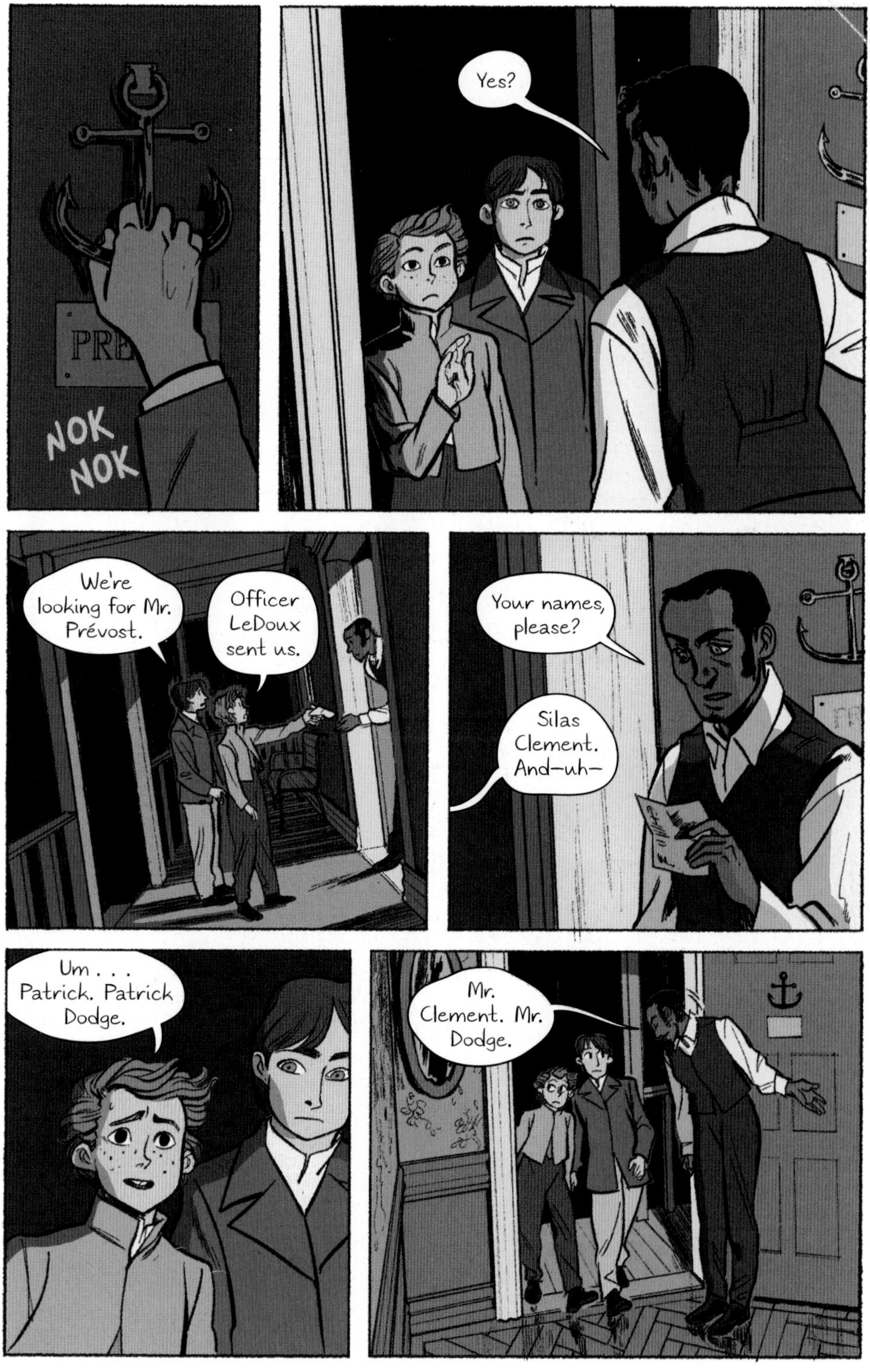
PRE
NOK
NOK
Yes?
We're looking for Mr. Prévost.
Officer LeDoux sent us.
Your names, please?
Silas Clement. And—uh—
Um . . . Patrick. Patrick Dodge.
Mr. Clement. Mr. Dodge.

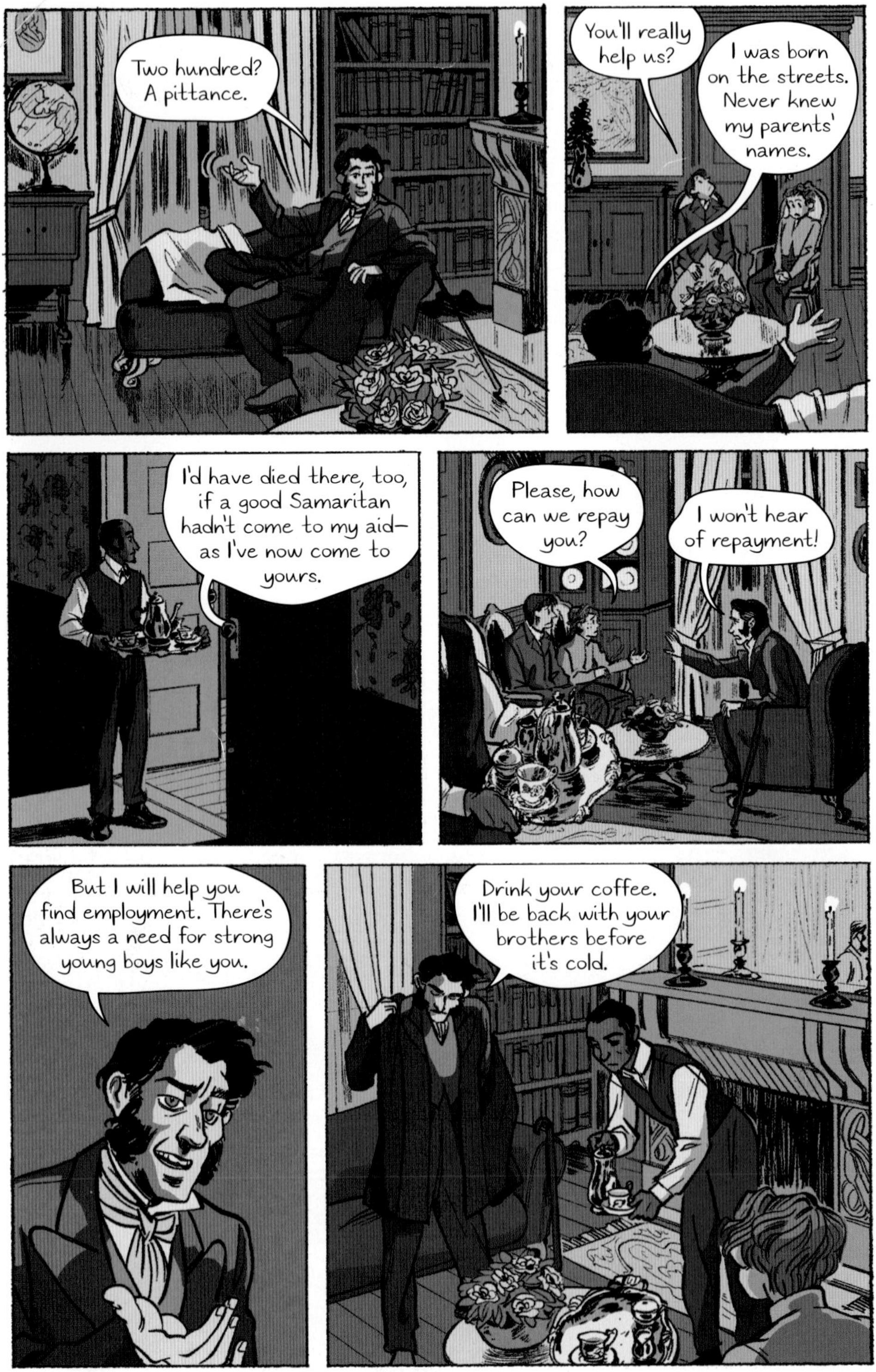
Two hundred? A pittance.
You'll really help us?
I was born on the streets. Never knew my parents' names.
I'd have died there, too, if a good Samaritan hadn't come to my aid—as I've now come to yours.
Please, how can we repay you?
I won't hear of repayment!
But I will help you find employment. There's always a need for strong young boys like you.
Drink your coffee. I'll be back with your brothers before it's cold.

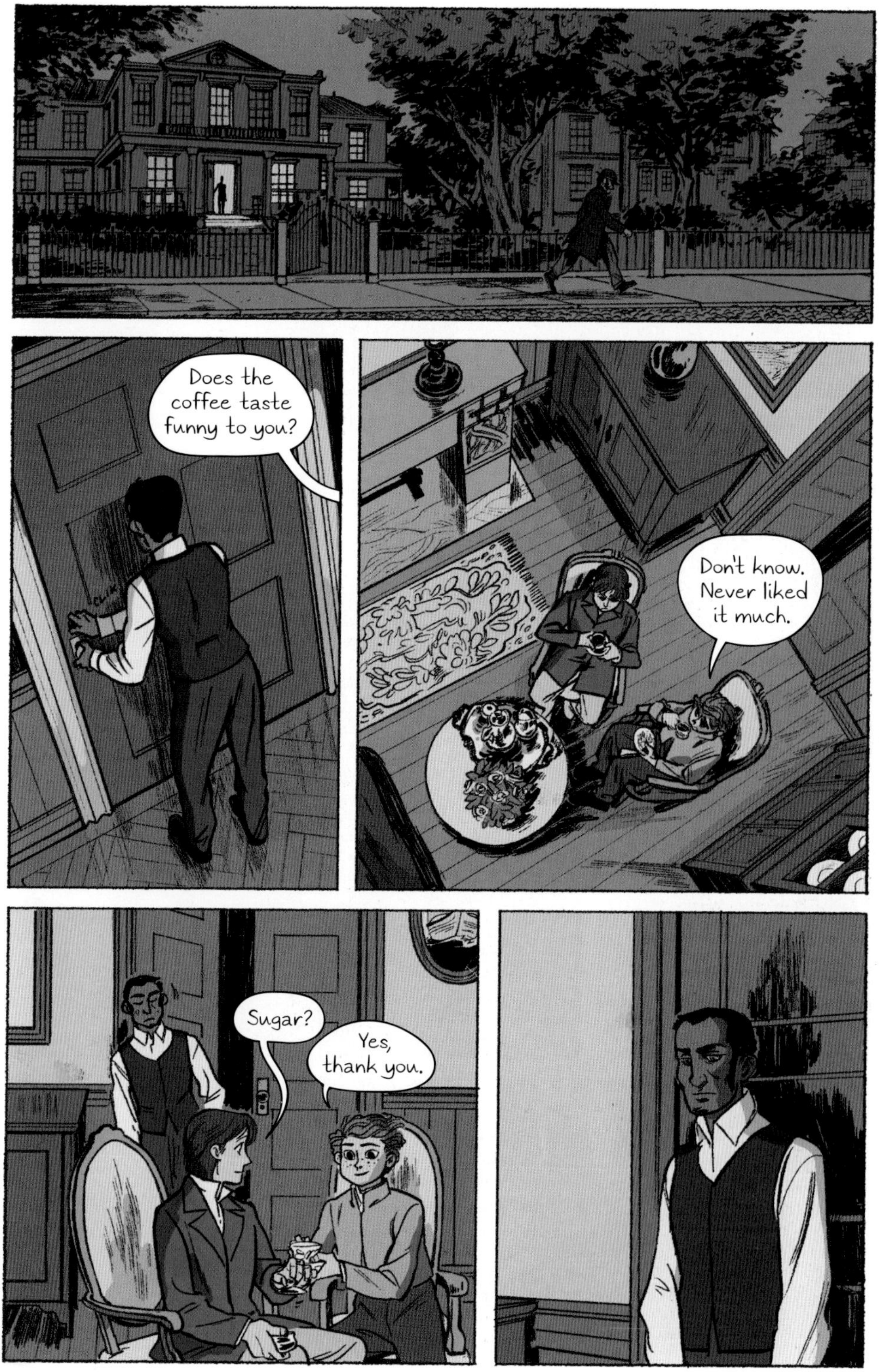
Does the coffee taste funny to you?
Don't know. Never liked it much.
Sugar?
Yes, thank you.

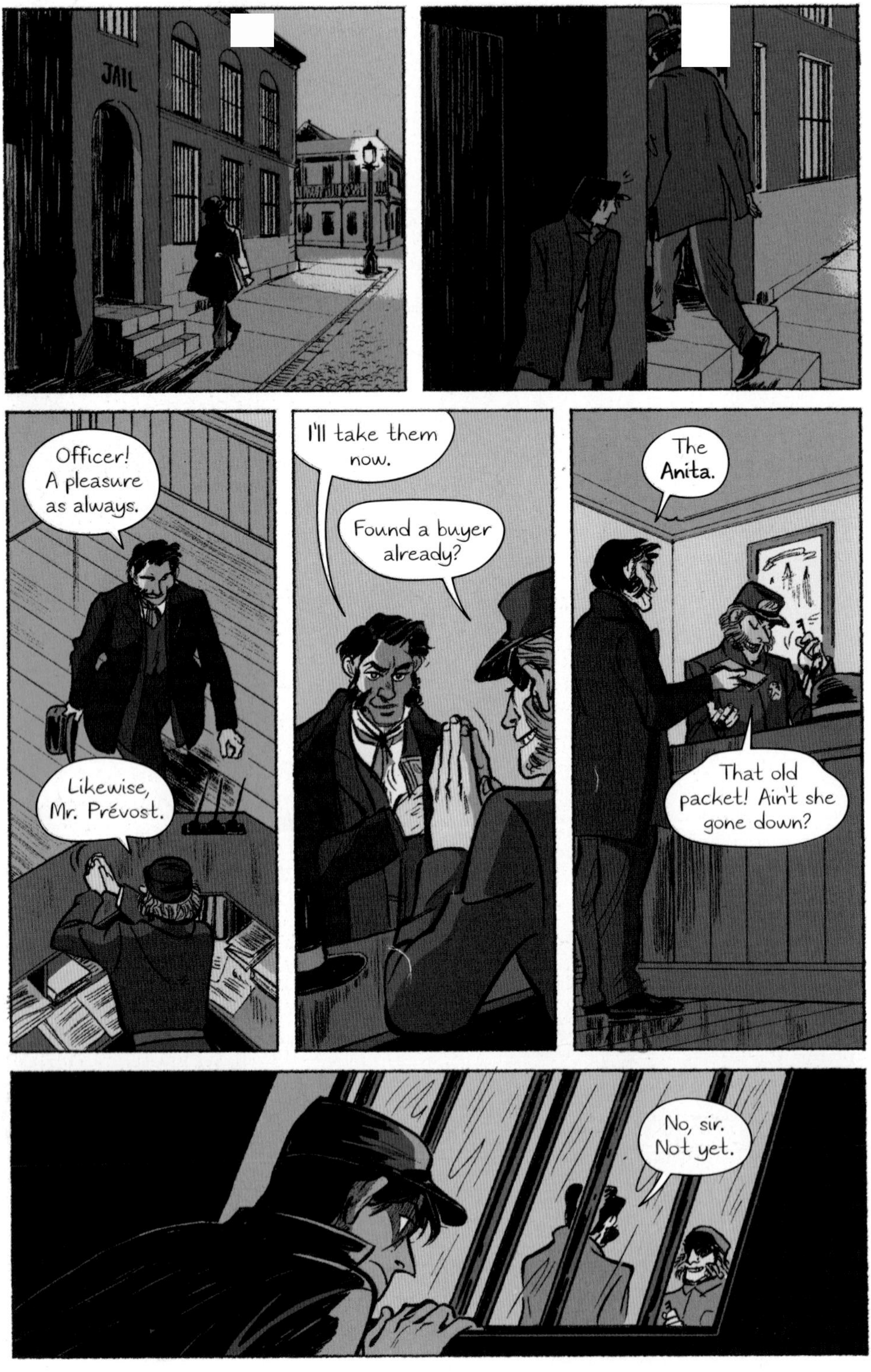
JAIL
Officer! A pleasure as always.
Likewise, Mr. Prévost.
I'll take them now.
Found a buyer already?
The **Anita.**
That old packet! Ain't she gone down?
No, sir. Not yet.

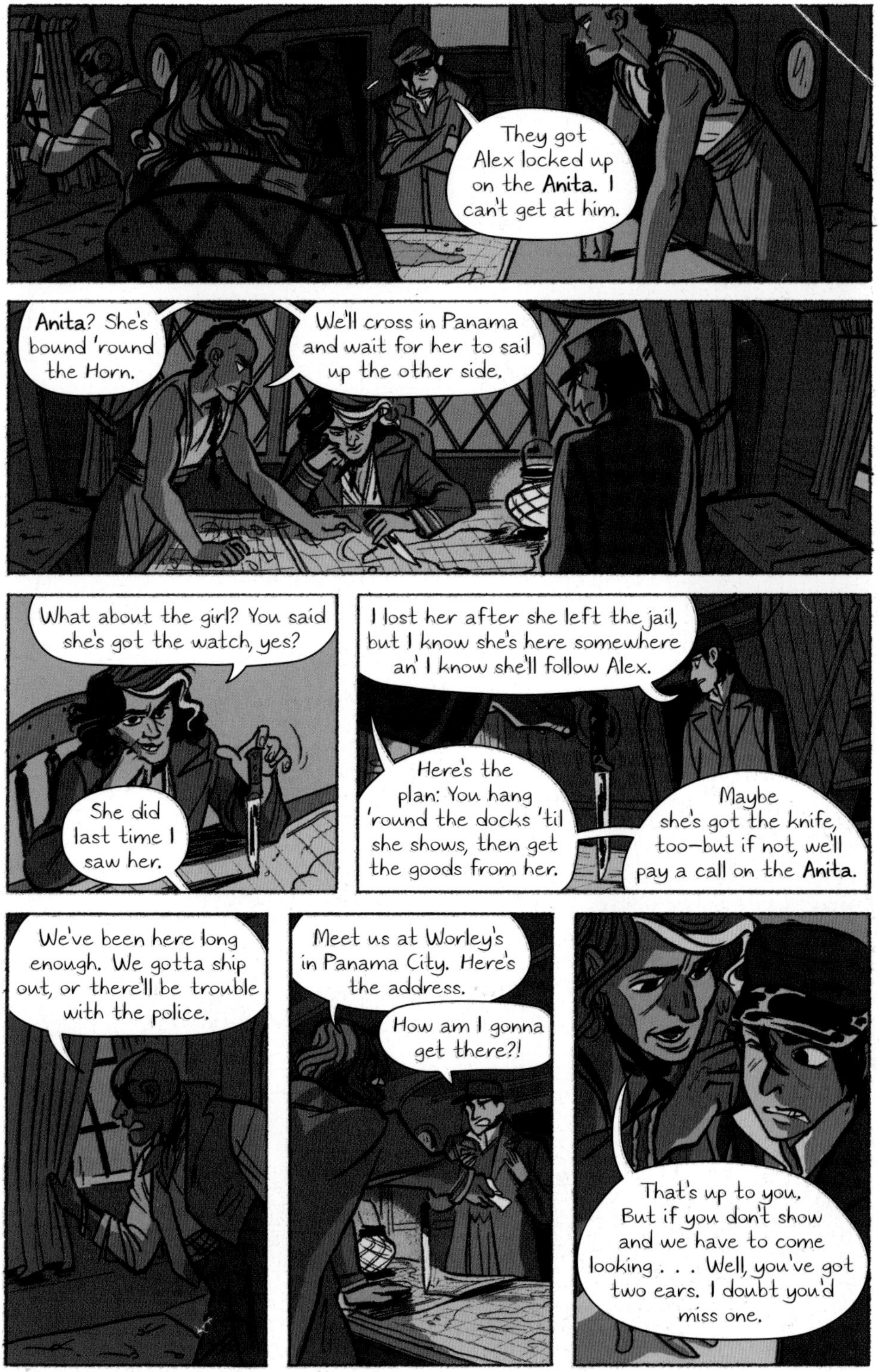
They got Alex locked up on the Anita. I can't get at him.
Anita? She's bound 'round the Horn.
We'll cross in Panama and wait for her to sail up the other side.
What about the girl? You said she's got the watch, yes?
She did last time I saw her.
I lost her after she left the jail, but I know she's here somewhere an' I know she'll follow Alex.
Here's the plan: You hang 'round the docks 'til she shows, then get the goods from her.
Maybe she's got the knife, too—but if not, we'll pay a call on the Anita.
We've been here long enough. We gotta ship out, or there'll be trouble with the police.
Meet us at Worley's in Panama City. Here's the address.
How am I gonna get there?!
That's up to you. But if you don't show and we have to come looking . . . Well, you've got two ears. I doubt you'd miss one.

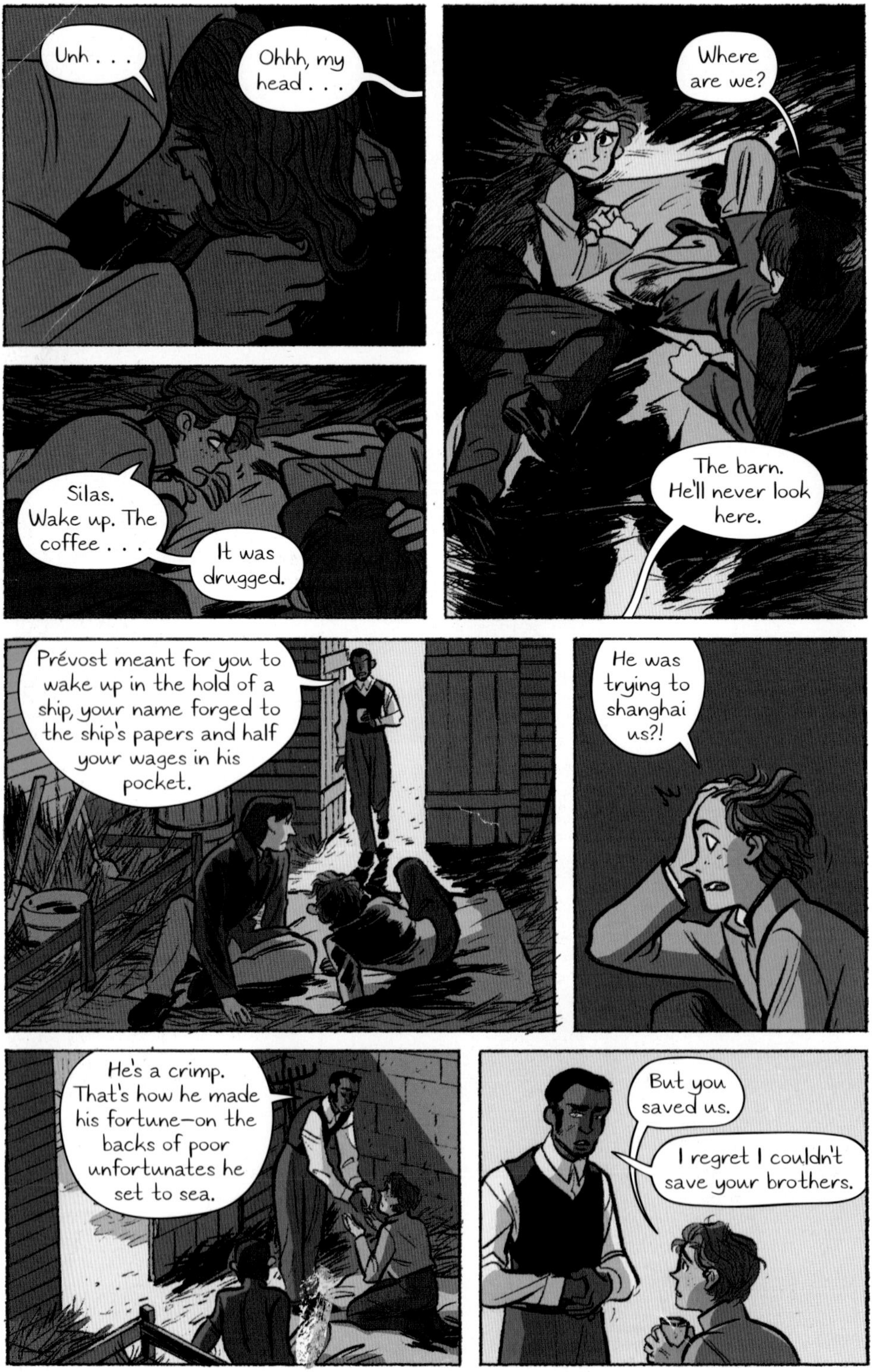
Unh . . .
Ohhh, my head . . .
Where are we?
Silas. Wake up. The coffee . . .
It was drugged.
The barn. He'll never look here.
Prévost meant for you to wake up in the hold of a ship, your name forged to the ship's papers and half your wages in his pocket.
He was trying to shanghai us?!
He's a crimp. That's how he made his fortune—on the backs of poor unfortunates he set to sea.
But you saved us.
I regret I couldn't save your brothers.

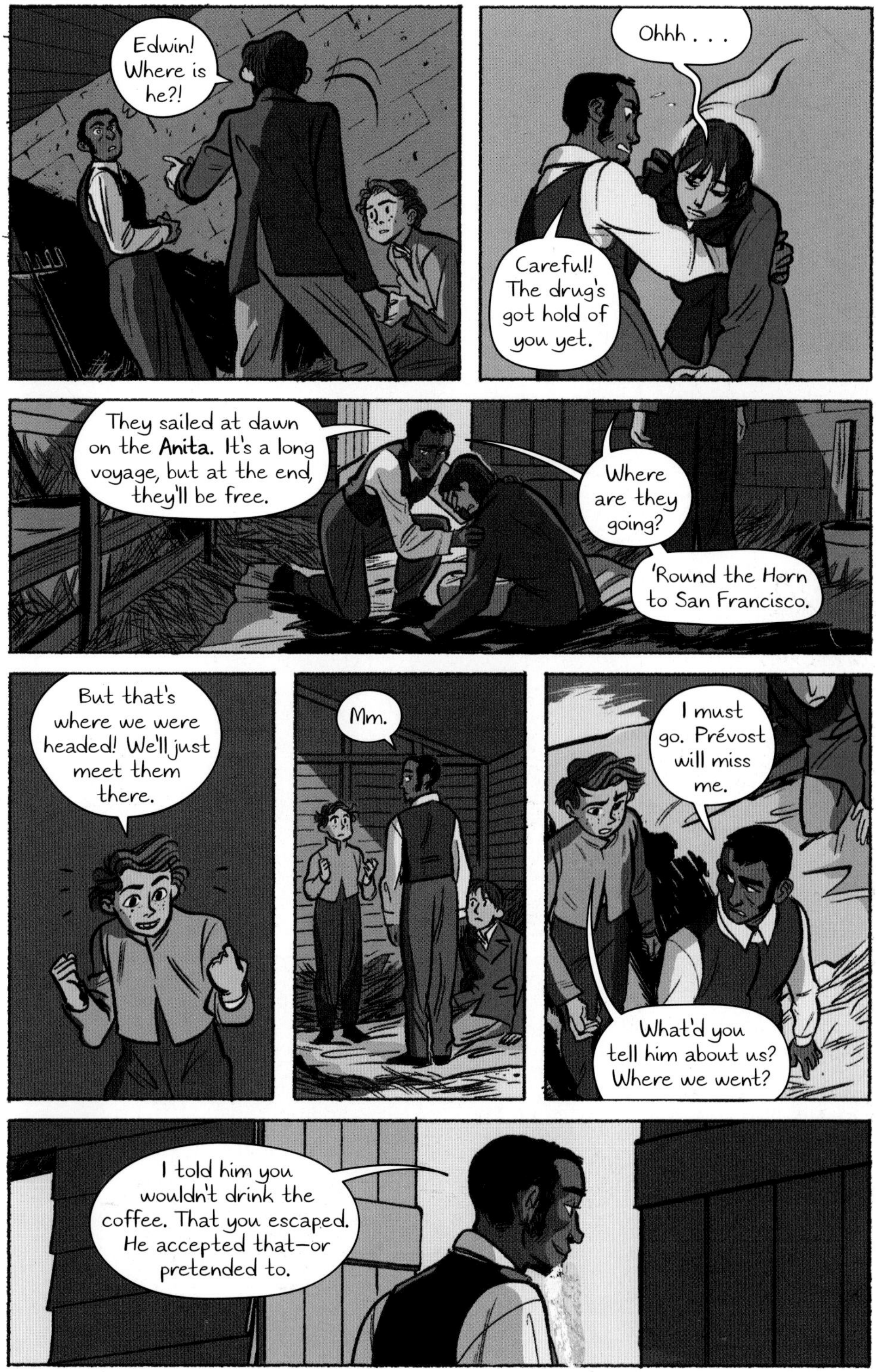
Edwin! Where is he?!
Ohhh . . .
Careful! The drug's got hold of you yet.
They sailed at dawn on the **Anita.** It's a long voyage, but at the end, they'll be free.
Where are they going?
'Round the Horn to San Francisco.
But that's where we were headed! We'll just meet them there.
Mm.
I must go. Prévost will miss me.
What'd you tell him about us? Where we went?
I told him you wouldn't drink the coffee. That you escaped. He accepted that—or pretended to.

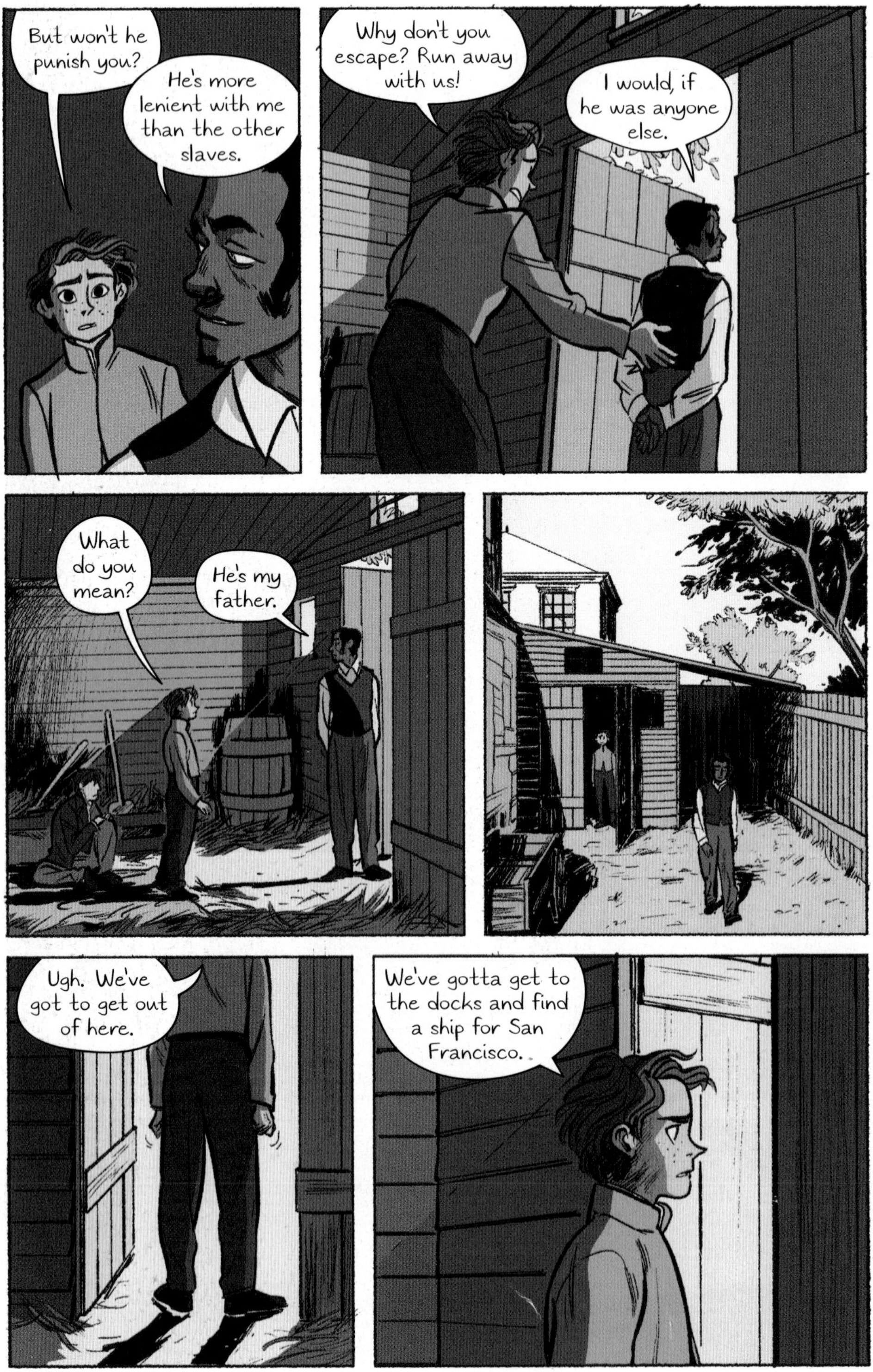
But won't he punish you?
He's more lenient with me than the other slaves.
Why don't you escape? Run away with us!
I would, if he was anyone else.
What do you mean?
He's my father.
Ugh. We've got to get out of here.
We've gotta get to the docks and find a ship for San Francisco.

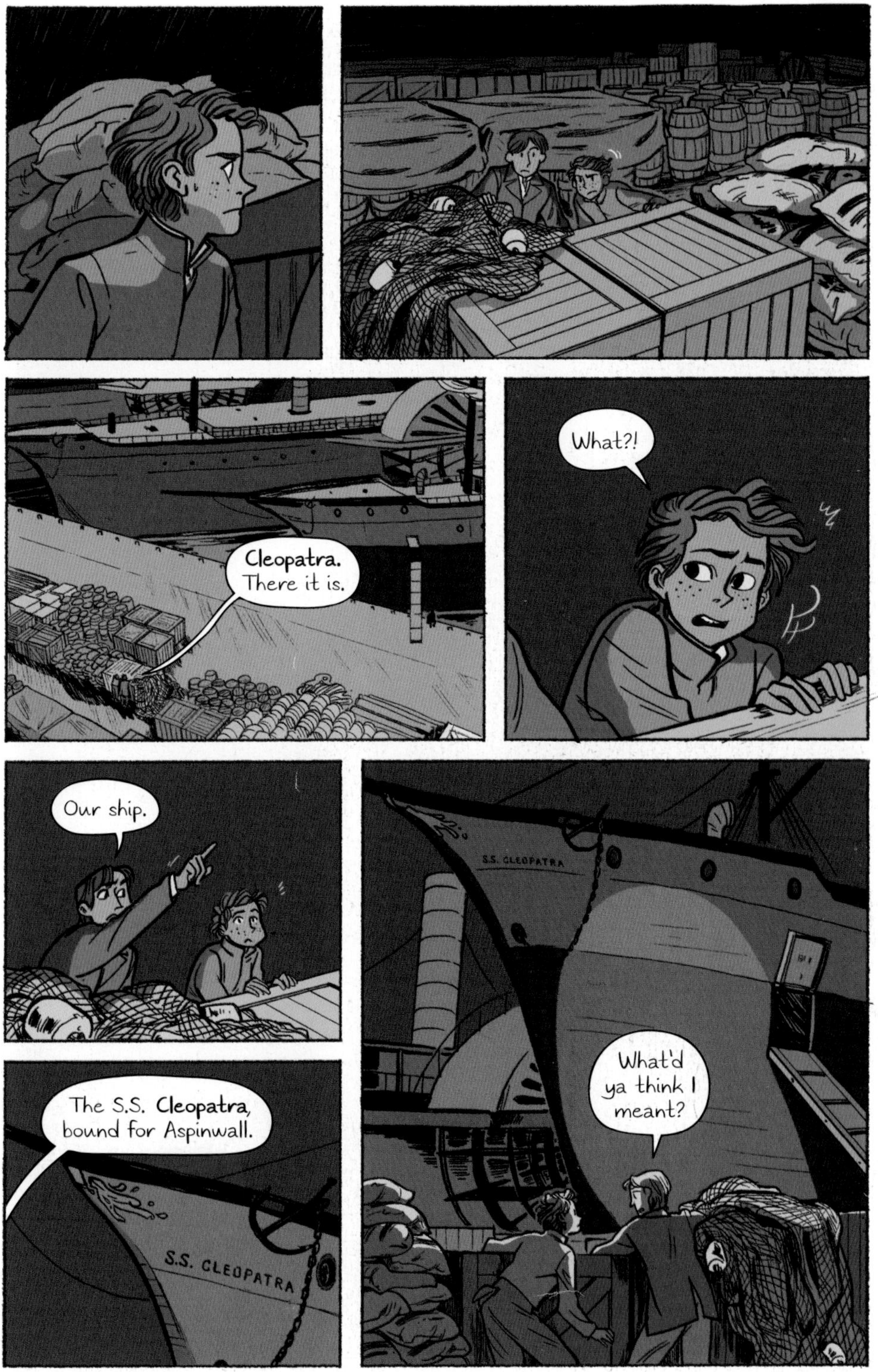

Cleopatra. There it is.
What?!
Our ship.
The S.S. Cleopatra, bound for Aspinwall.
S.S. CLEOPATRA
S.S. CLEOPATRA
What'd ya think I meant?

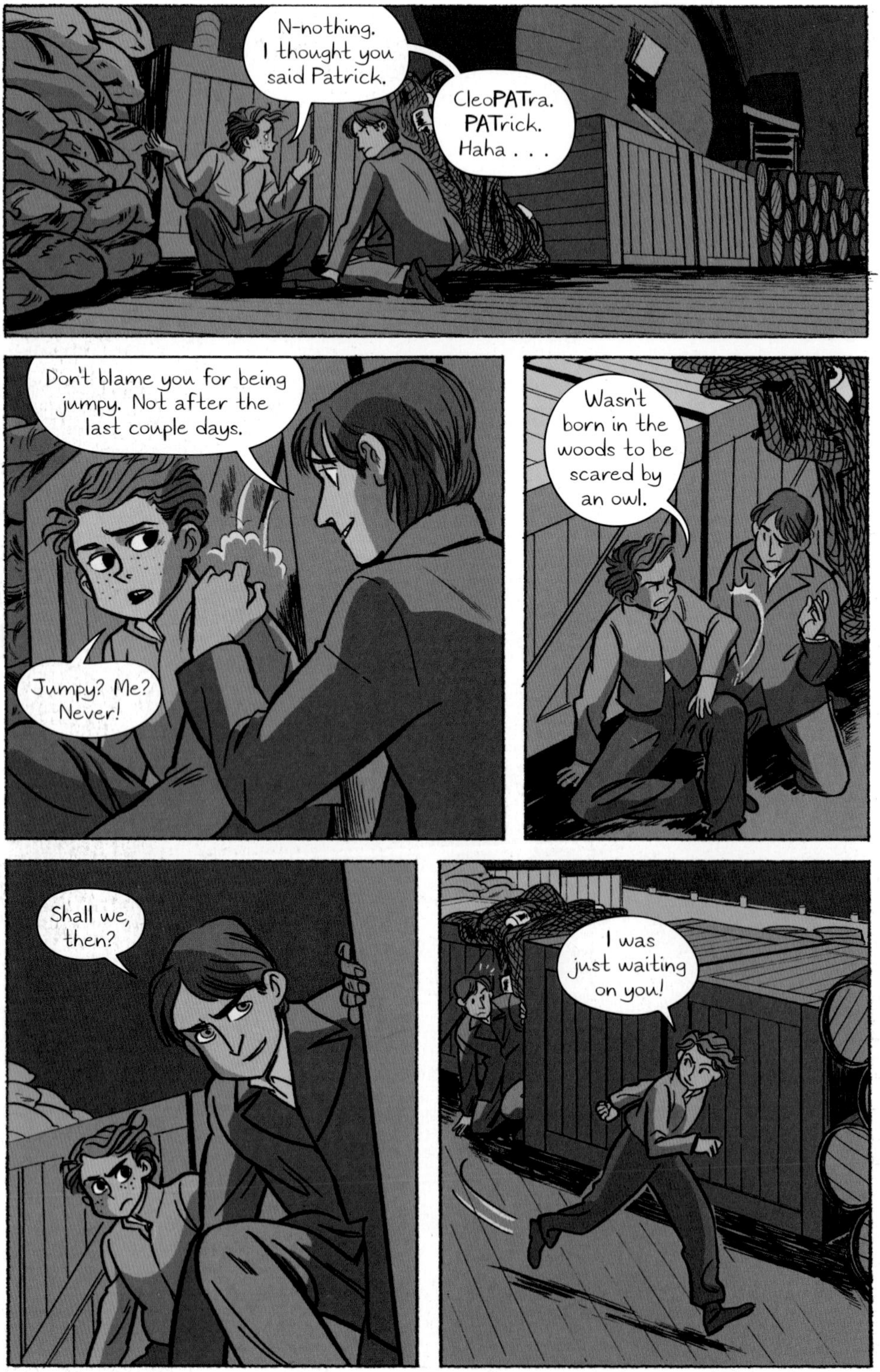
N-nothing. I thought you said Patrick.
CleoPATra. PATrick. Haha . . .
Don't blame you for being jumpy. Not after the last couple days.
Jumpy? Me? Never!
Wasn't born in the woods to be scared by an owl.
Shall we, then?
I was just waiting on you!

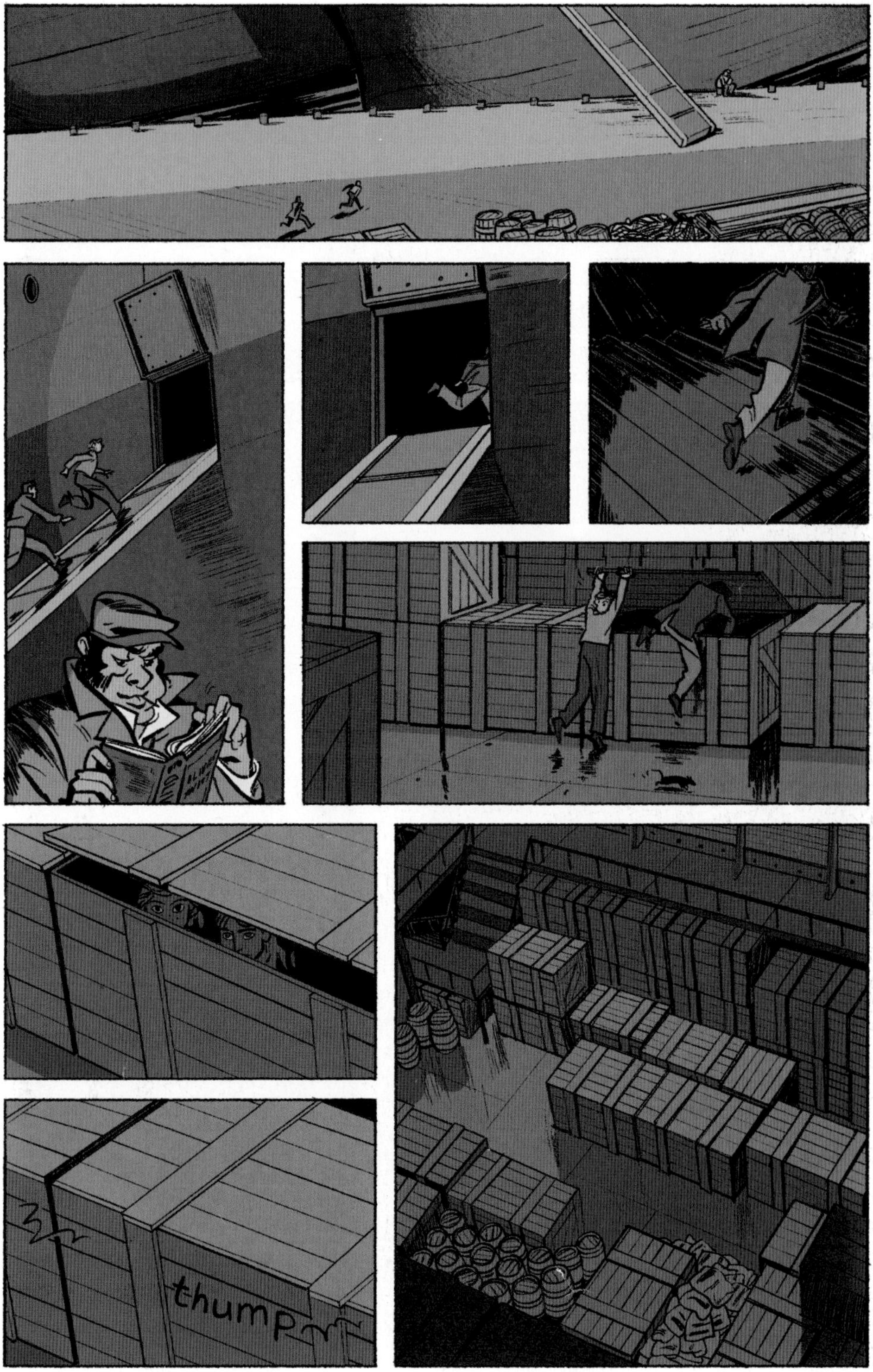
thump

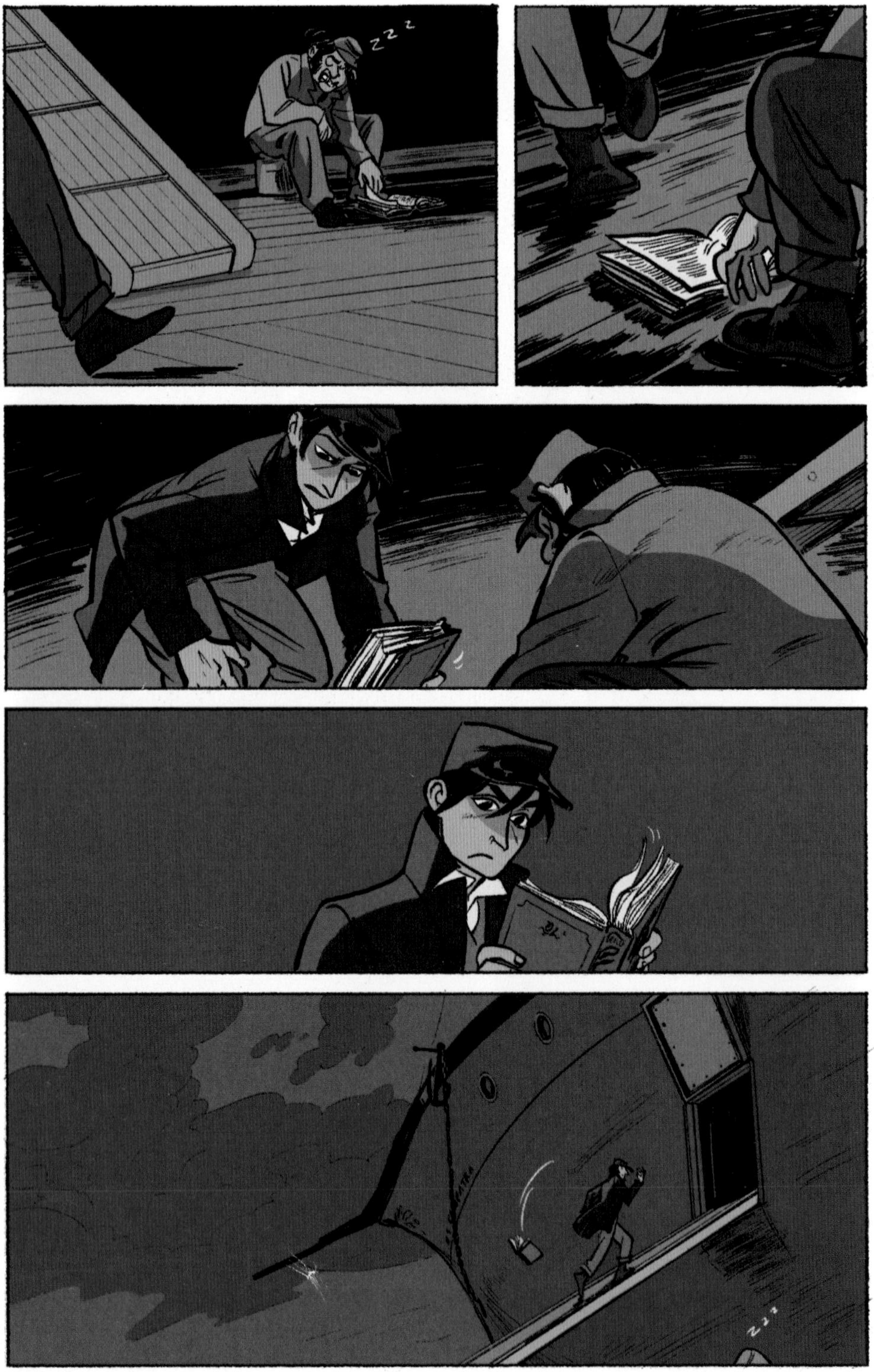

CHAPTER THREE
TO SEA

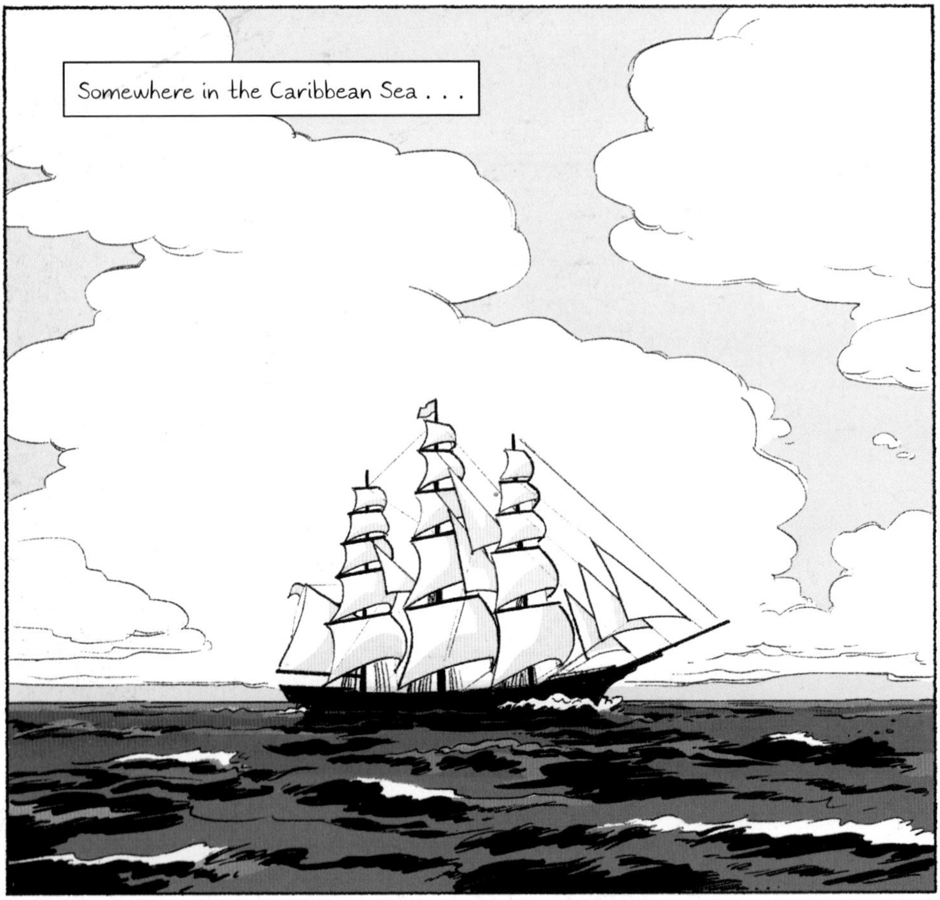
Somewhere in the Caribbean Sea . . .

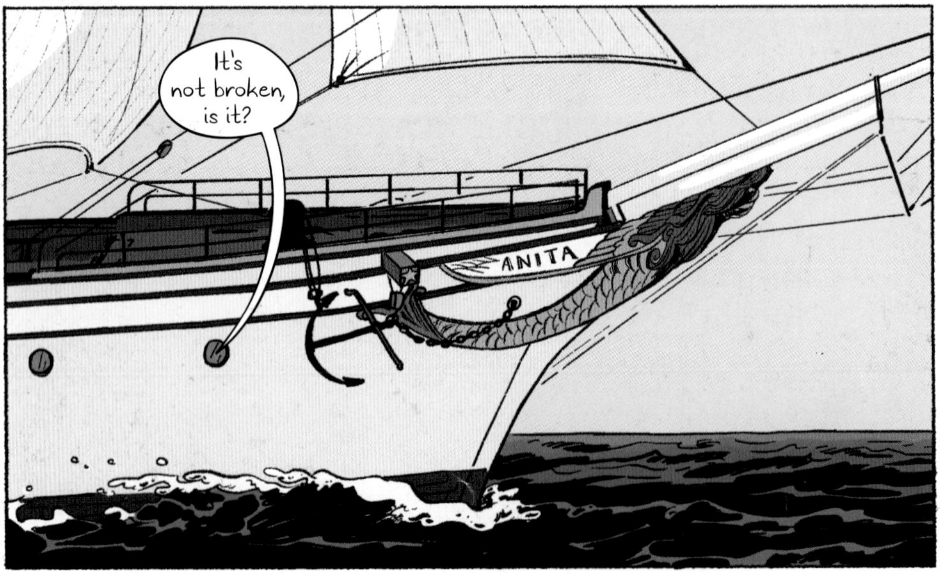
It's not broken, is it?
ANITA

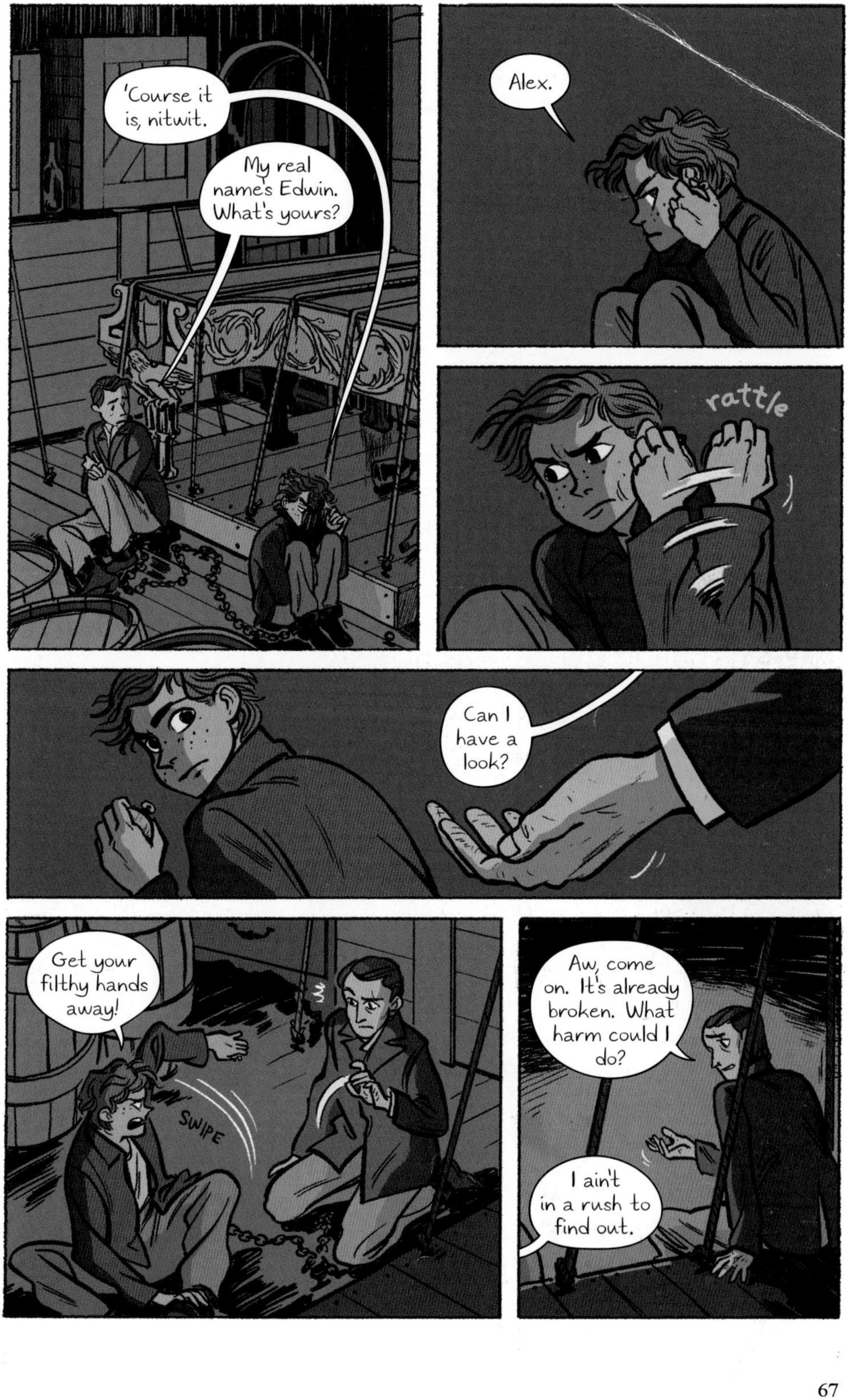
'Course it is, nitwit.
My real name's Edwin. What's yours?
Alex.
rattle
Can I have a look?
Get your filthy hands away!
SWIPE
Aw, come on. It's already broken. What harm could I do?
I ain't in a rush to find out.

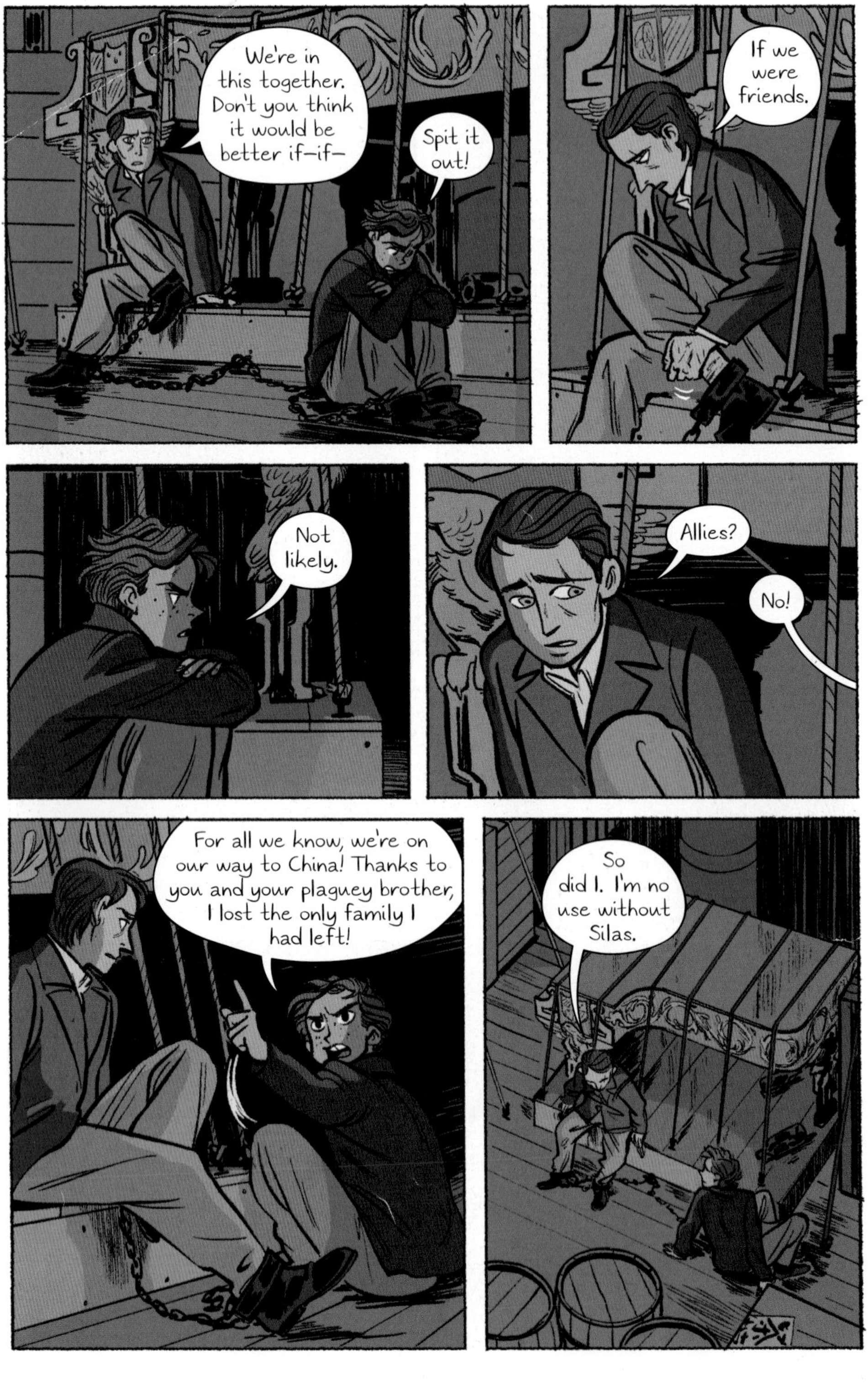
We're in this together. Don't you think it would be better if—if—
Spit it out!
If we were friends.
Not likely.
Allies?
No!
For all we know, we're on our way to China! Thanks to you and your plaguey brother, I lost the only family I had left!
So did I. I'm no use without Silas.

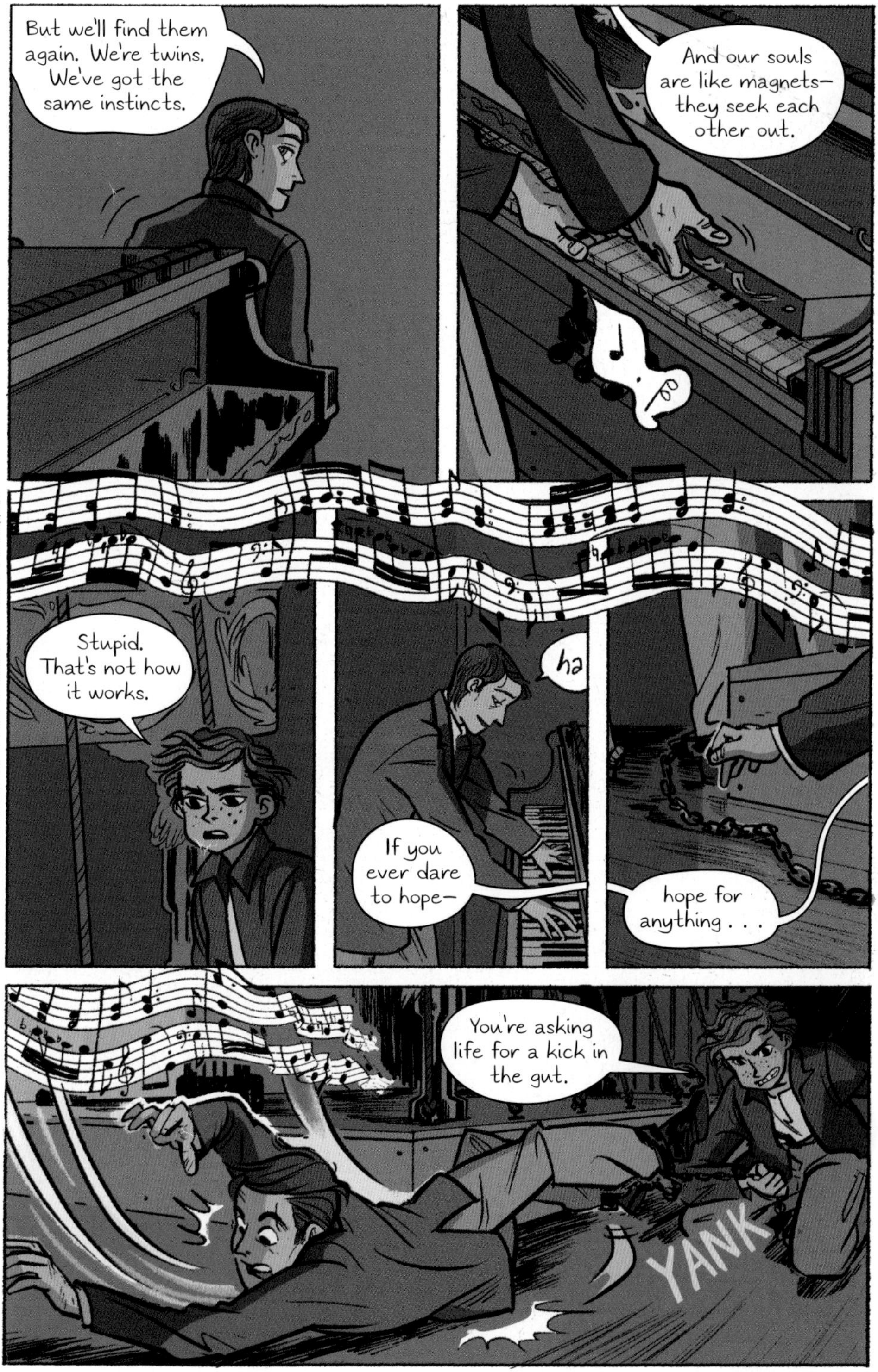
But we'll find them again. We're twins. We've got the same instincts.
And our souls are like magnets— they seek each other out.
Stupid. That's not how it works.
ha
If you ever dare to hope—
hope for anything . . .
You're asking life for a kick in the gut.
YANK

*SOUVENIR DE PORTO RICO BY GOTTSCHALK

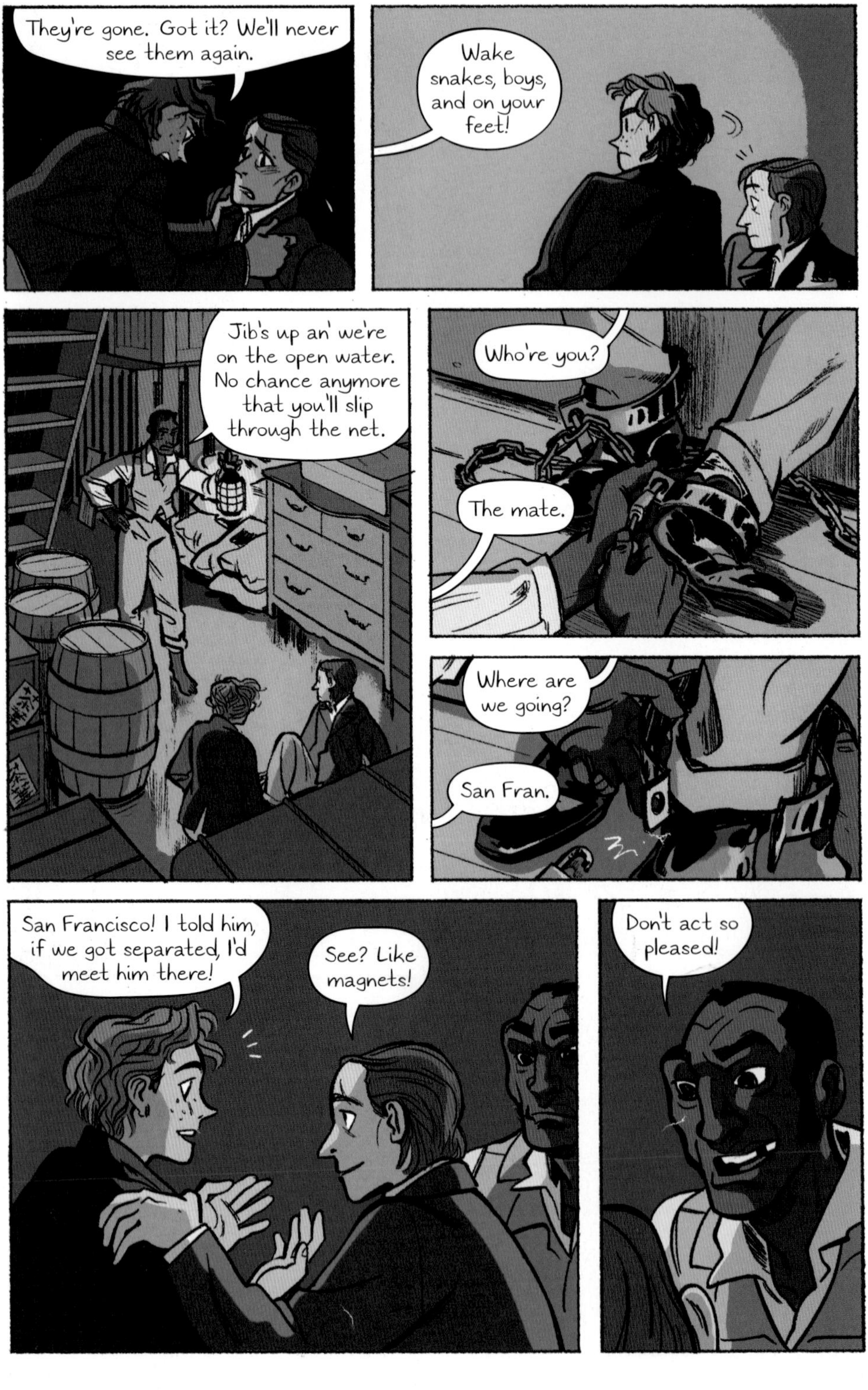
They're gone. Got it? We'll never see them again.
Wake snakes, boys, and on your feet!
Jib's up an' we're on the open water. No chance anymore that you'll slip through the net.
Who're you?
The mate.
Where are we going?
San Fran.
San Francisco! I told him, if we got separated, I'd meet him there!
See? Like magnets!
Don't act so pleased!

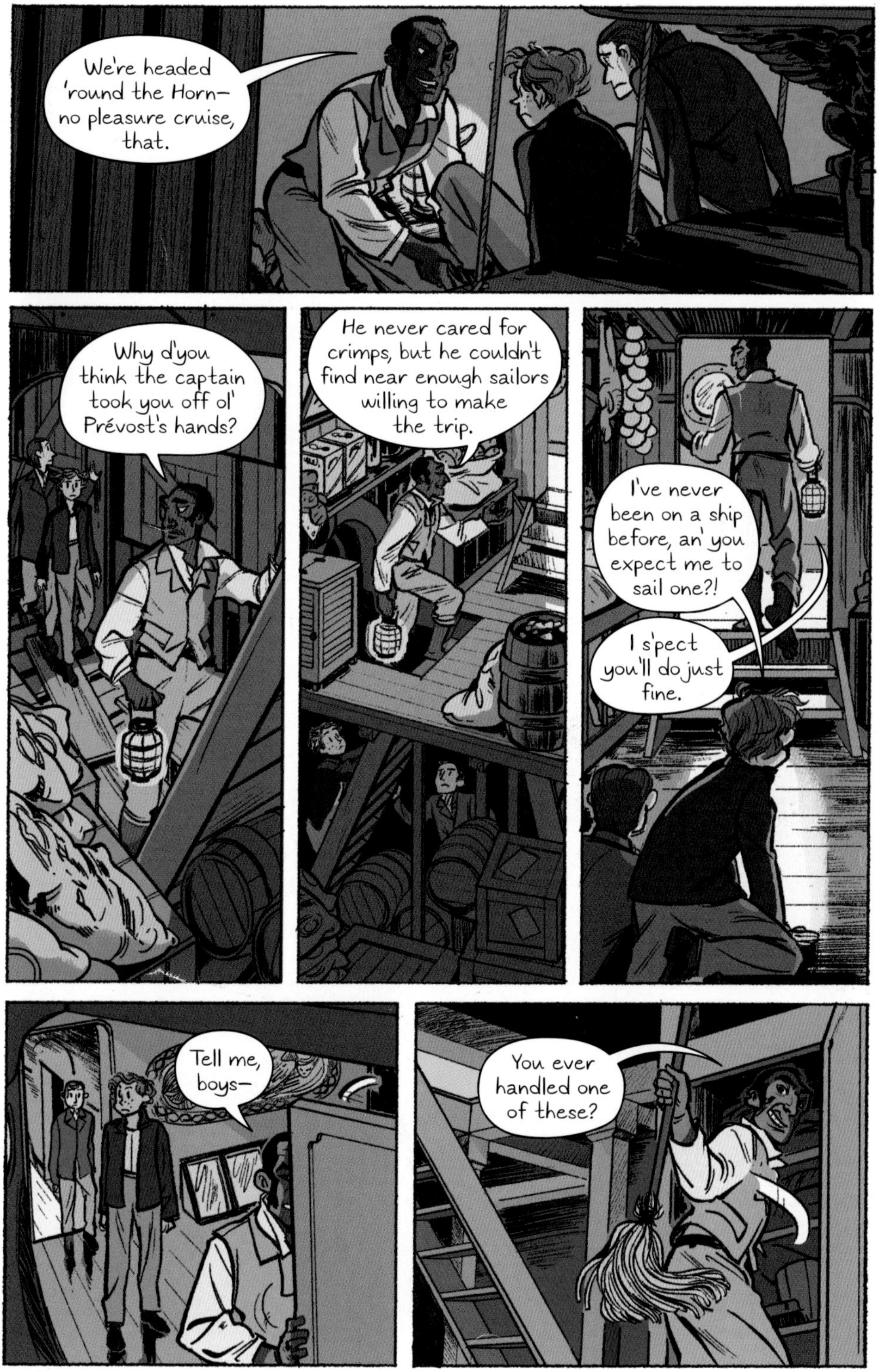
We're headed 'round the Horn— no pleasure cruise, that.
Why d'you think the captain took you off ol' Prévost's hands?
He never cared for crimps, but he couldn't find near enough sailors willing to make the trip.
I've never been on a ship before, an' you expect me to sail one?!
I s'pect you'll do just fine.
Tell me, boys—
You ever handled one of these?

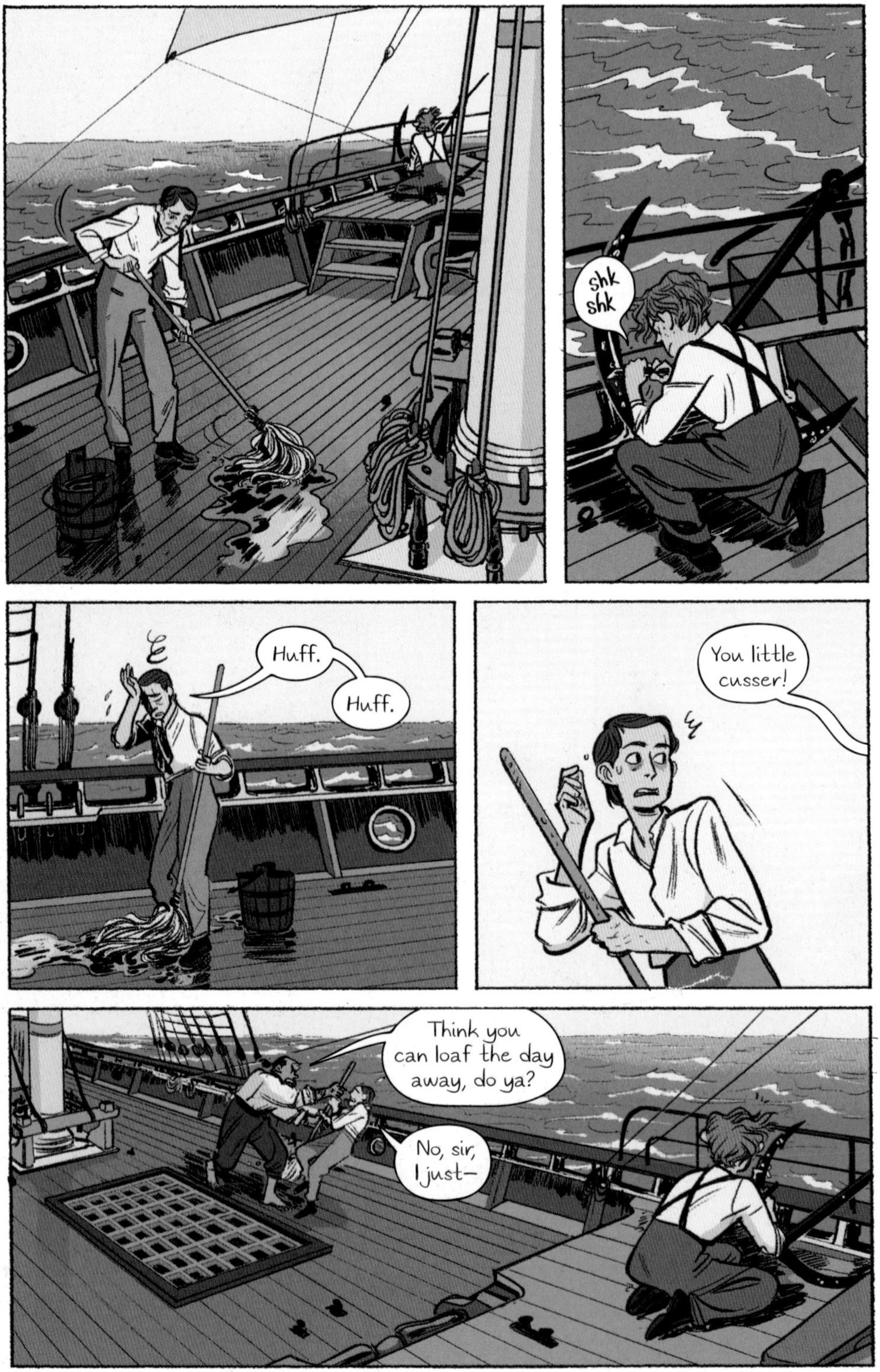
shk shk
Huff.
Huff.
You little cusser!
Think you can loaf the day away, do ya?
No, sir, I just—

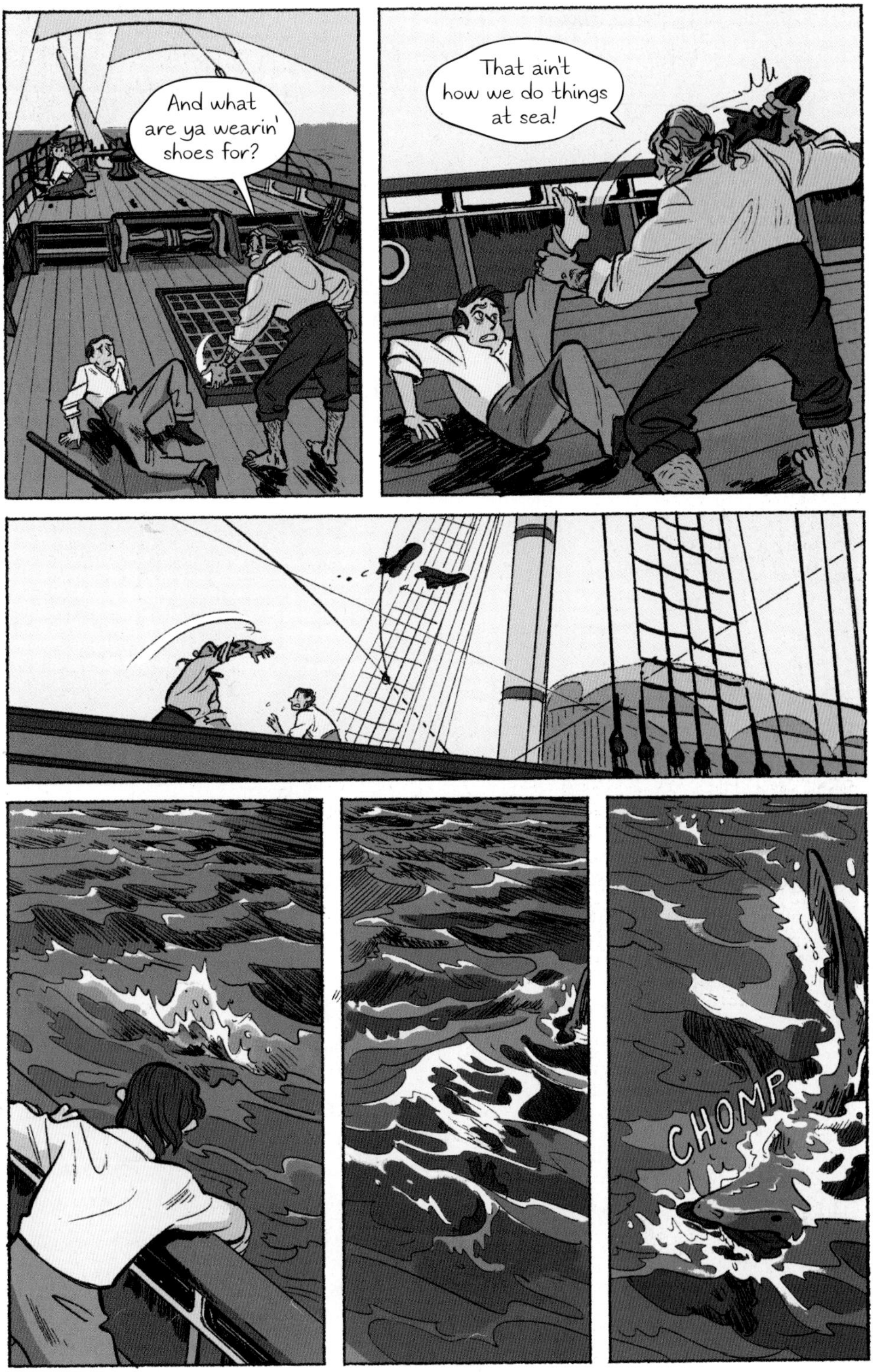
And what are ya wearin' shoes for?
That ain't how we do things at sea!
CHOMP

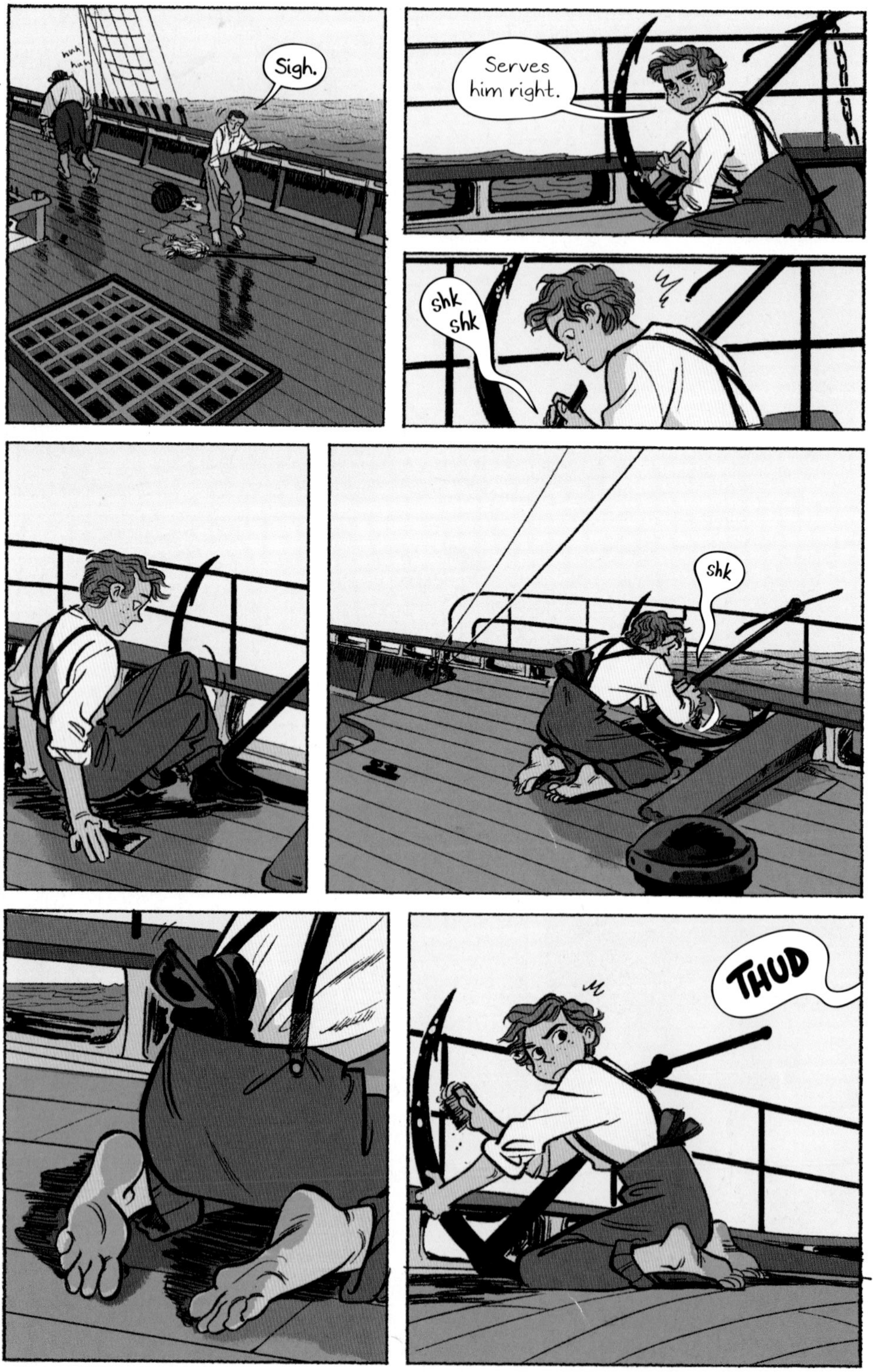
hnh
hah
Sigh.
Serves him right.
shk shk
shk
THUD

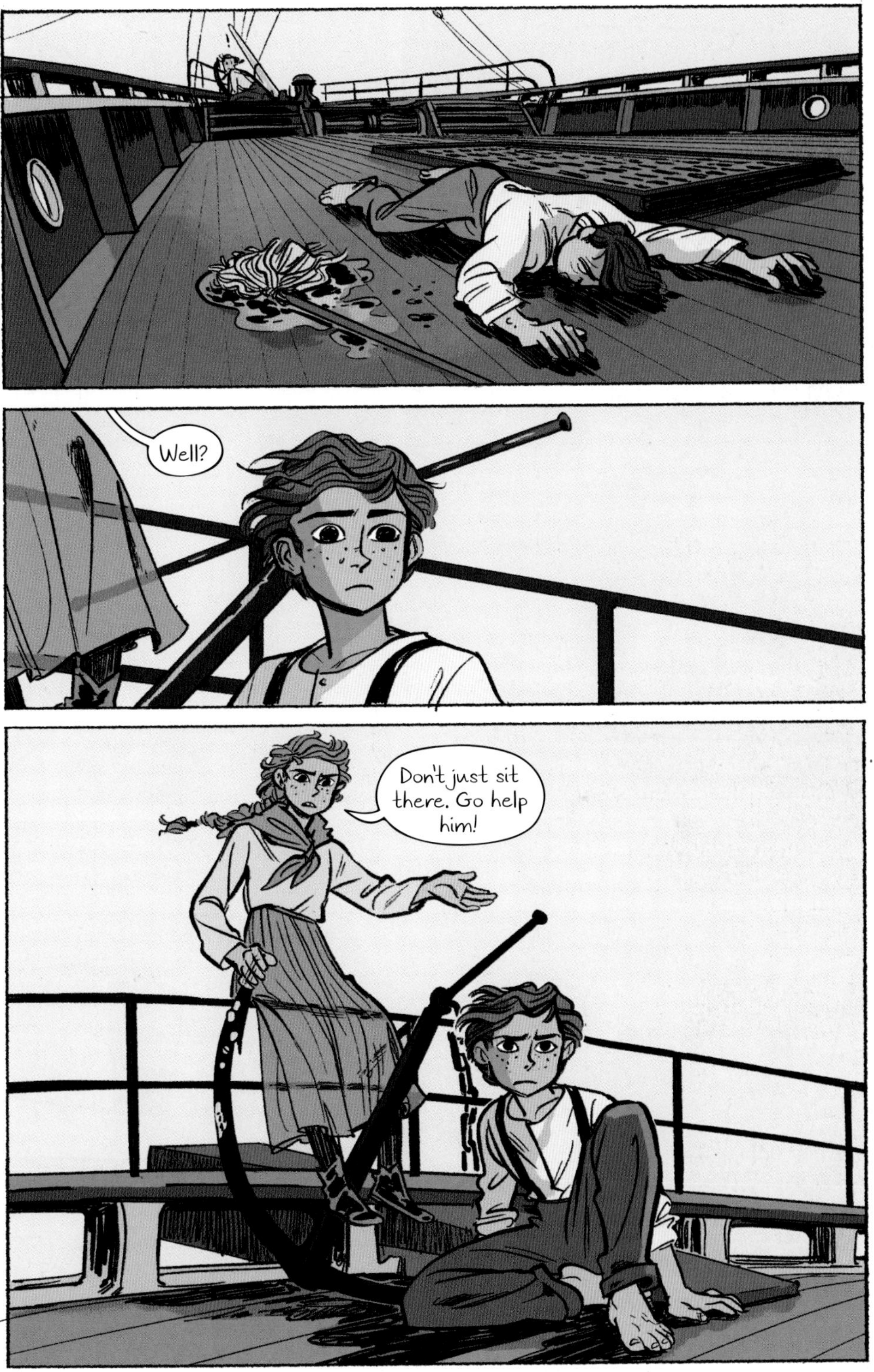
Well?
Don't just sit there. Go help him!

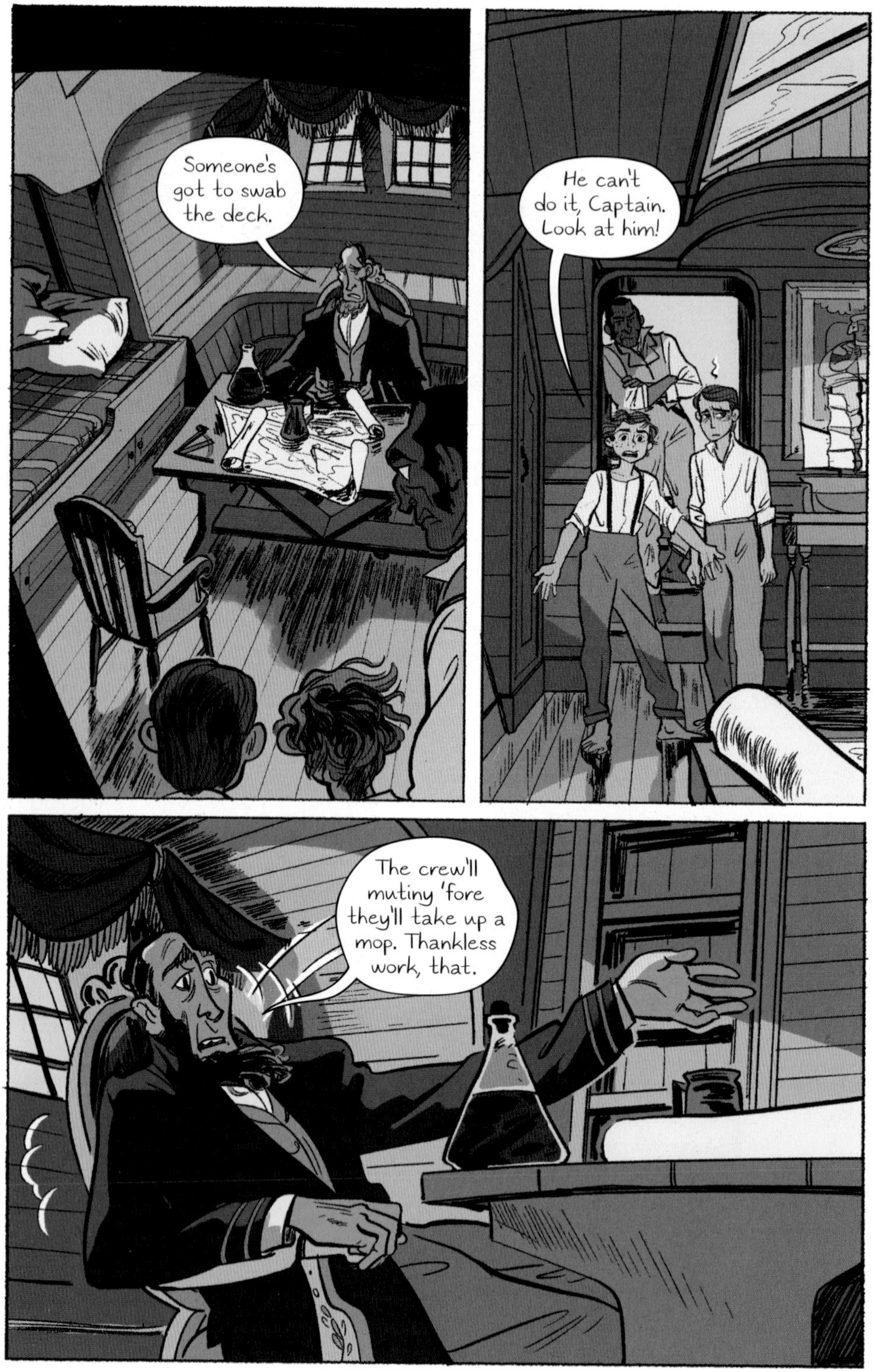
Someone's got to swab the deck.
He can't do it, Captain. Look at him!
The crew'll mutiny 'fore they'll take up a mop. Thankless work, that.

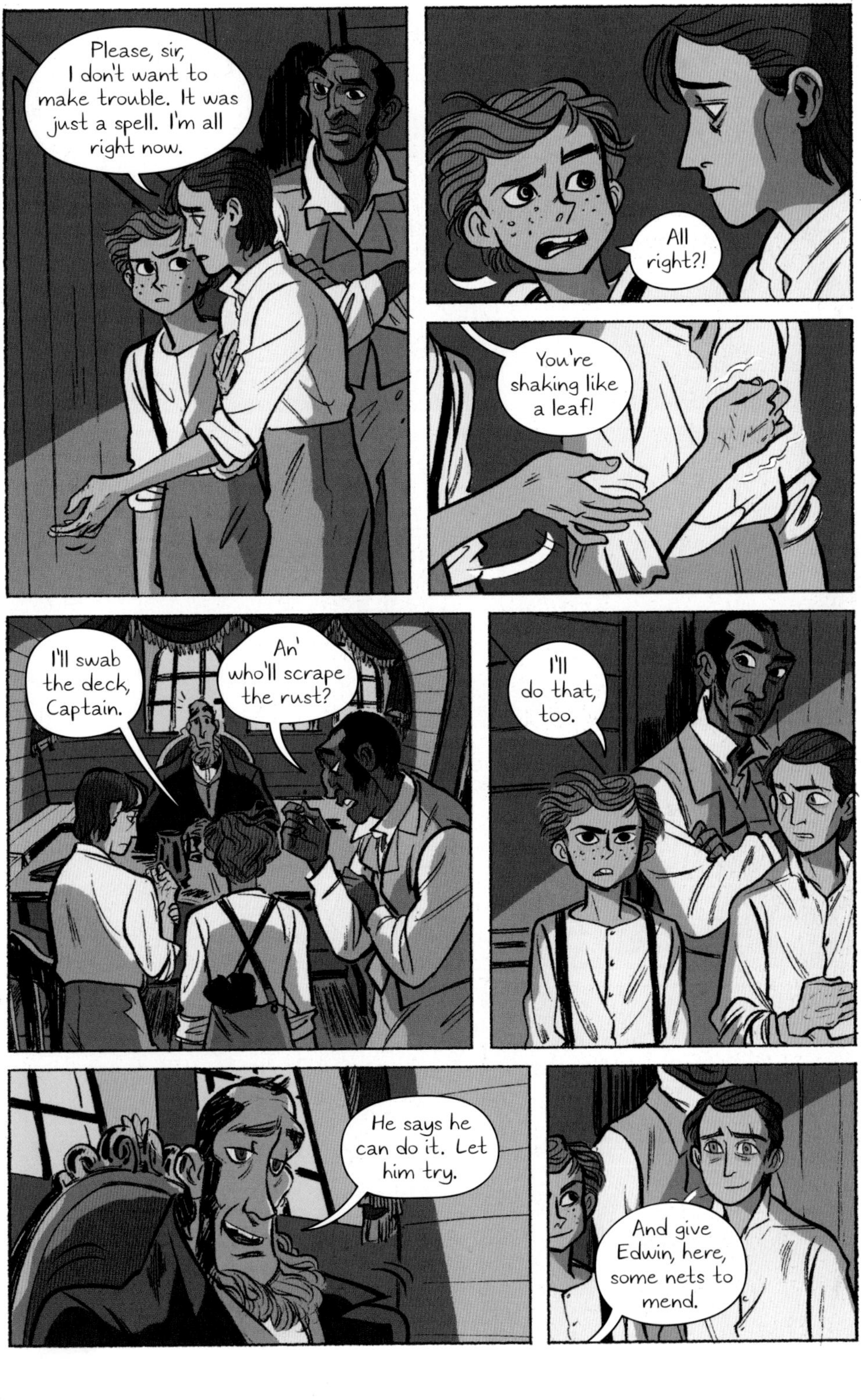
Please, sir, I don't want to make trouble. It was just a spell. I'm all right now.
All right?!
You're shaking like a leaf!
I'll swab the deck, Captain.
An' who'll scrape the rust?
I'll do that, too.
He says he can do it. Let him try.
And give Edwin, here, some nets to mend.

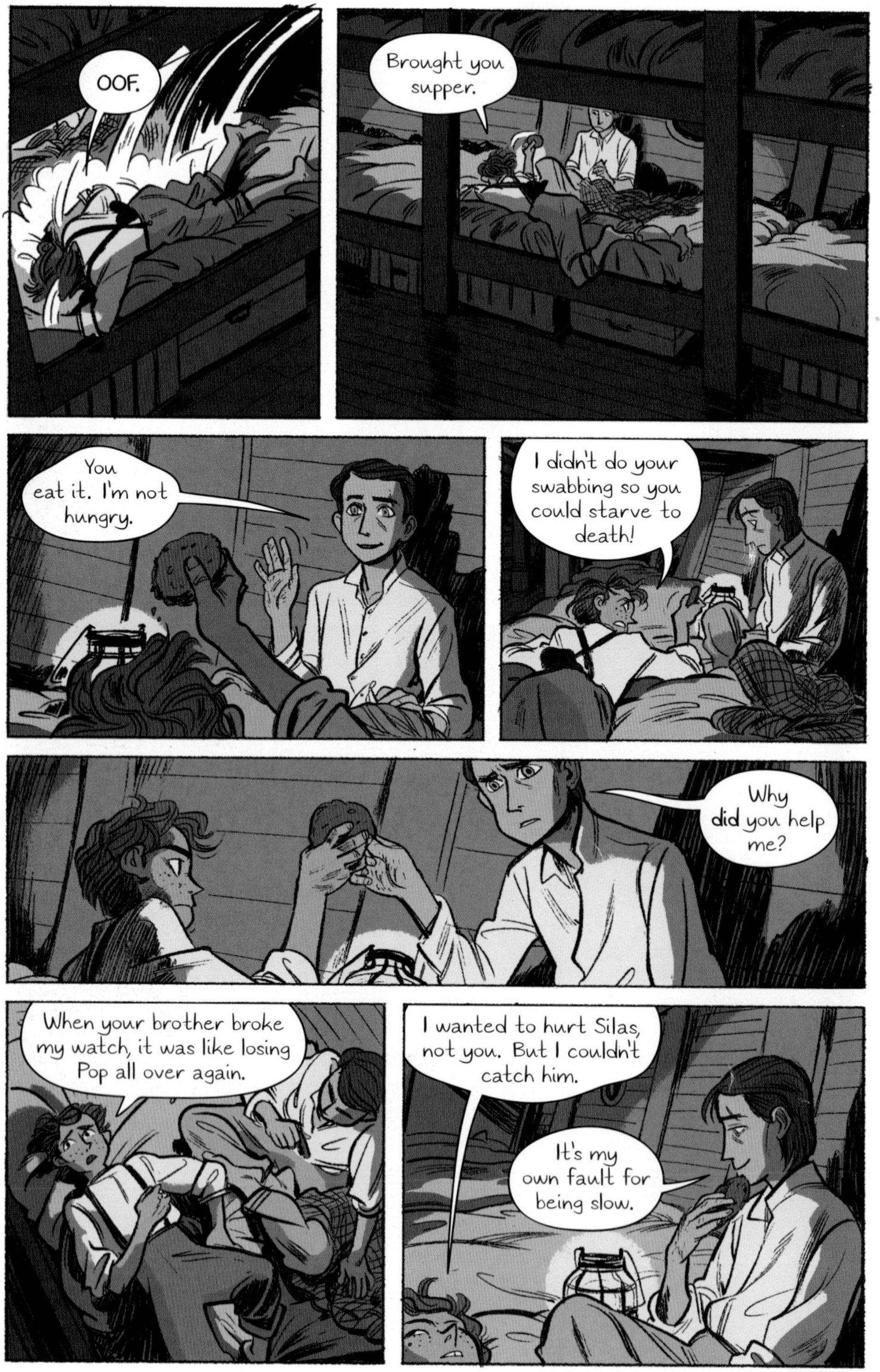
OOF.
Brought you supper.
You eat it. I'm not hungry.
I didn't do your swabbing so you could starve to death!
Why did you help me?
When your brother broke my watch, it was like losing Pop all over again.
I wanted to hurt Silas, not you. But I couldn't catch him.
It's my own fault for being slow.

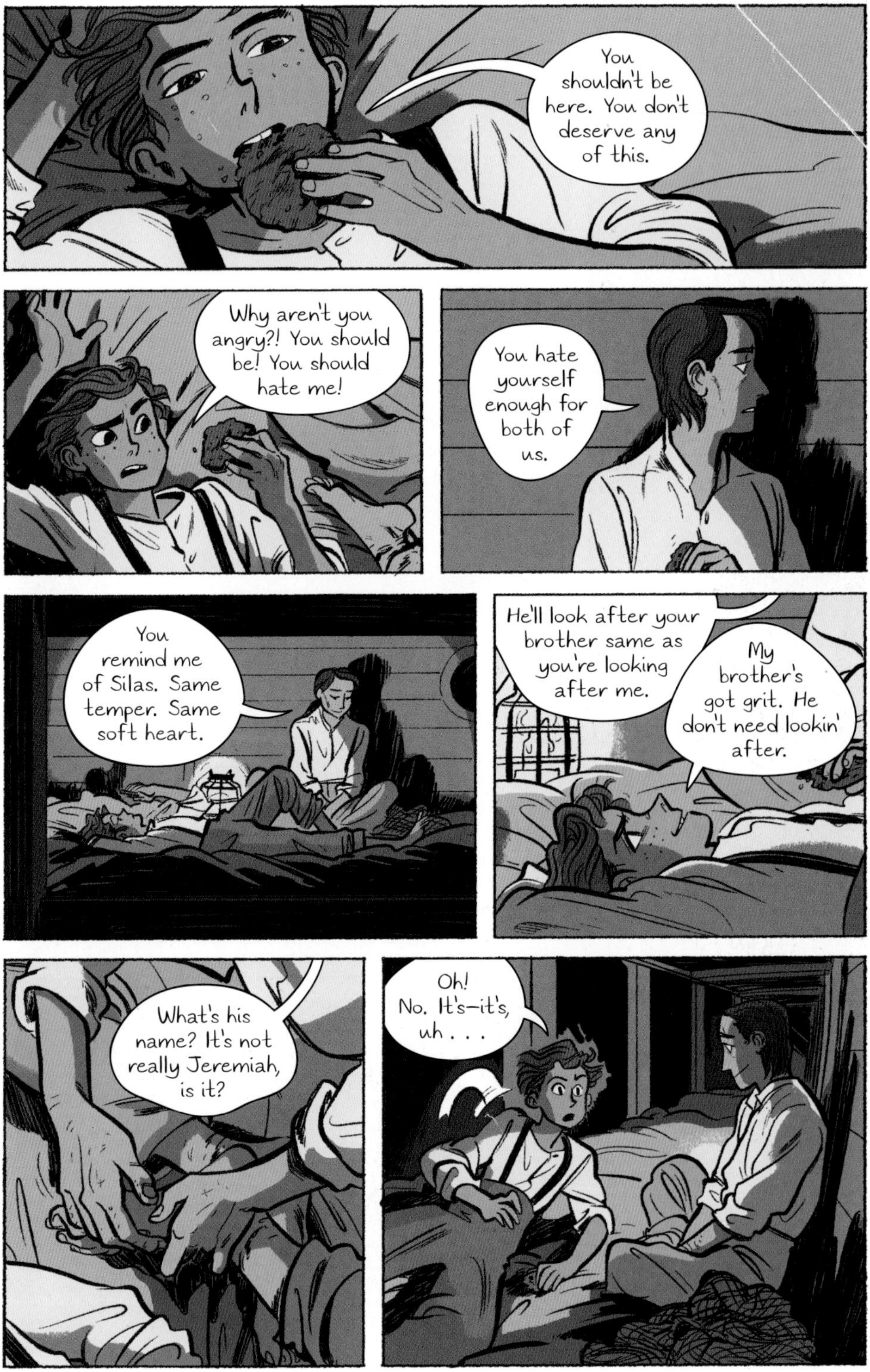
You shouldn't be here. You don't deserve any of this.
Why aren't you angry?! You should be! You should hate me!
You hate yourself enough for both of us.
You remind me of Silas. Same temper. Same soft heart.
He'll look after your brother same as you're looking after me.
My brother's got grit. He don't need lookin' after.
What's his name? It's not really Jeremiah, is it?
Oh! No. It's—it's, uh . . .

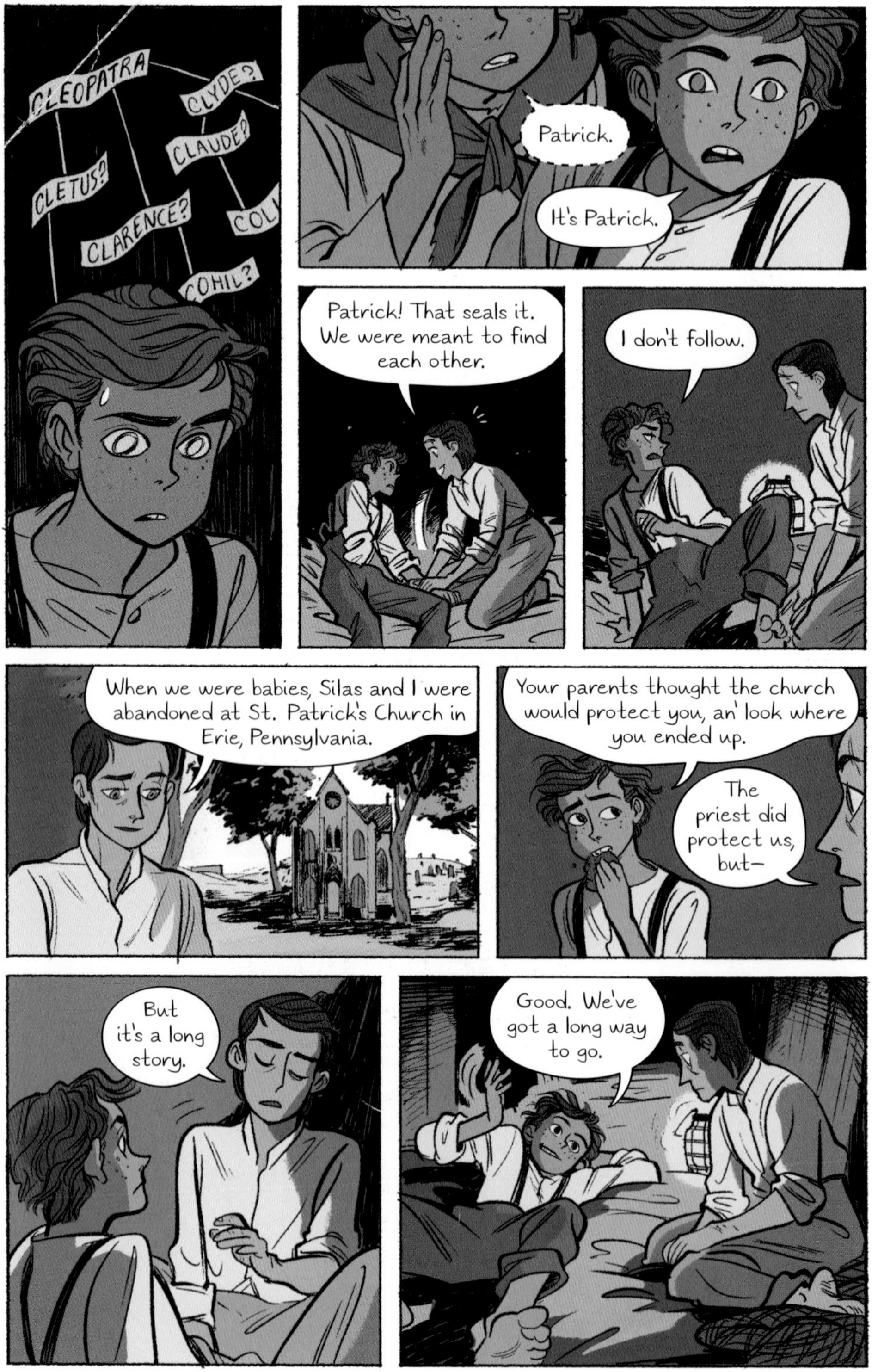
CLEOPATRA
CLYDE?
CLAUDE?
CLETUS?
CLARENCE?
COHIL?
Patrick.
It's Patrick.
Patrick! That seals it. We were meant to find each other.
I don't follow.
When we were babies, Silas and I were abandoned at St. Patrick's Church in Erie, Pennsylvania.
Your parents thought the church would protect you, an' look where you ended up.
The priest did protect us, but—
But it's a long story.
Good. We've got a long way to go.

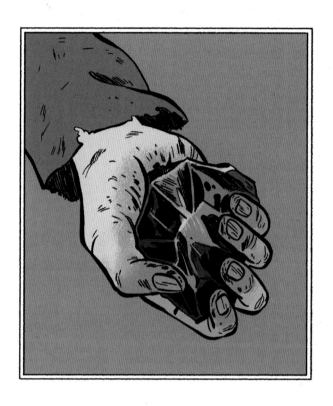

CHAPTER FOUR

THE BREAKER
AND THE BOILER

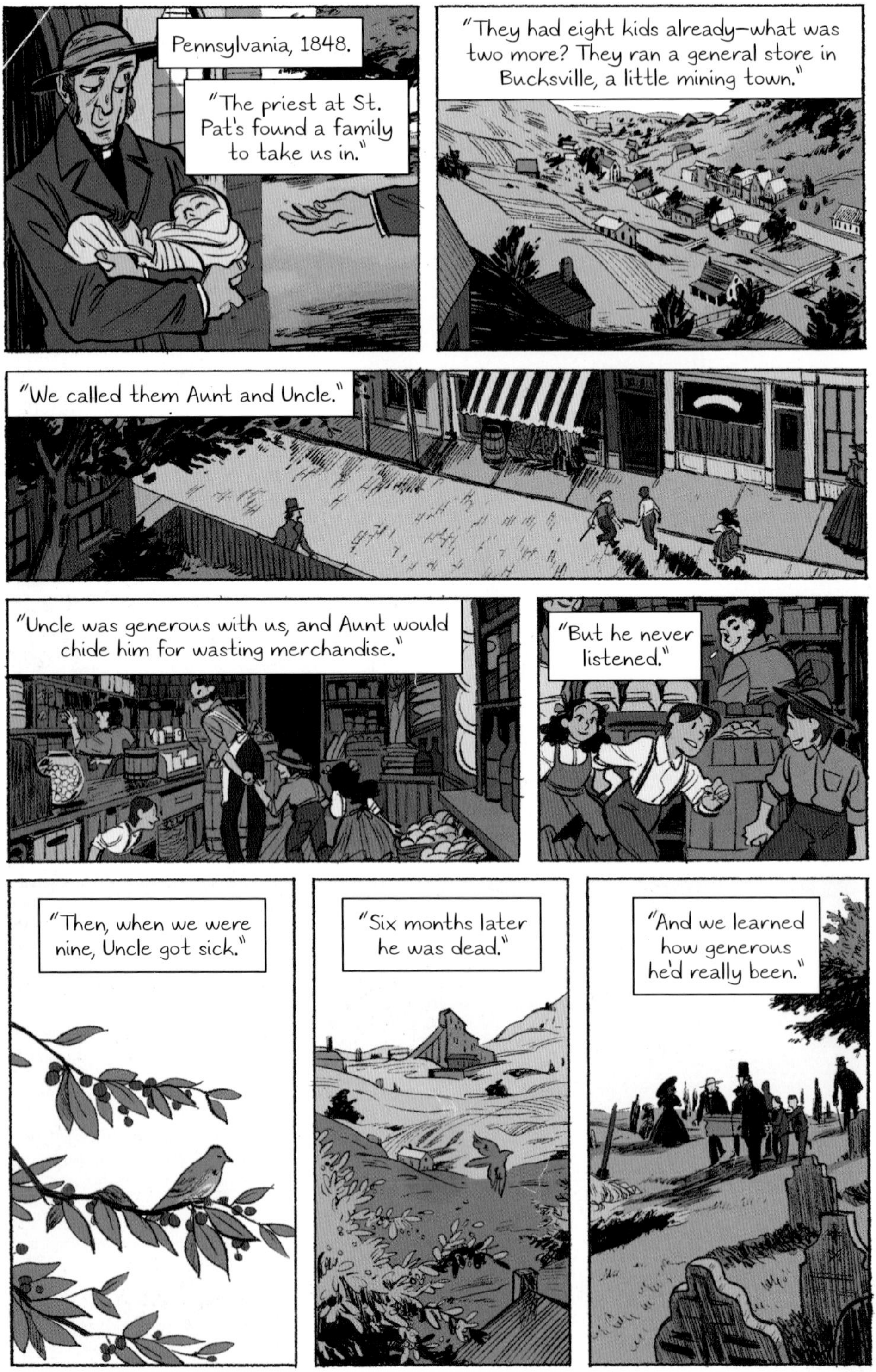
Pennsylvania, 1848.
"The priest at St. Pat's found a family to take us in."
"They had eight kids already—what was two more? They ran a general store in Bucksville, a little mining town."
"We called them Aunt and Uncle."
"Uncle was generous with us, and Aunt would chide him for wasting merchandise."
"But he never listened."
"Then, when we were nine, Uncle got sick."
"Six months later he was dead."
"And we learned how generous he'd really been."

"He could never bear to see a neighbor suffer."

"He'd given loans to half the town—friends, strangers, anyone who asked."

"When they didn't repay him, he was the one borrowing, just to keep the store afloat."

"Wasn't long 'til the vultures came to pick his corpse clean."

Is Mrs. Clement home?

No! Go away!

"In the end she lost the house."

"Aunt's sister took them in, her and the cousins, but there wasn't room for us."

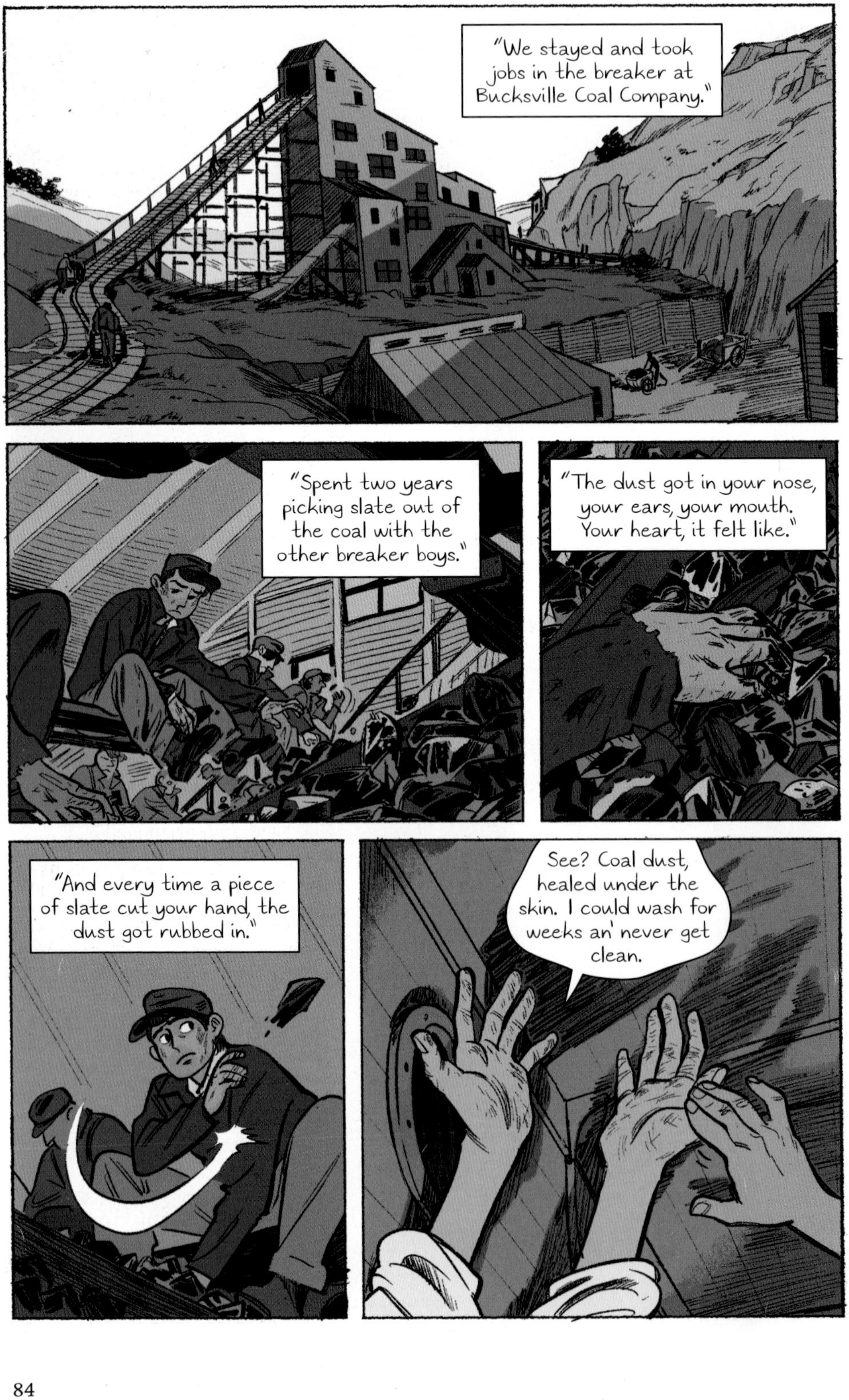
"We stayed and took jobs in the breaker at Bucksville Coal Company."
"Spent two years picking slate out of the coal with the other breaker boys."
"The dust got in your nose, your ears, your mouth. Your heart, it felt like."
"And every time a piece of slate cut your hand, the dust got rubbed in."
See? Coal dust, healed under the skin. I could wash for weeks an' never get clean.

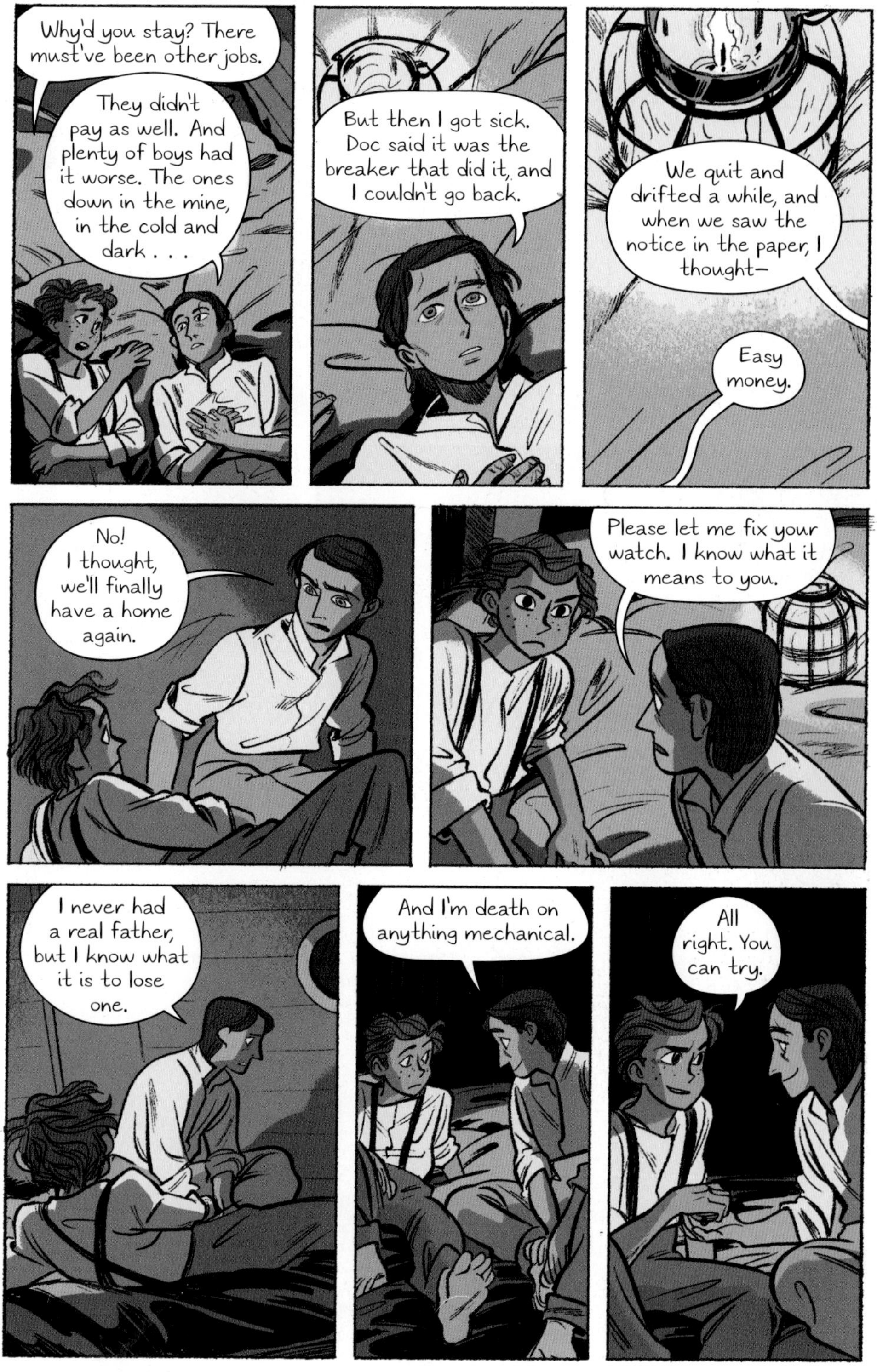
Why'd you stay? There must've been other jobs.
They didn't pay as well. And plenty of boys had it worse. The ones down in the mine, in the cold and dark . . .
But then I got sick. Doc said it was the breaker that did it, and I couldn't go back.
We quit and drifted a while, and when we saw the notice in the paper, I thought—
Easy money.
No! I thought, we'll finally have a home again.
Please let me fix your watch. I know what it means to you.
I never had a real father, but I know what it is to lose one.
And I'm death on anything mechanical.
All right. You can try.

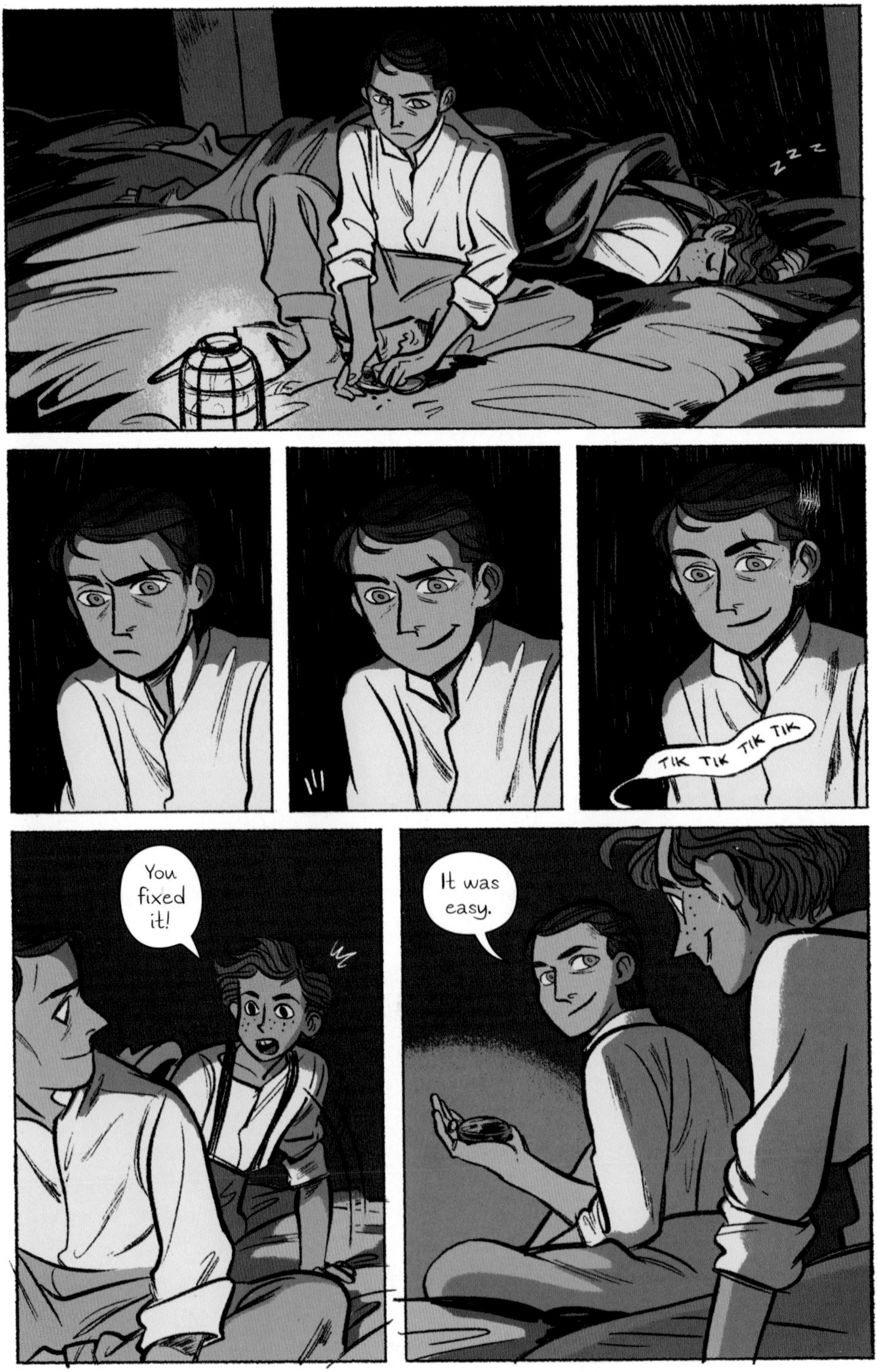
Z Z Z
TIK TIK TIK TIK
You fixed it!
It was easy.

Wait. I gotta show you something.
Look.
See this?
CLICK
POP

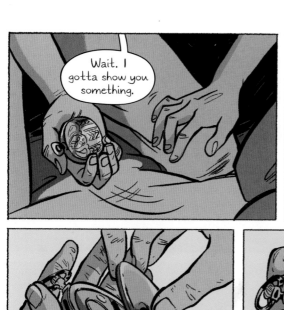

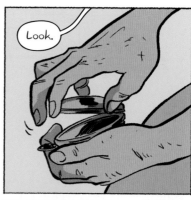

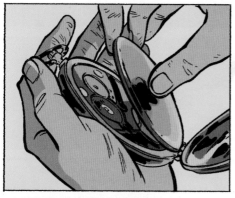

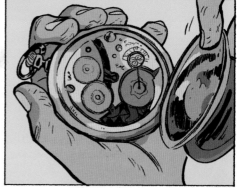

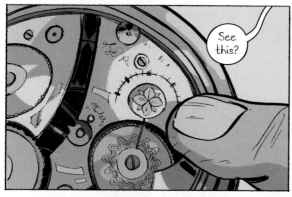

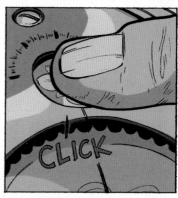

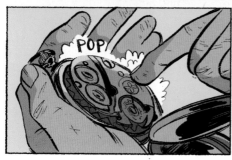

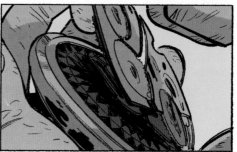

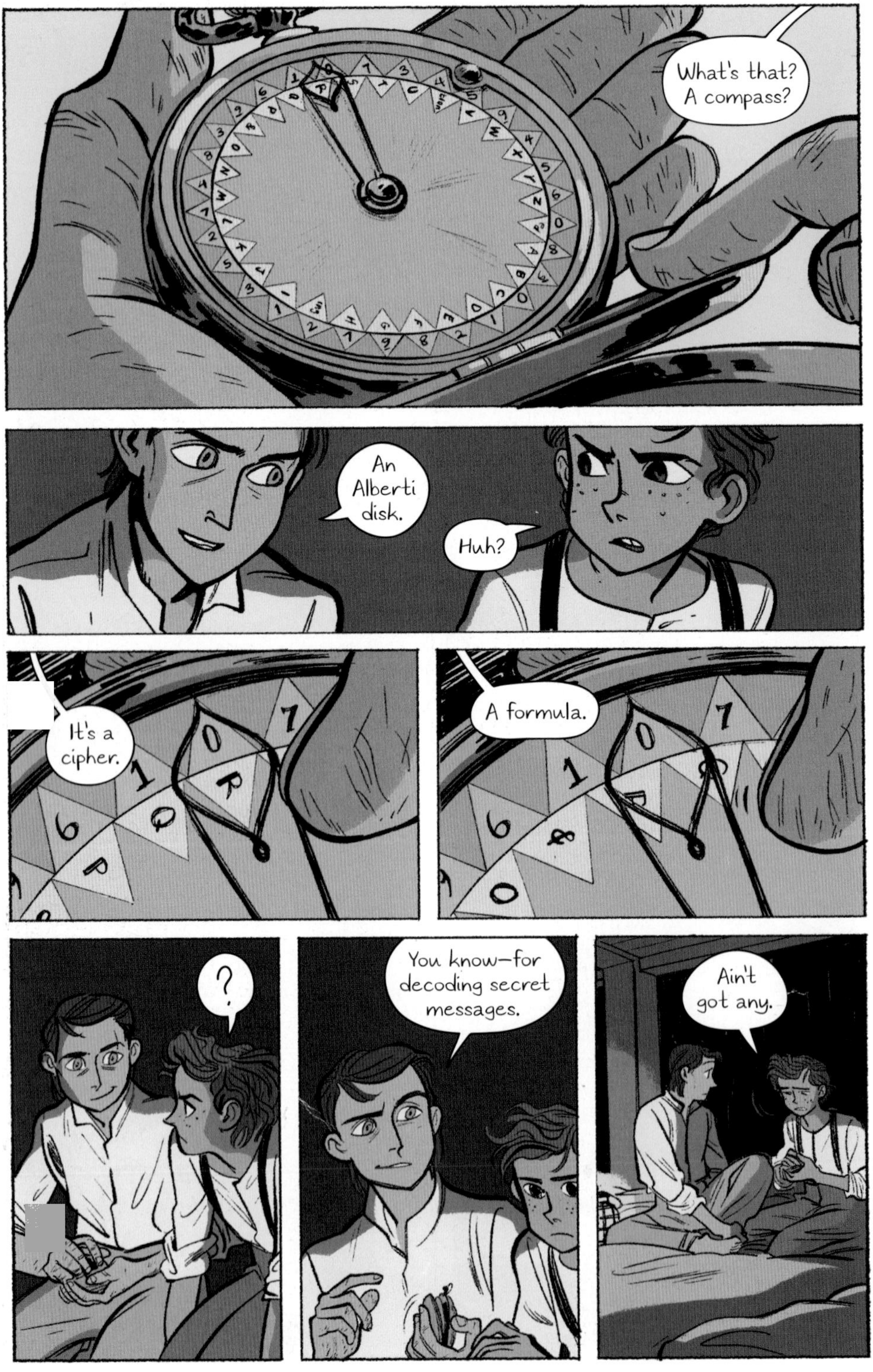

What's that? A compass?
An Alberti disk.
Huh?
It's a cipher.
A formula.
?
You know—for decoding secret messages.
Ain't got any.

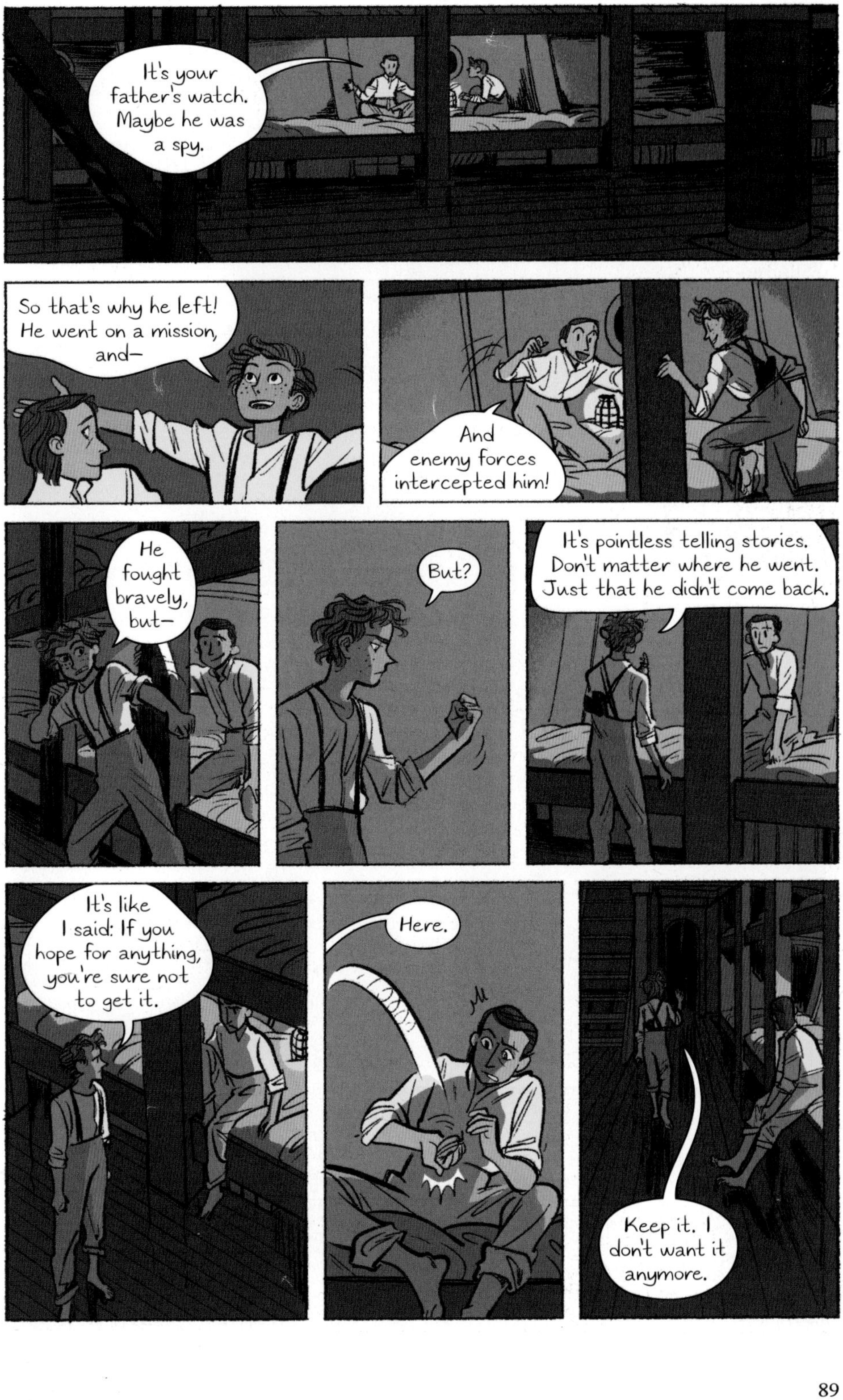
It's your father's watch. Maybe he was a spy.
So that's why he left! He went on a mission, and—
And enemy forces intercepted him!
He fought bravely, but—
But?
It's pointless telling stories. Don't matter where he went. Just that he didn't come back.
It's like I said: If you hope for anything, you're sure not to get it.
Here.
Keep it. I don't want it anymore.

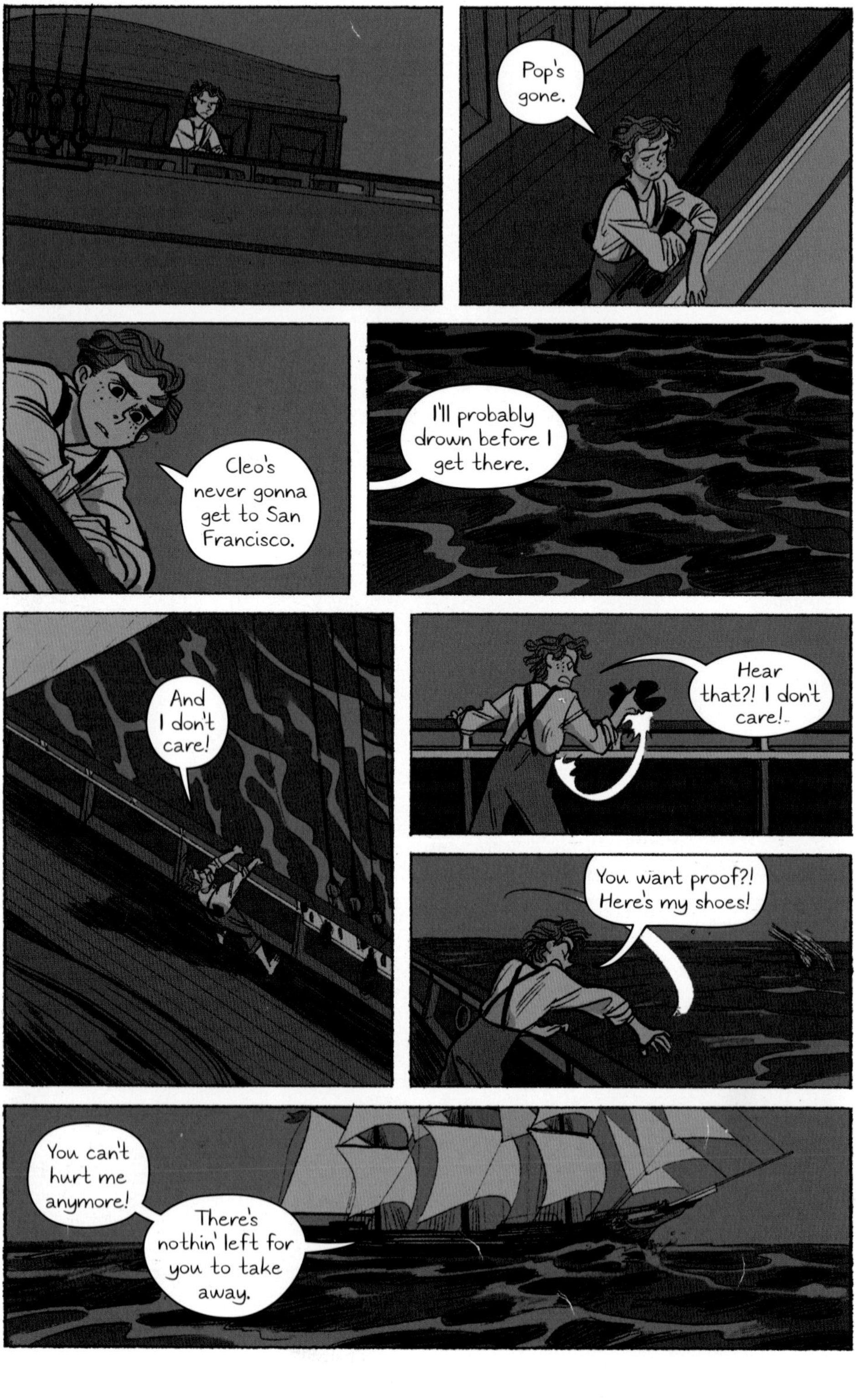
Pop's gone.
Cleo's never gonna get to San Francisco.
I'll probably drown before I get there.
And I don't care!
Hear that?! I don't care!
You want proof?! Here's my shoes!
You can't hurt me anymore!
There's nothin' left for you to take away.

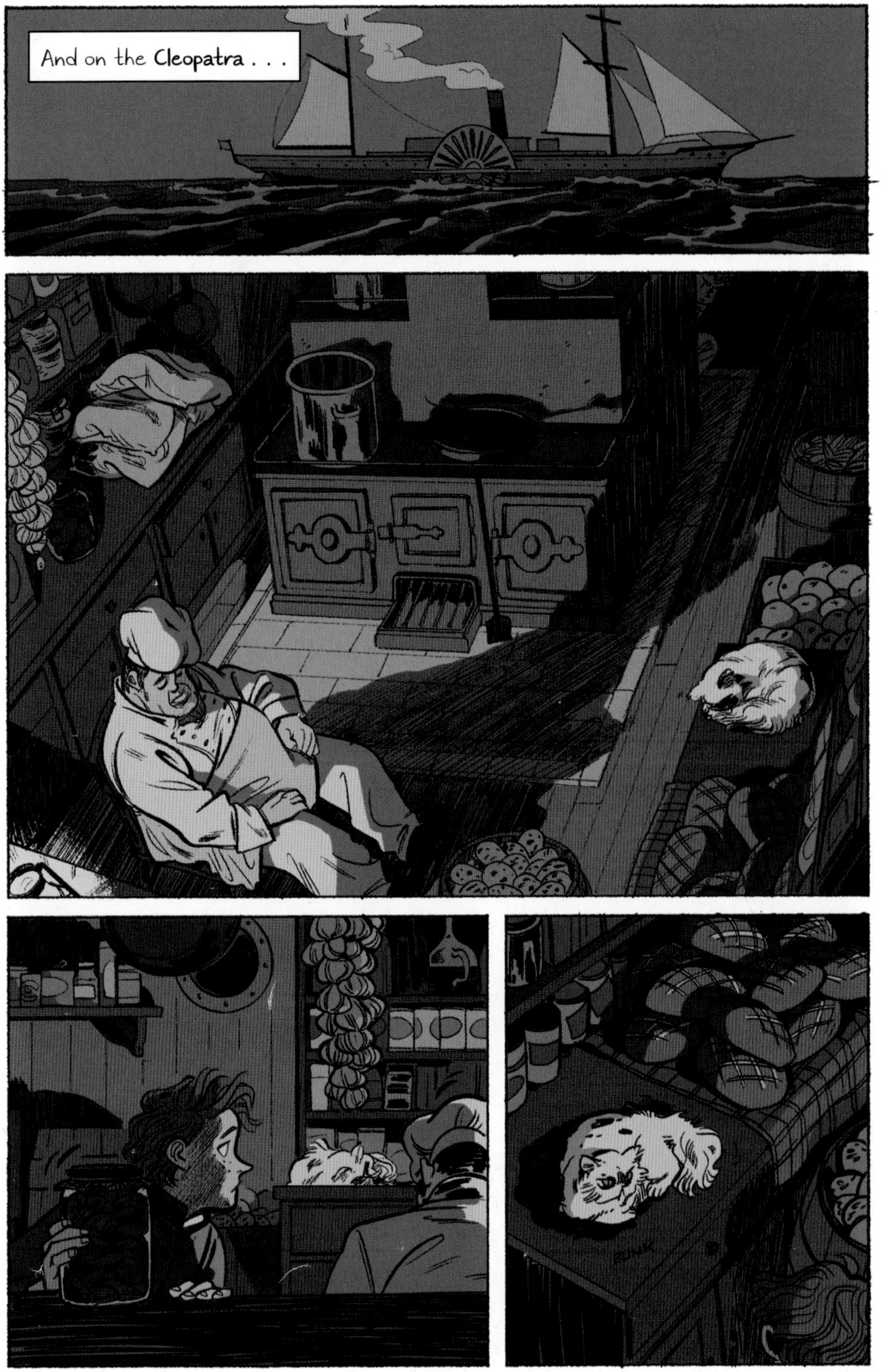
And on the **Cleopatra** . . .

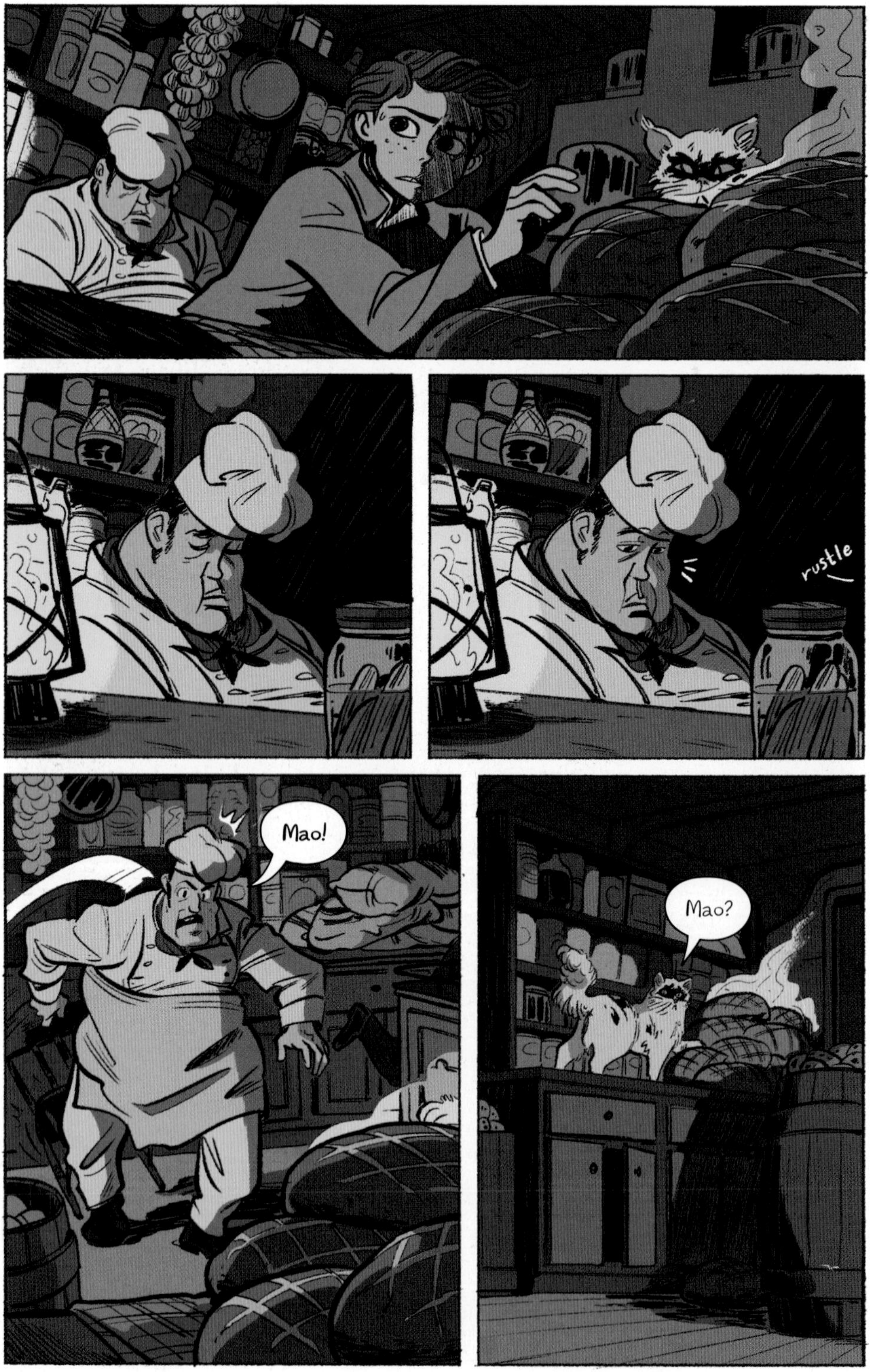
rustle
Mao!
Mao?

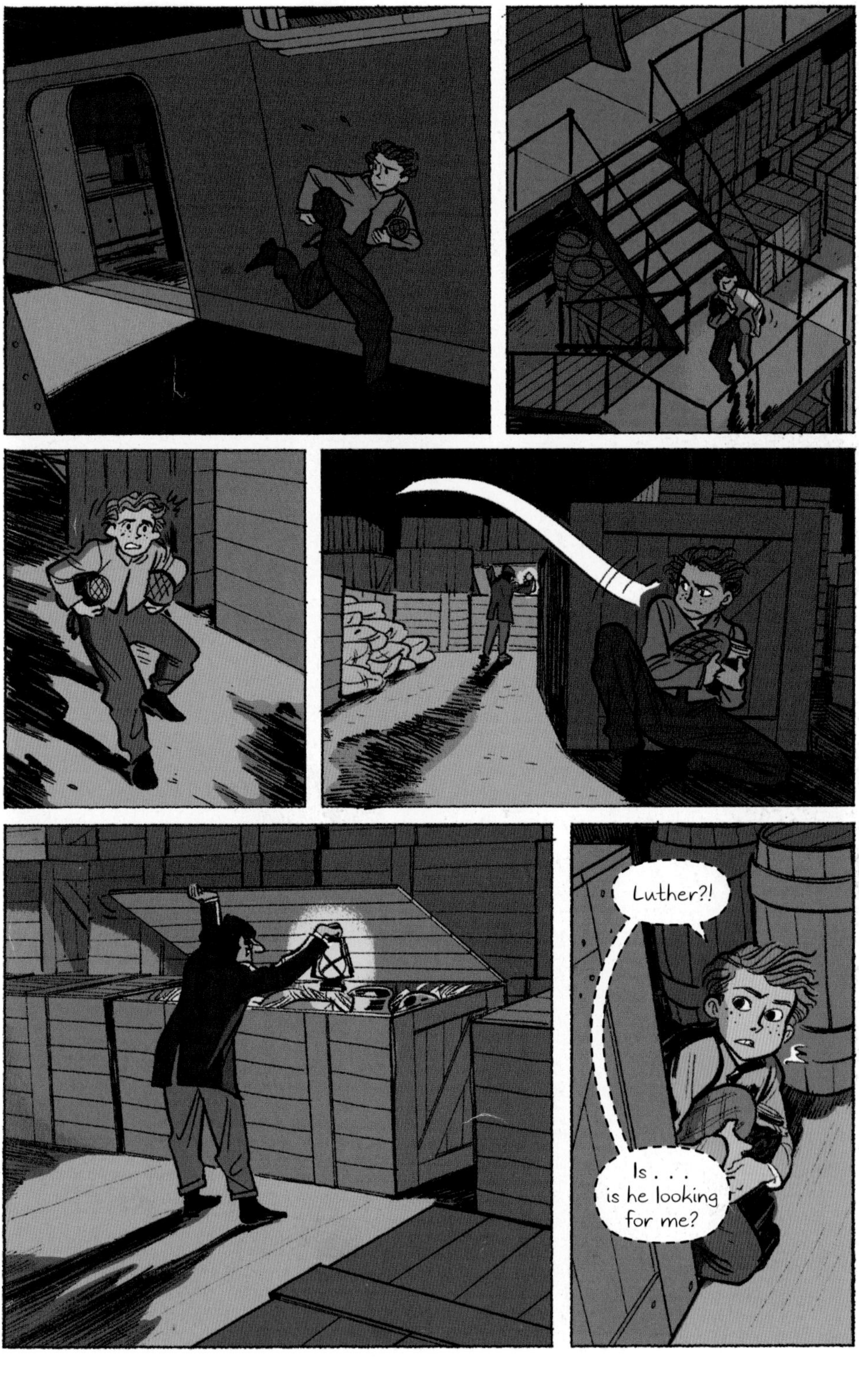
Luther?!
Is . . .
is he looking
for me?

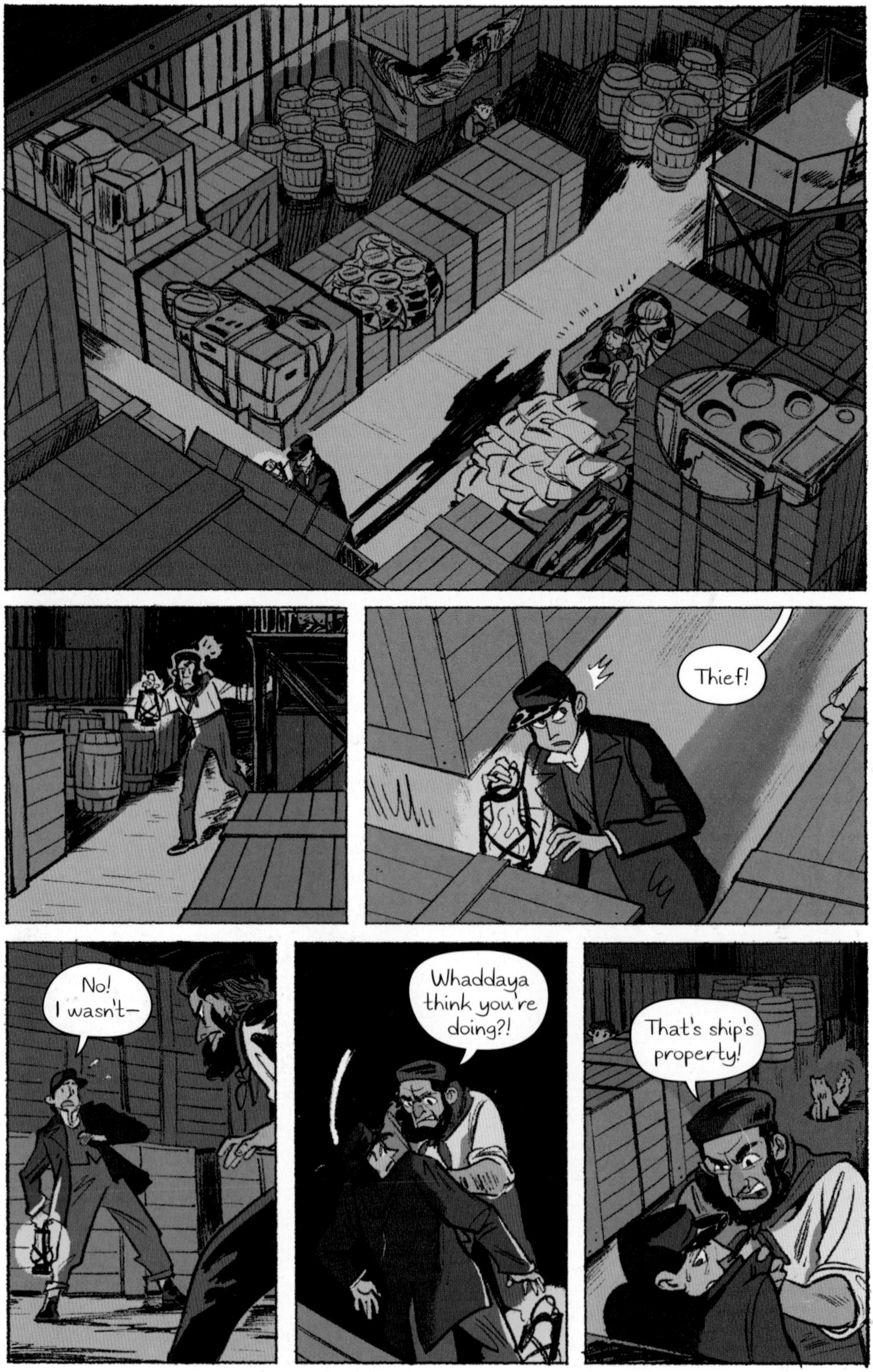
Thief!
No! I wasn't–
Whaddaya think you're doing?!
That's ship's property!

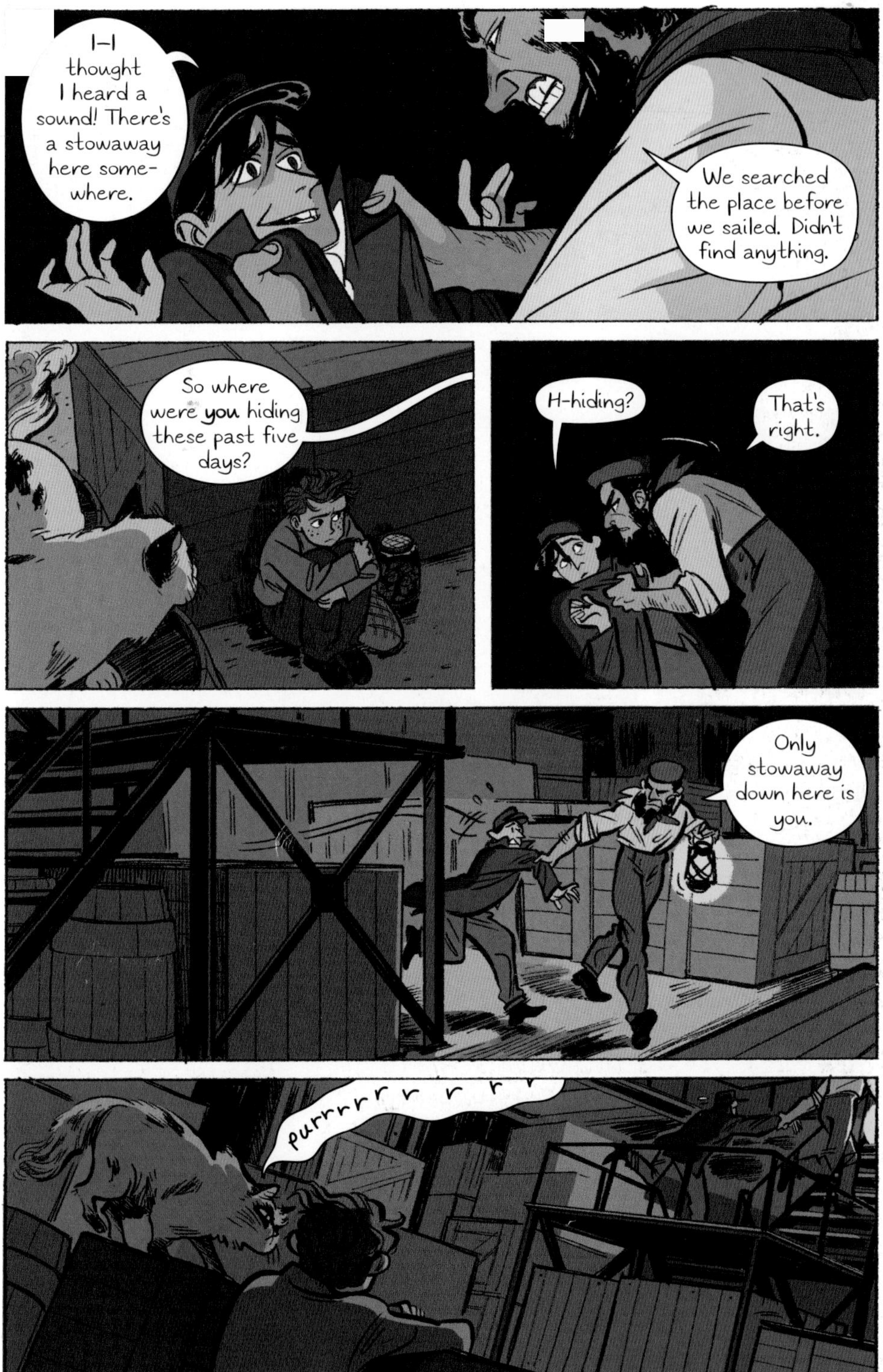

I-I thought I heard a sound! There's a stowaway here some-where.
We searched the place before we sailed. Didn't find anything.
So where were **you** hiding these past five days?
H-hiding?
That's right.
Only stowaway down here is you.
purrrrr r r r r

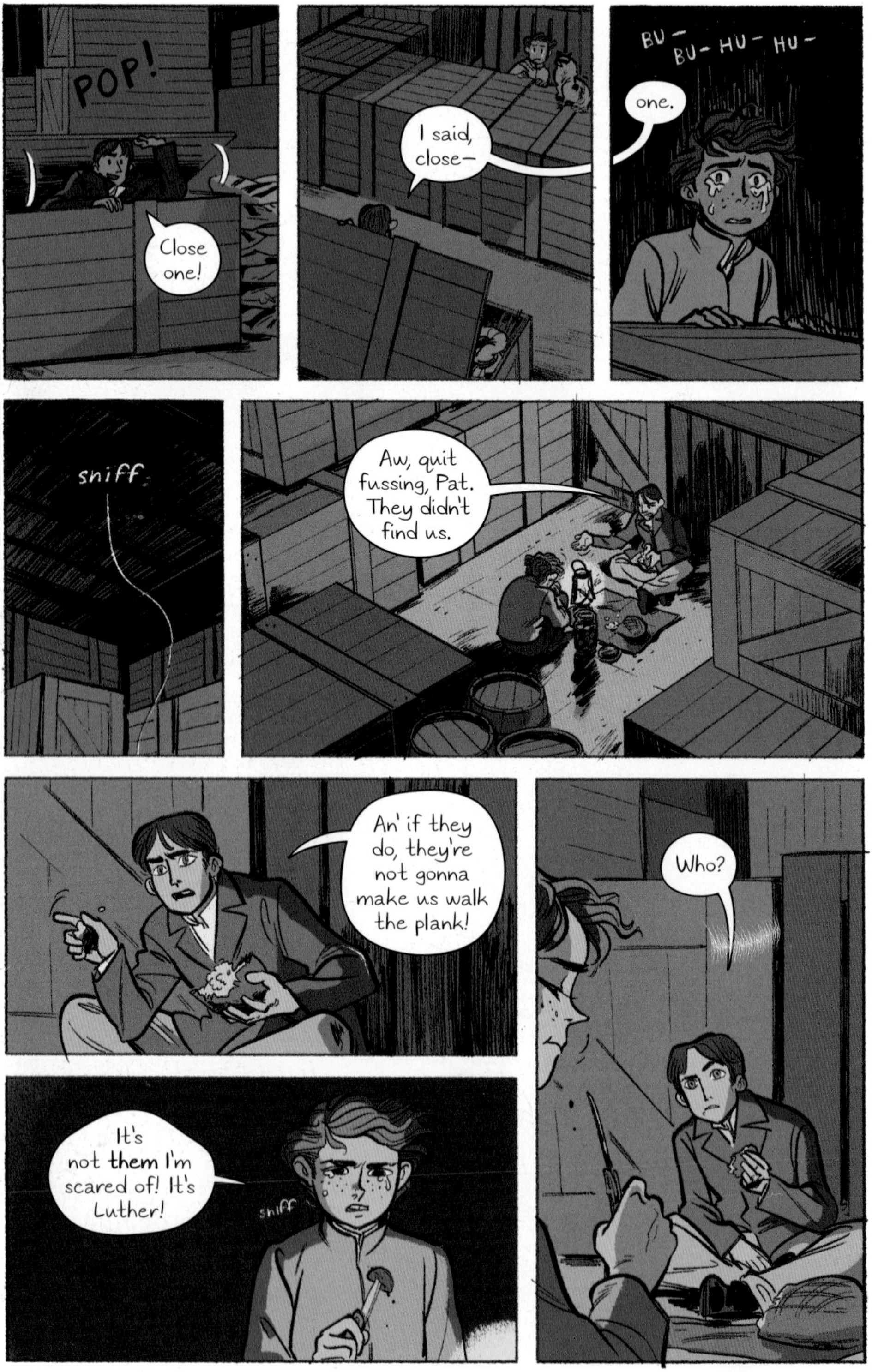
POP!
Close one!
I said, close—
BU— BU—HU—HU—
one.
sniff.
Aw, quit fussing, Pat. They didn't find us.
An' if they do, they're not gonna make us walk the plank!
Who?
It's not **them** I'm scared of! It's Luther!
sniff

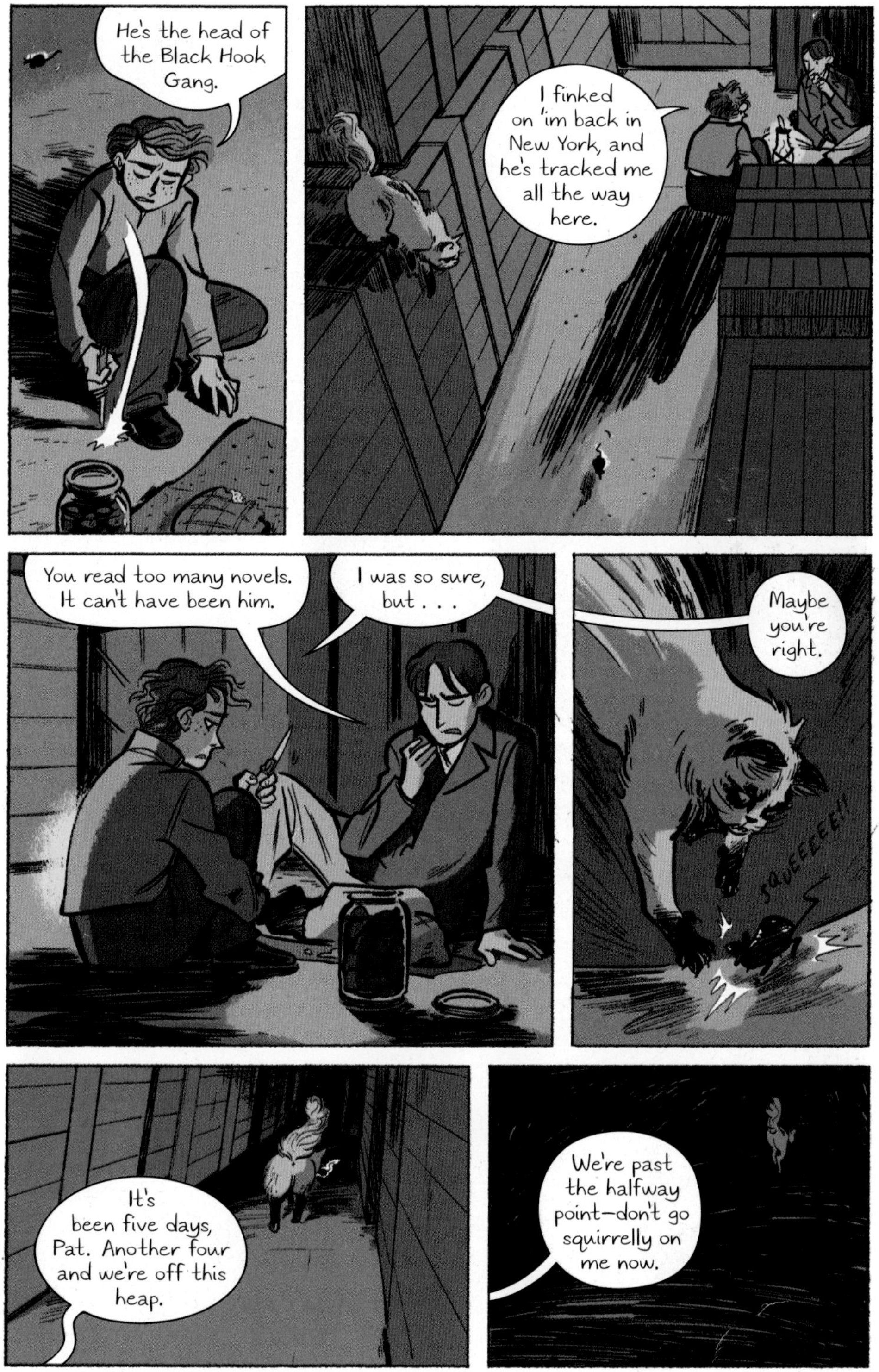
He's the head of the Black Hook Gang.
I finked on 'im back in New York, and he's tracked me all the way here.
You read too many novels. It can't have been him.
I was so sure, but . . .
Maybe you're right.
SQUEEEEE!!
It's been five days, Pat. Another four and we're off this heap.
We're past the halfway point—don't go squirrelly on me now.

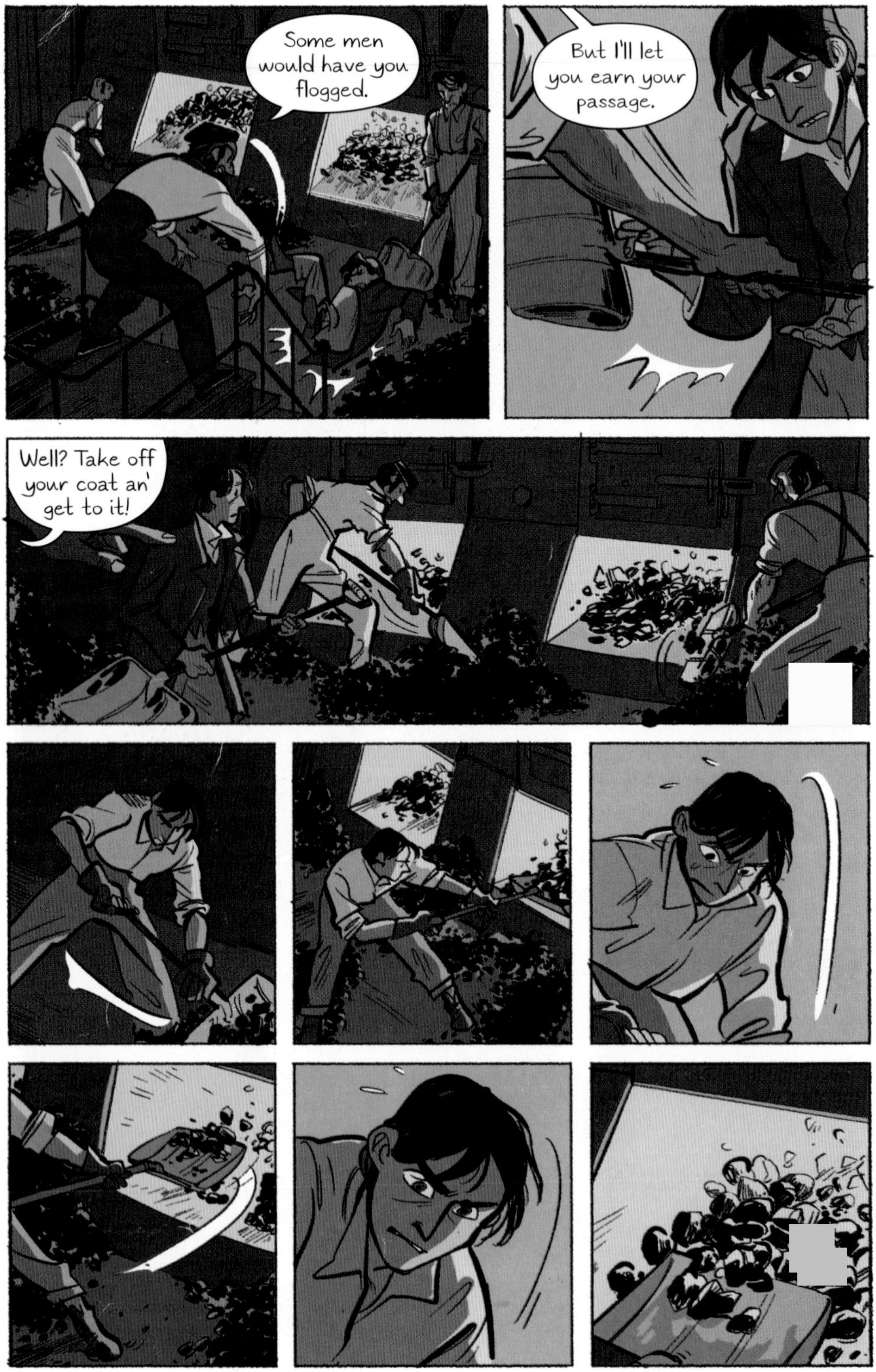
Some men would have you flogged.
But I'll let you earn your passage.
Well? Take off your coat an' get to it!

CHAPTER FIVE
THE POCKETKNIFE

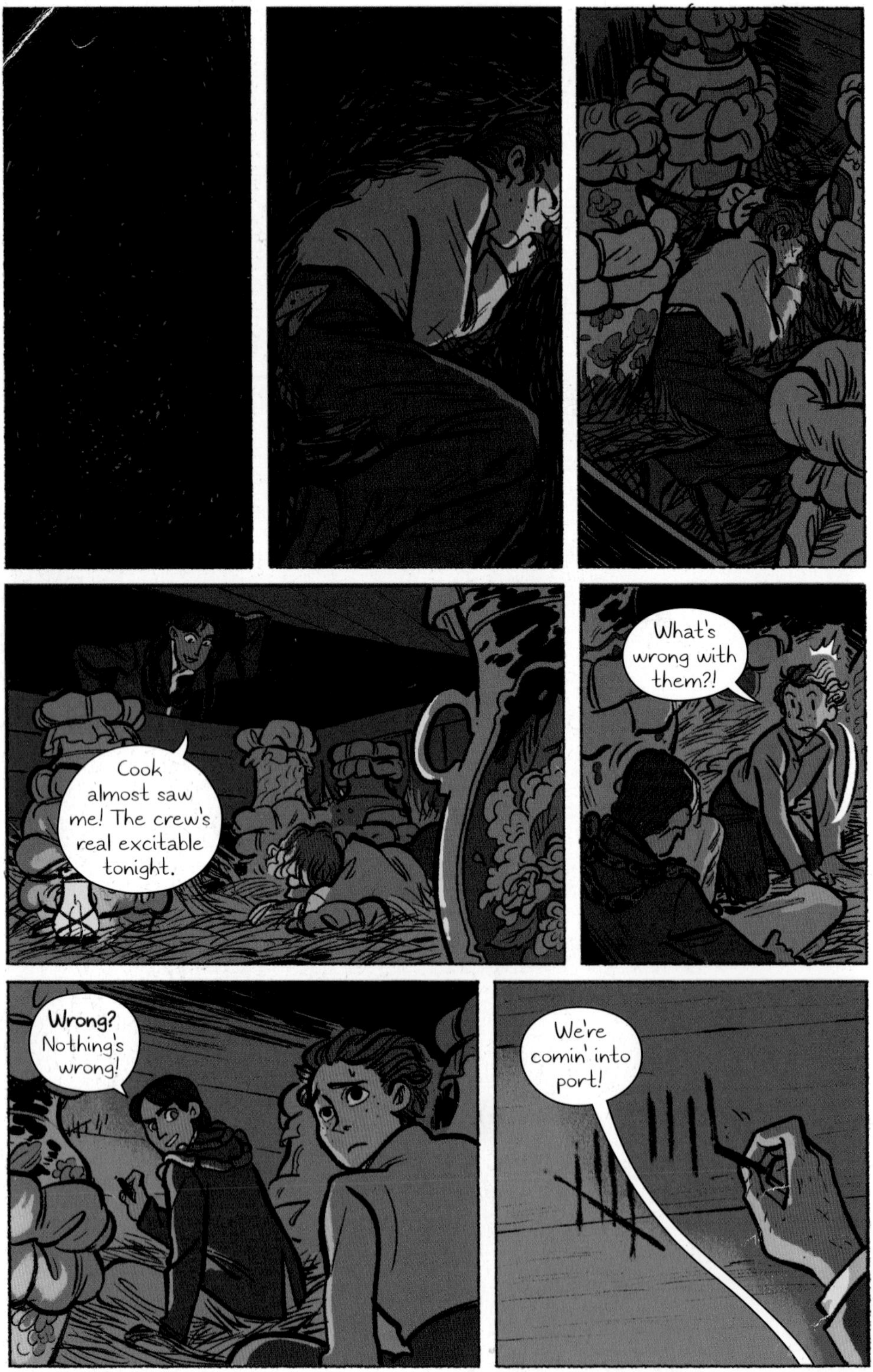
Cook almost saw me! The crew's real excitable tonight.
What's wrong with them?!
Wrong? Nothing's wrong!
We're comin' into port!

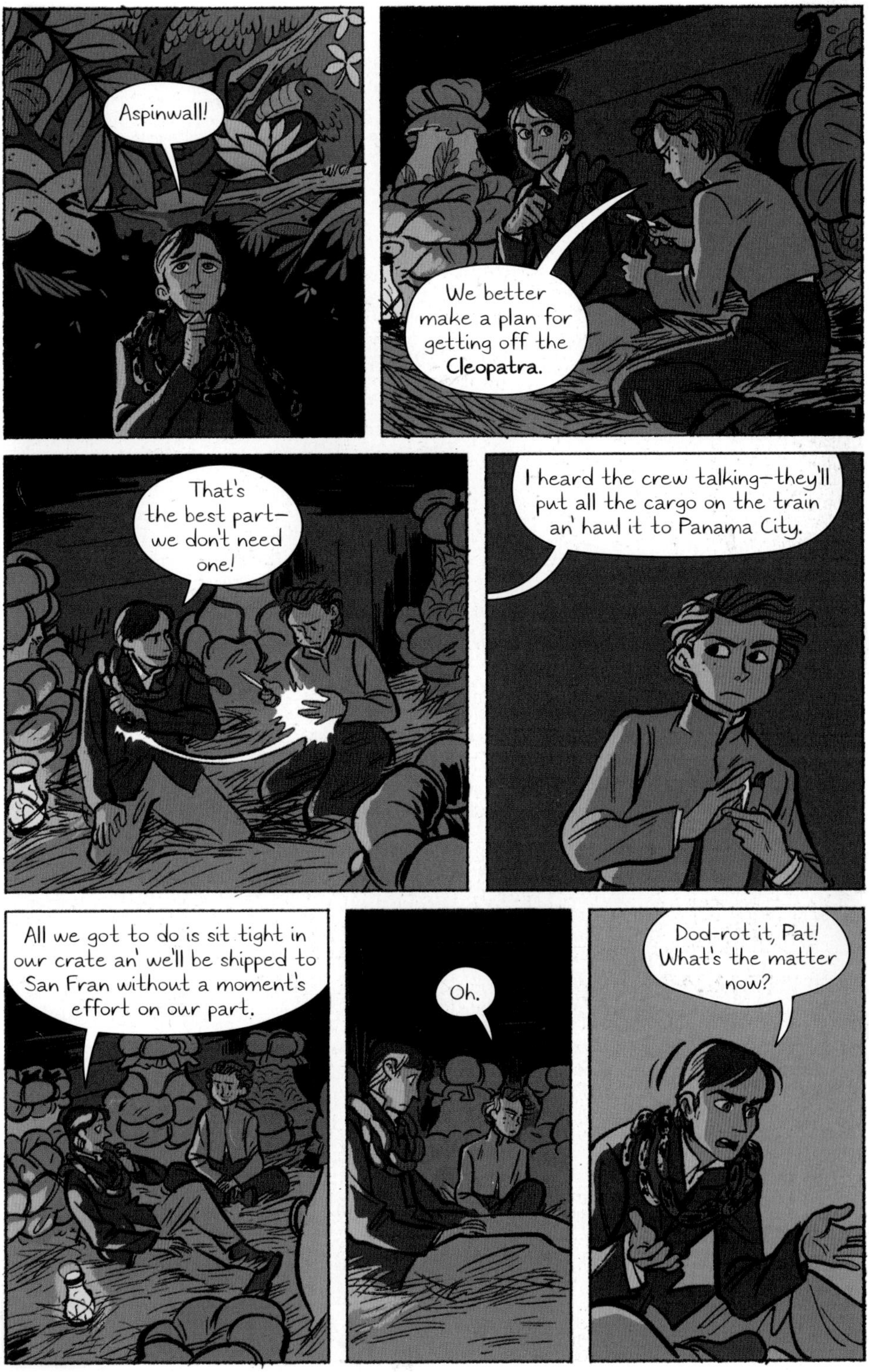
Aspinwall!
We better make a plan for getting off the **Cleopatra.**
That's the best part—we don't need one!
I heard the crew talking—they'll put all the cargo on the train an' haul it to Panama City.
All we got to do is sit tight in our crate an' we'll be shipped to San Fran without a moment's effort on our part.
Oh.
Dod-rot it, Pat! What's the matter now?

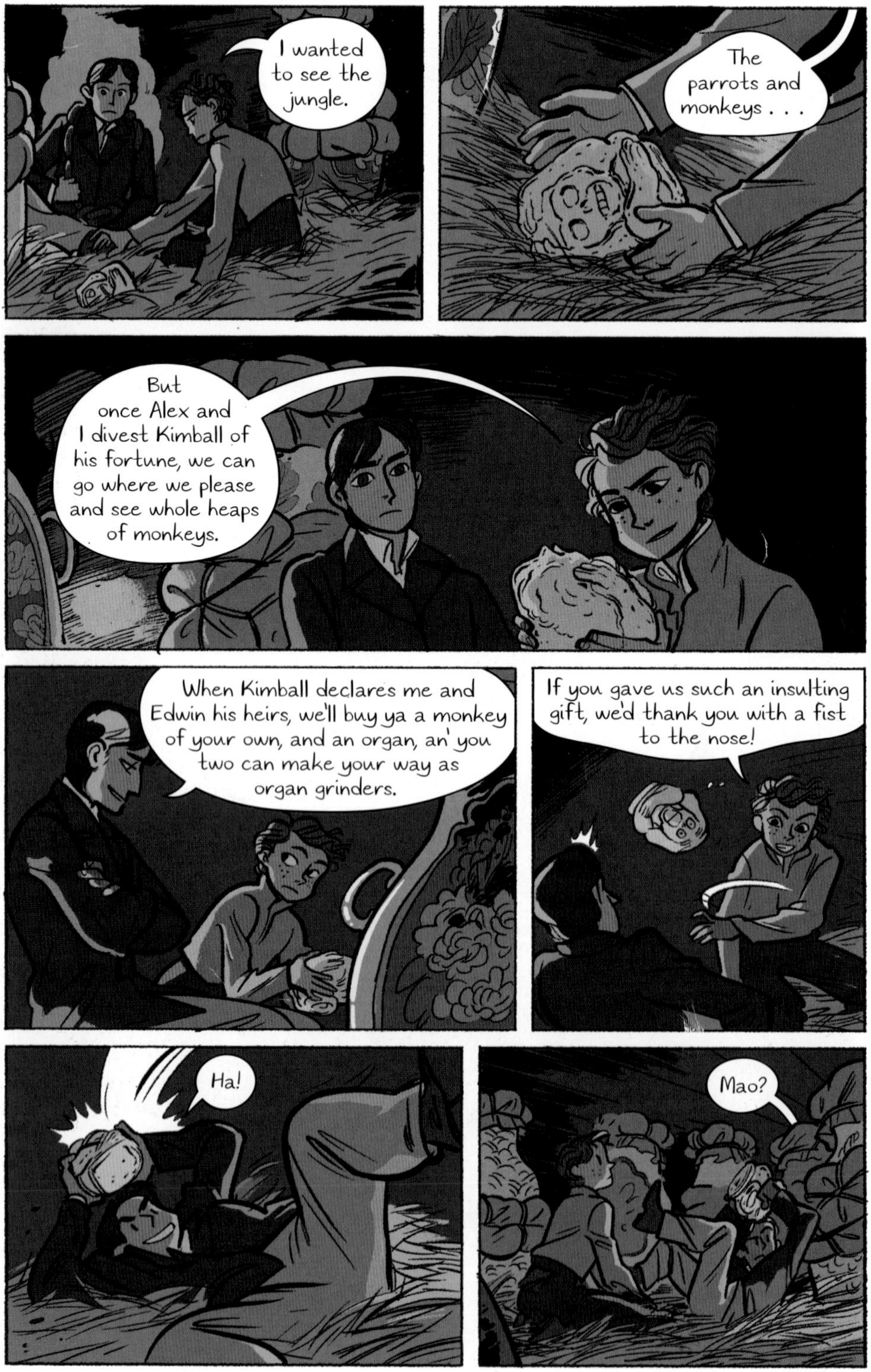
I wanted to see the jungle.
The parrots and monkeys . . .
But once Alex and I divest Kimball of his fortune, we can go where we please and see whole heaps of monkeys.
When Kimball declares me and Edwin his heirs, we'll buy ya a monkey of your own, and an organ, an' you two can make your way as organ grinders.
If you gave us such an insulting gift, we'd thank you with a fist to the nose!
Ha!
Mao?

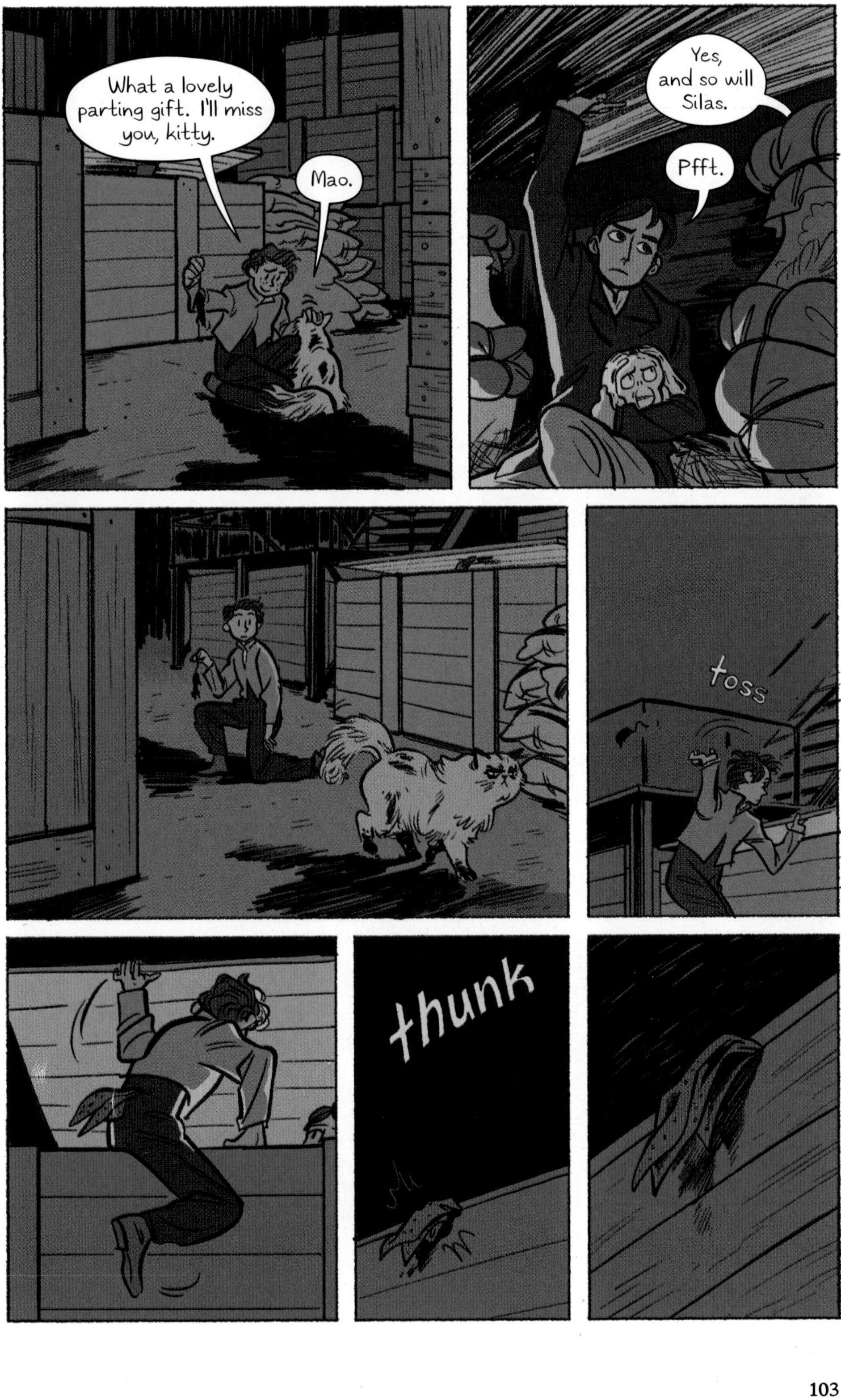
What a lovely parting gift. I'll miss you, kitty.
Mao.
Yes, and so will Silas.
Pfft.
toss
thunk

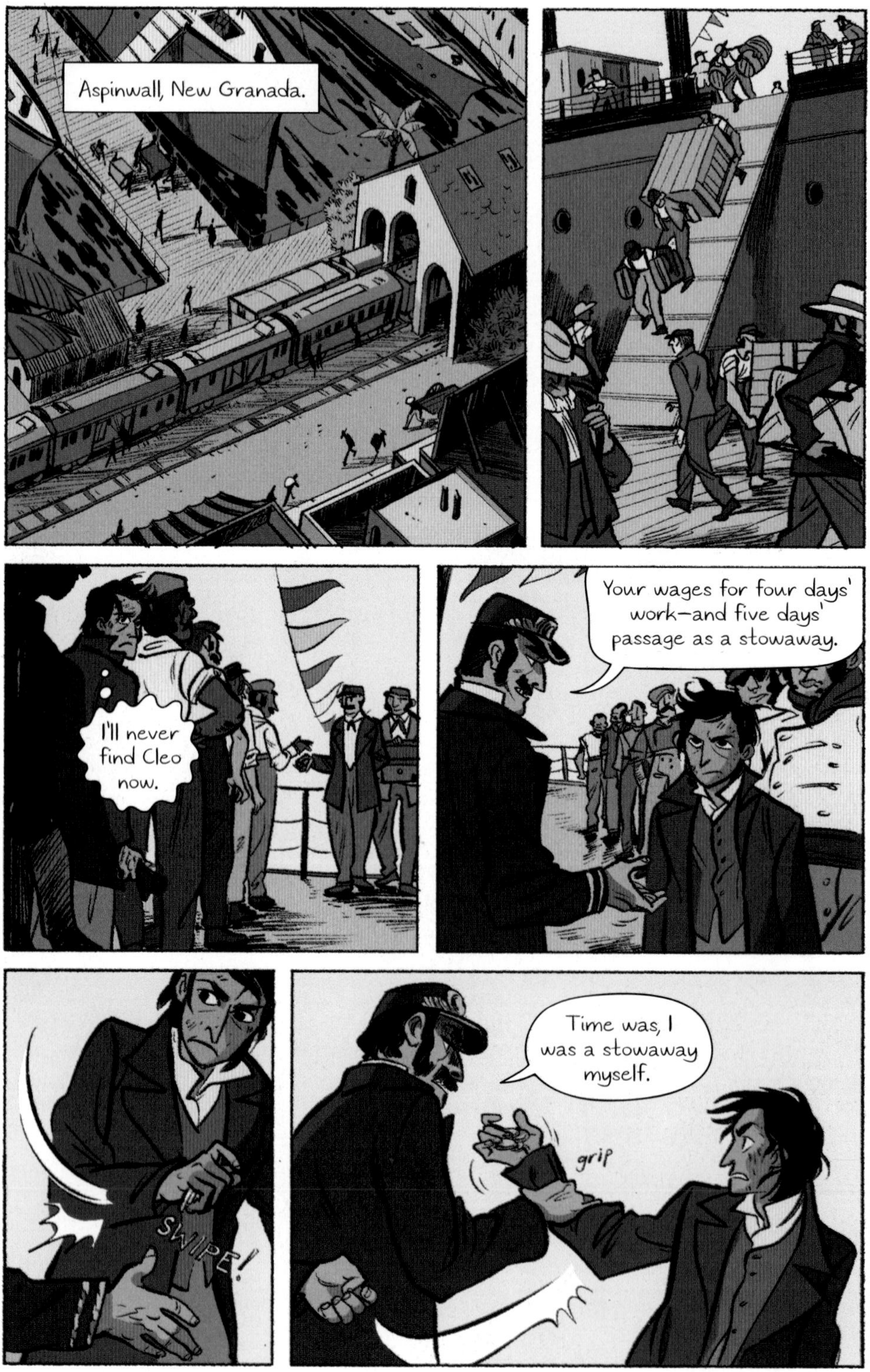
Aspinwall, New Granada.
I'll never find Cleo now.
Your wages for four days' work—and five days' passage as a stowaway.
SWIPE!
Time was, I was a stowaway myself.
grip

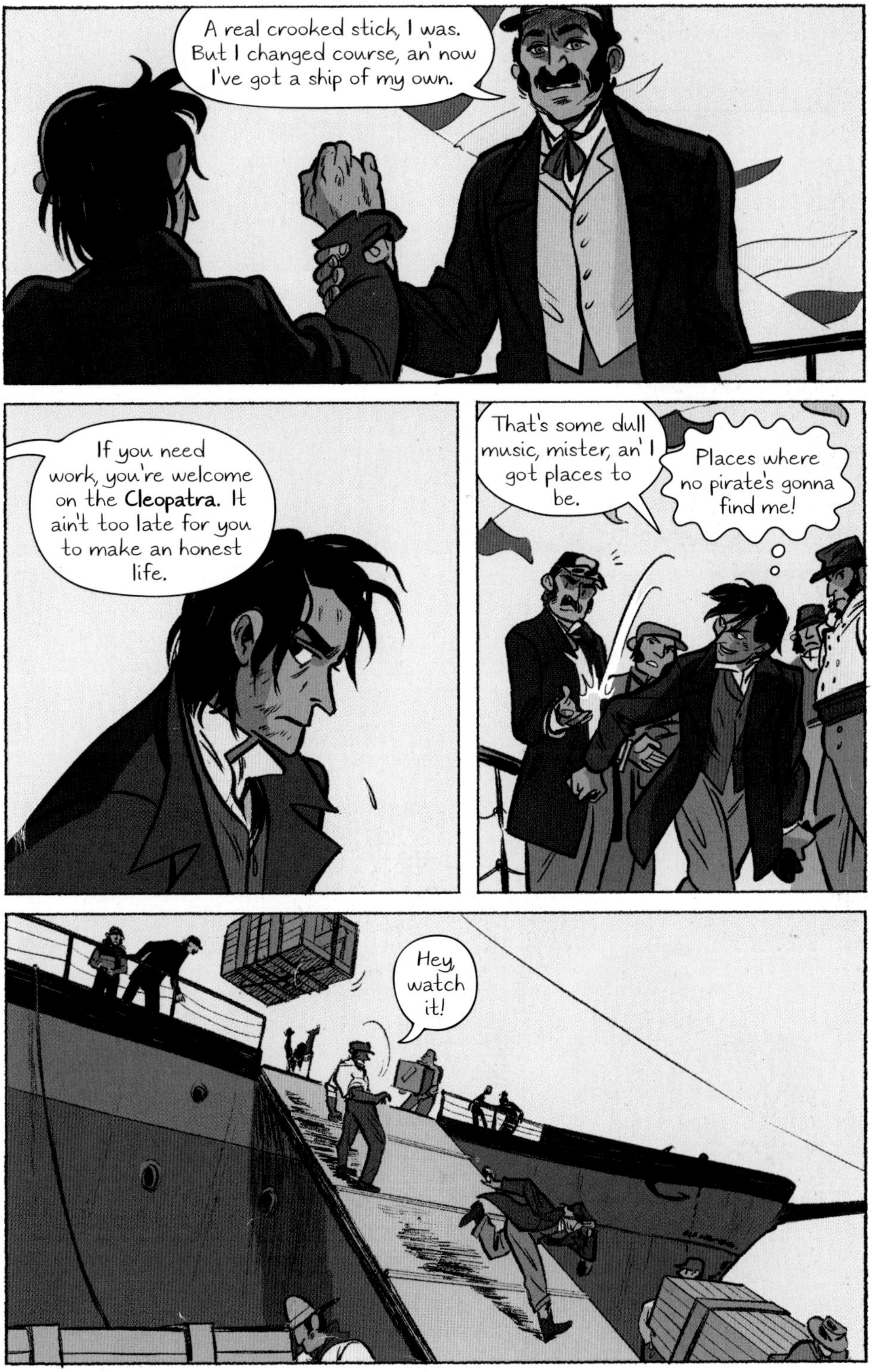
A real crooked stick, I was. But I changed course, an' now I've got a ship of my own.
If you need work, you're welcome on the **Cleopatra.** It ain't too late for you to make an honest life.
That's some dull music, mister, an' I got places to be.
Places where no pirate's gonna find me!
Hey, watch it!

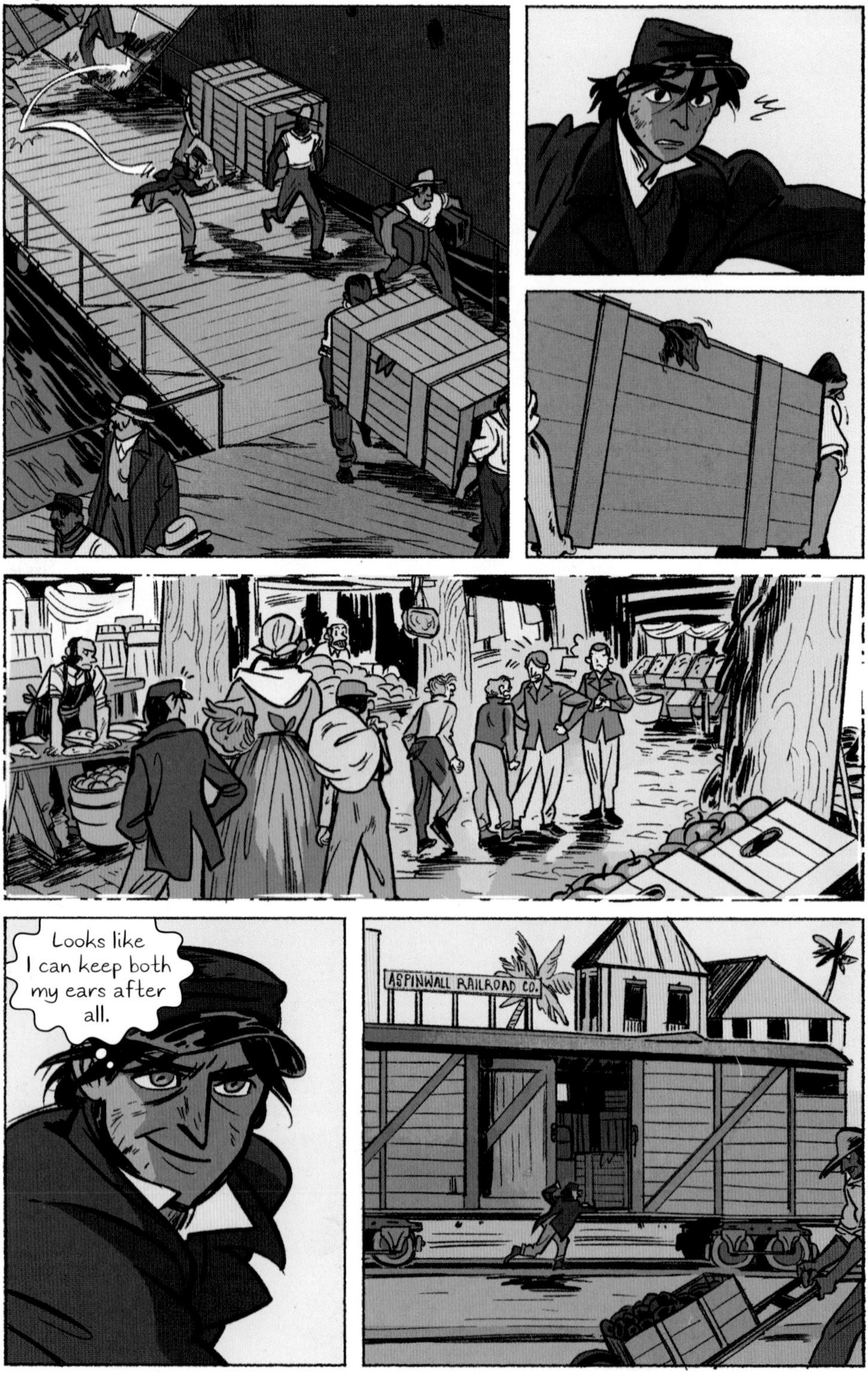
Looks like I can keep both my ears after all.
ASPINWALL RAILROAD CO.

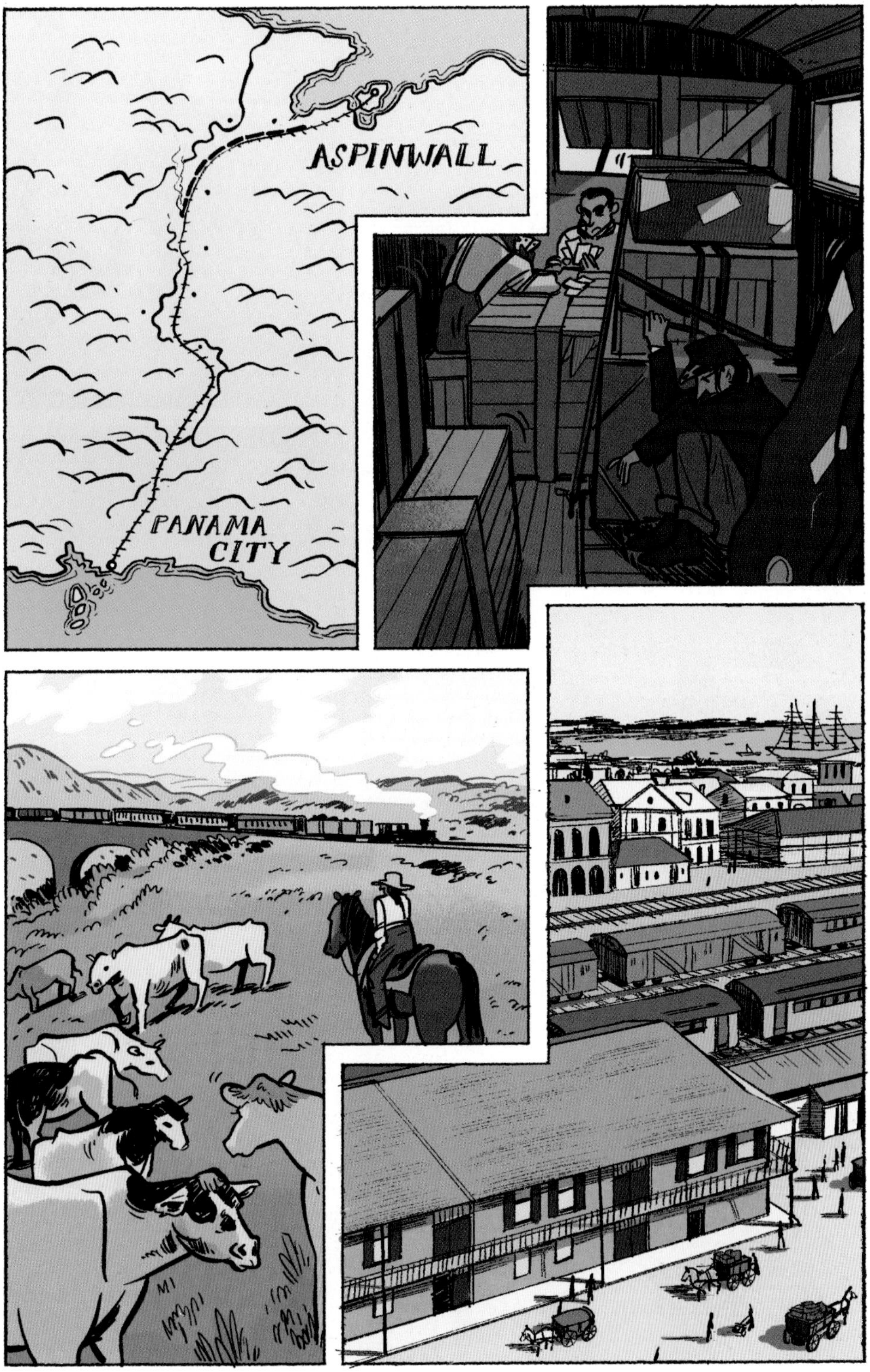
ASPINWALL
PANAMA CITY

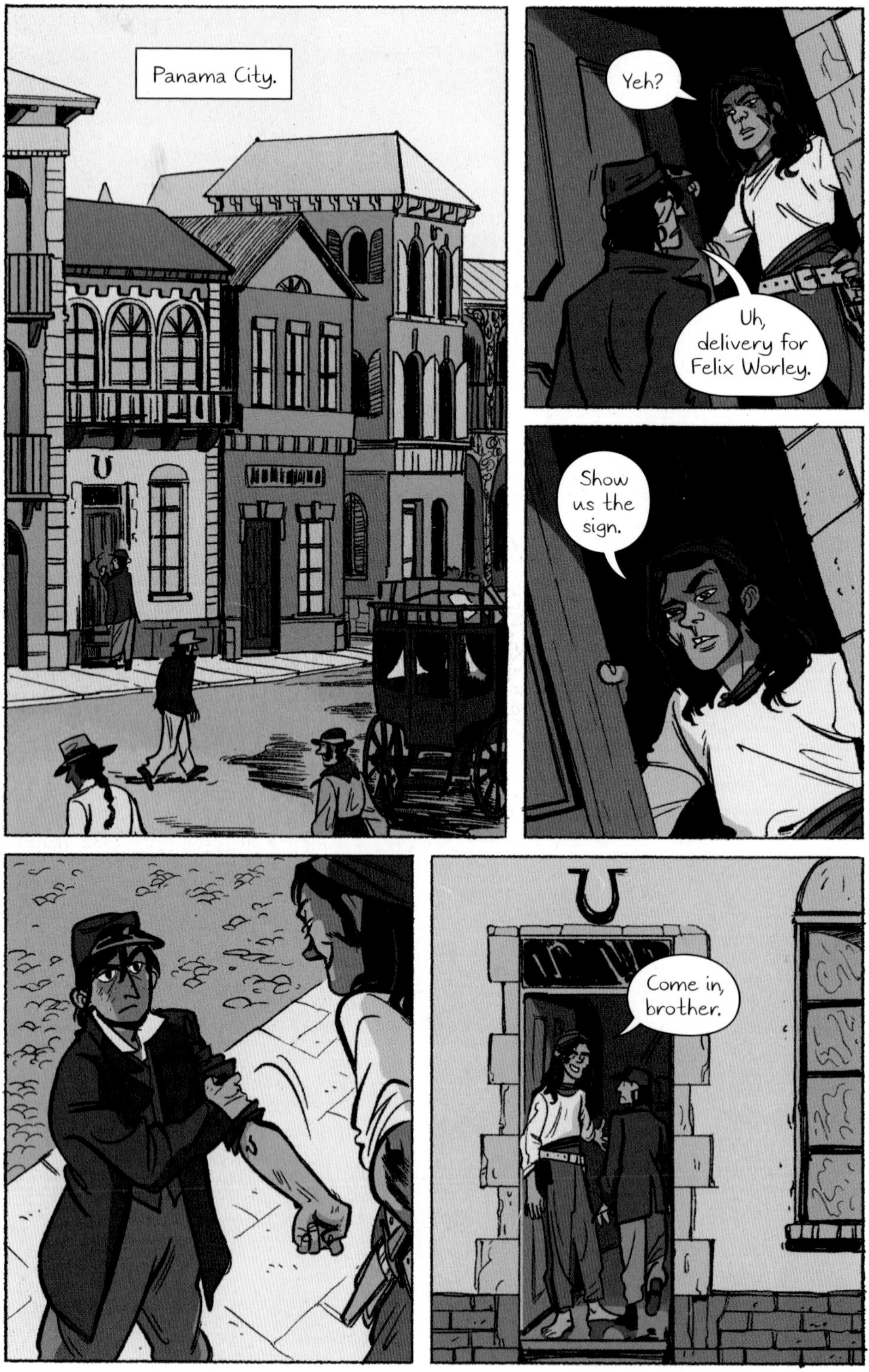
Panama City.
Yeh?
Uh, delivery for Felix Worley.
Show us the sign.
Come in, brother.

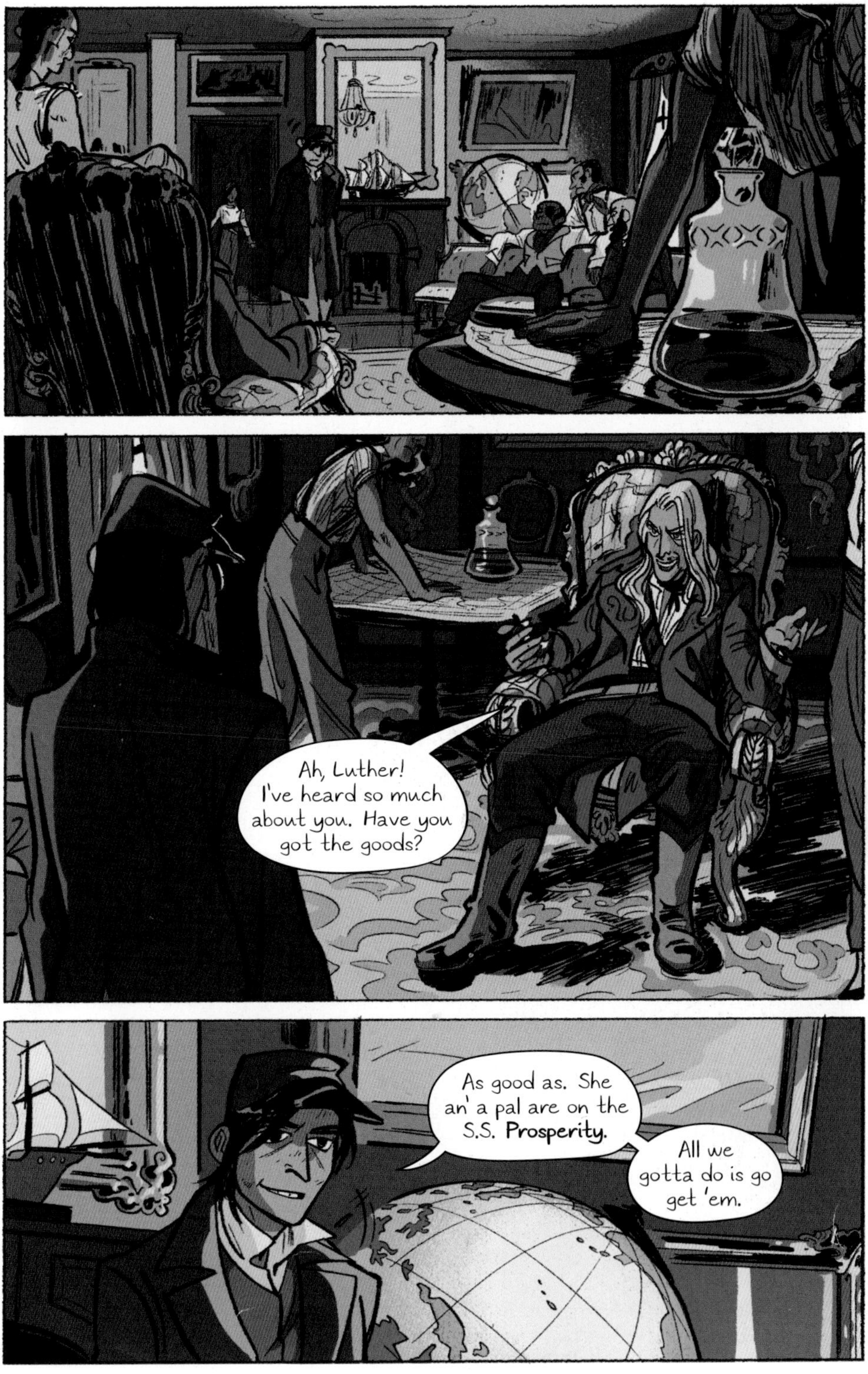
Ah, Luther! I've heard so much about you. Have you got the goods?
As good as. She an' a pal are on the S.S. **Prosperity.**
All we gotta do is go get 'em.

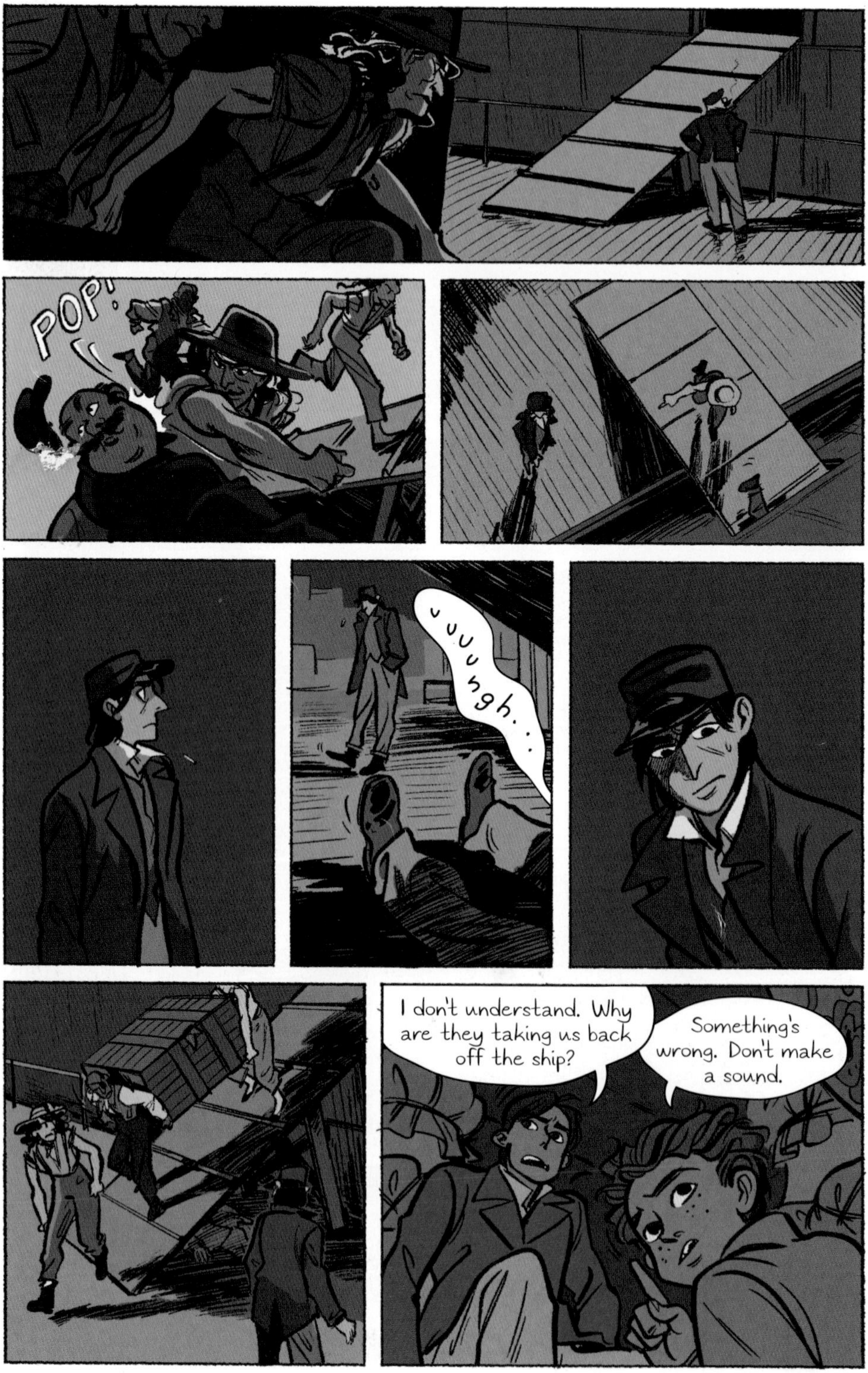
POP!
vuuungh...
I don't understand. Why are they taking us back off the ship?
Something's wrong. Don't make a sound.

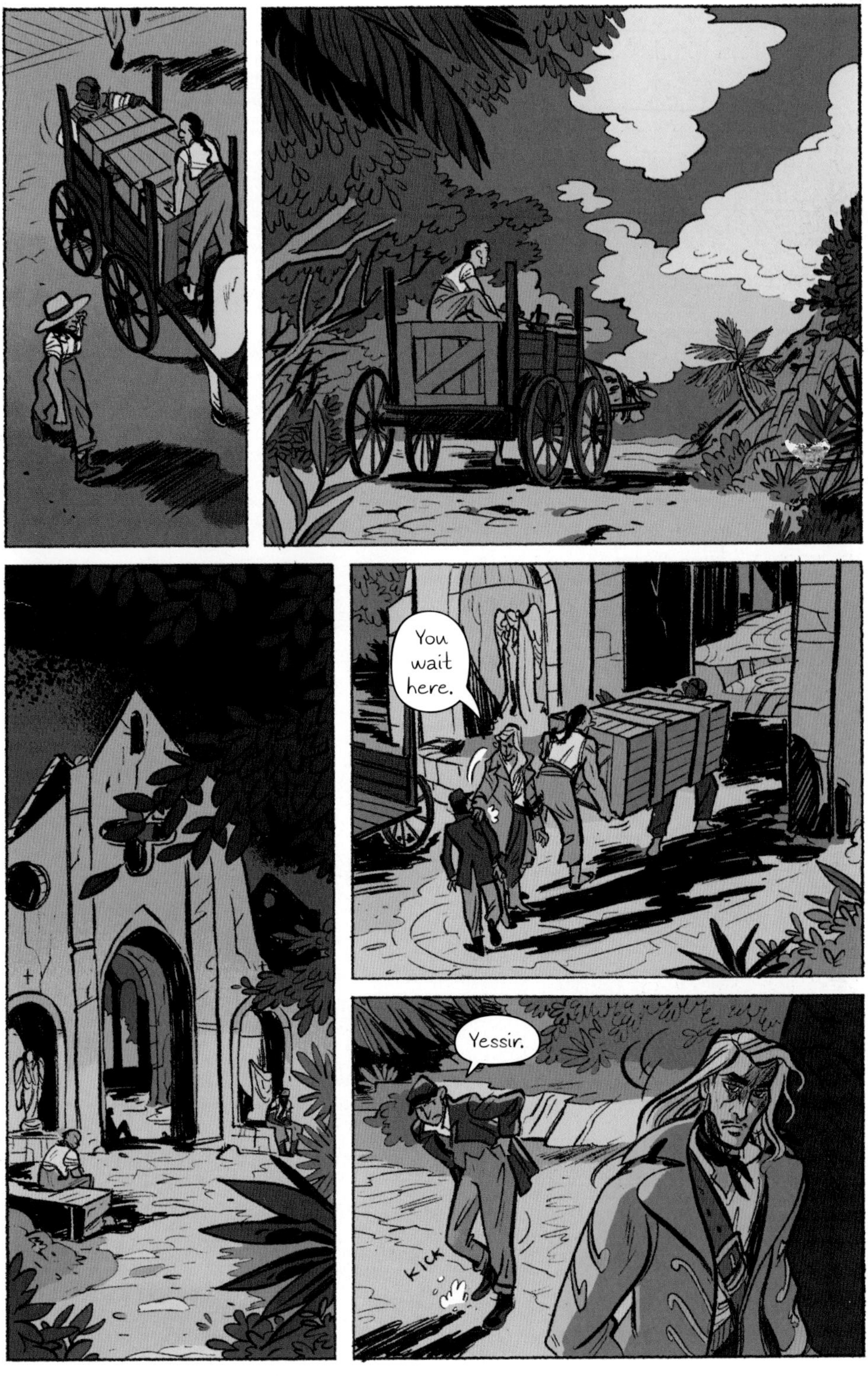
You wait here.
Yessir.
KICK

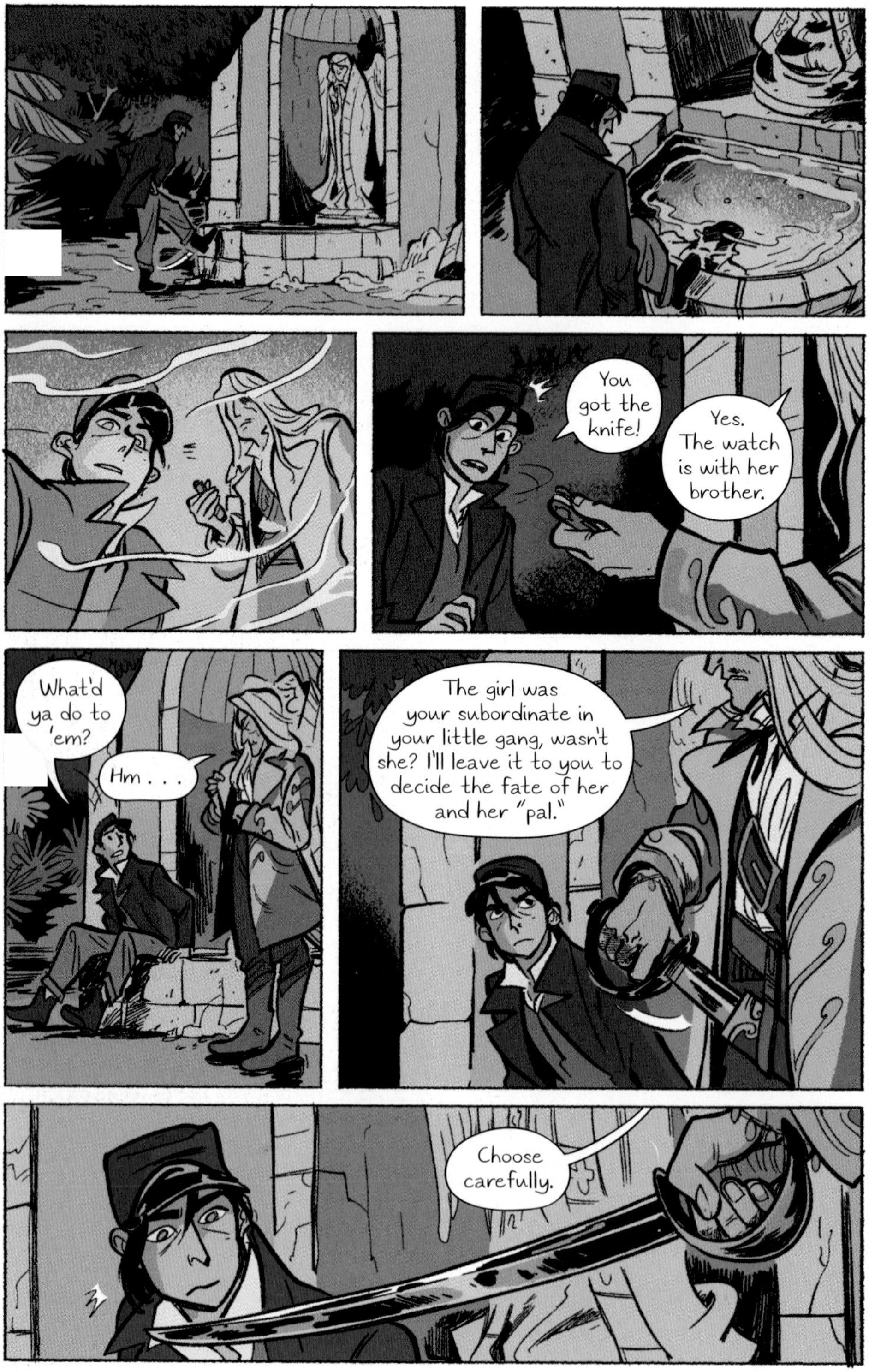
You got the knife!
Yes. The watch is with her brother.
What'd ya do to 'em?
Hm . . .
The girl was your subordinate in your little gang, wasn't she? I'll leave it to you to decide the fate of her and her "pal."
Choose carefully.

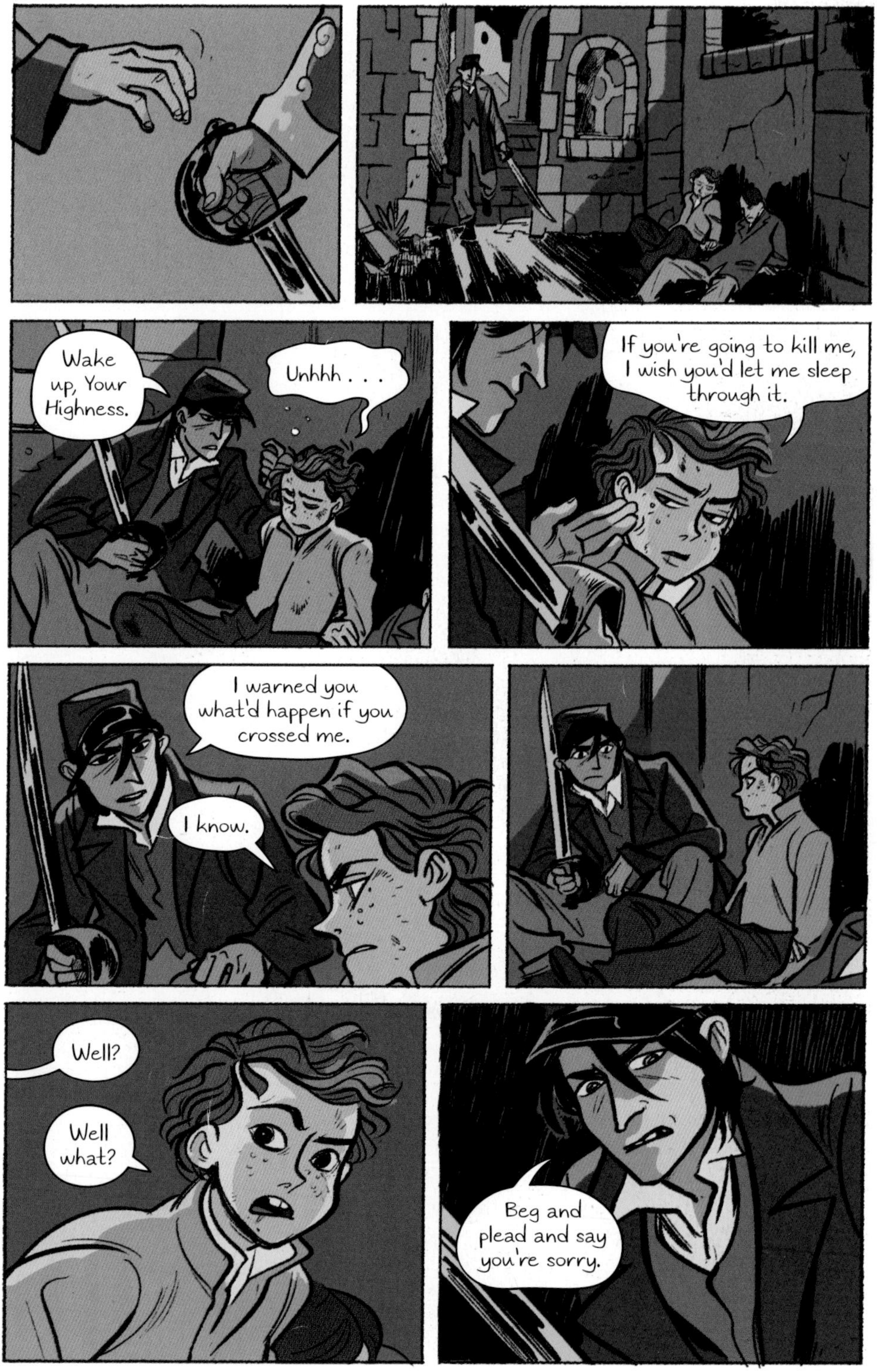

Wake up, Your Highness.
Unhhh . . .
If you're going to kill me, I wish you'd let me sleep through it.
I warned you what'd happen if you crossed me.
I know.
Well?
Well what?
Beg and plead and say you're sorry.

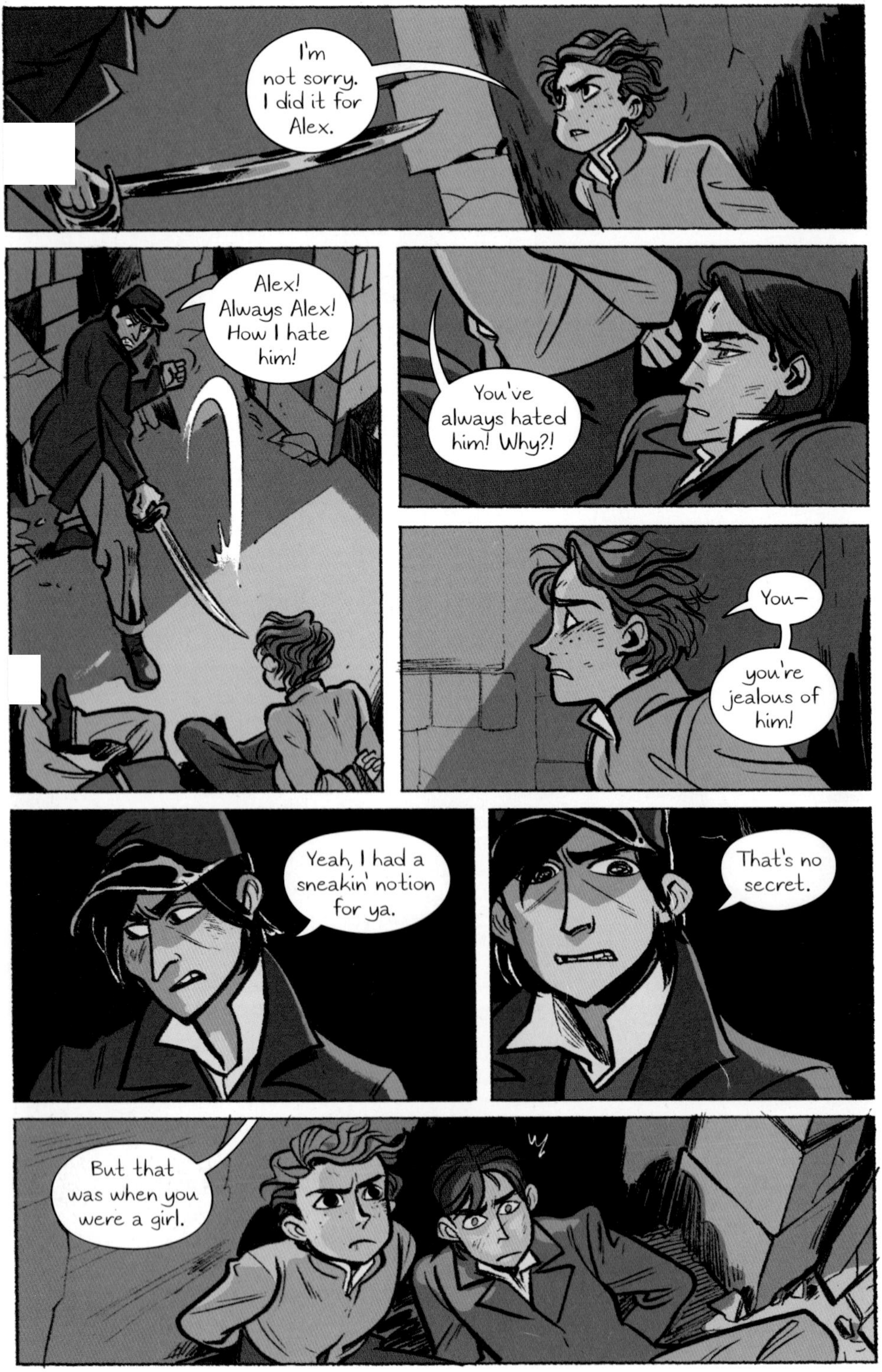
I'm not sorry. I did it for Alex.
Alex! Always Alex! How I hate him!
You've always hated him! Why?!
You—
you're jealous of him!
Yeah, I had a sneakin' notion for ya.
That's no secret.
But that was when you were a girl.

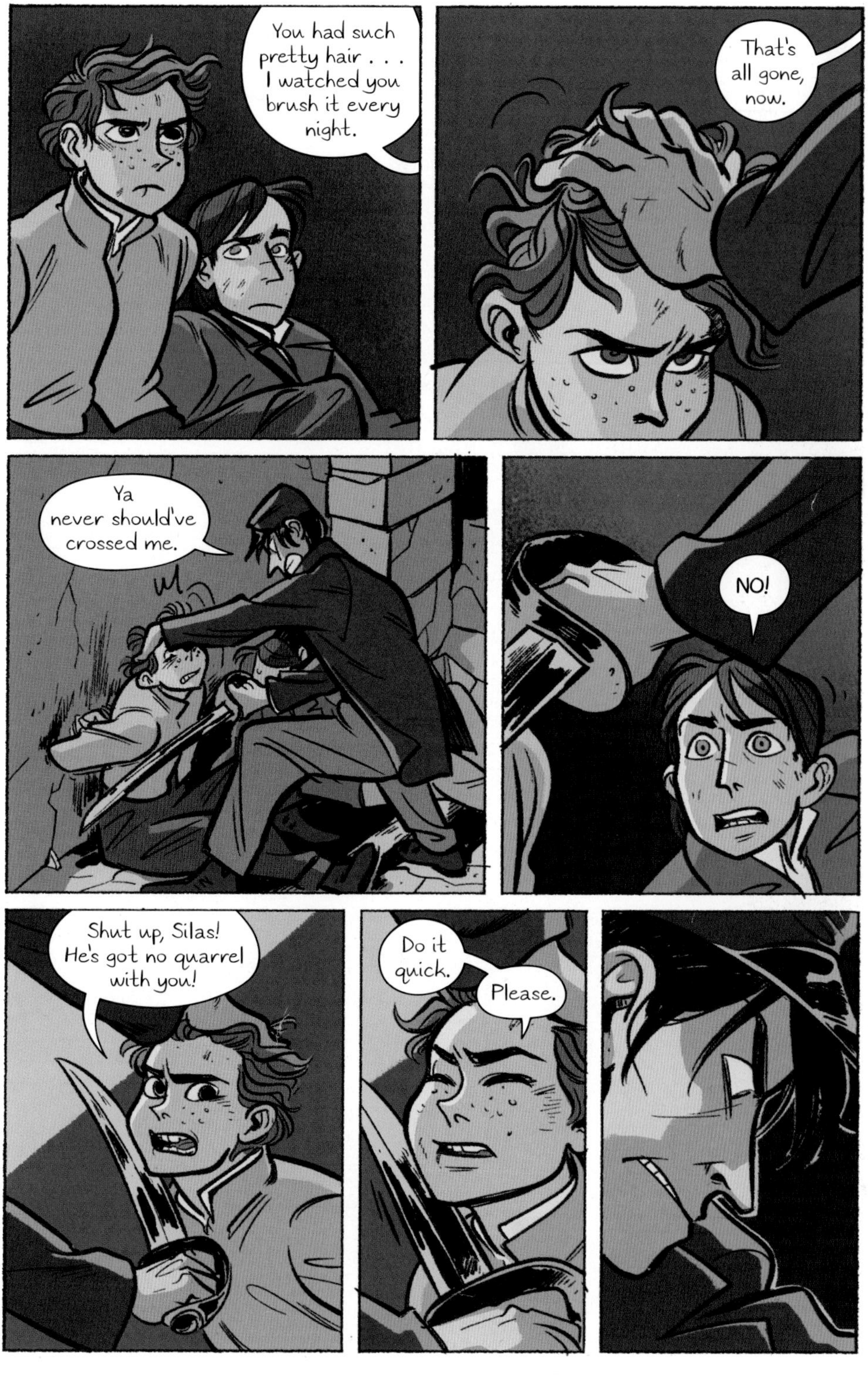
You had such pretty hair . . . I watched you brush it every night.
That's all gone, now.
Ya never should've crossed me.
NO!
Shut up, Silas! He's got no quarrel with you!
Do it quick.
Please.

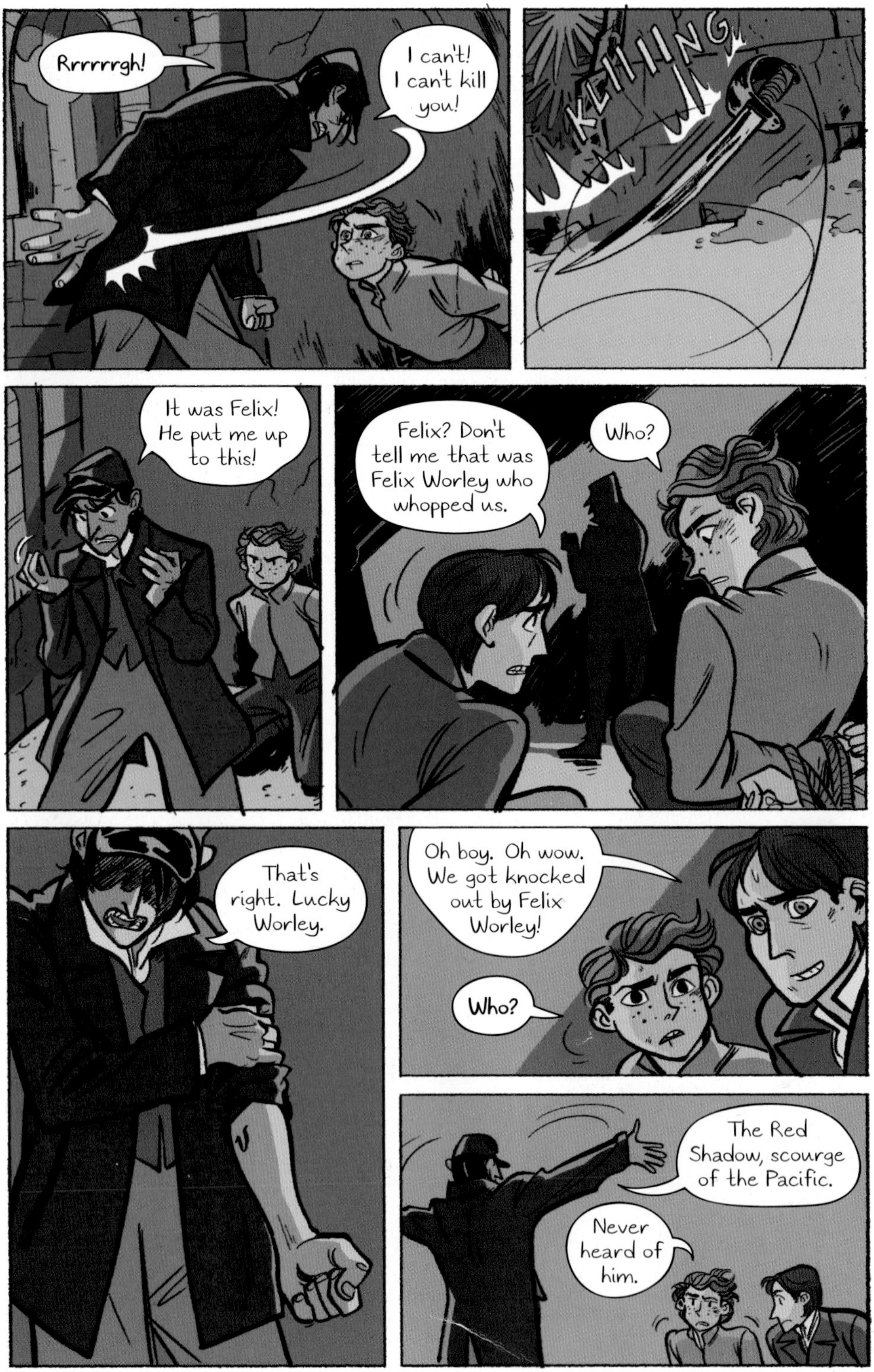
Rrrrrrgh!
I can't! I can't kill you!
KLIIIING
It was Felix! He put me up to this!
Felix? Don't tell me that was Felix Worley who whopped us.
Who?
That's right. Lucky Worley.
Oh boy. Oh wow. We got knocked out by Felix Worley!
Who?
The Red Shadow, scourge of the Pacific.
Never heard of him.

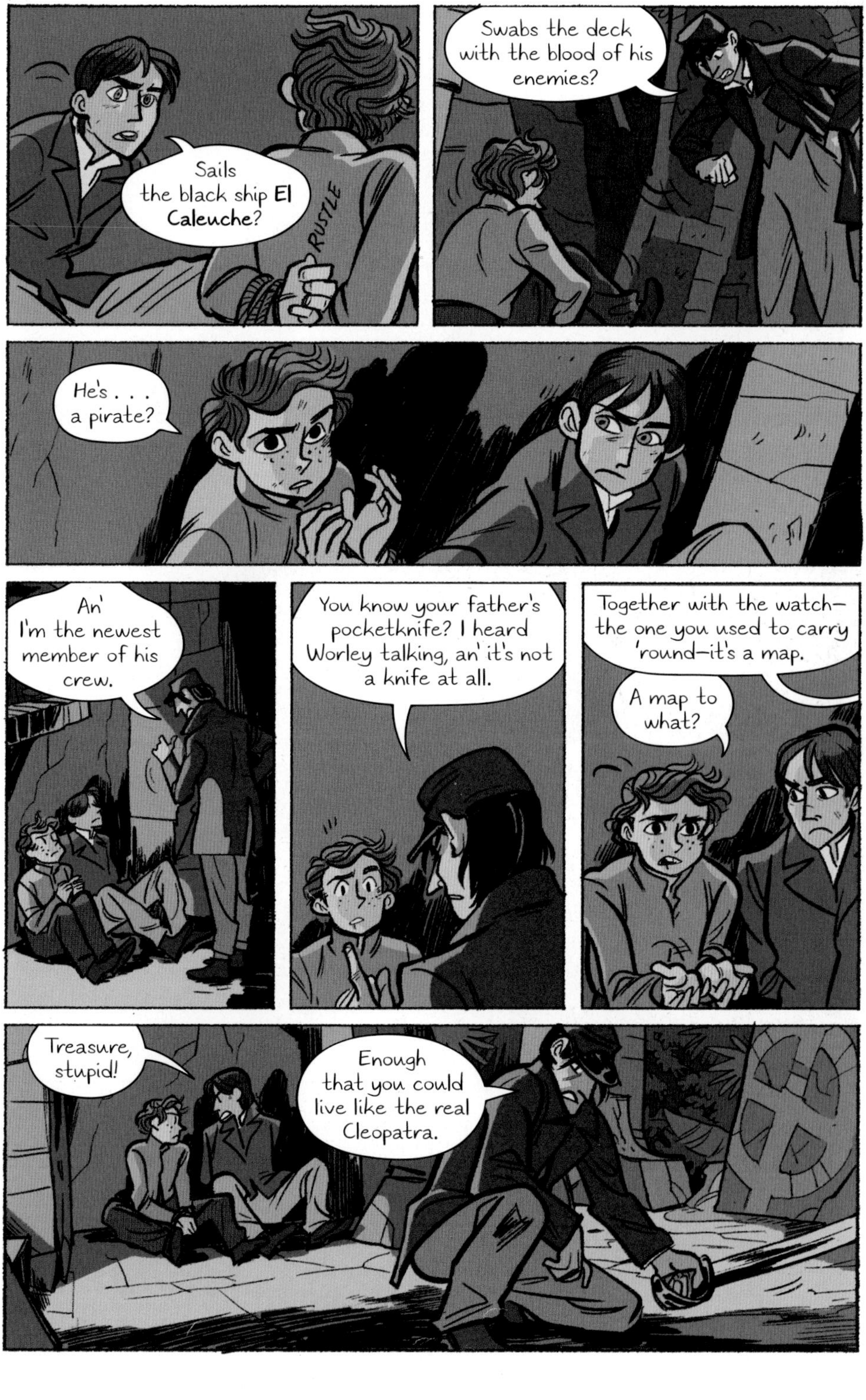
Sails the black ship **El Caleuche**?
RUSTLE
Swabs the deck with the blood of his enemies?
He's . . . a pirate?
An' I'm the newest member of his crew.
You know your father's pocketknife? I heard Worley talking, an' it's not a knife at all.
Together with the watch—the one you used to carry 'round—it's a map.
A map to what?
Treasure, stupid!
Enough that you could live like the real Cleopatra.

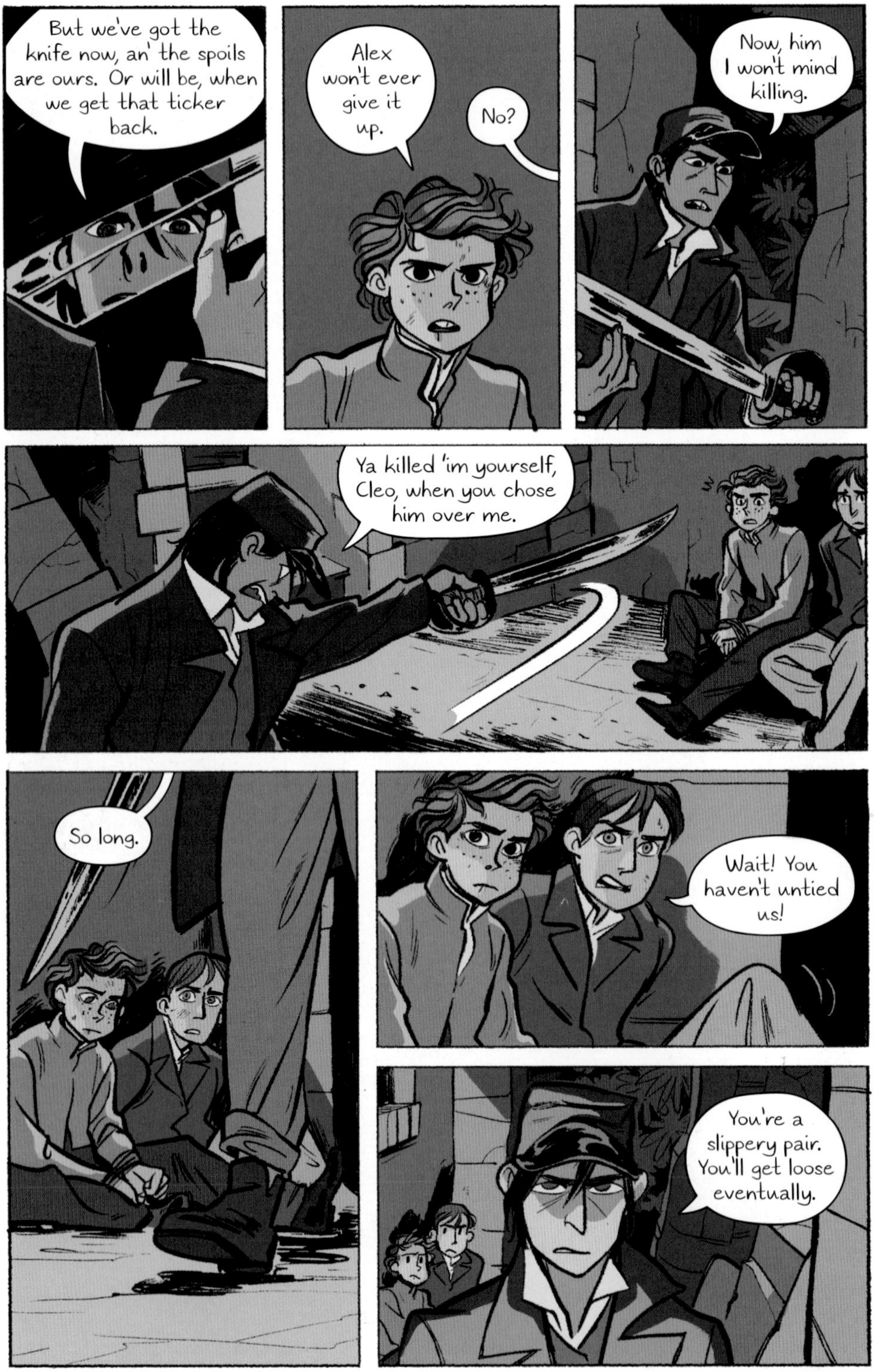

But we've got the knife now, an' the spoils are ours. Or will be, when we get that ticker back.
Alex won't ever give it up.
No?
Now, him I won't mind killing.
Ya killed 'im yourself, Cleo, when you chose him over me.
So long.
Wait! You haven't untied us!
You're a slippery pair. You'll get loose eventually.

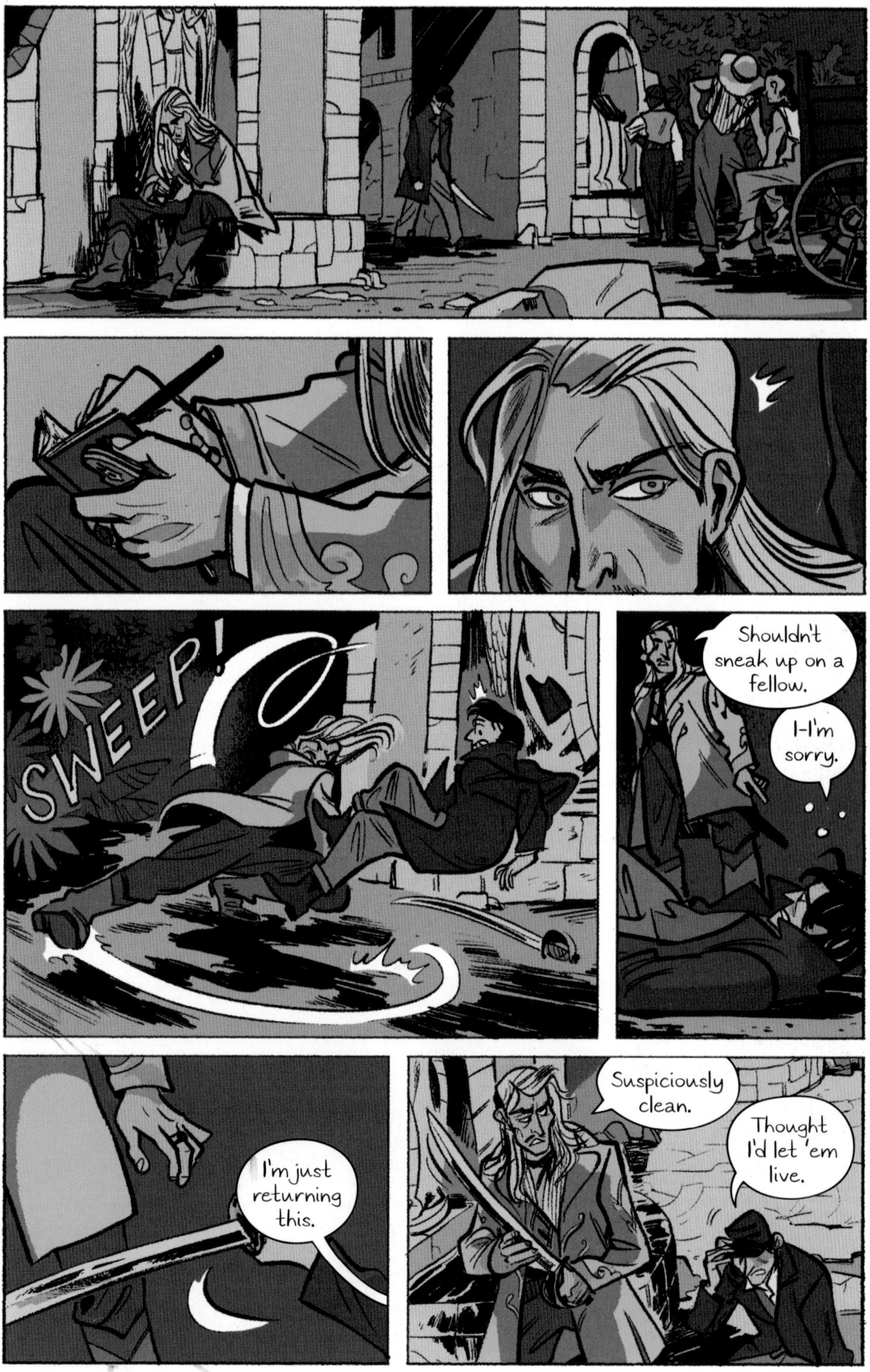
SWEEP!
Shouldn't sneak up on a fellow.
I-I'm sorry.
I'm just returning this.
Suspiciously clean.
Thought I'd let 'em live.

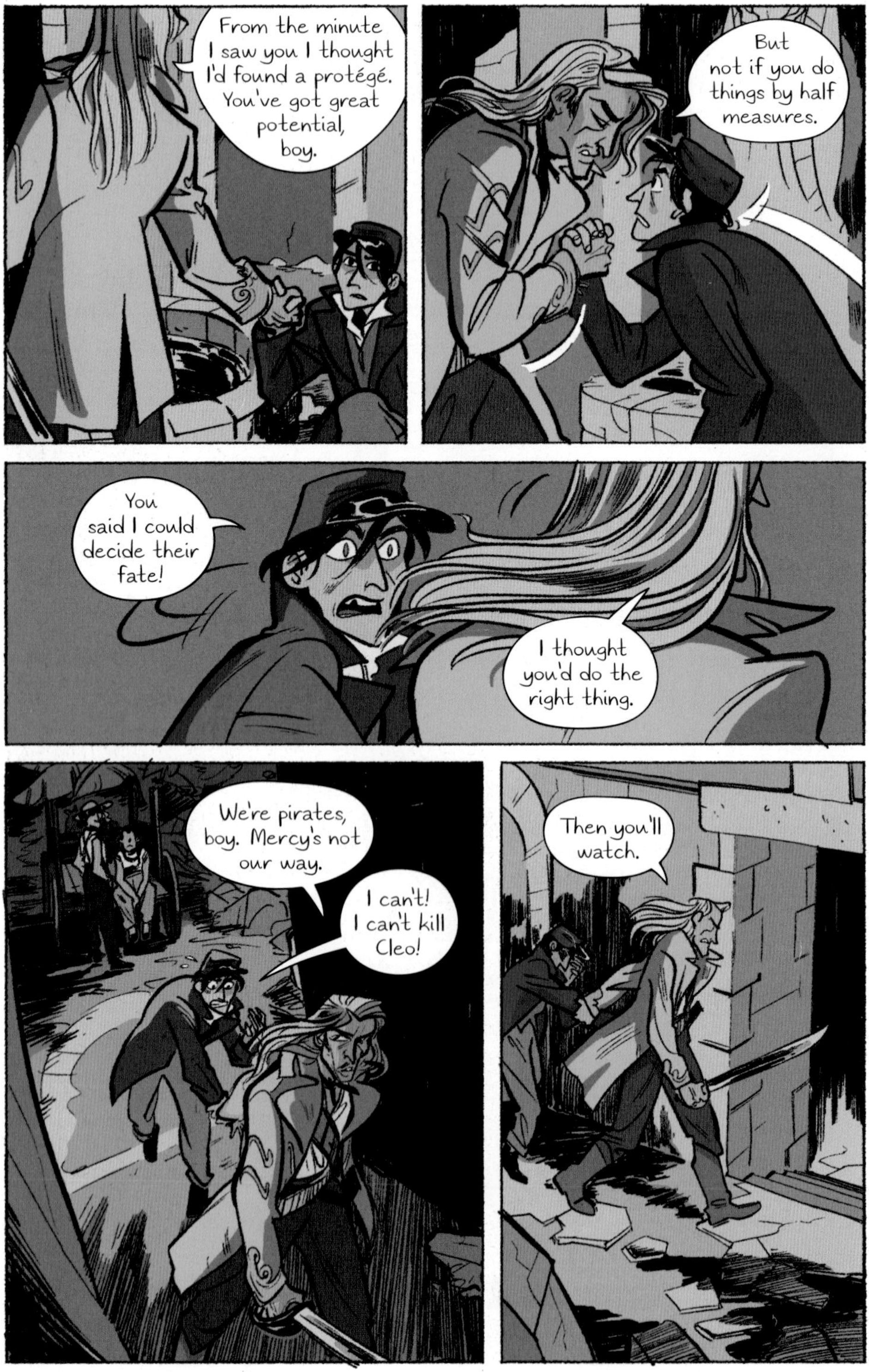
From the minute I saw you I thought I'd found a protégé. You've got great potential, boy.
But not if you do things by half measures.
You said I could decide their fate!
I thought you'd do the right thing.
We're pirates, boy. Mercy's not our way.
I can't! I can't kill Cleo!
Then you'll watch.

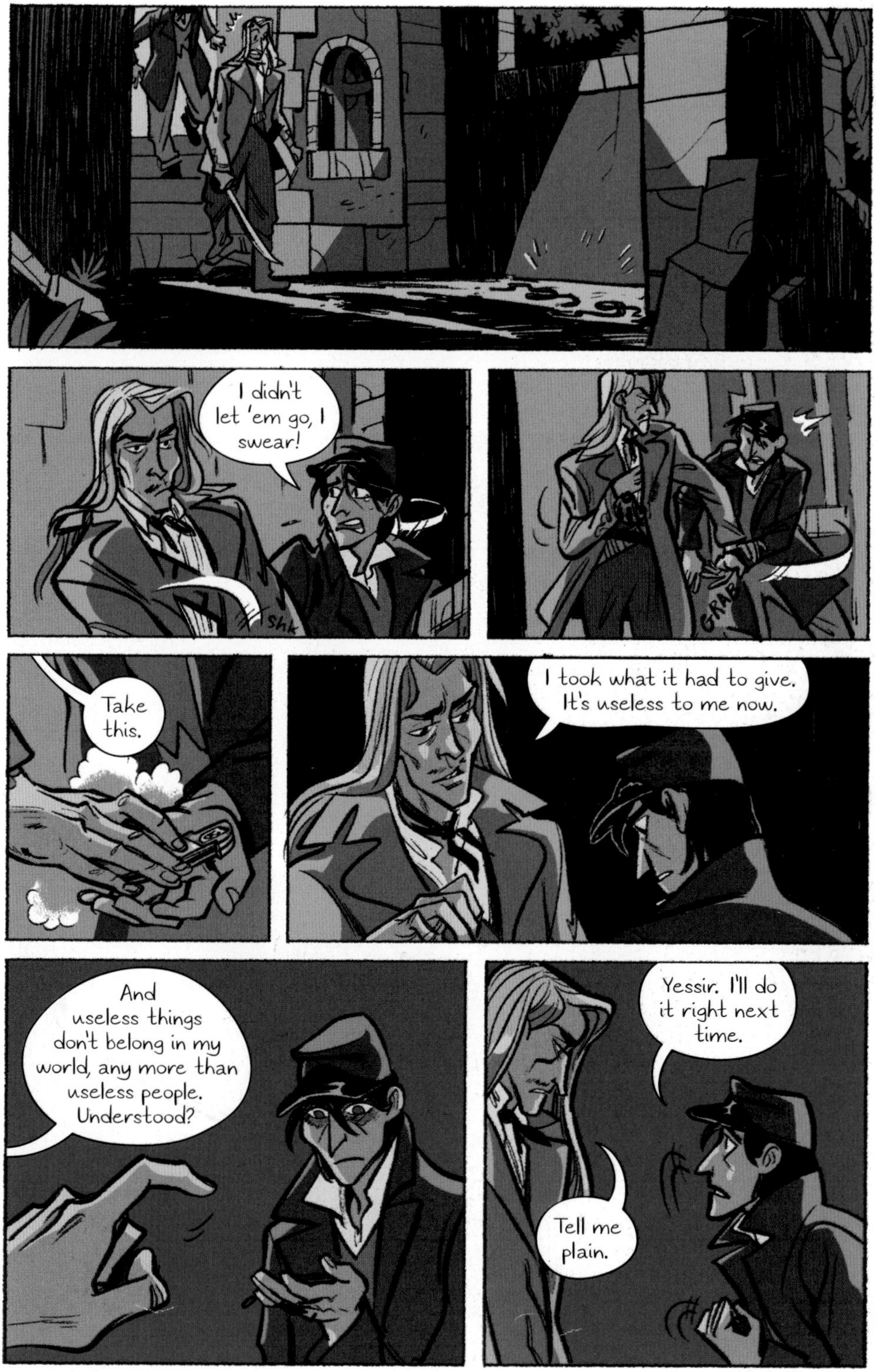
I didn't let 'em go, I swear!
shk
GRAB
Take this.
I took what it had to give. It's useless to me now.
And useless things don't belong in my world, any more than useless people. Understood?
Yessir. I'll do it right next time.
Tell me plain.

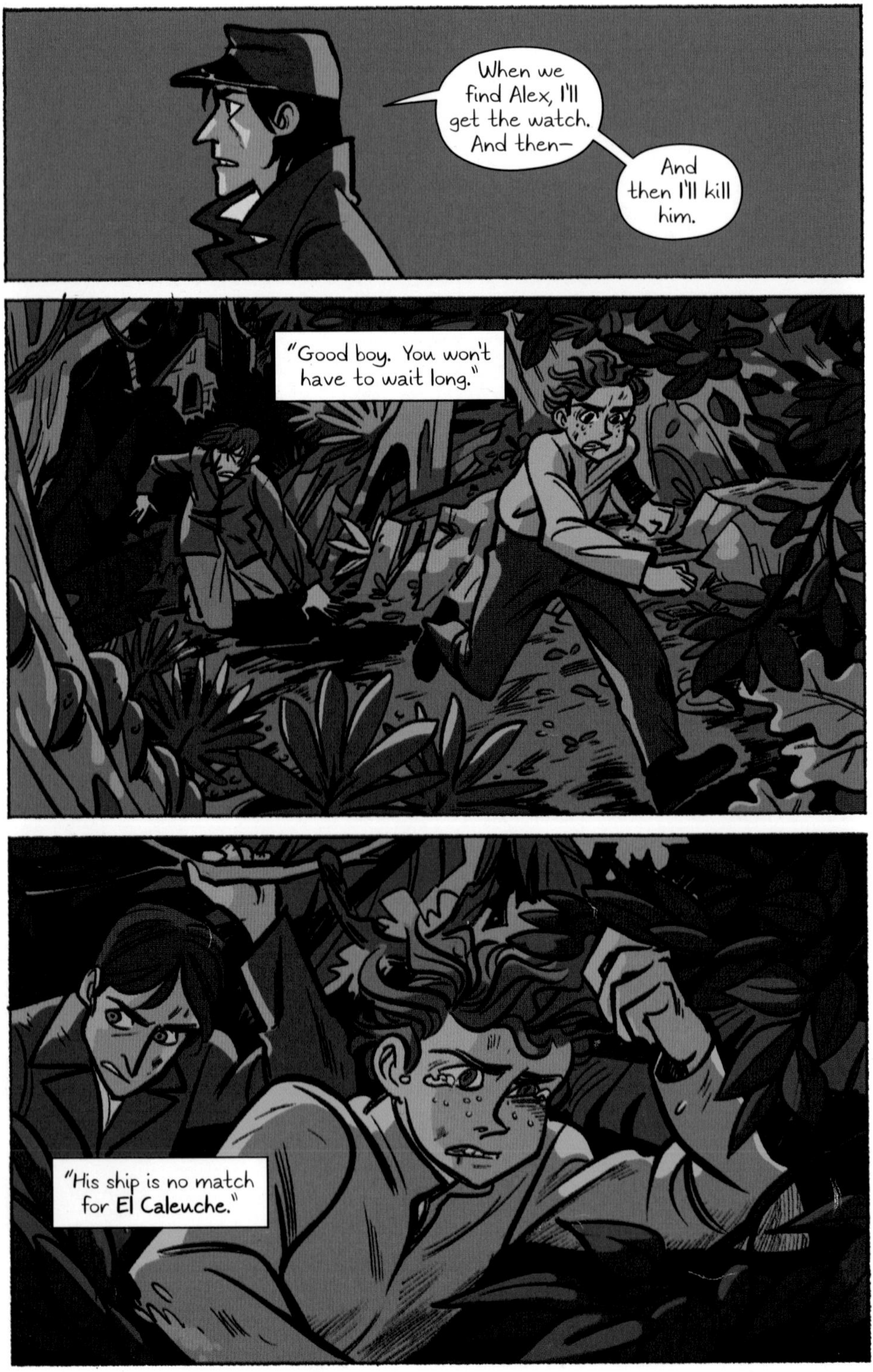
When we find Alex, I'll get the watch. And then—
And then I'll kill him.
"Good boy. You won't have to wait long."
"His ship is no match for El Caleuche."

CHAPTER SIX
CAPE HORN

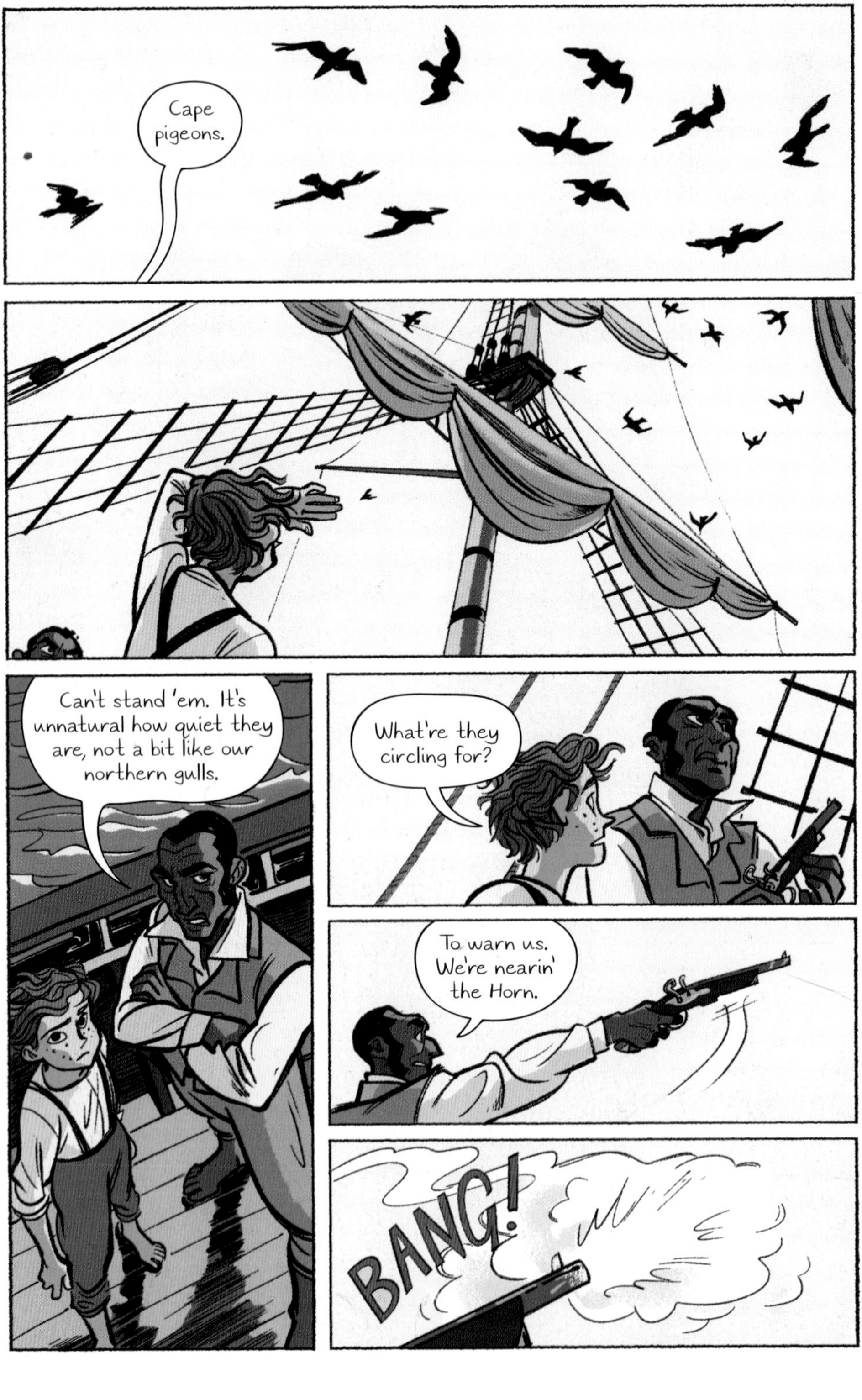
Cape pigeons.
Can't stand 'em. It's unnatural how quiet they are, not a bit like our northern gulls.
What're they circling for?
To warn us. We're nearin' the Horn.
BANG!

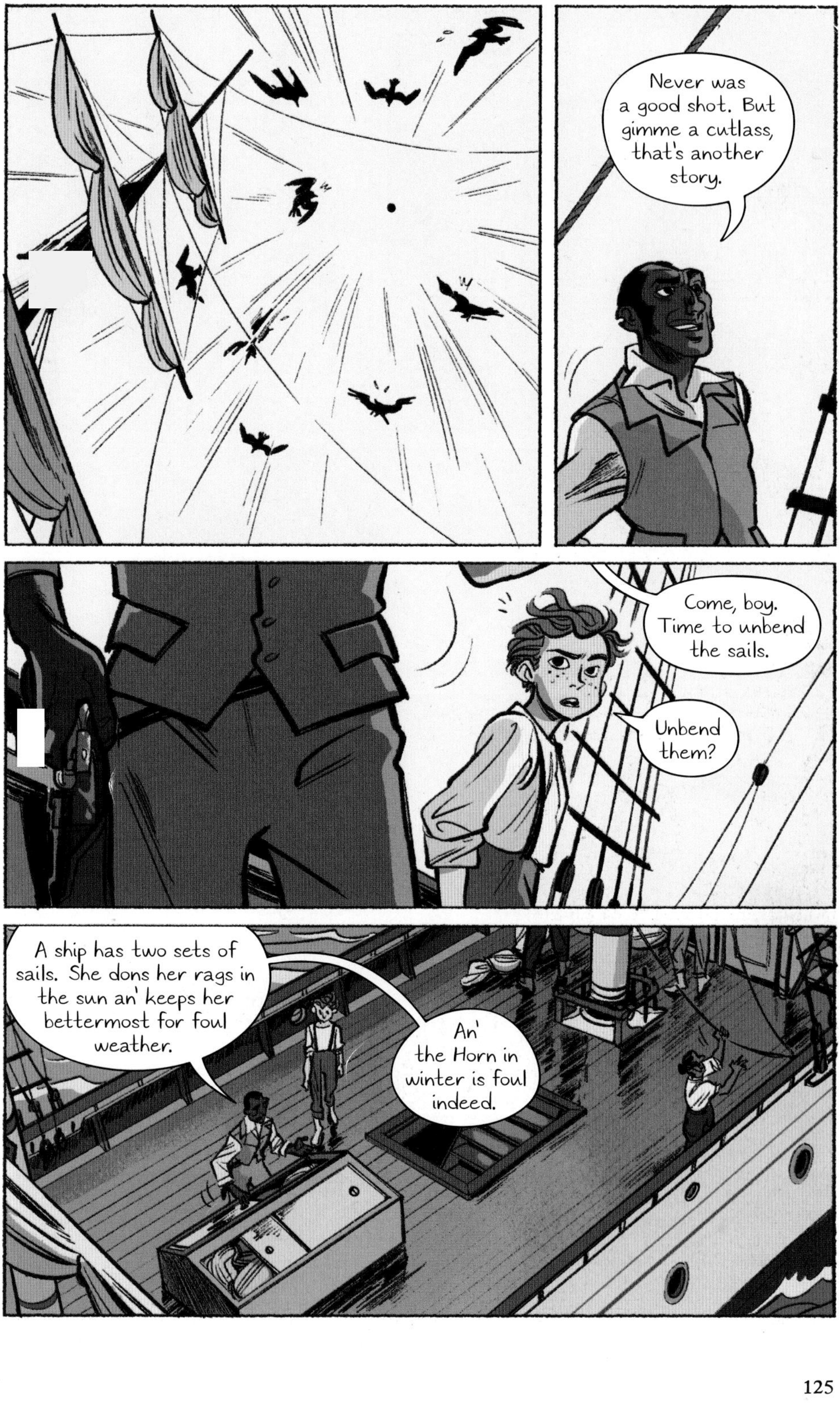
Never was a good shot. But gimme a cutlass, that's another story.
Come, boy. Time to unbend the sails.
Unbend them?
A ship has two sets of sails. She dons her rags in the sun an' keeps her bettermost for foul weather.
An' the Horn in winter is foul indeed.

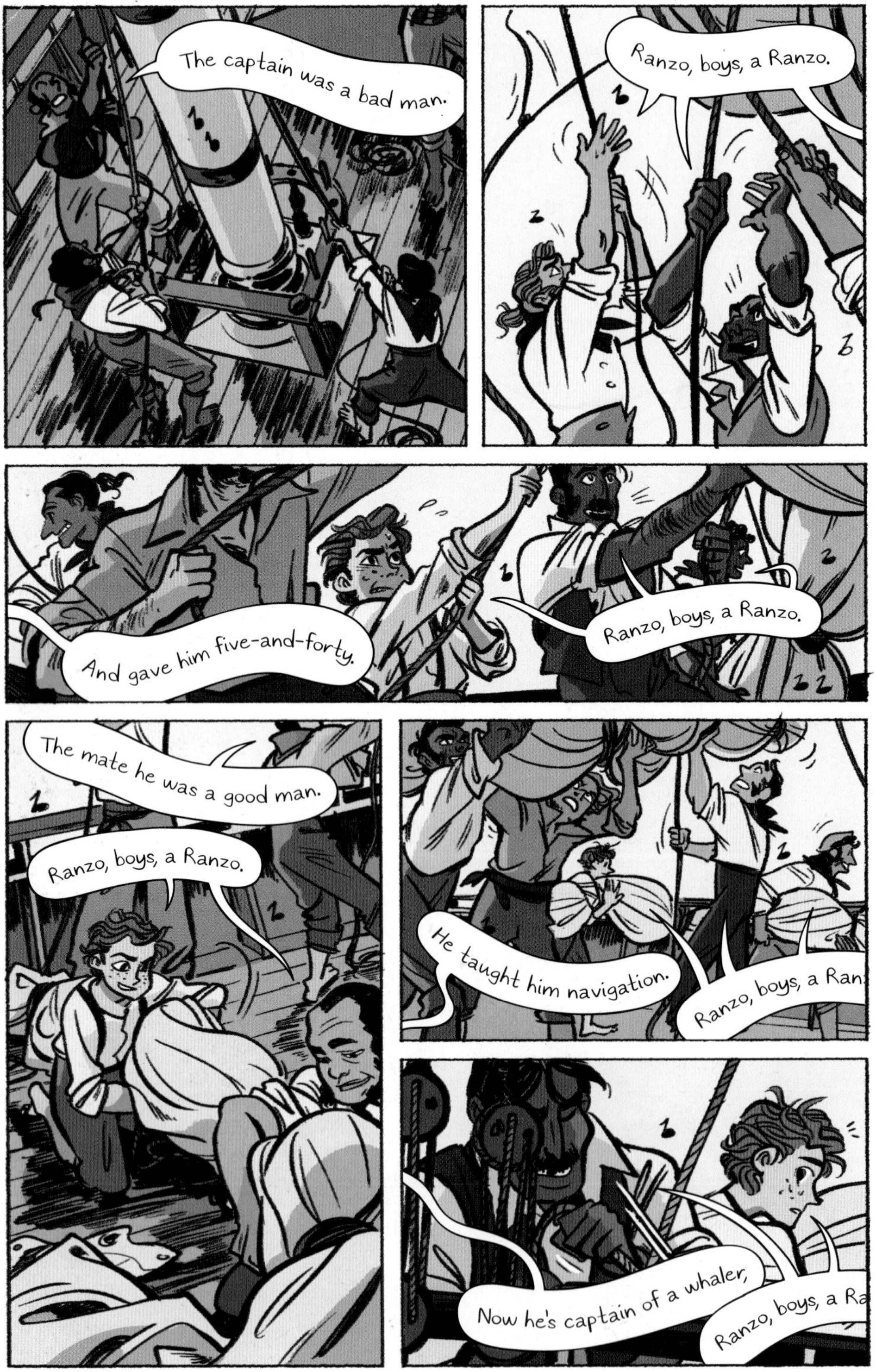

The captain was a bad man.
Ranzo, boys, a Ranzo.
And gave him five-and-forty.
Ranzo, boys, a Ranzo.
The mate he was a good man.
Ranzo, boys, a Ranzo.
He taught him navigation.
Ranzo, boys, a Ran
Now he's captain of a whaler,
Ranzo, boys, a Ra

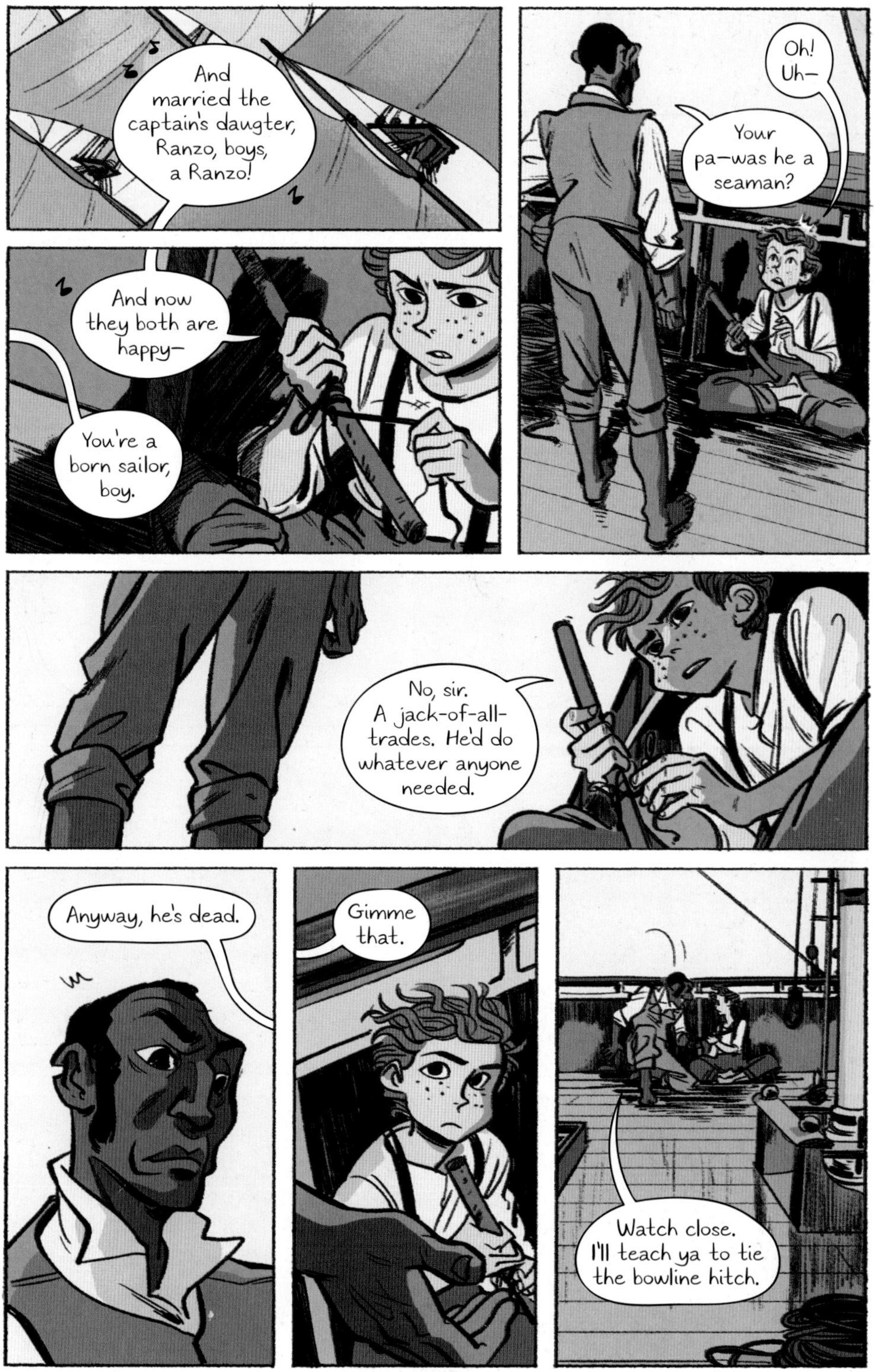
And married the captain's daugter, Ranzo, boys, a Ranzo!
Oh! Uh—
Your pa—was he a seaman?
And now they both are happy—
You're a born sailor, boy.
No, sir. A jack-of-all-trades. He'd do whatever anyone needed.
Anyway, he's dead.
Gimme that.
Watch close. I'll teach ya to tie the bowline hitch.

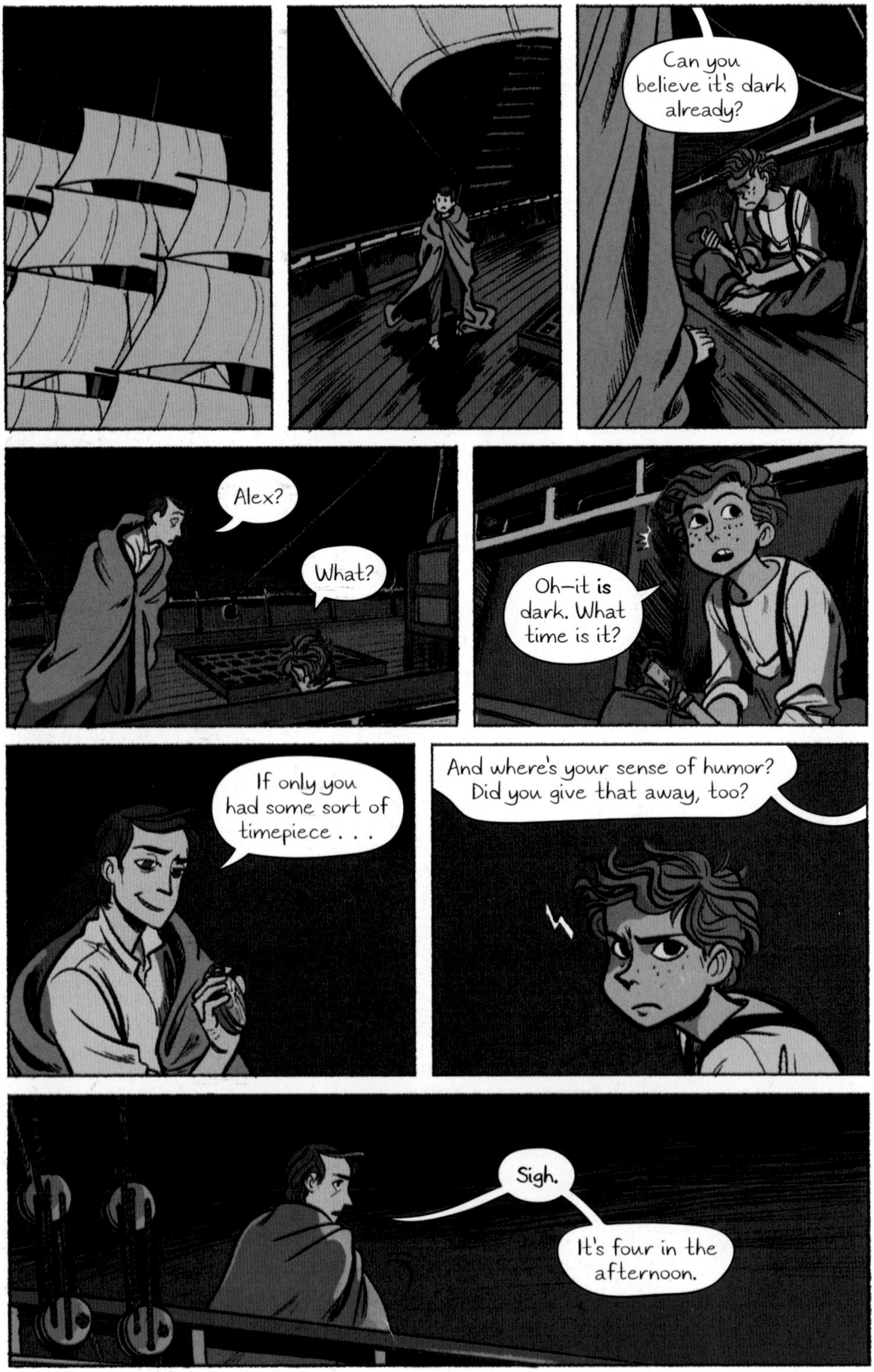
Can you believe it's dark already?
Alex?
What?
Oh—it **is** dark. What time is it?
If only you had some sort of timepiece . . .
And where's your sense of humor? Did you give that away, too?
Sigh.
It's four in the afternoon.

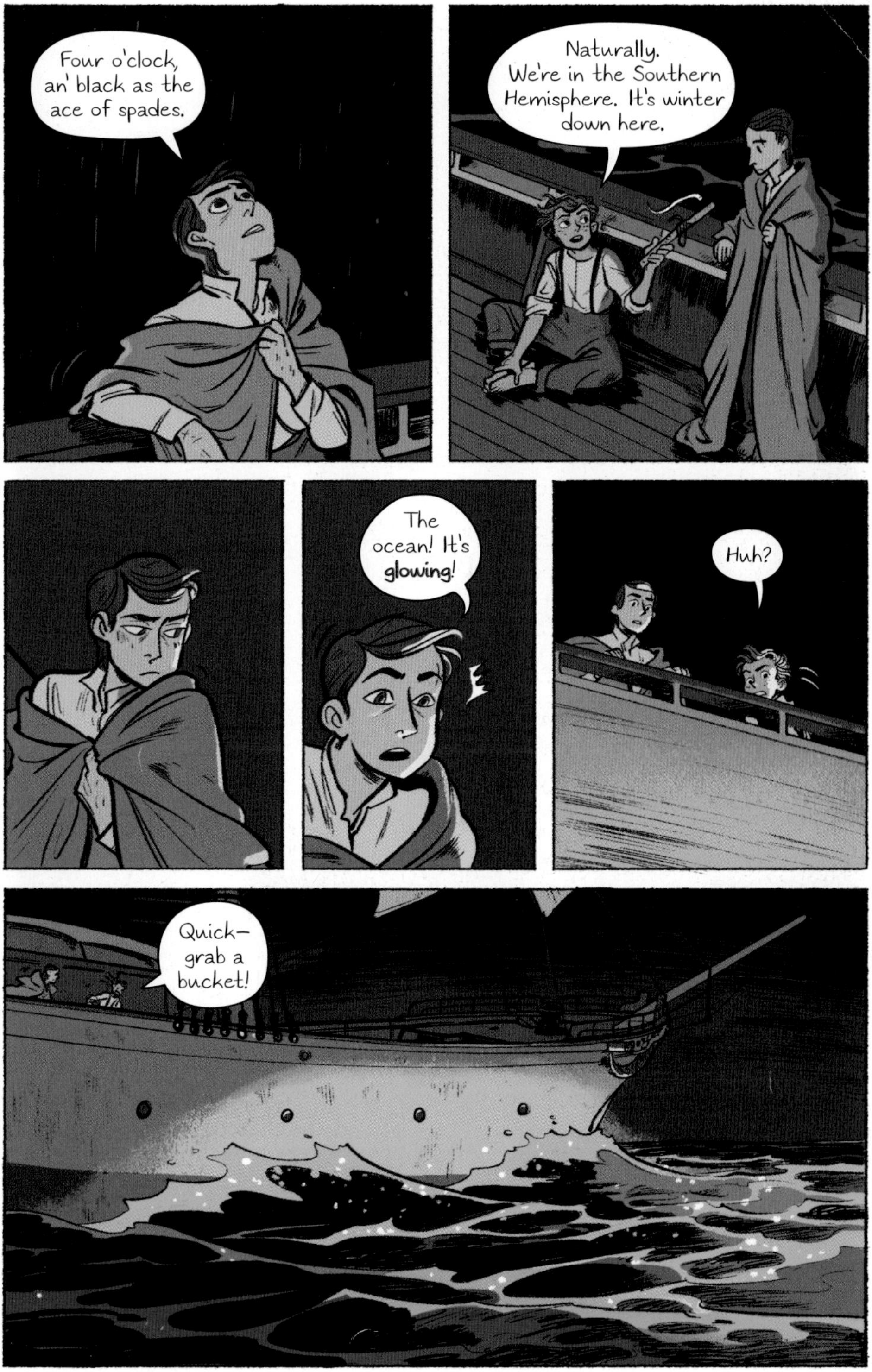
Four o'clock, an' black as the ace of spades.
Naturally. We're in the Southern Hemisphere. It's winter down here.
The ocean! It's **glowing**!
Huh?
Quick—grab a bucket!

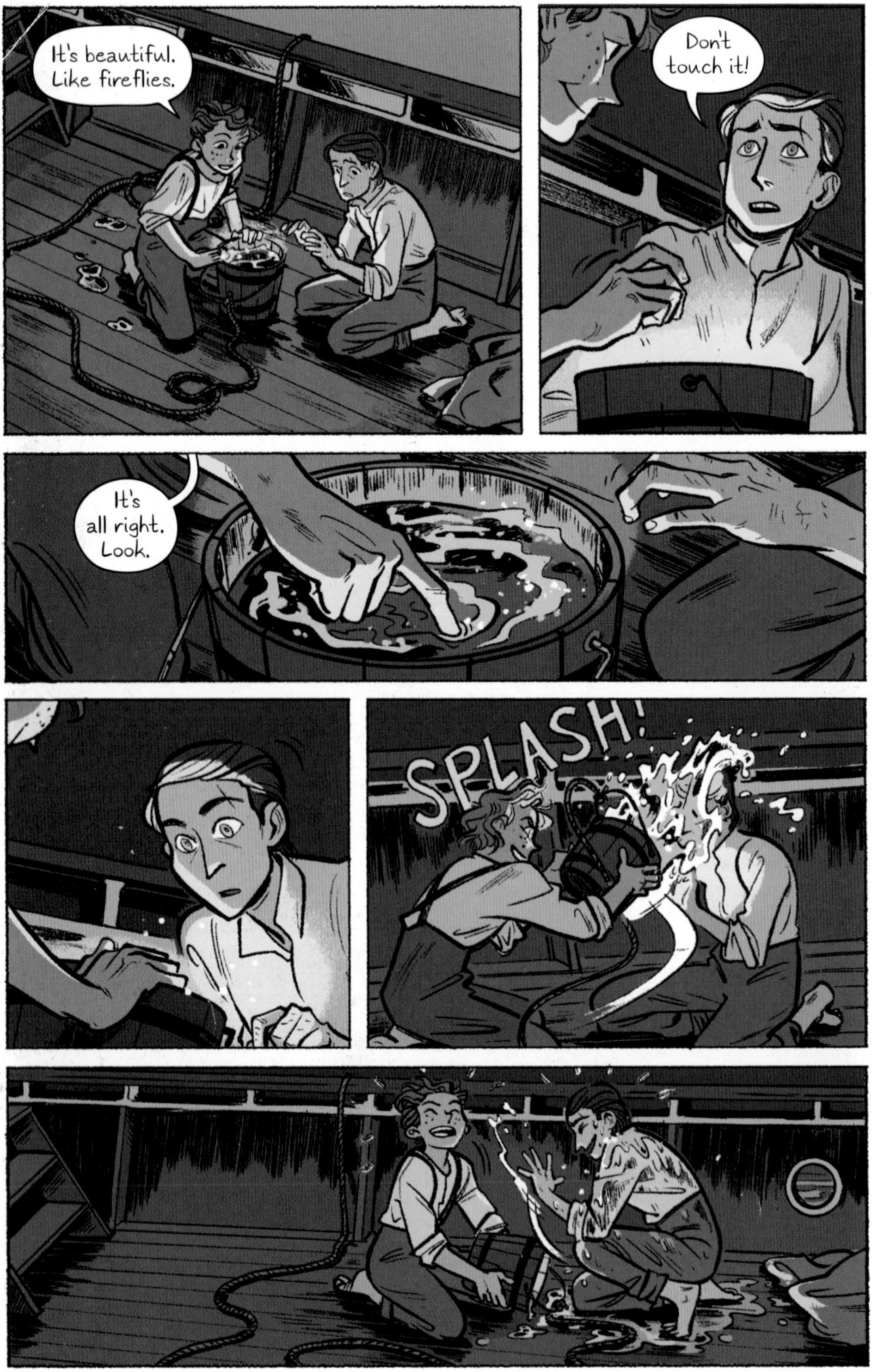
It's beautiful. Like fireflies.
Don't touch it!
It's all right. Look.
SPLASH!

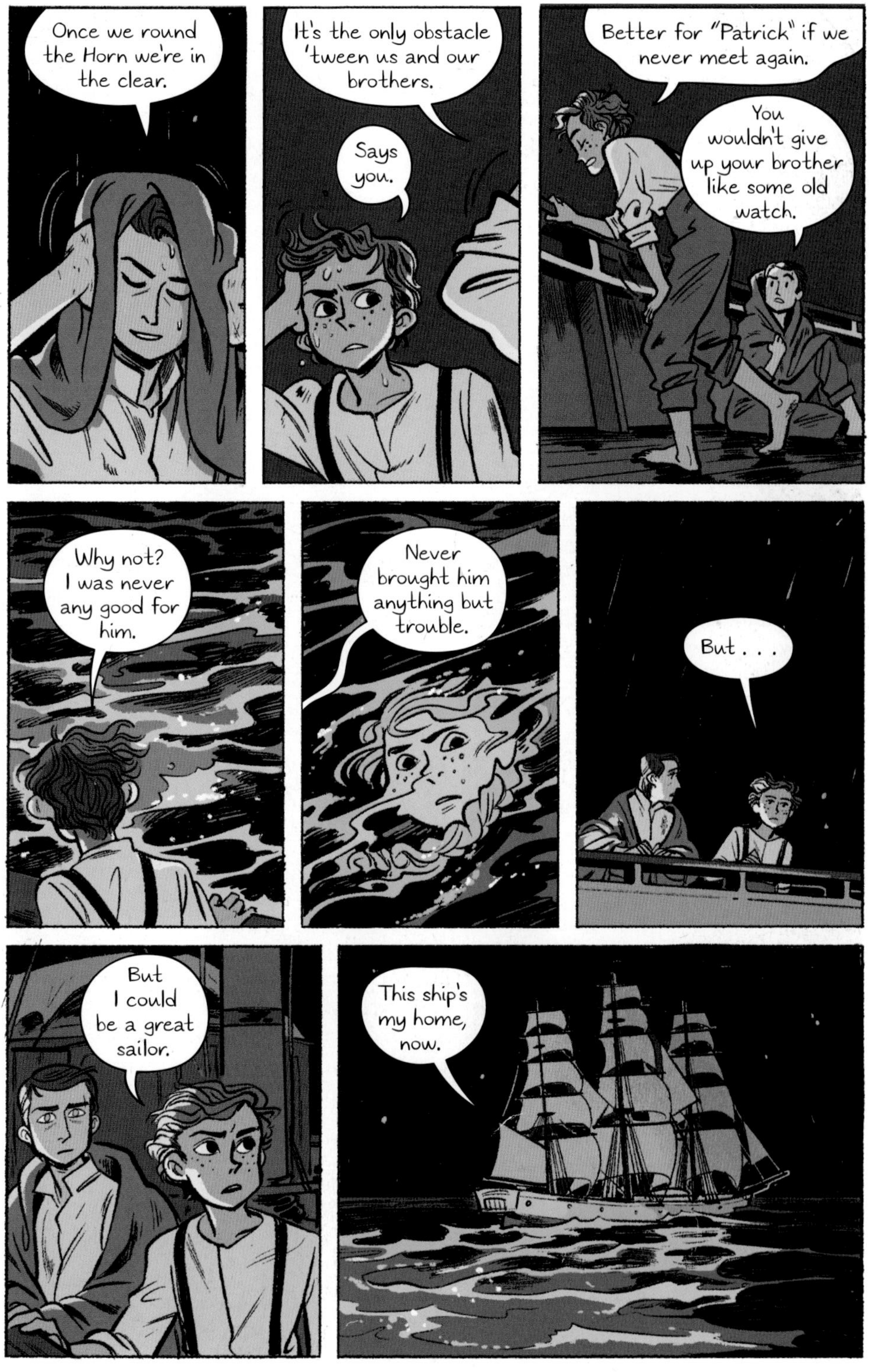
Once we round the Horn we're in the clear.
It's the only obstacle 'tween us and our brothers.
Says you.
Better for "Patrick" if we never meet again.
You wouldn't give up your brother like some old watch.
Why not? I was never any good for him.
Never brought him anything but trouble.
But . . .
But I could be a great sailor.
This ship's my home, now.

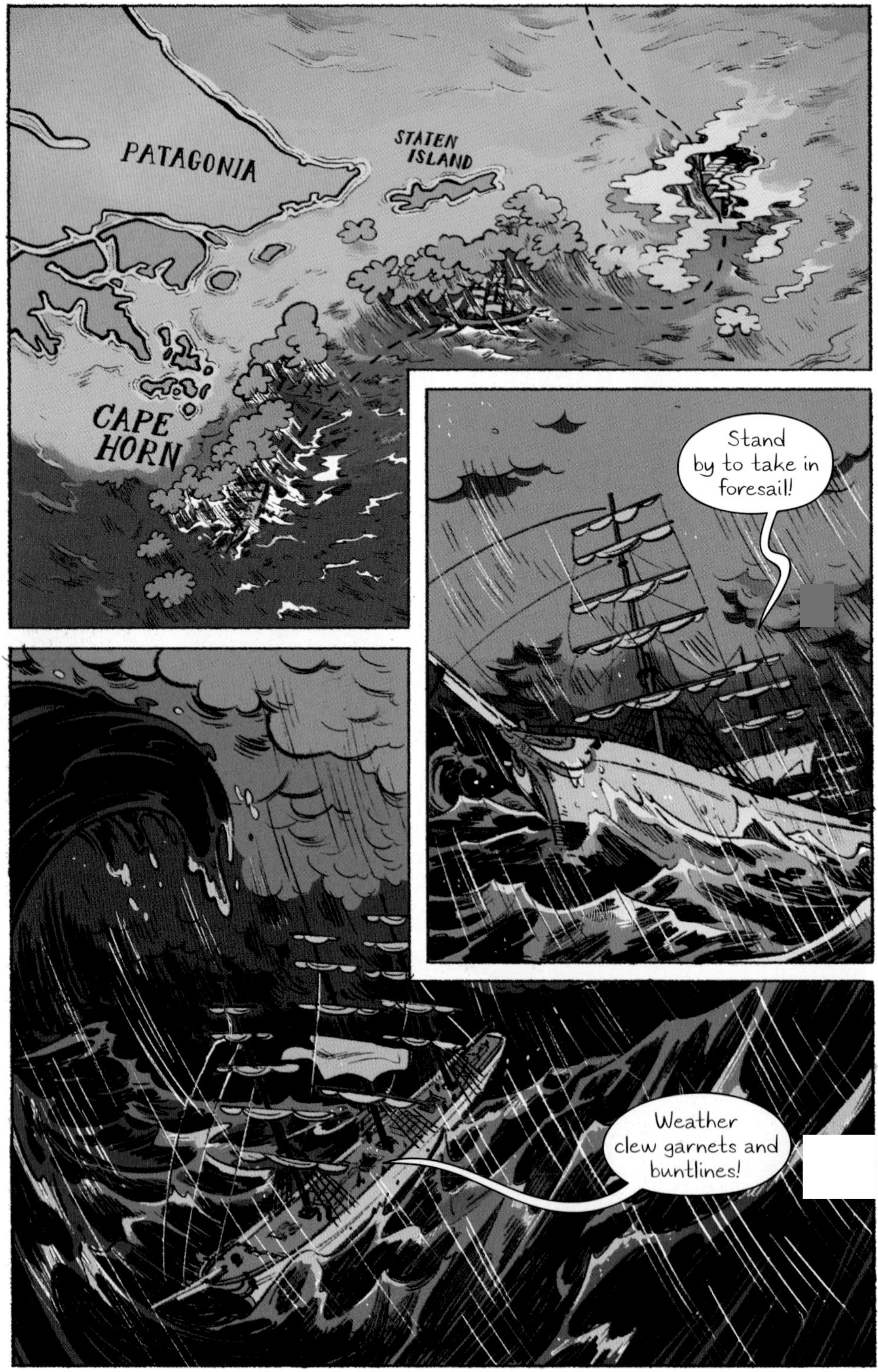
PATAGONIA
STATEN ISLAND
CAPE HORN
Stand by to take in foresail!
Weather clew garnets and buntlines!

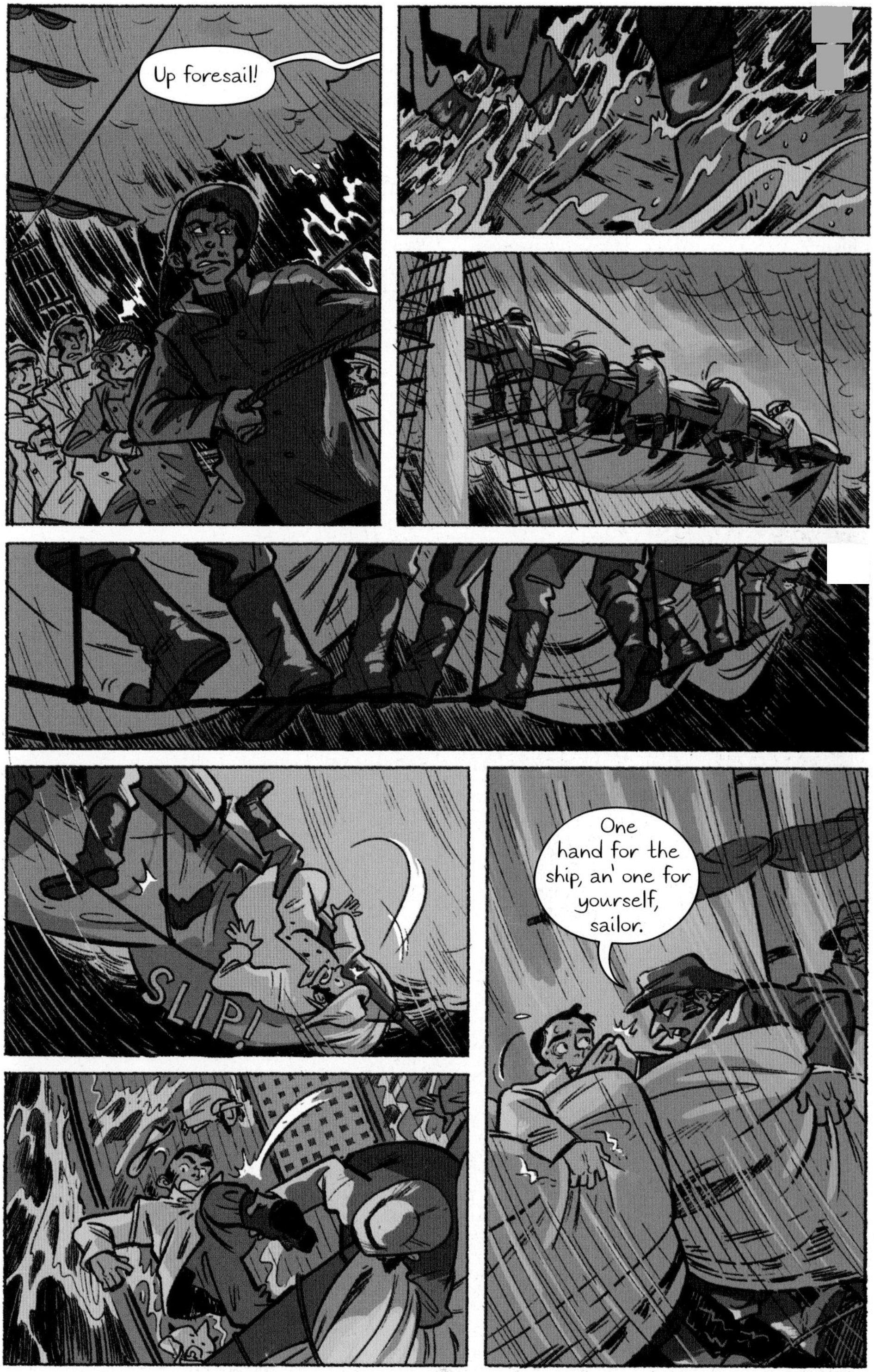
Up foresail!
SLIP!
One hand for the ship, an' one for yourself, sailor.

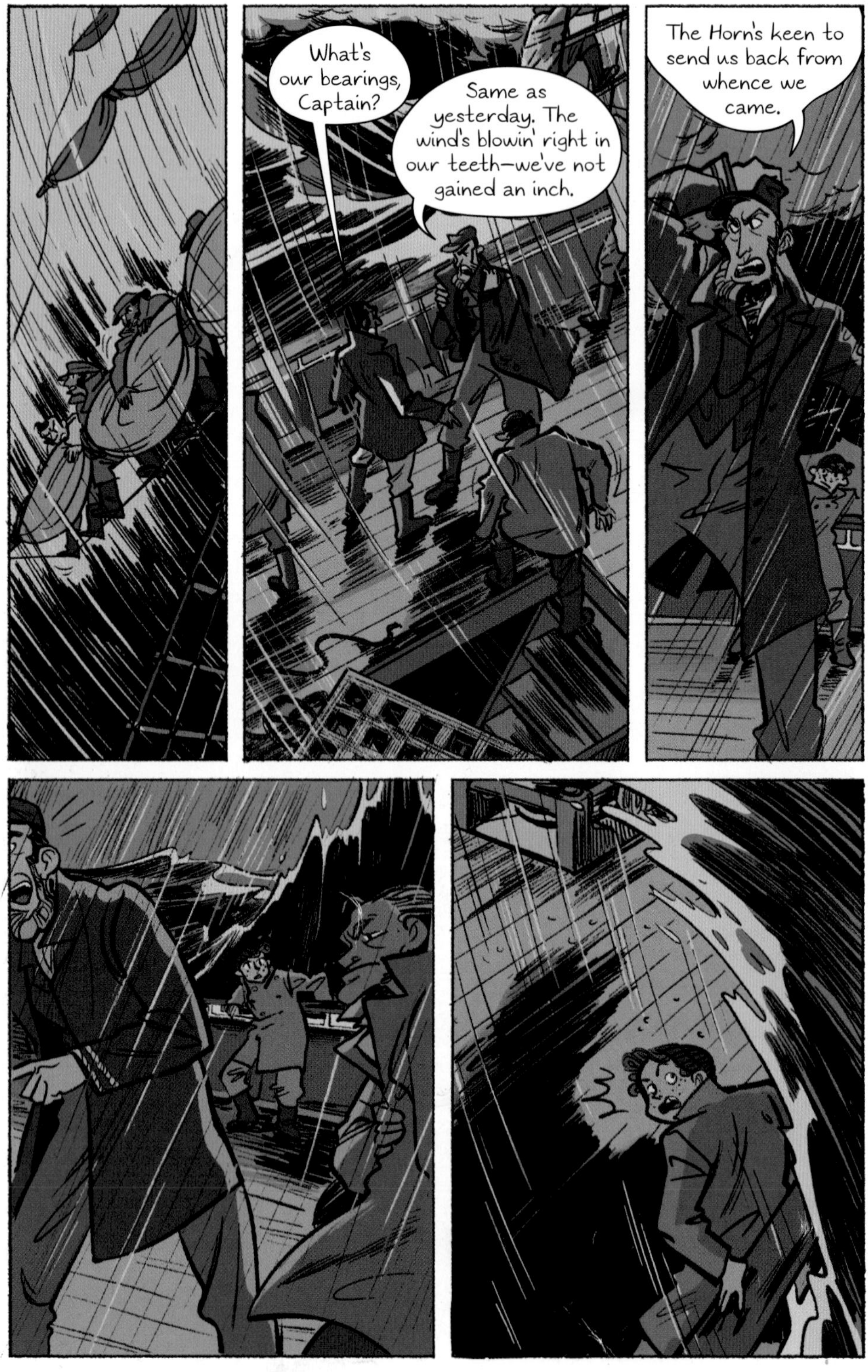
What's our bearings, Captain?
Same as yesterday. The wind's blowin' right in our teeth—we've not gained an inch.
The Horn's keen to send us back from whence we came.

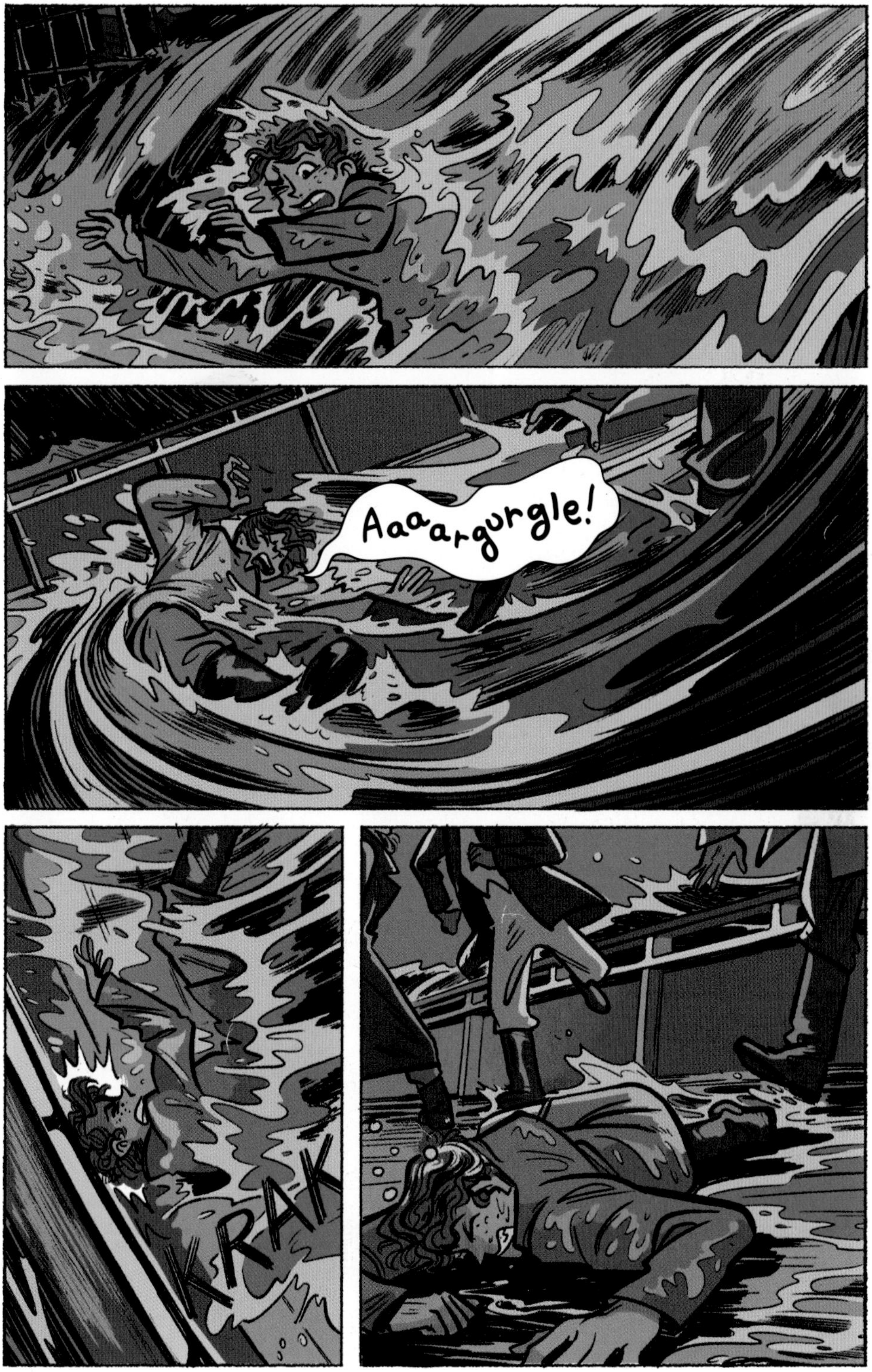
Aaaargurgle!
KRAK

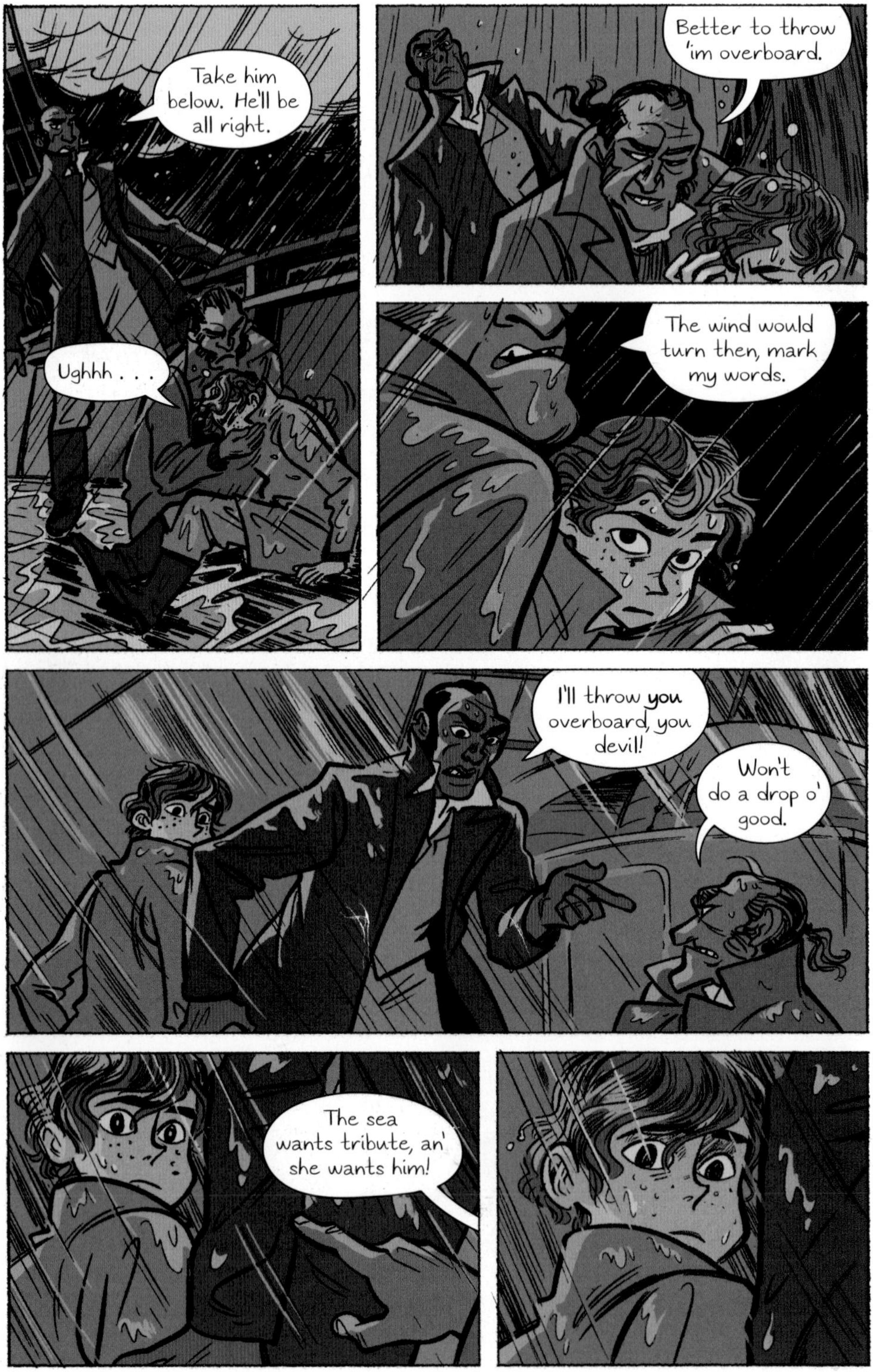
Take him below. He'll be all right.
Ughhh . . .
Better to throw 'im overboard.
The wind would turn then, mark my words.
I'll throw **you** overboard, you devil!
Won't do a drop o' good.
The sea wants tribute, an' she wants him!

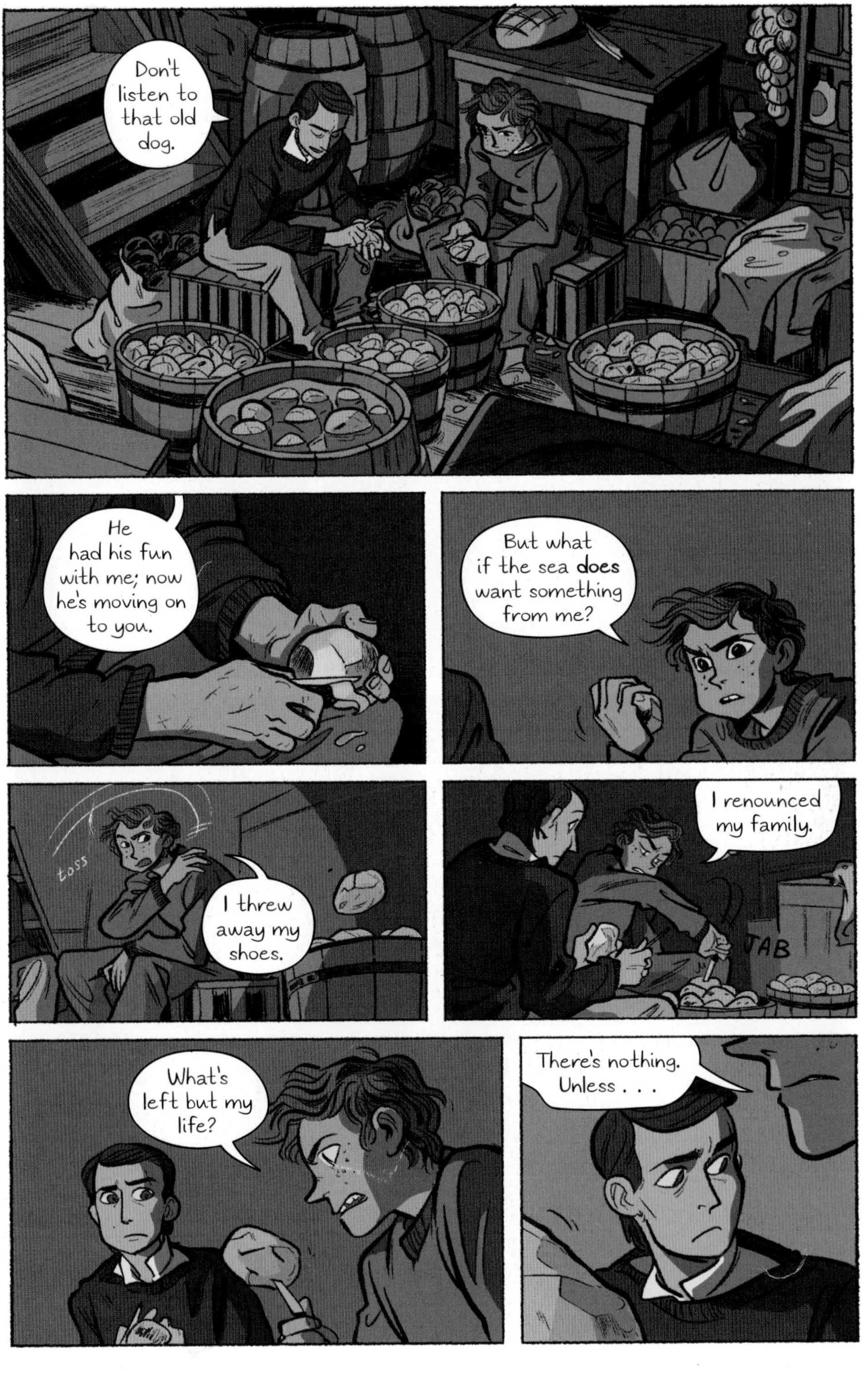
Don't listen to that old dog.
He had his fun with me; now he's moving on to you.
But what if the sea **does** want something from me?
toss
I threw away my shoes.
I renounced my family.
TAB
What's left but my life?
There's nothing. Unless . . .

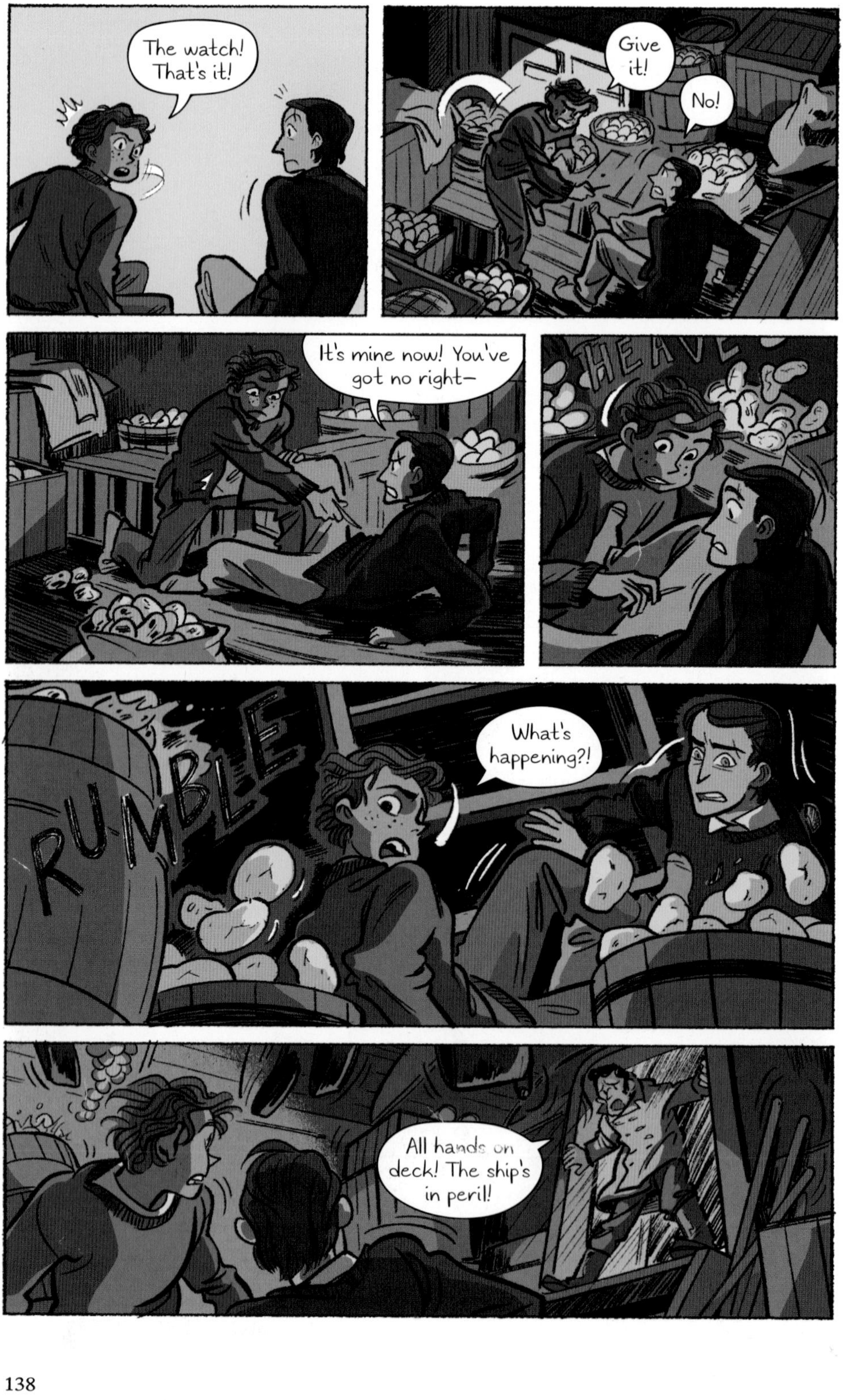
The watch! That's it!
Give it!
No!
It's mine now! You've got no right—
HEAVE
RUMBLE
What's happening?!
All hands on deck! The ship's in peril!

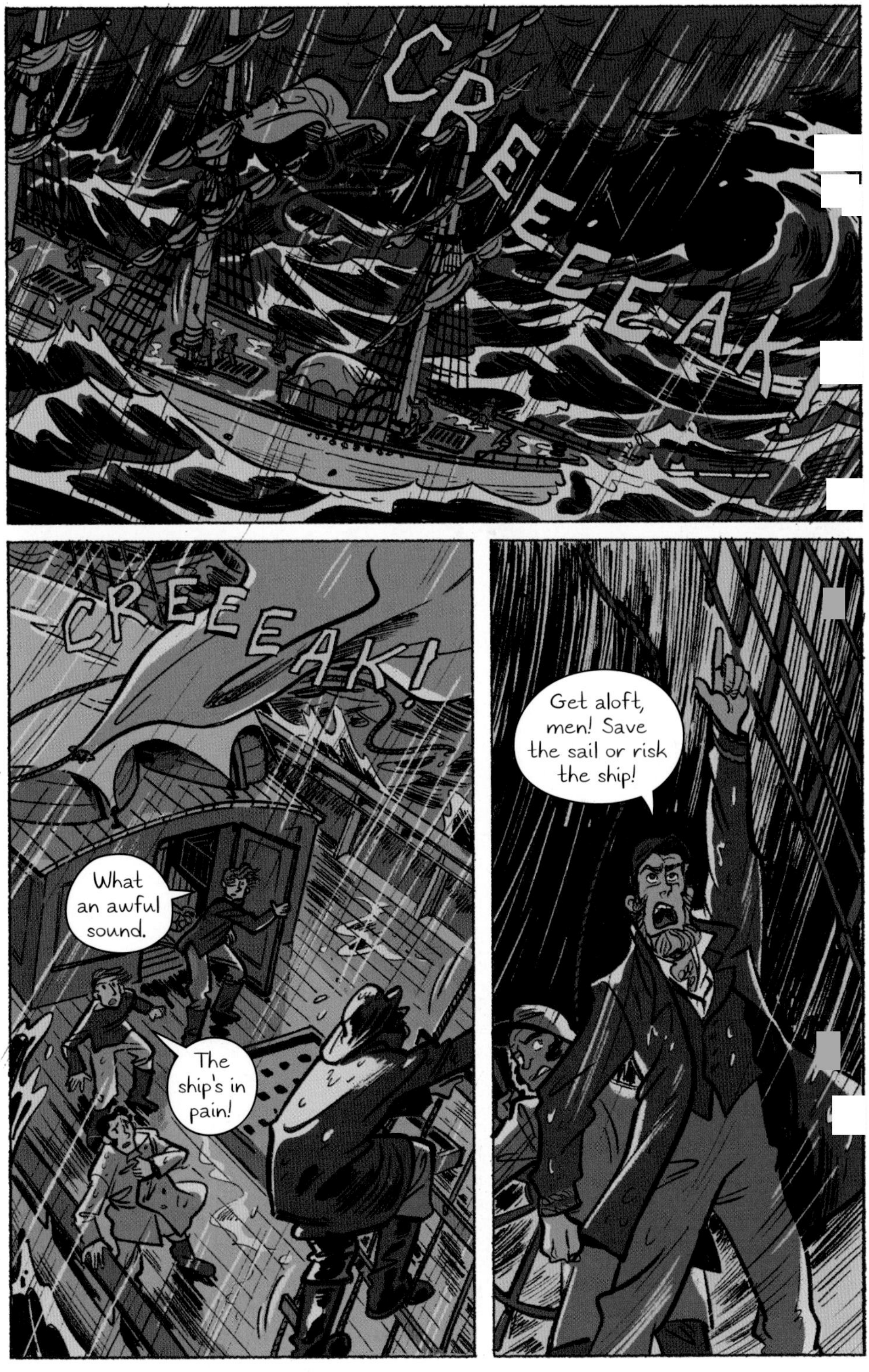
CREEEEAK!
CREEEAK!
What an awful sound.
The ship's in pain!
Get aloft, men! Save the sail or risk the ship!

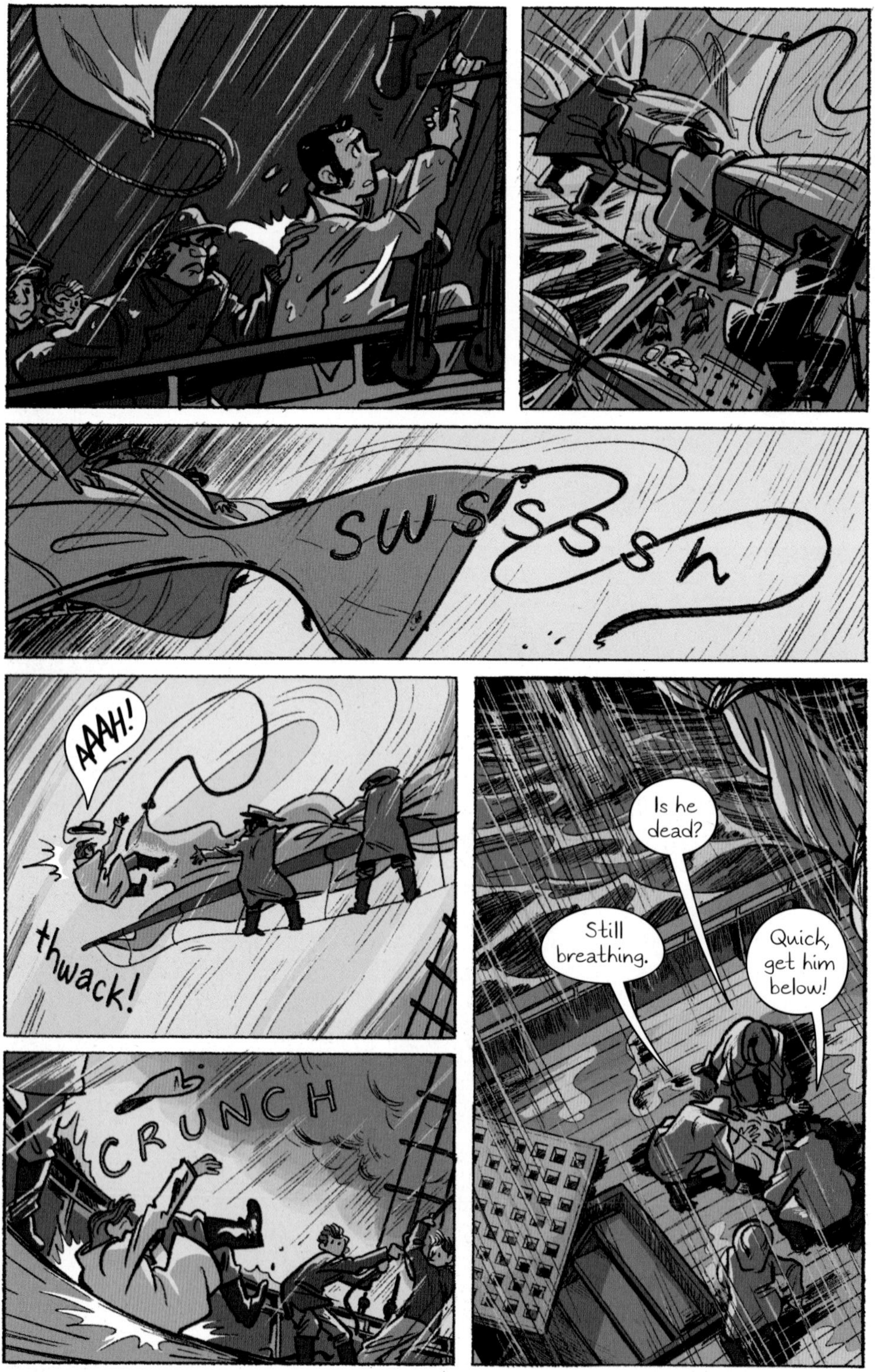
SWSSSSh
AAAH!
thwack!
CRUNCH
Is he dead?
Still breathing.
Quick, get him below!

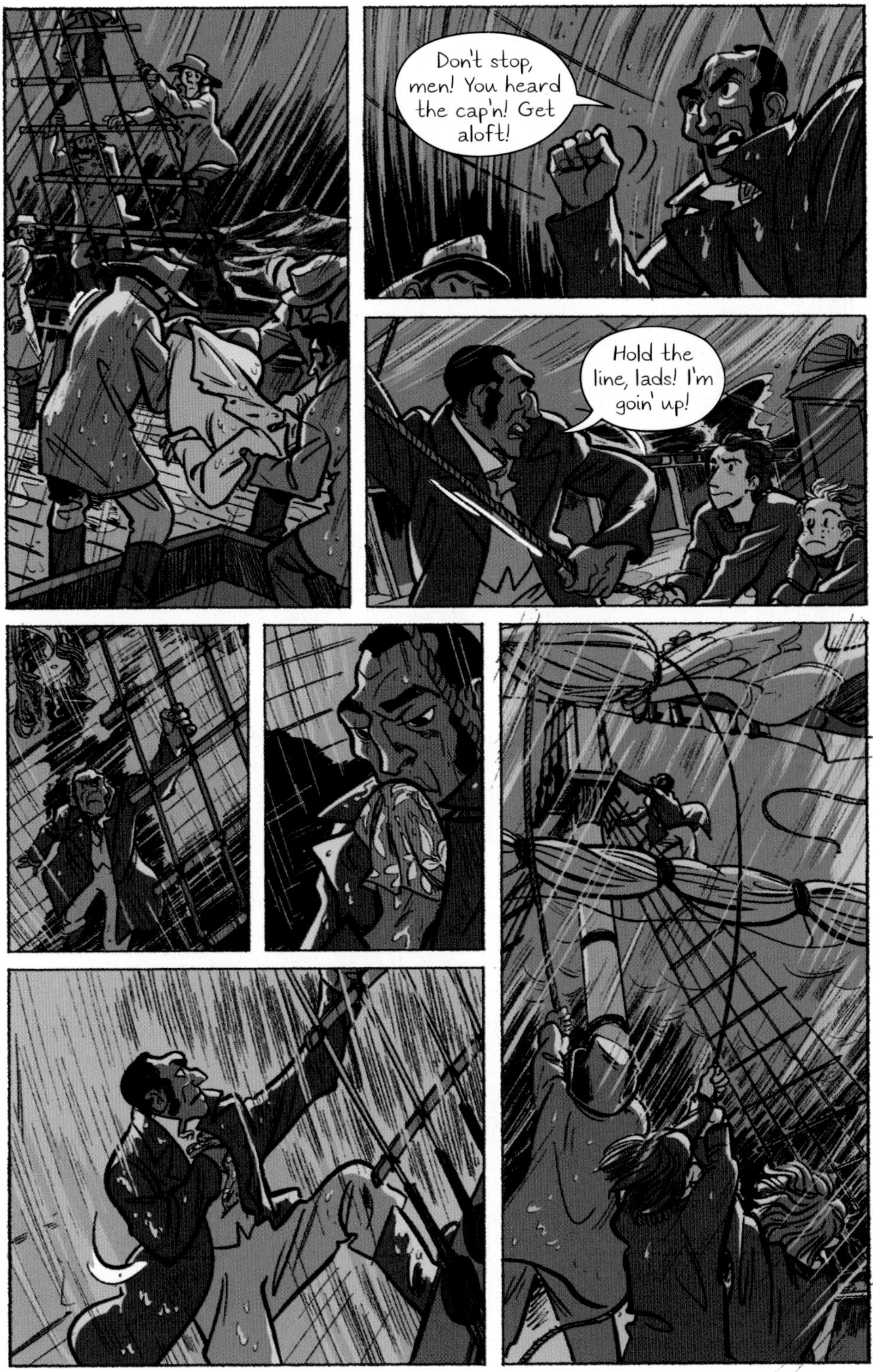
Don't stop, men! You heard the cap'n! Get aloft!
Hold the line, lads! I'm goin' up!

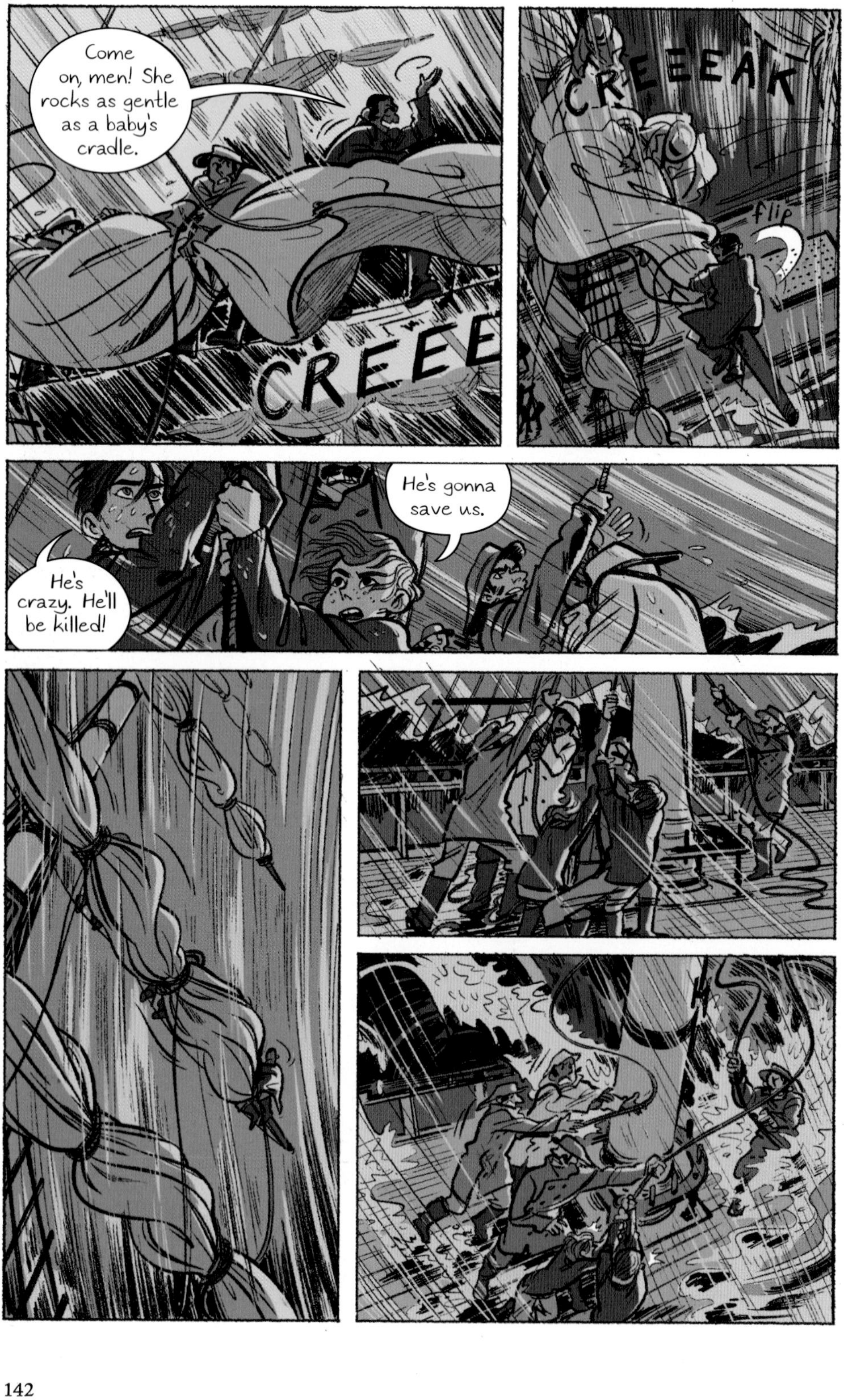
Come on, men! She rocks as gentle as a baby's cradle.
CREEE
CREEEAK
flip
He's crazy. He'll be killed!
He's gonna save us.

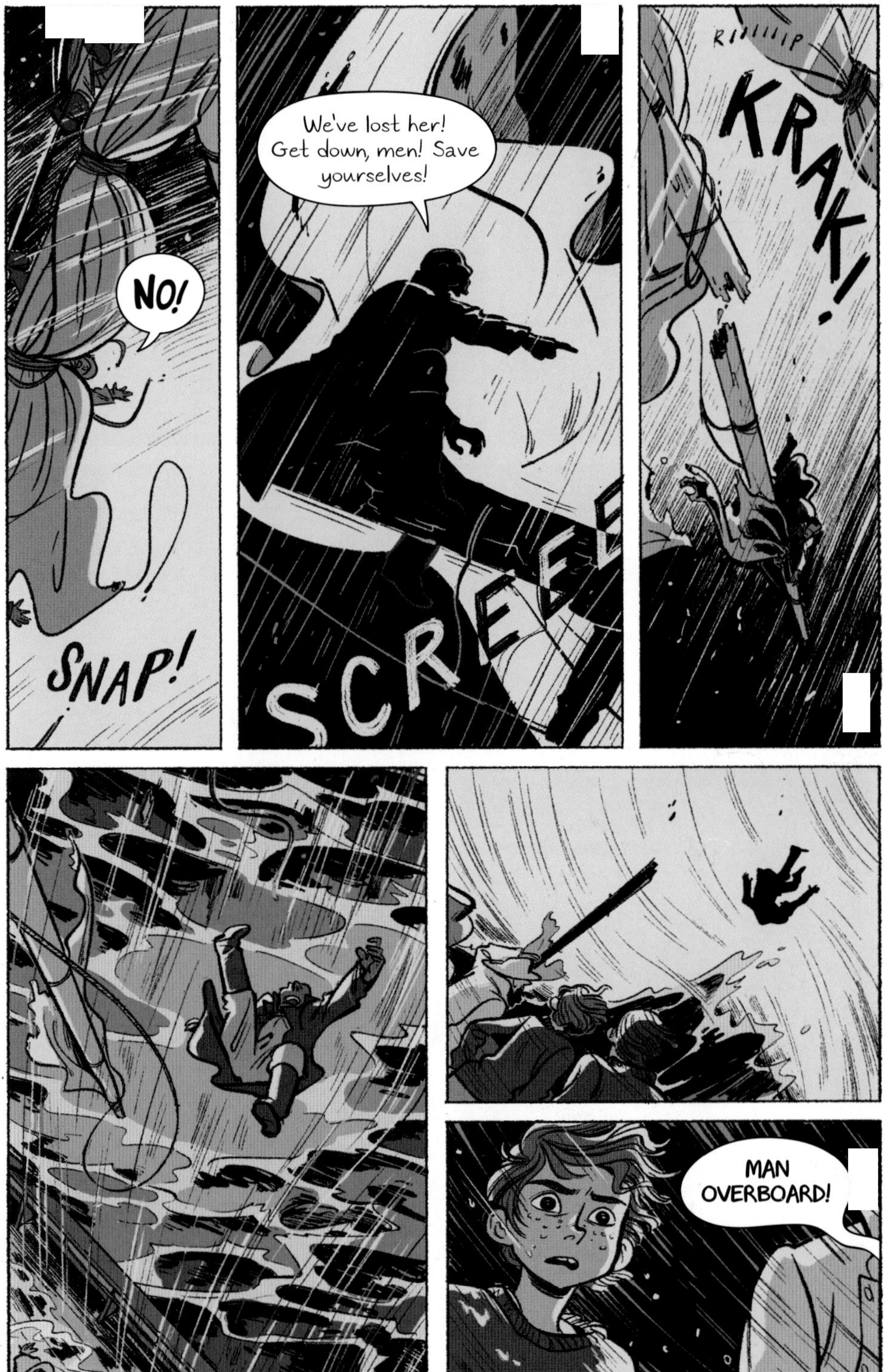
NO!
SNAP!
We've lost her! Get down, men! Save yourselves!
SCREEE
RIIIIIIP
KRAK!
MAN OVERBOARD!

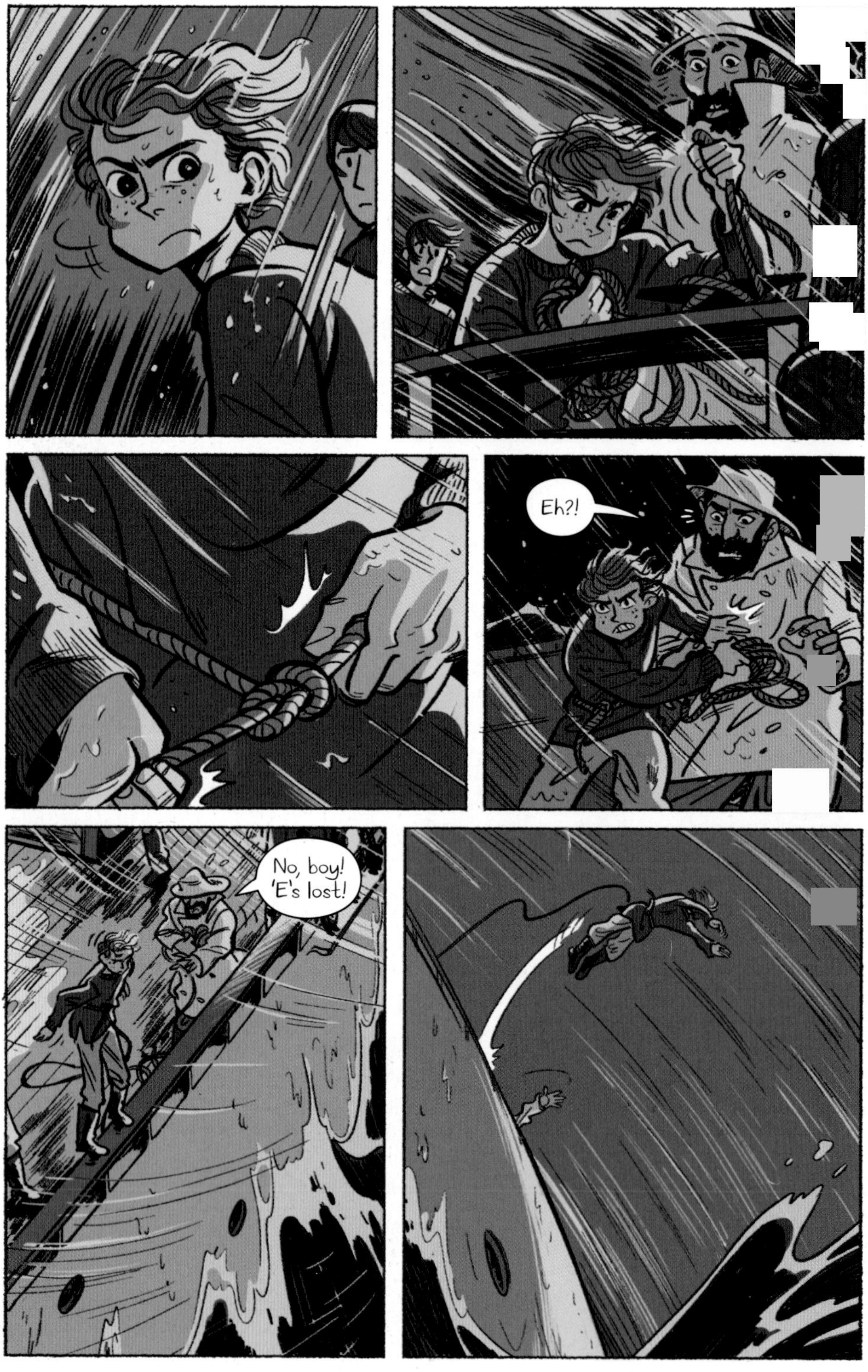
Eh?!
No, boy! 'E's lost!

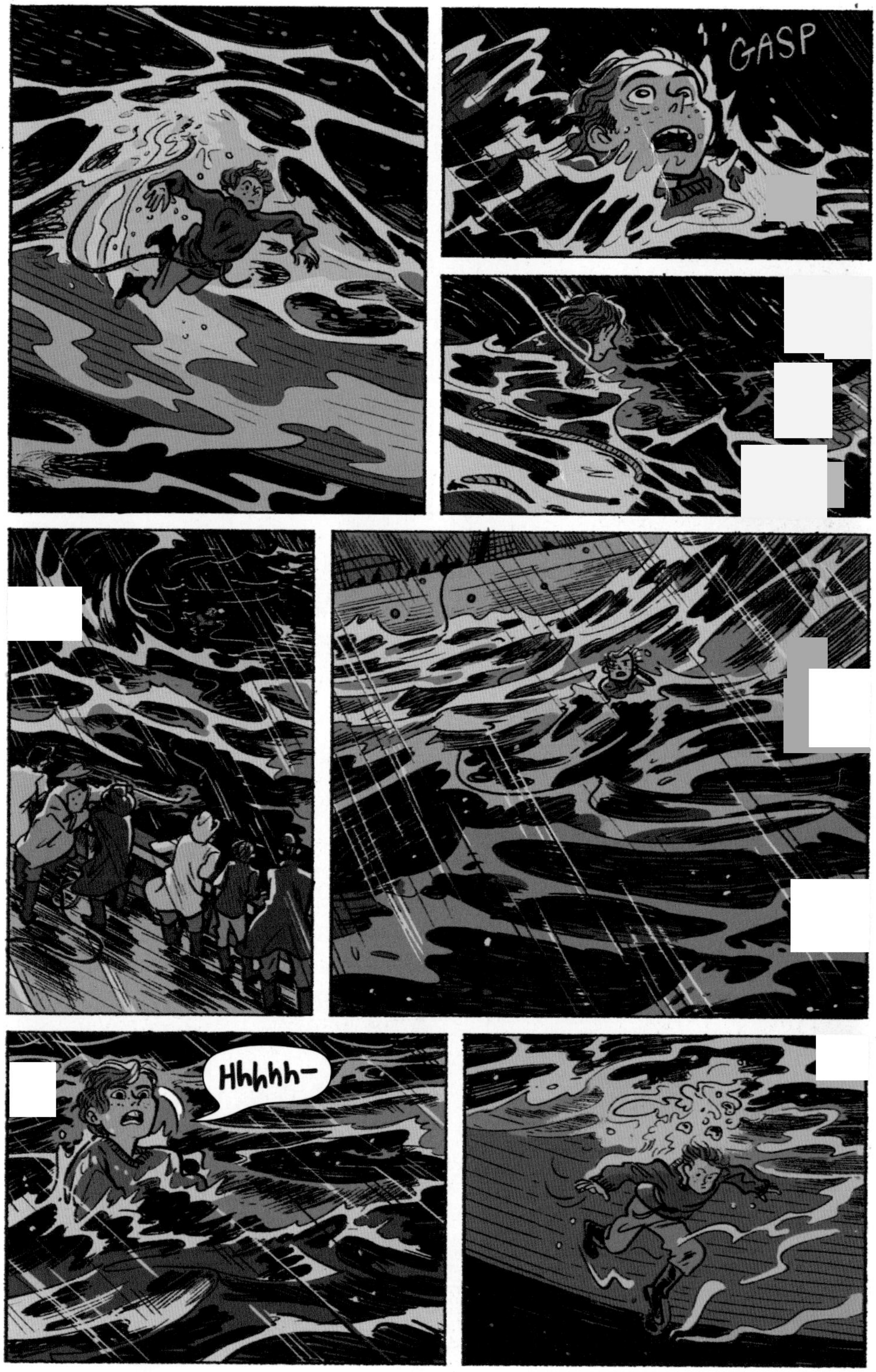
GASP
Hhhhh-

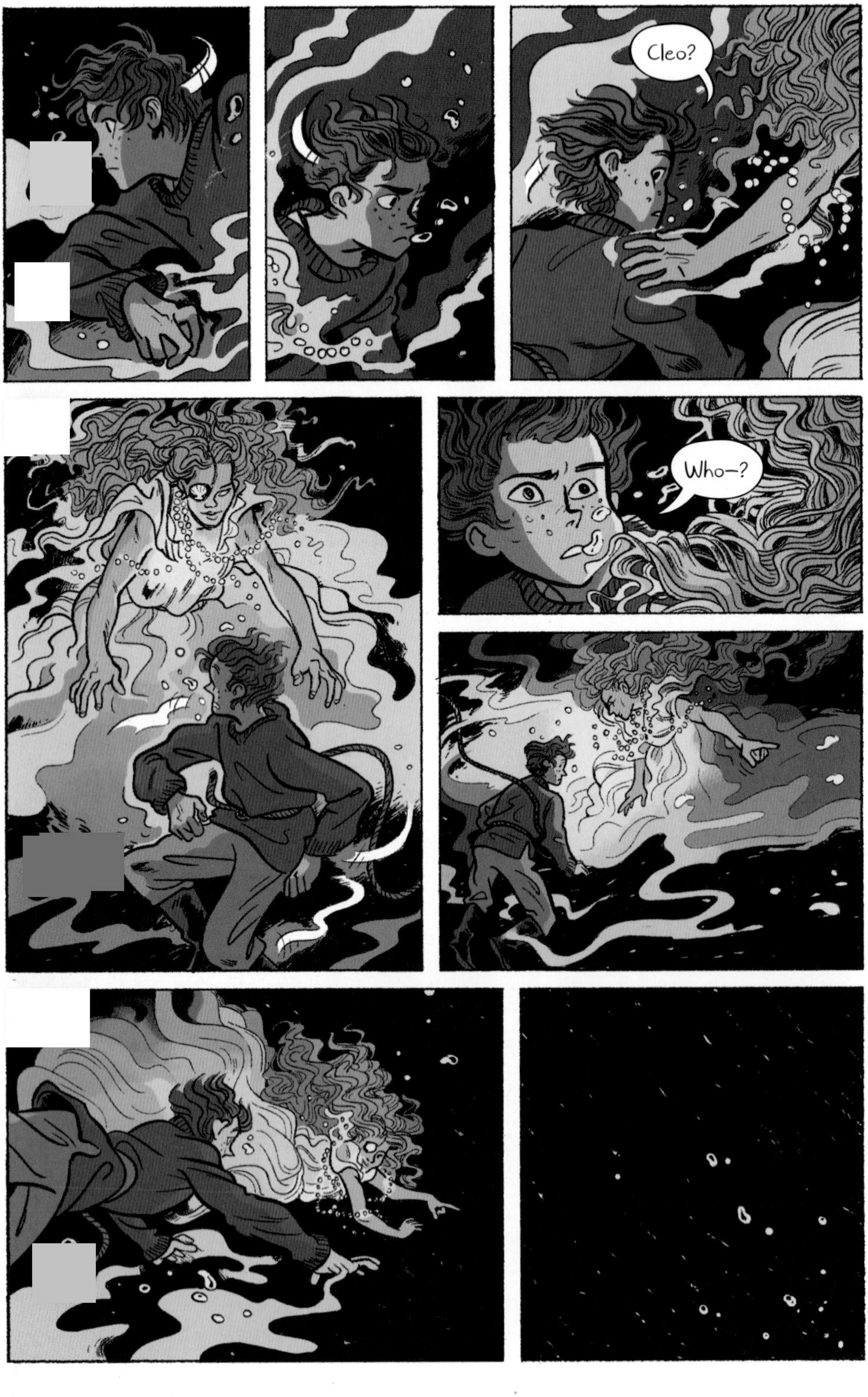
Cleo?
Who-?

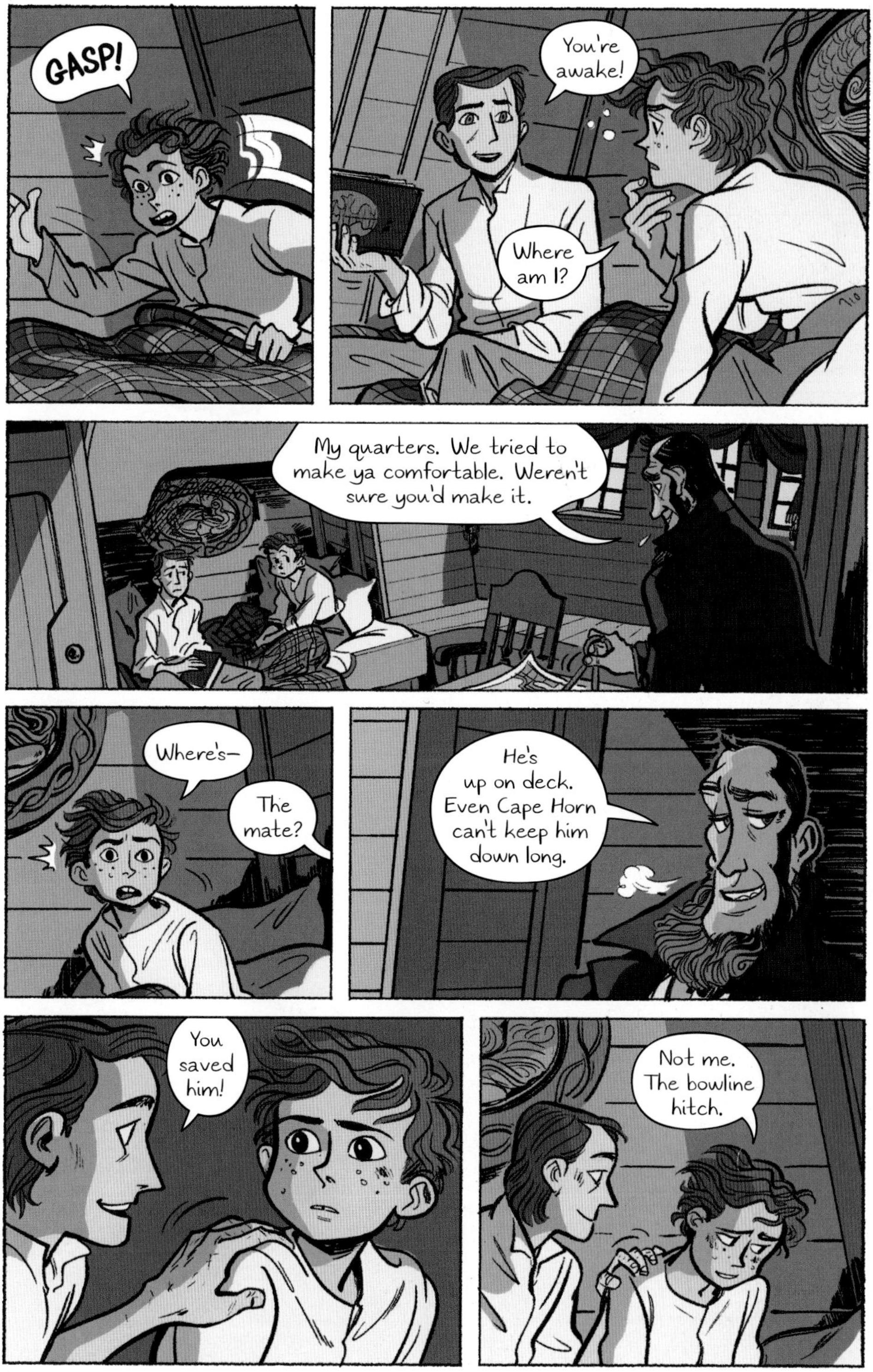
GASP!
You're awake!
Where am I?
My quarters. We tried to make ya comfortable. Weren't sure you'd make it.
Where's—
The mate?
He's up on deck. Even Cape Horn can't keep him down long.
You saved him!
Not me. The bowline hitch.

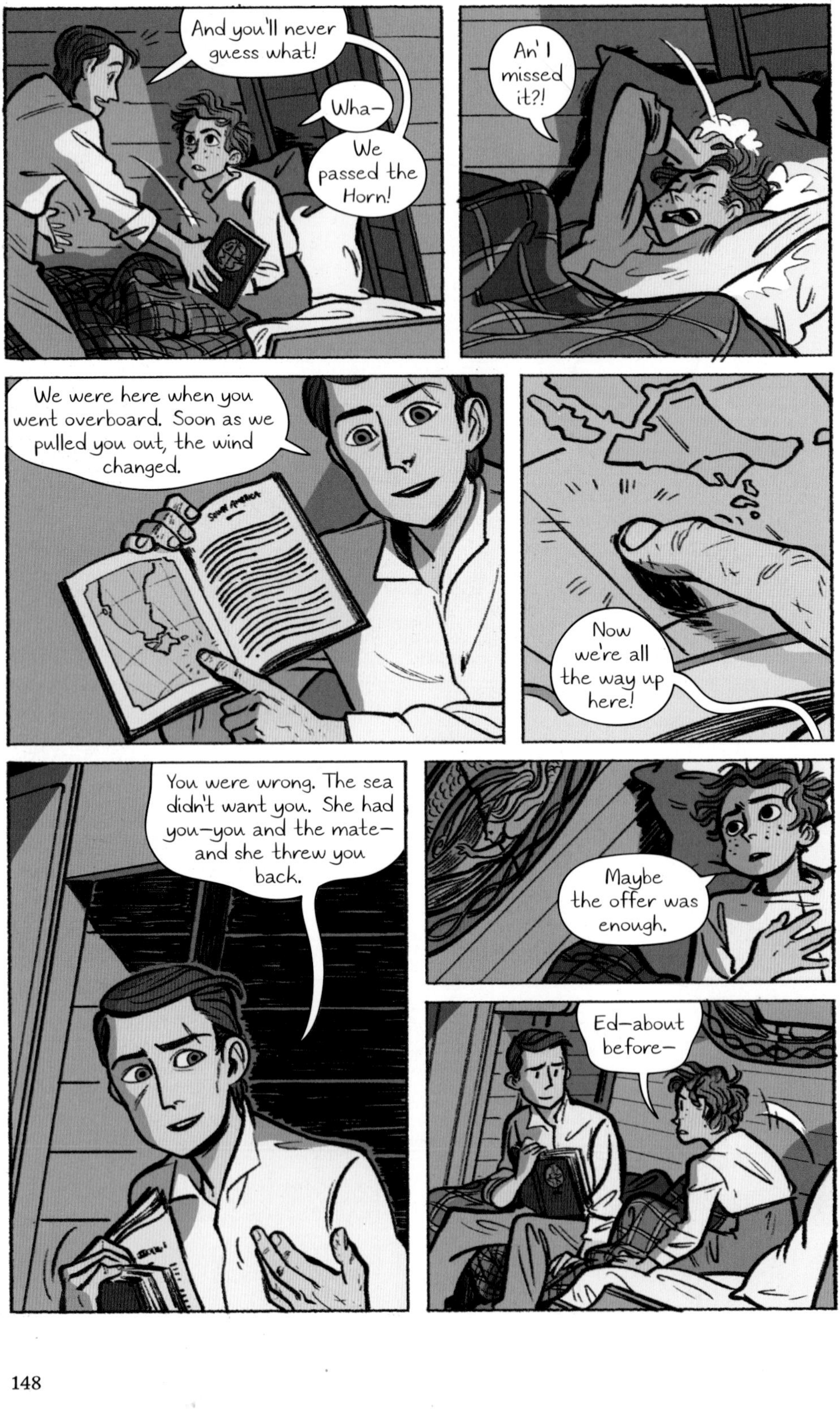
And you'll never guess what!
Wha—
We passed the Horn!
An' I missed it?!
We were here when you went overboard. Soon as we pulled you out, the wind changed.
Now we're all the way up here!
You were wrong. The sea didn't want you. She had you—you and the mate—and she threw you back.
Maybe the offer was enough.
Ed—about before—

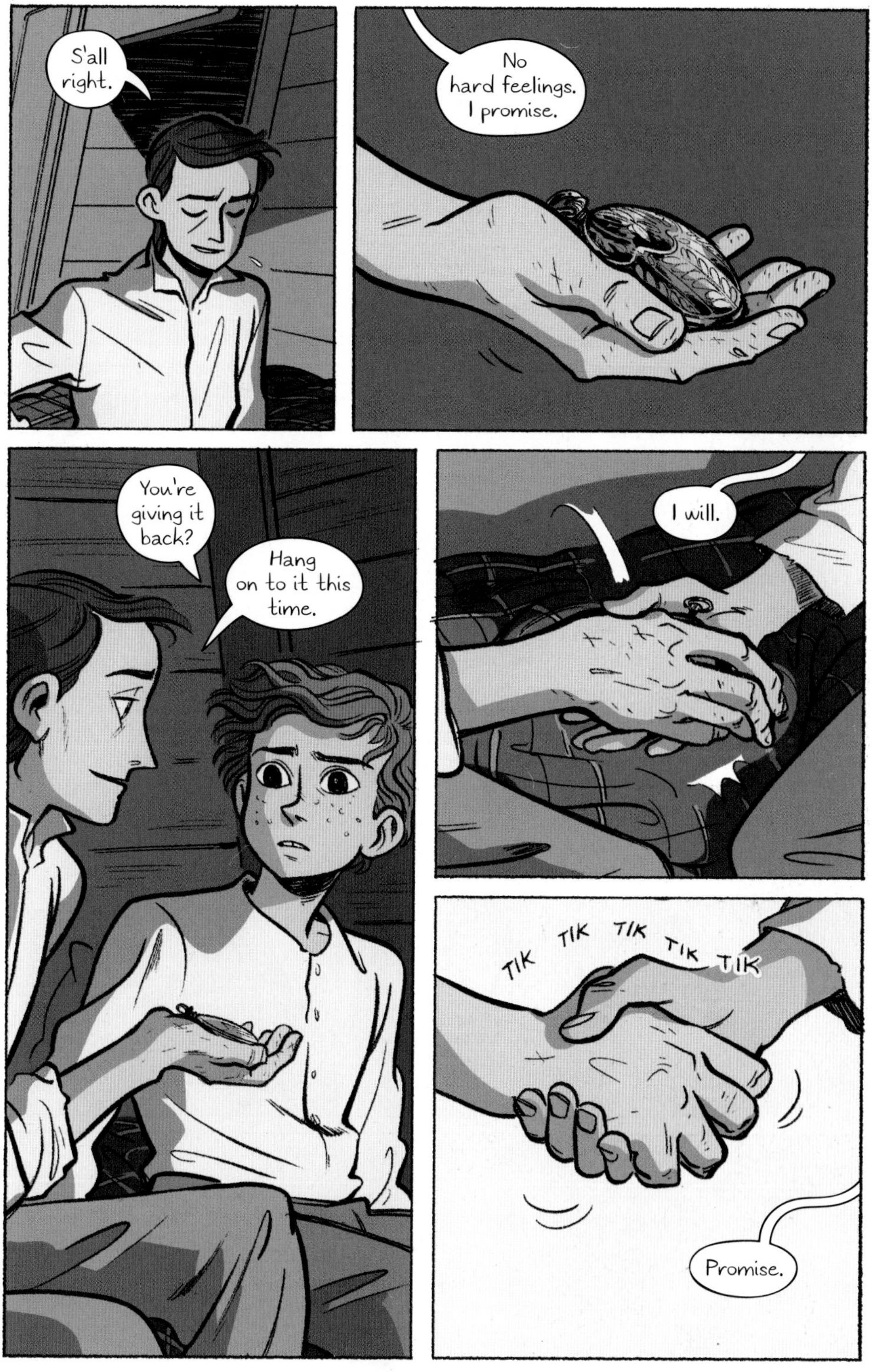
S'all right.
No hard feelings. I promise.
You're giving it back?
Hang on to it this time.
I will.
TIK TIK TIK TIK TIK
Promise.

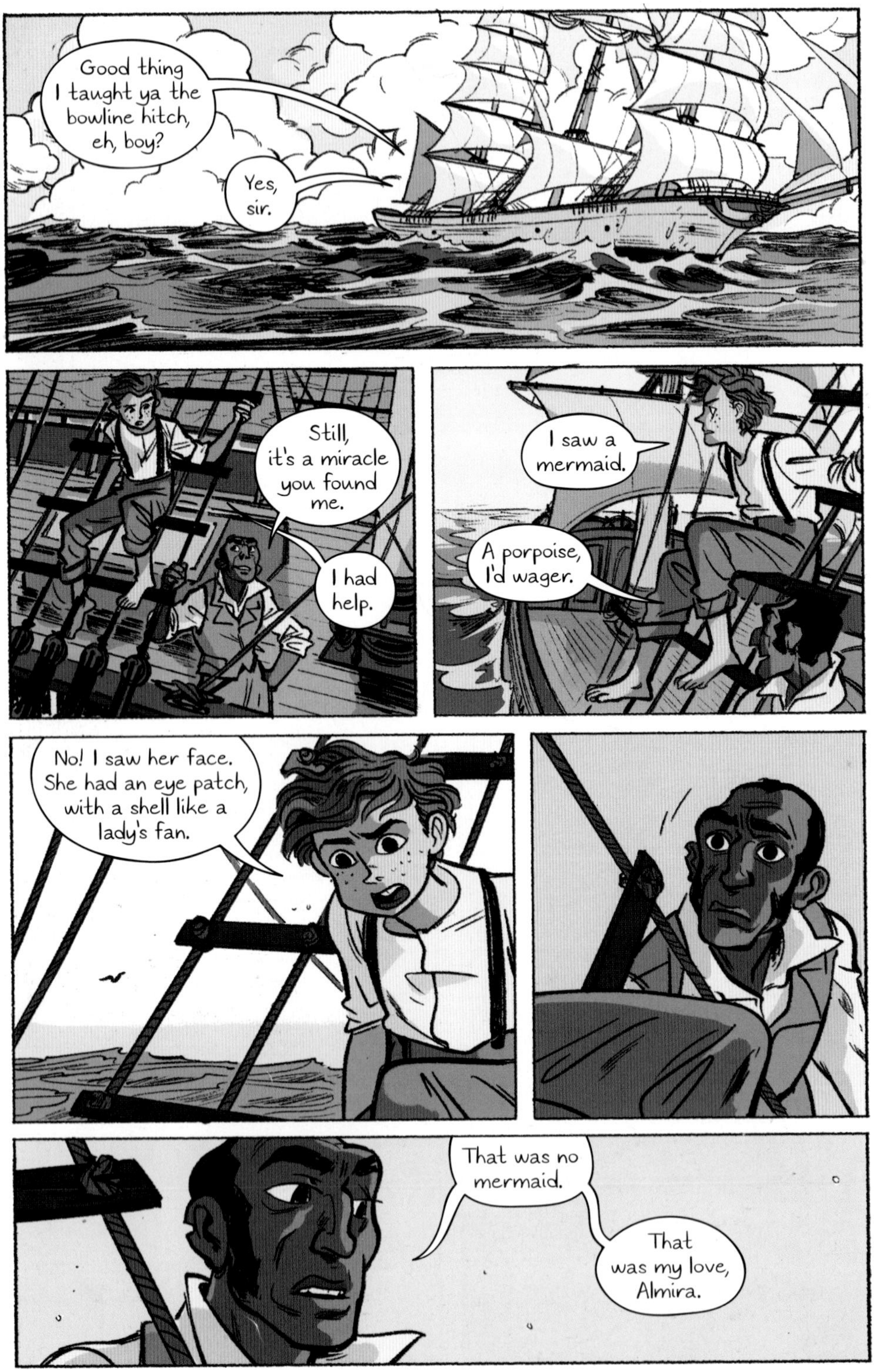
Good thing I taught ya the bowline hitch, eh, boy?
Yes, sir.
Still, it's a miracle you found me.
I had help.
I saw a mermaid.
A porpoise, I'd wager.
No! I saw her face. She had an eye patch, with a shell like a lady's fan.
That was no mermaid.
That was my love, Almira.

"I brought 'er that shell from Tahiti."

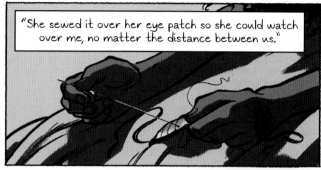

"She sewed it over her eye patch so she could watch over me, no matter the distance between us."

"Our moments together are few, but she never leaves my thoughts."

"She's there when I wake in the morning, an' she walks my dreams at night."

"An' when I'm in danger, my only prayer is that I may return to her."

"An' somehow I find the strength to do what must be done, an' I've always come out right."

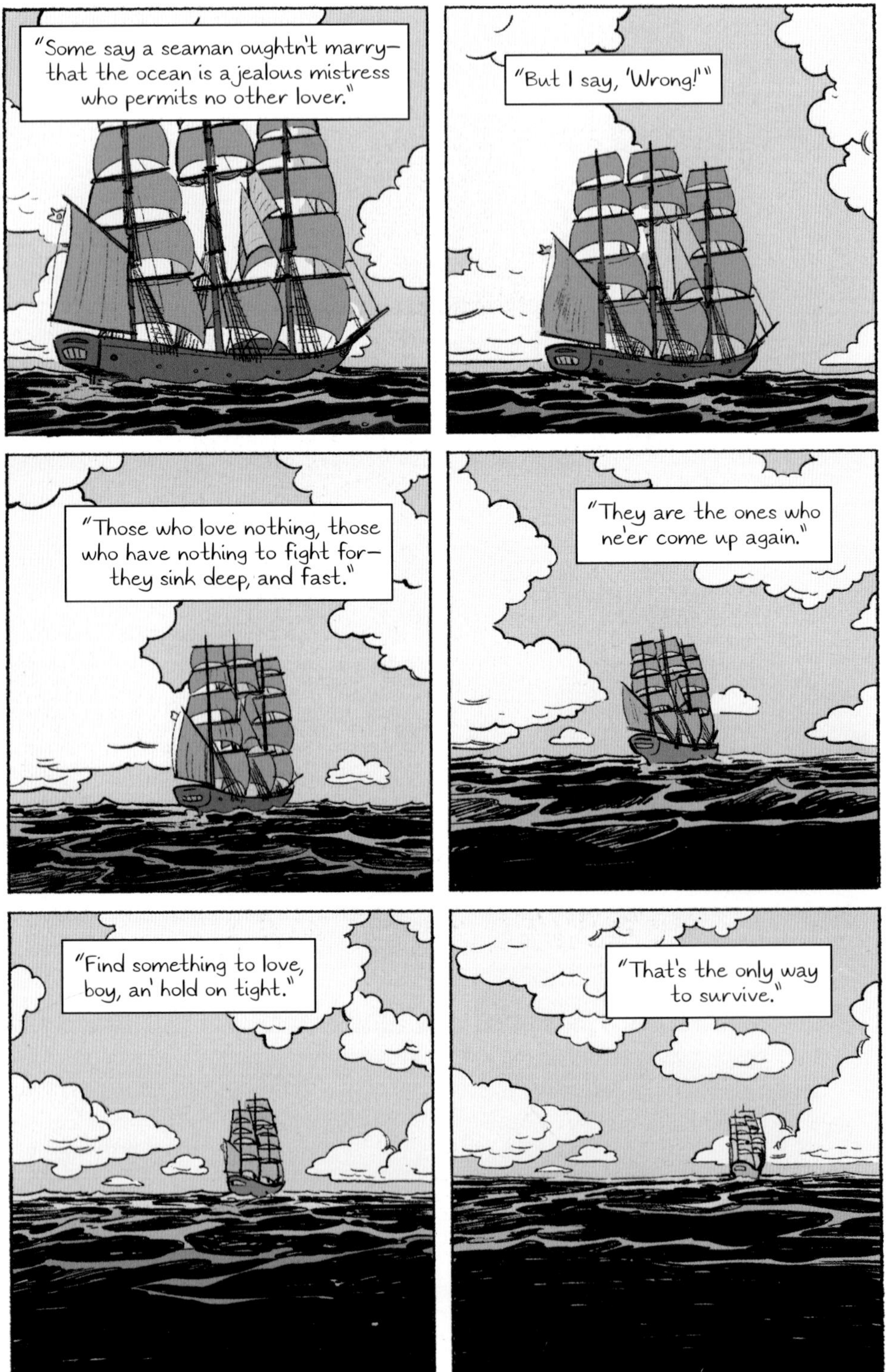
"Some say a seaman oughtn't marry—that the ocean is a jealous mistress who permits no other lover."
"But I say, 'Wrong!'"
"Those who love nothing, those who have nothing to fight for—they sink deep, and fast."
"They are the ones who ne'er come up again."
"Find something to love, boy, an' hold on tight."
"That's the only way to survive."

CHAPTER SEVEN
TOOTH AND NAIL

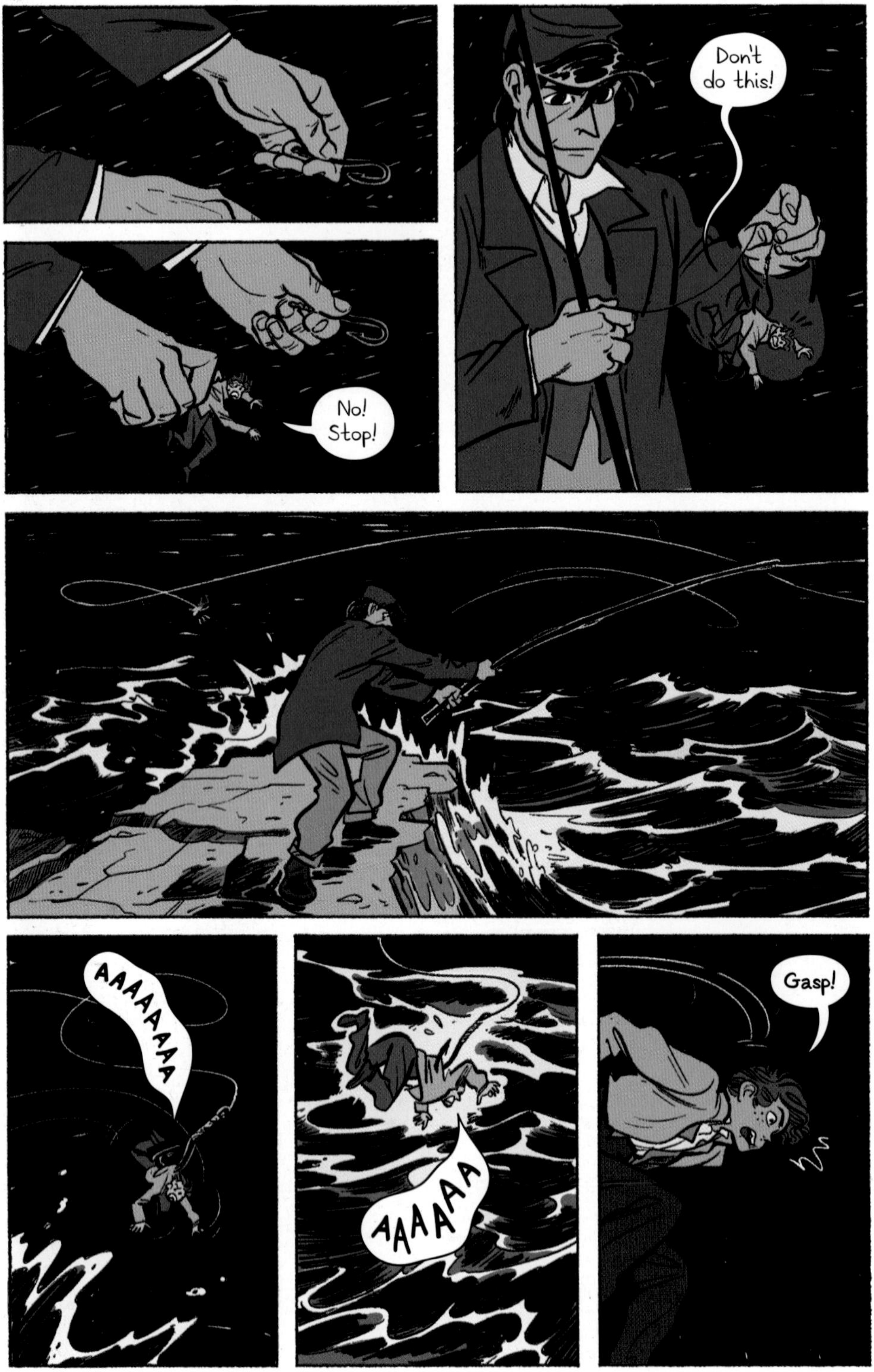
No!
Stop!
Don't
do this!
AAAAAAAA
AAAAA
Gasp!

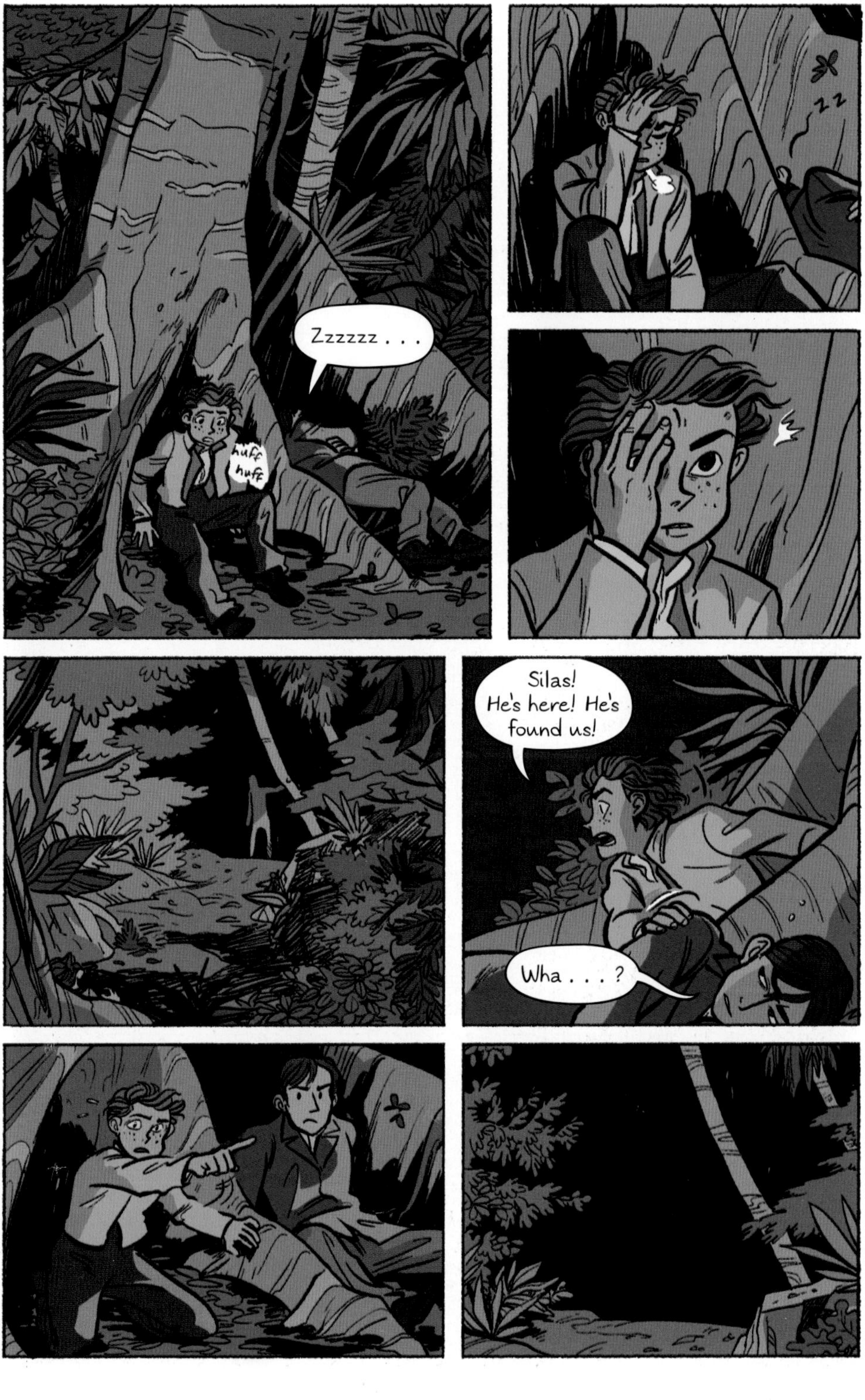
Zzzzzz . . .
huff huff
Silas! He's here! He's found us!
Wha . . . ?

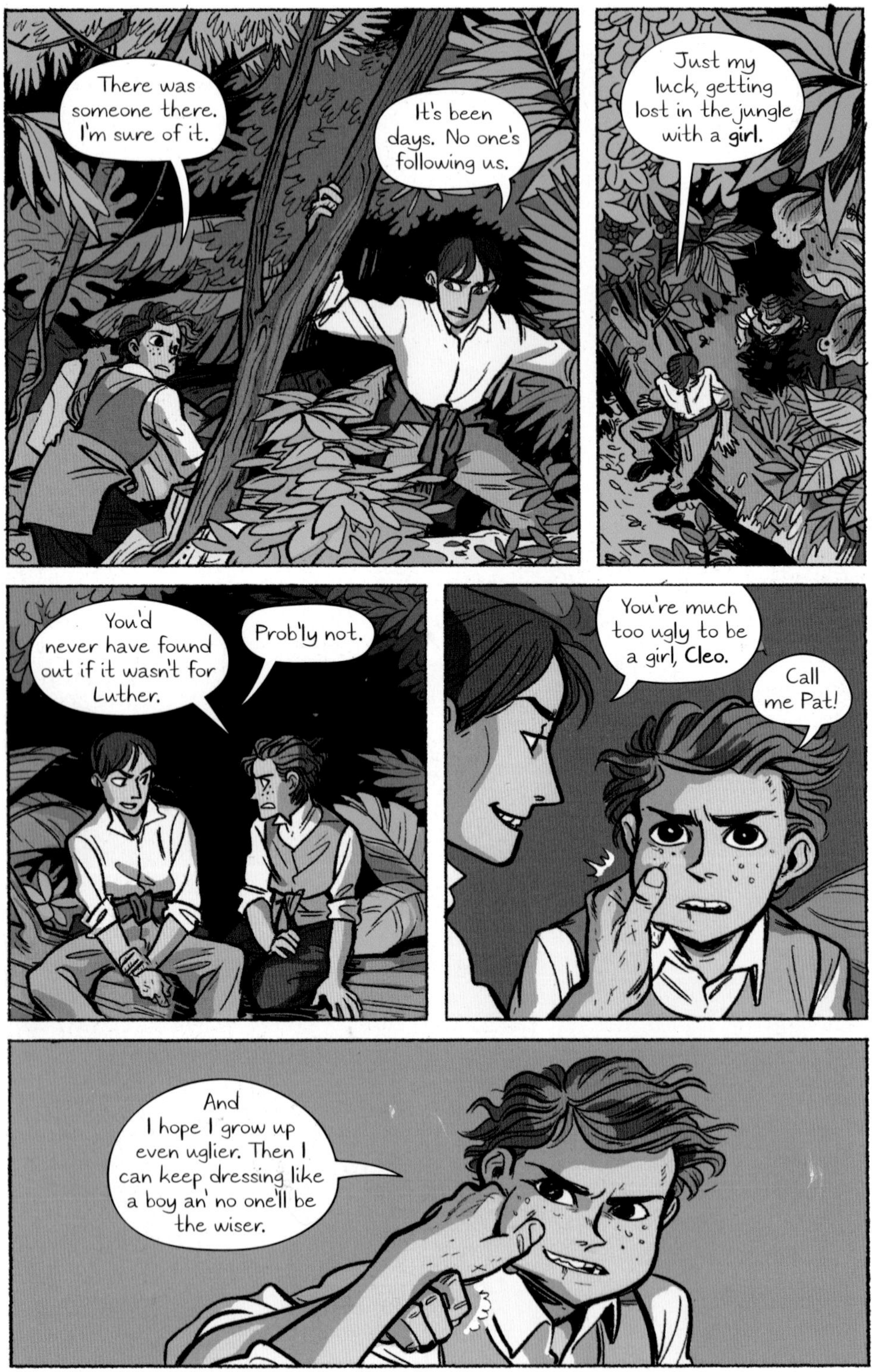
There was someone there. I'm sure of it.
It's been days. No one's following us.
Just my luck, getting lost in the jungle with a **girl**.
You'd never have found out if it wasn't for Luther.
Prob'ly not.
You're much too ugly to be a girl, **Cleo.**
Call me Pat!
And I hope I grow up even uglier. Then I can keep dressing like a boy an' no one'll be the wiser.

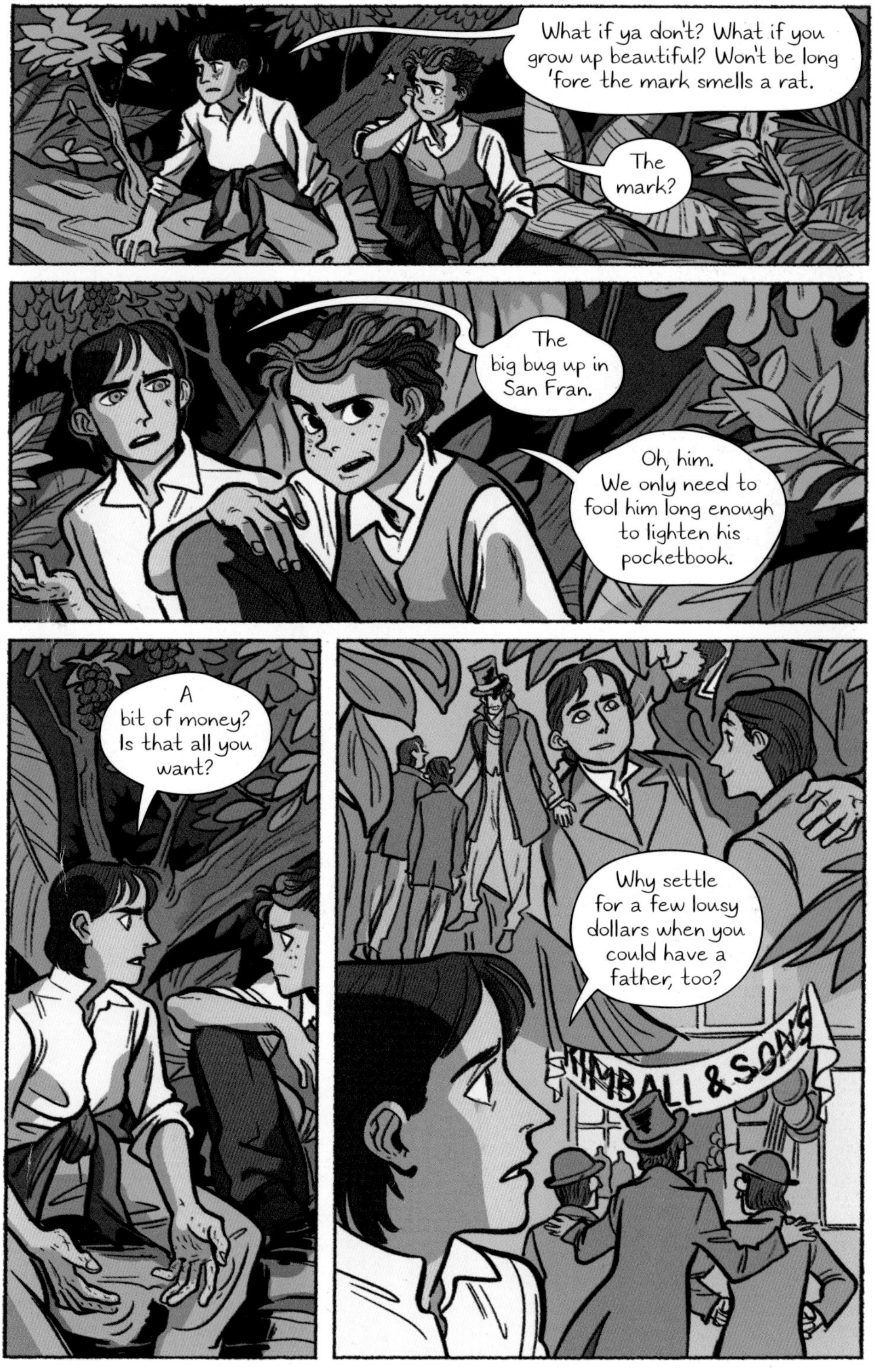

What if ya don't? What if you grow up beautiful? Won't be long 'fore the mark smells a rat.
The mark?
The big bug up in San Fran.
Oh, him. We only need to fool him long enough to lighten his pocketbook.
A bit of money? Is that all you want?
Why settle for a few lousy dollars when you could have a father, too?
KIMBALL & SONS

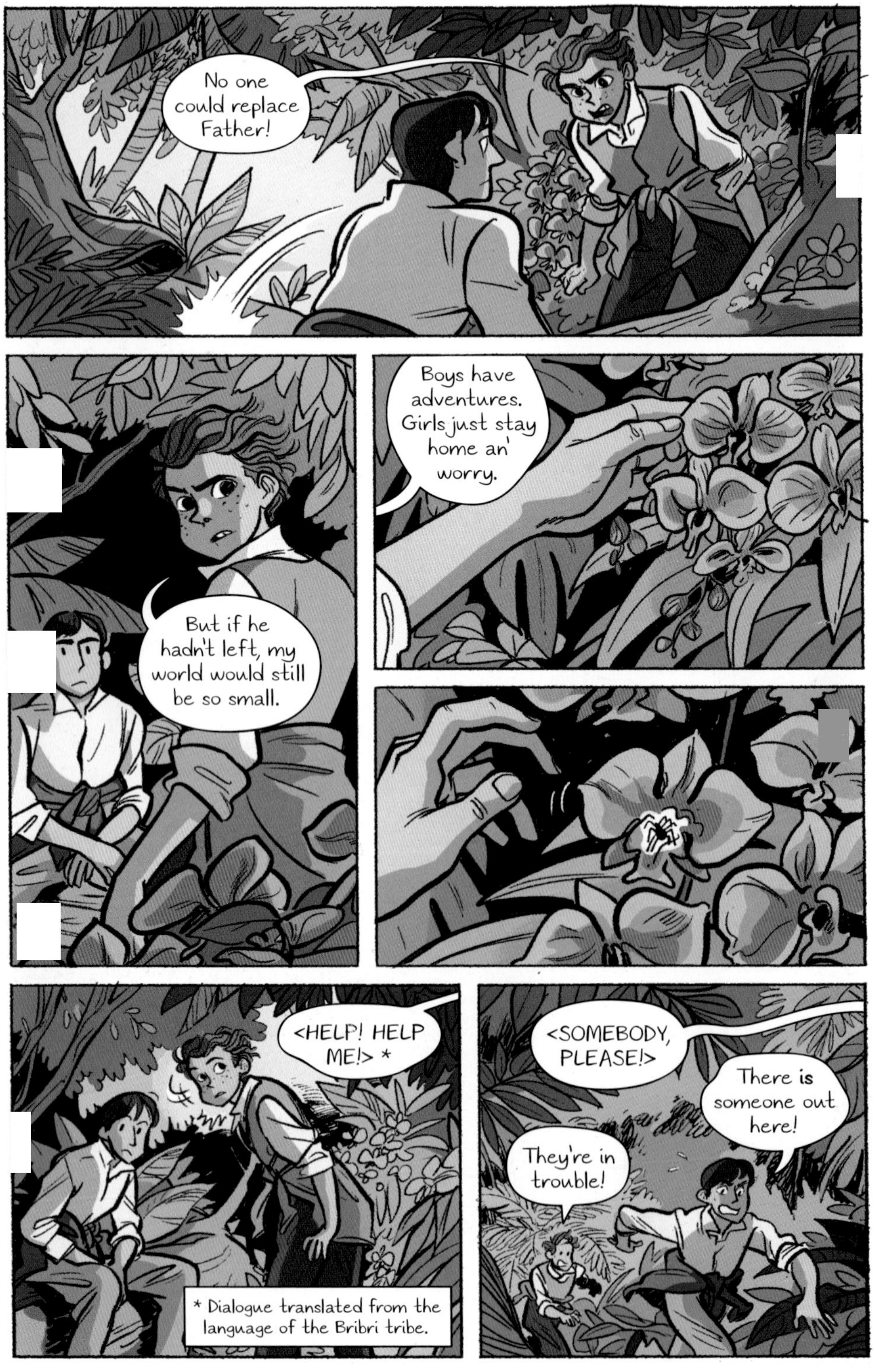
No one could replace Father!
But if he hadn't left, my world would still be so small.
Boys have adventures. Girls just stay home an' worry.
<HELP! HELP ME!> *
* Dialogue translated from the language of the Bribri tribe.
<SOMEBODY, PLEASE!>
There is someone out here!
They're in trouble!

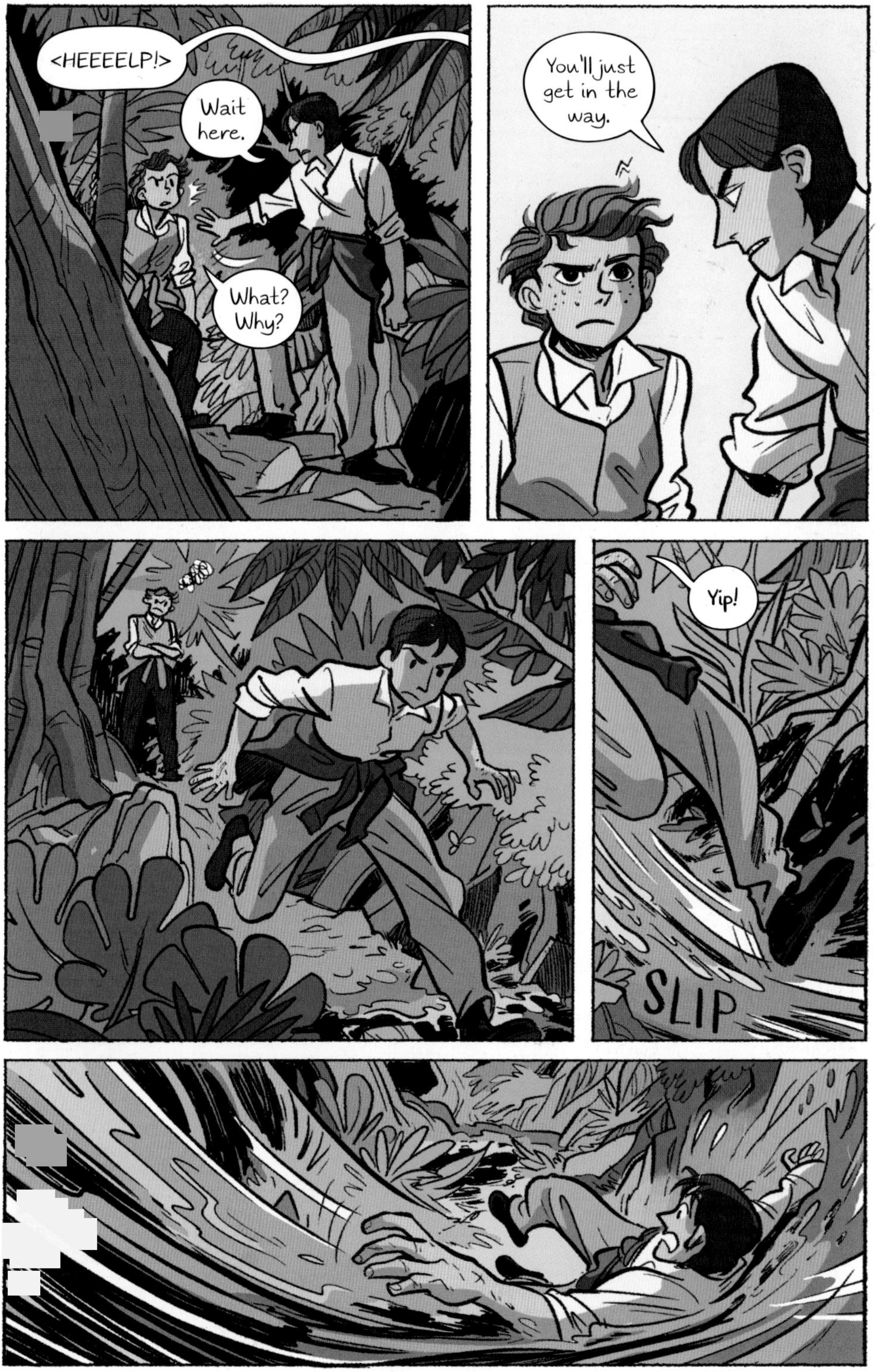
<HEEEELP!>
Wait here.
What? Why?
You'll just get in the way.
Yip!
SLIP

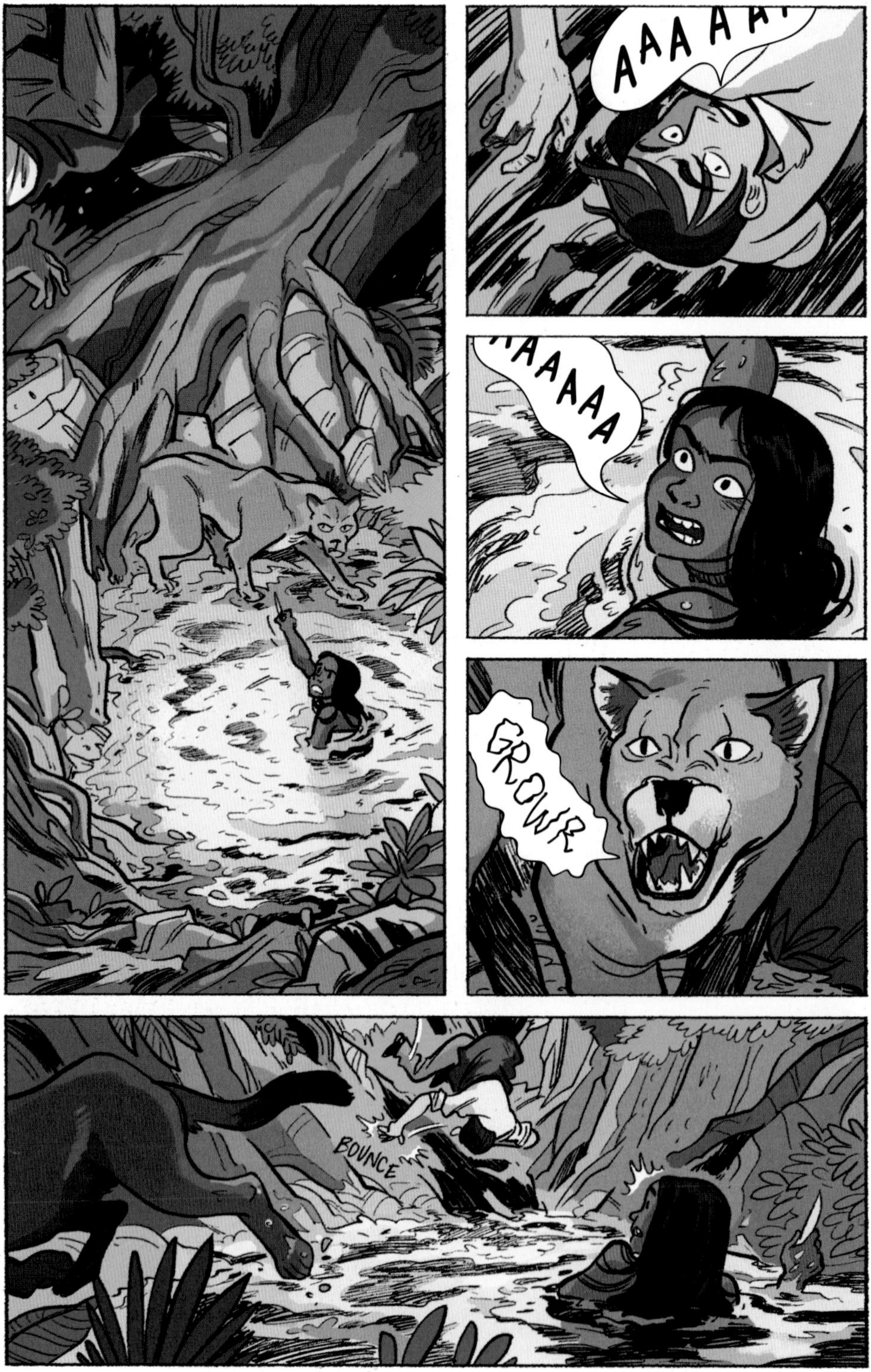
AAAAA
AAAAAA
GROWR
BOUNCE

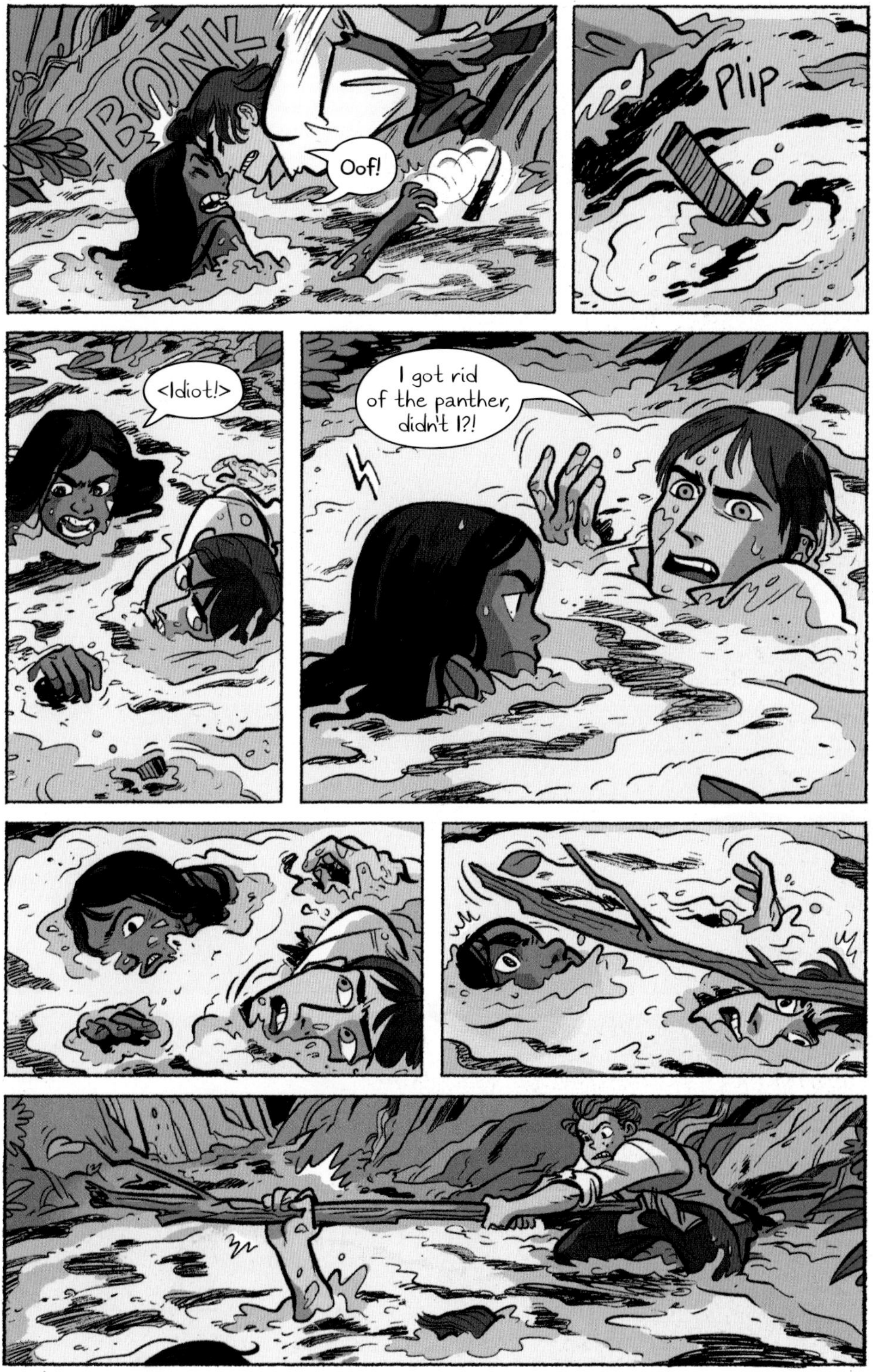
BONK
Oof!
PLIP
<Idiot!>
I got rid of the panther, didn't I?!

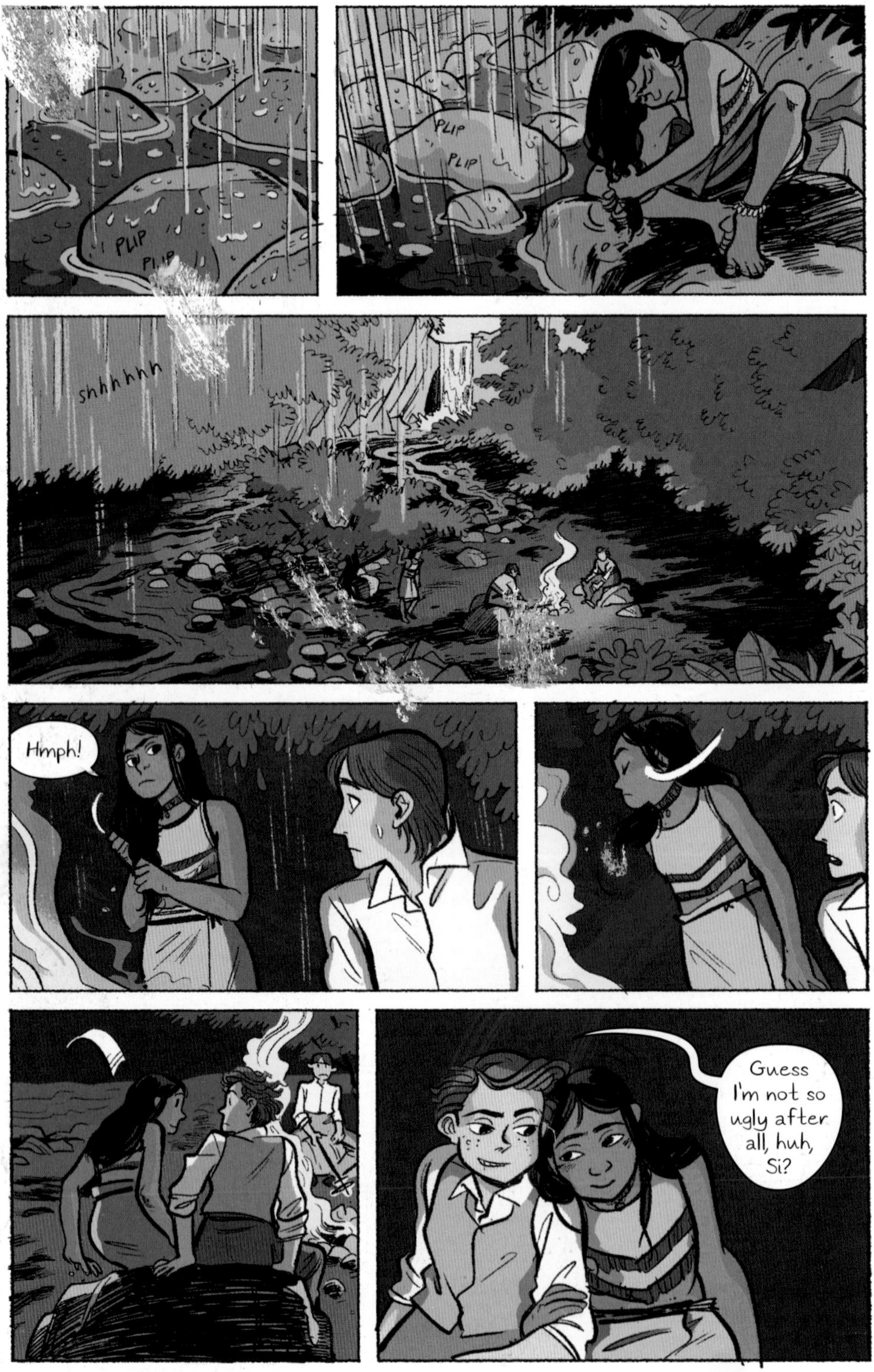
PLIP
PLIP
PLIP
PLIP
shhhhhh
Hmph!
Guess I'm not so ugly after all, huh, Si?

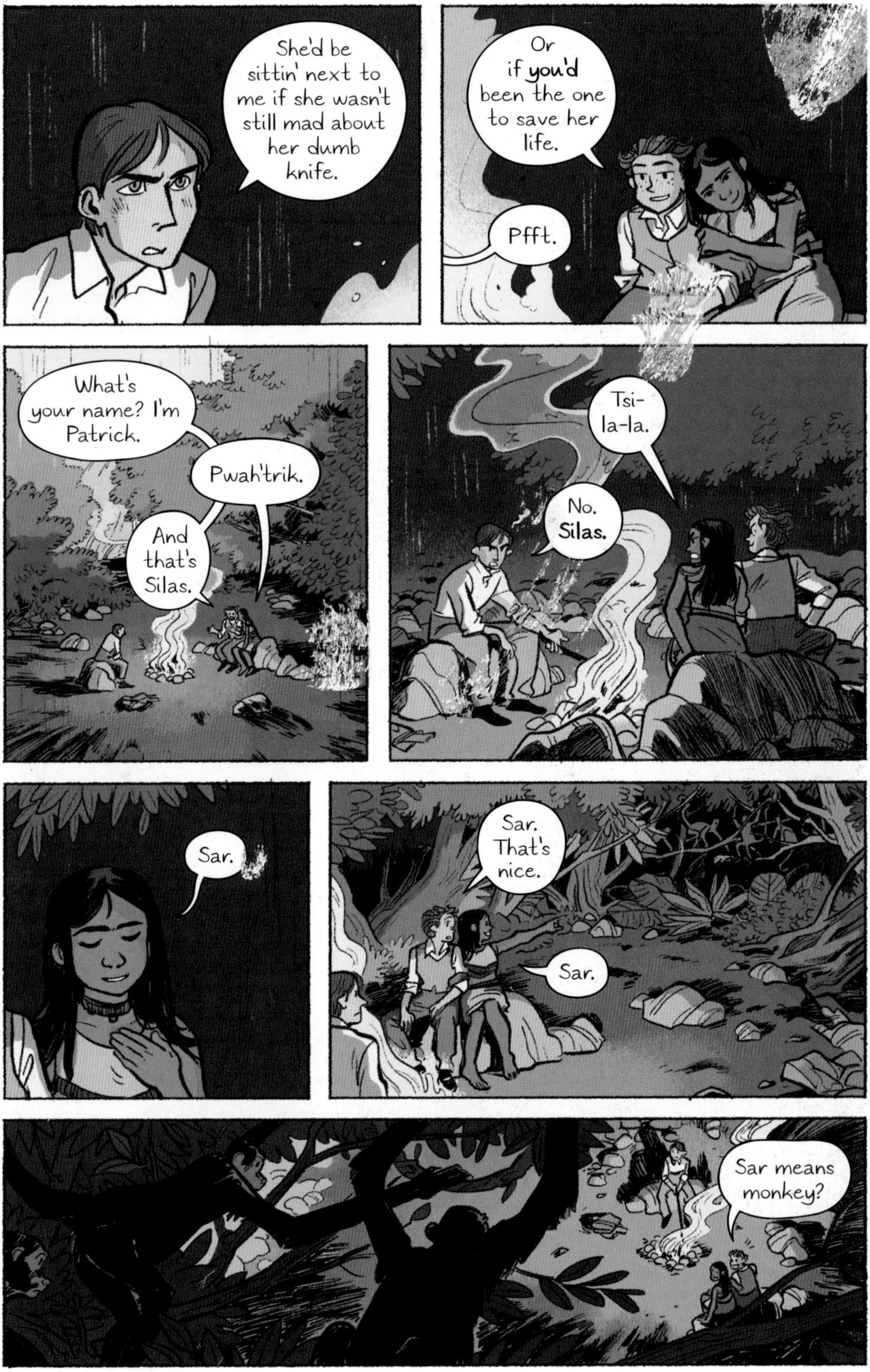
She'd be sittin' next to me if she wasn't still mad about her dumb knife.
Or if you'd been the one to save her life.
Pfft.
What's your name? I'm Patrick.
Pwah'trik.
And that's Silas.
Tsi-la-la.
No. Silas.
Sar.
Sar. That's nice.
Sar.
Sar means monkey?

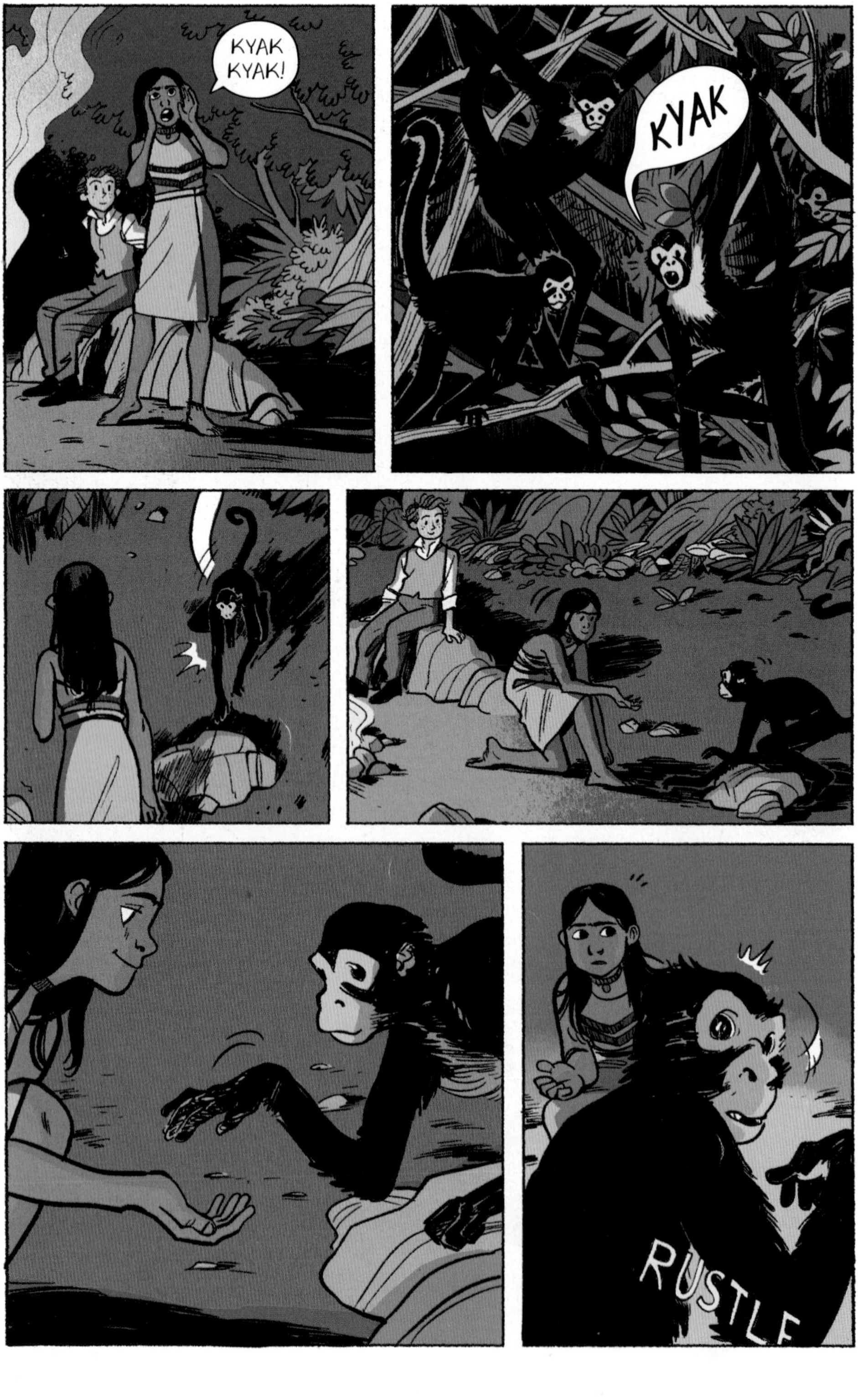
KYAK KYAK!
KYAK
RUSTLE

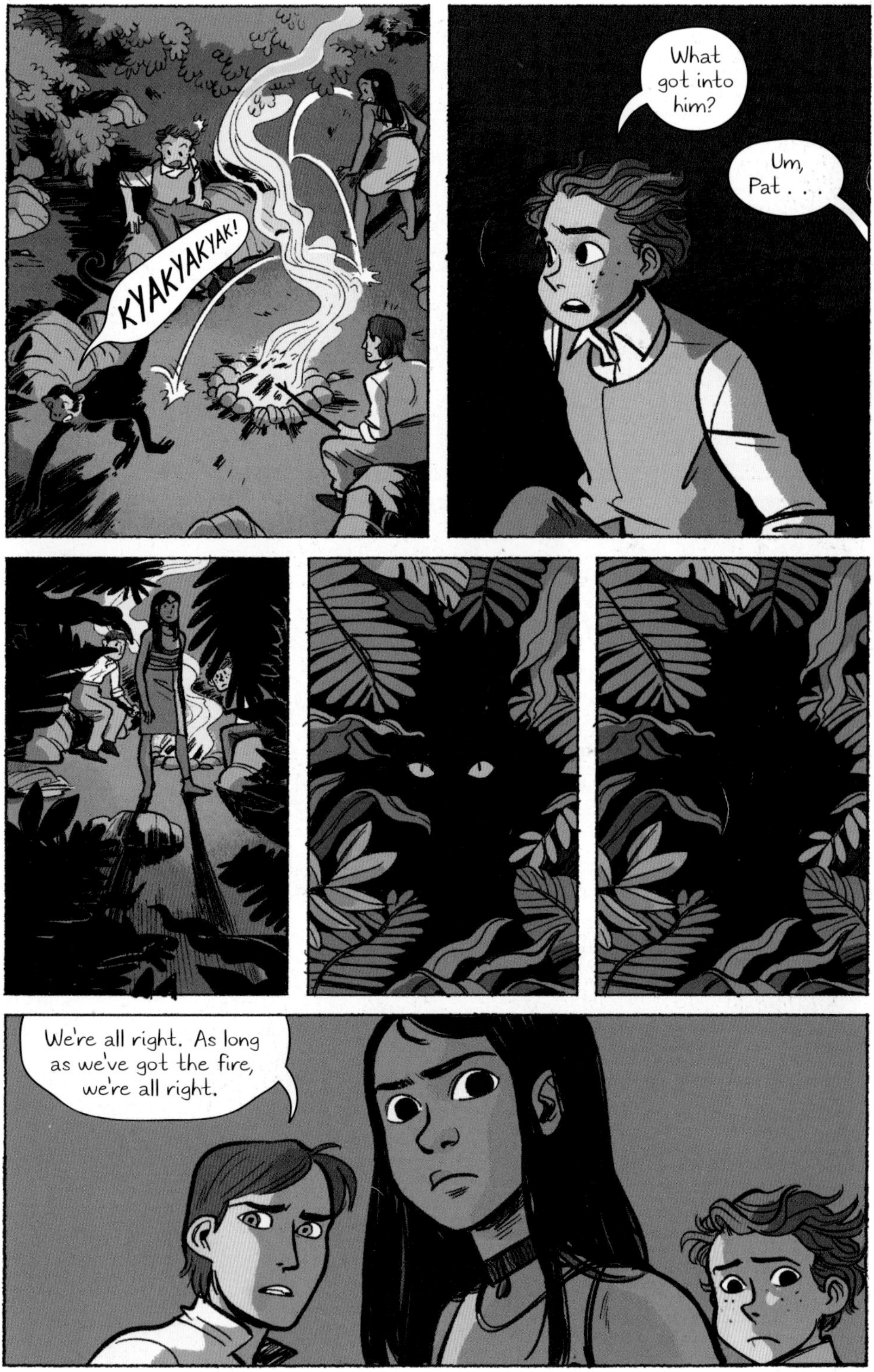
KYAKYAKYAK!
What got into him?
Um, Pat . . .
We're all right. As long as we've got the fire, we're all right.

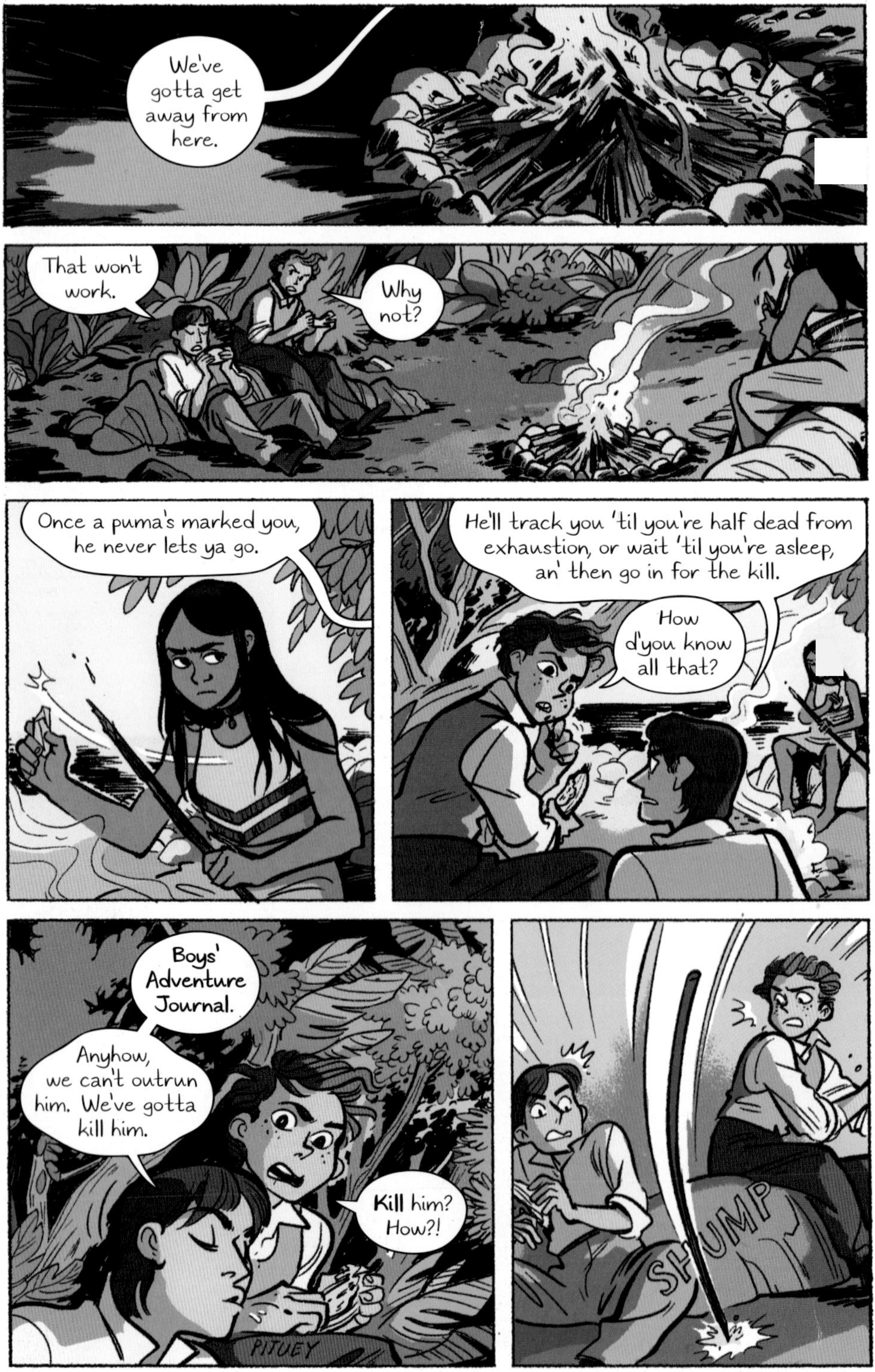
We've gotta get away from here.
That won't work.
Why not?
Once a puma's marked you, he never lets ya go.
He'll track you 'til you're half dead from exhaustion, or wait 'til you're asleep, an' then go in for the kill.
How d'you know all that?
Boys' Adventure Journal.
Anyhow, we can't outrun him. We've gotta kill him.
Kill him? How?!
PITUEY
SHUMP

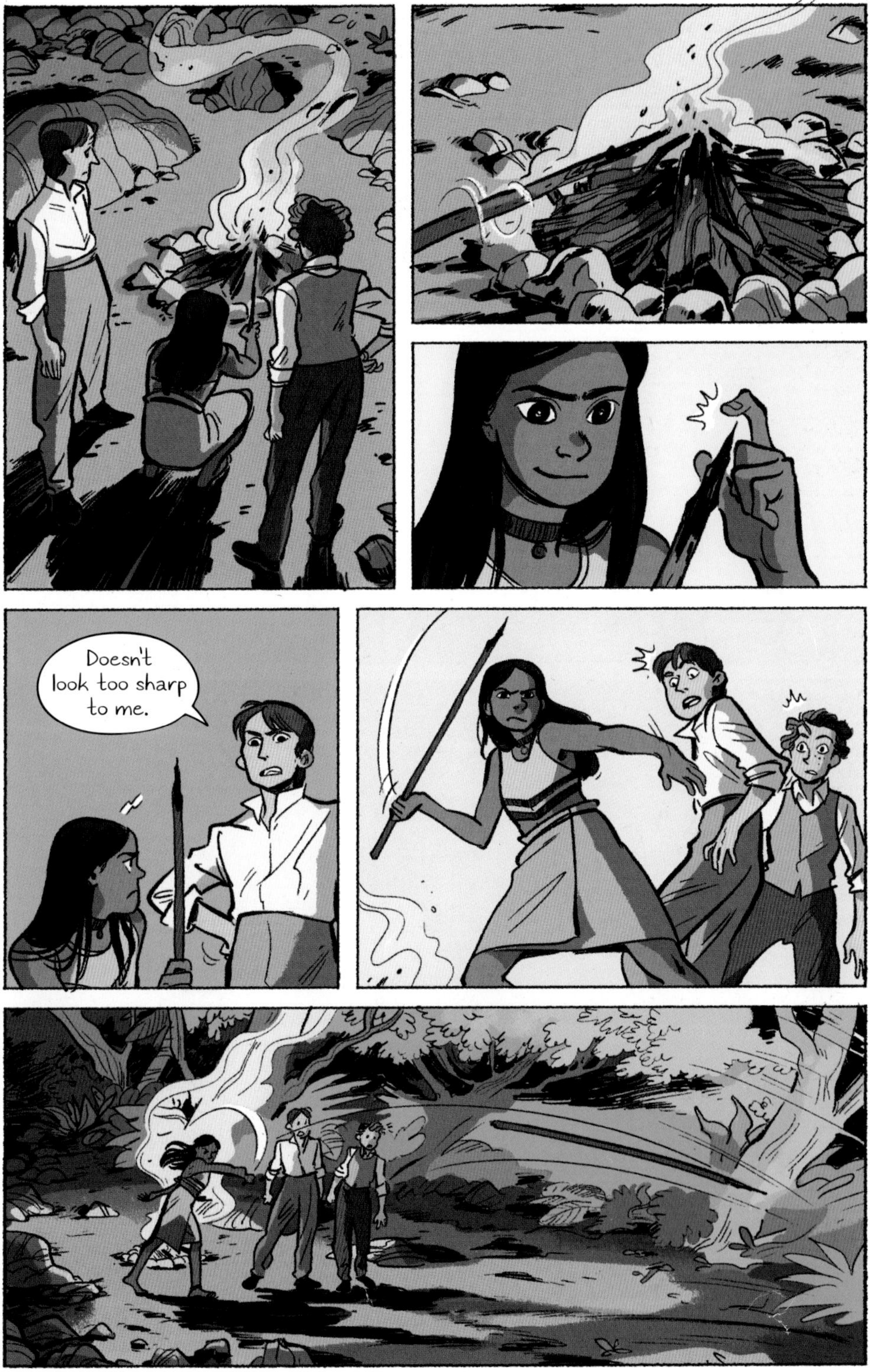
Doesn't look too sharp to me.

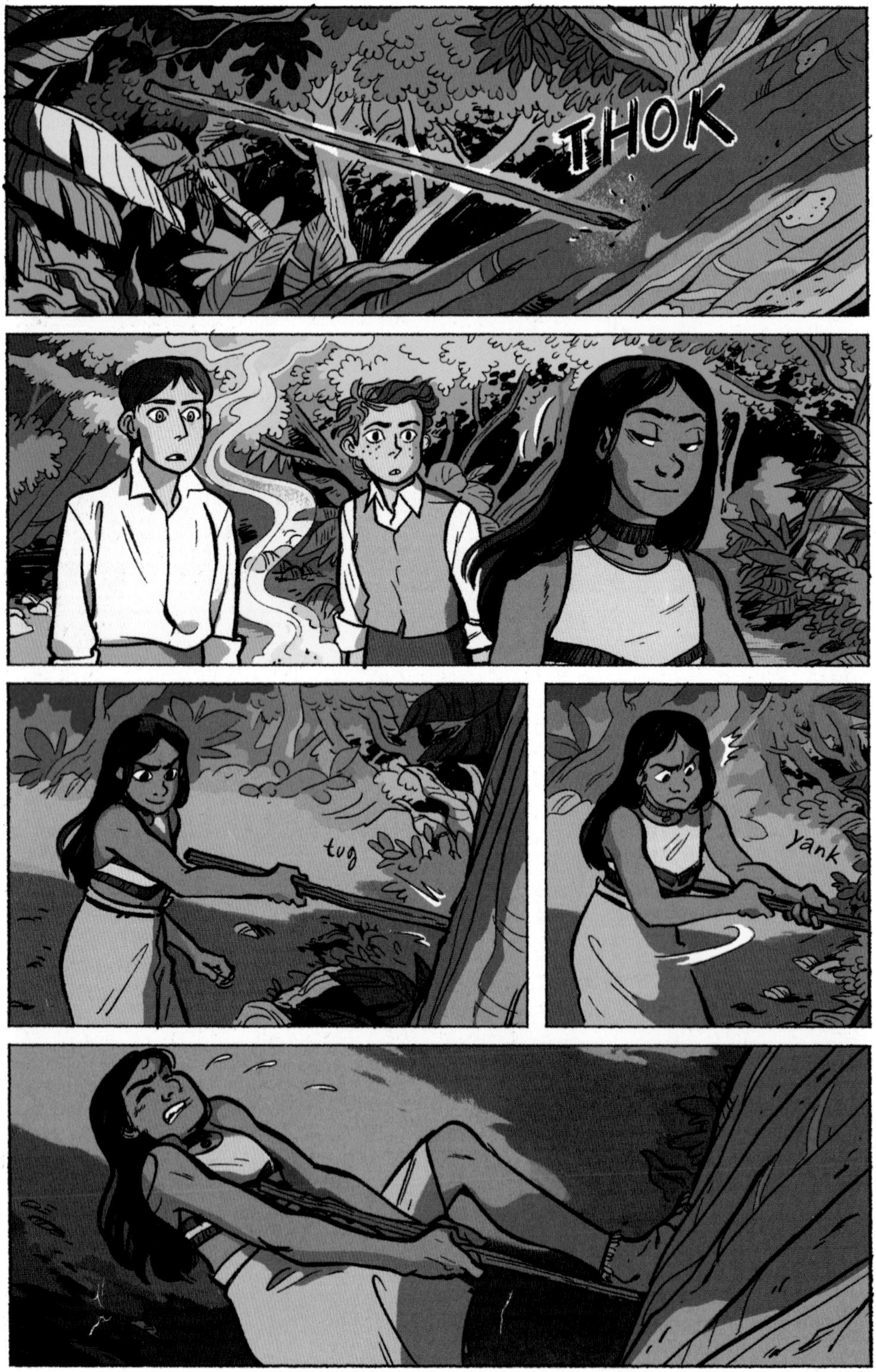
THOK
tug
yank

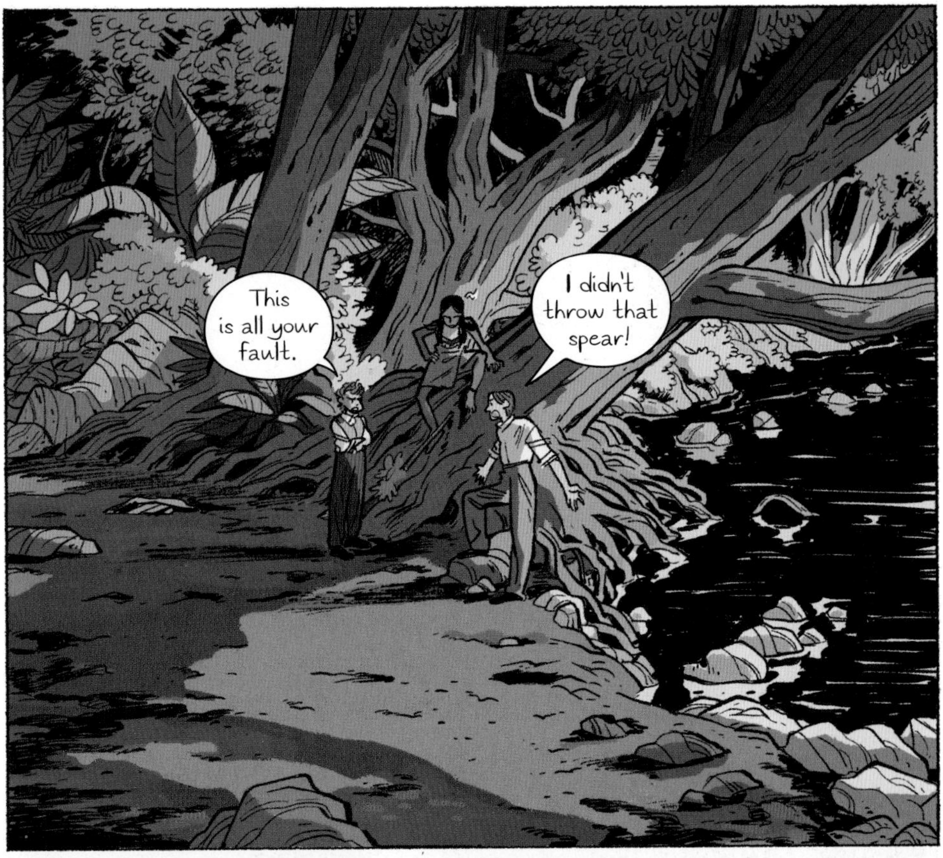
This is all your fault.
I didn't throw that spear!

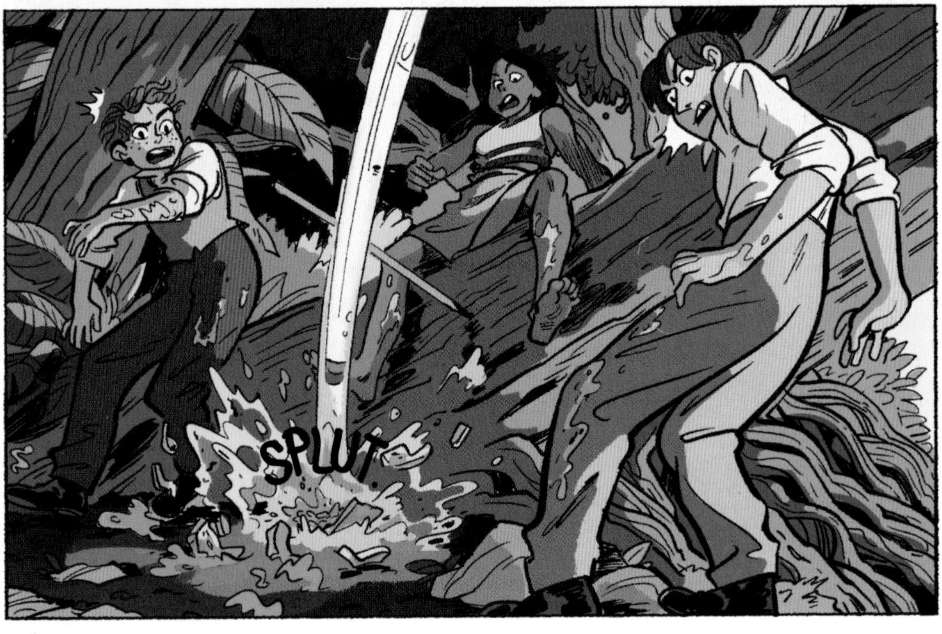
SPLUT

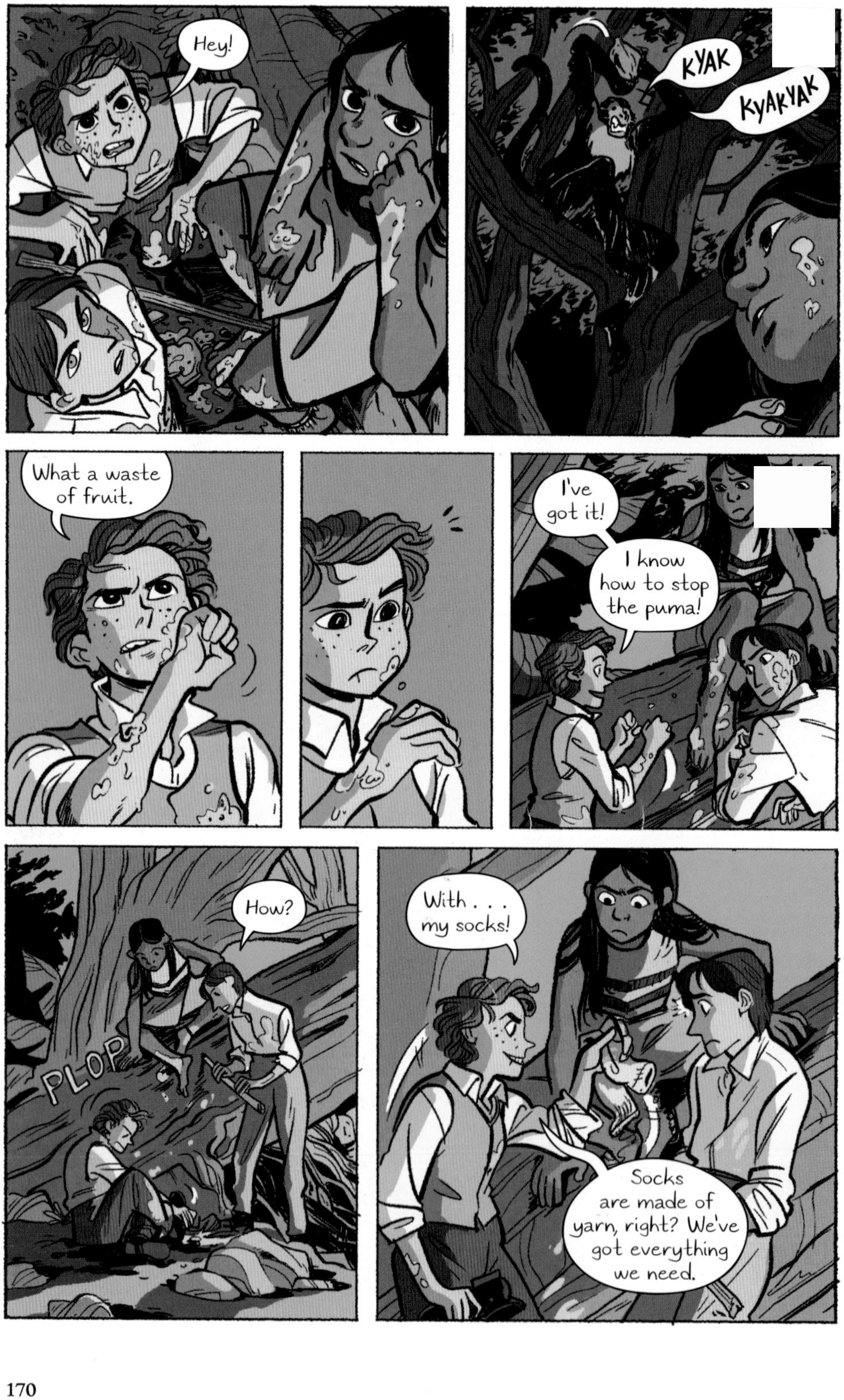
Hey!
KYAK
KYAKYAK
What a waste of fruit.
I've got it!
I know how to stop the puma!
How?
PLOP
With . . . my socks!
Socks are made of yarn, right? We've got everything we need.

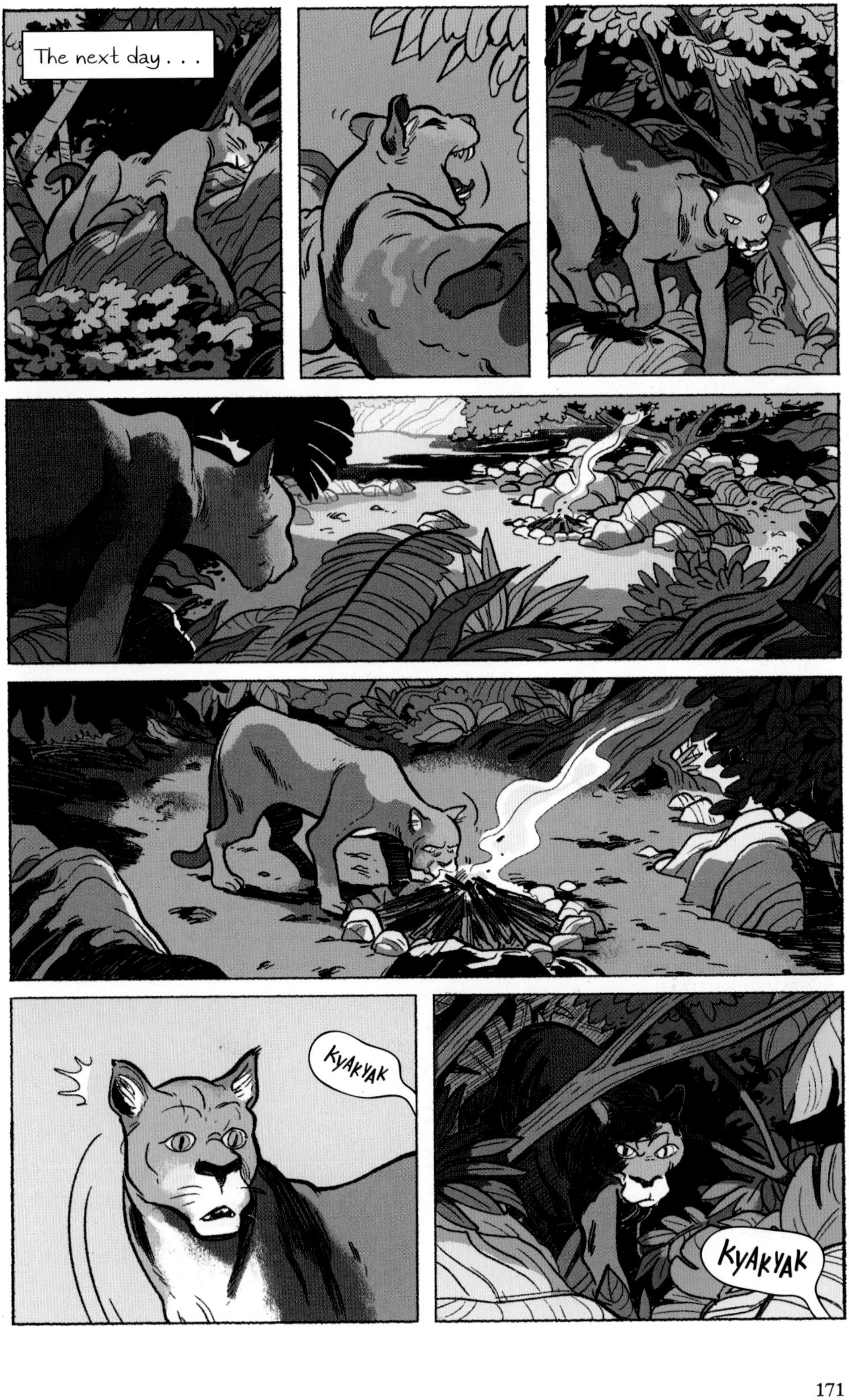
The next day . . .
KYAKYAK
KYAKYAK

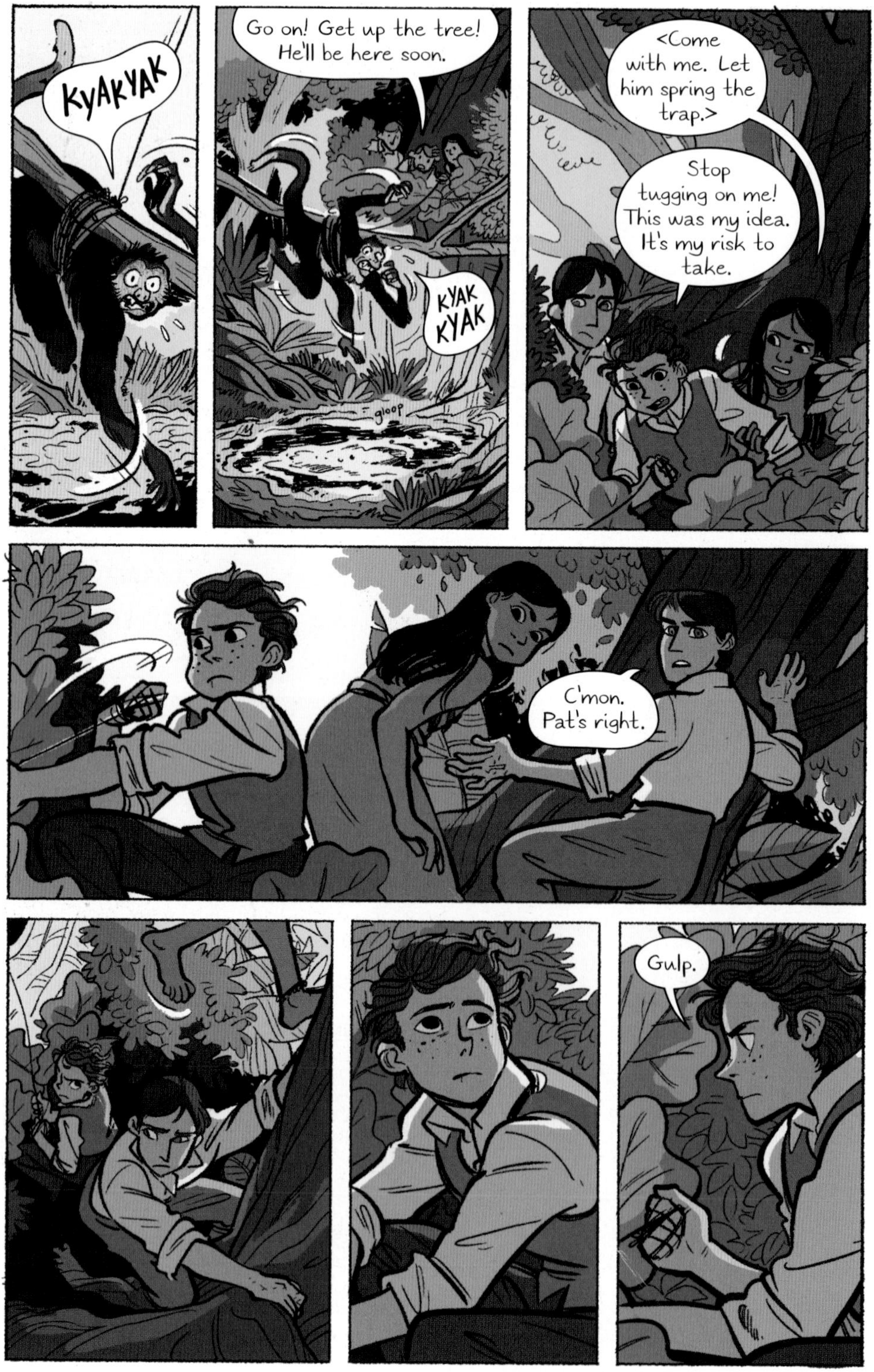
KYAKYAK
Go on! Get up the tree! He'll be here soon.
KYAK KYAK
gloop
<Come with me. Let him spring the trap.>
Stop tugging on me! This was my idea. It's my risk to take.
C'mon. Pat's right.
Gulp.

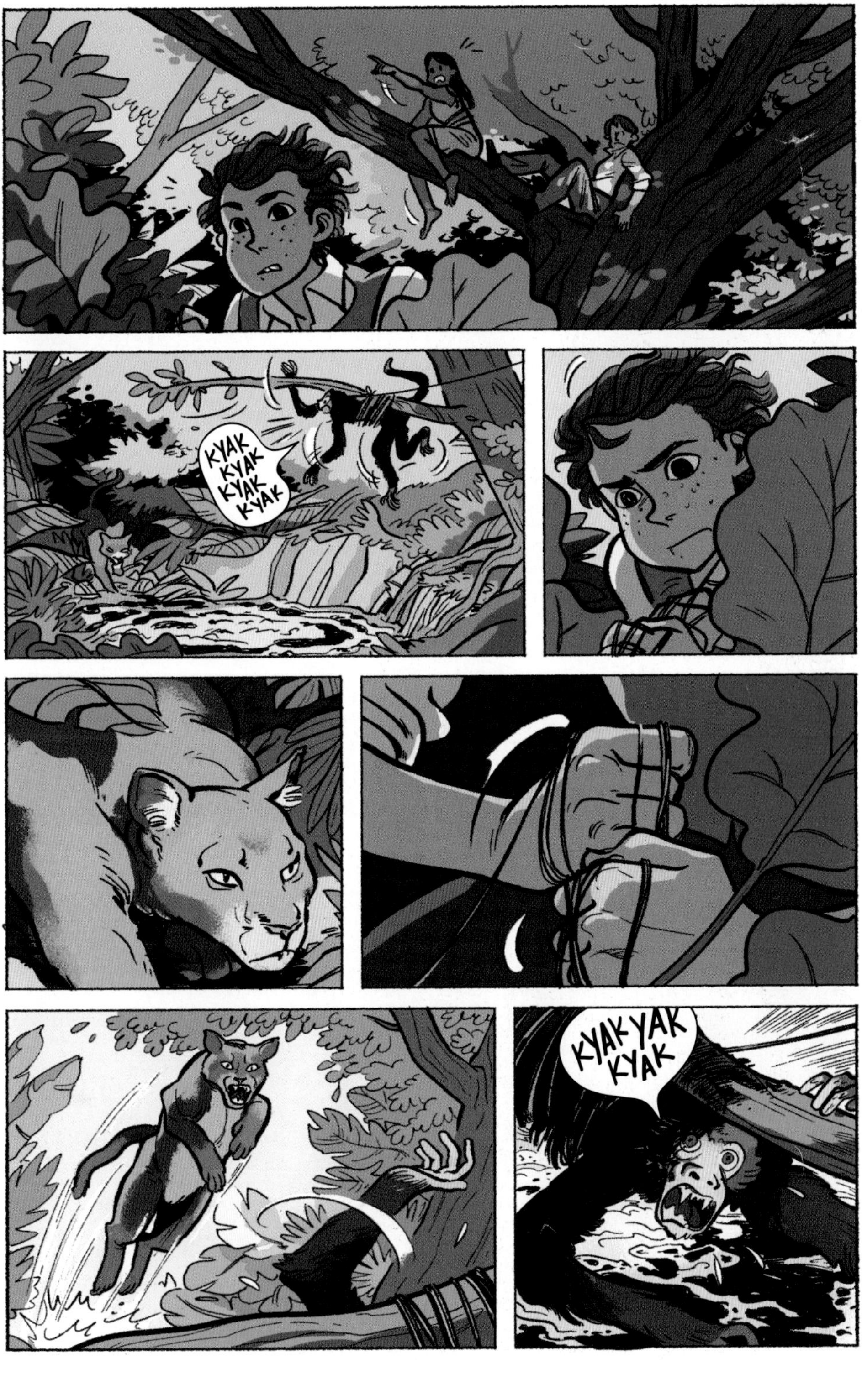
KYAK KYAK KYAK KYAK
KYAKYAK KYAK

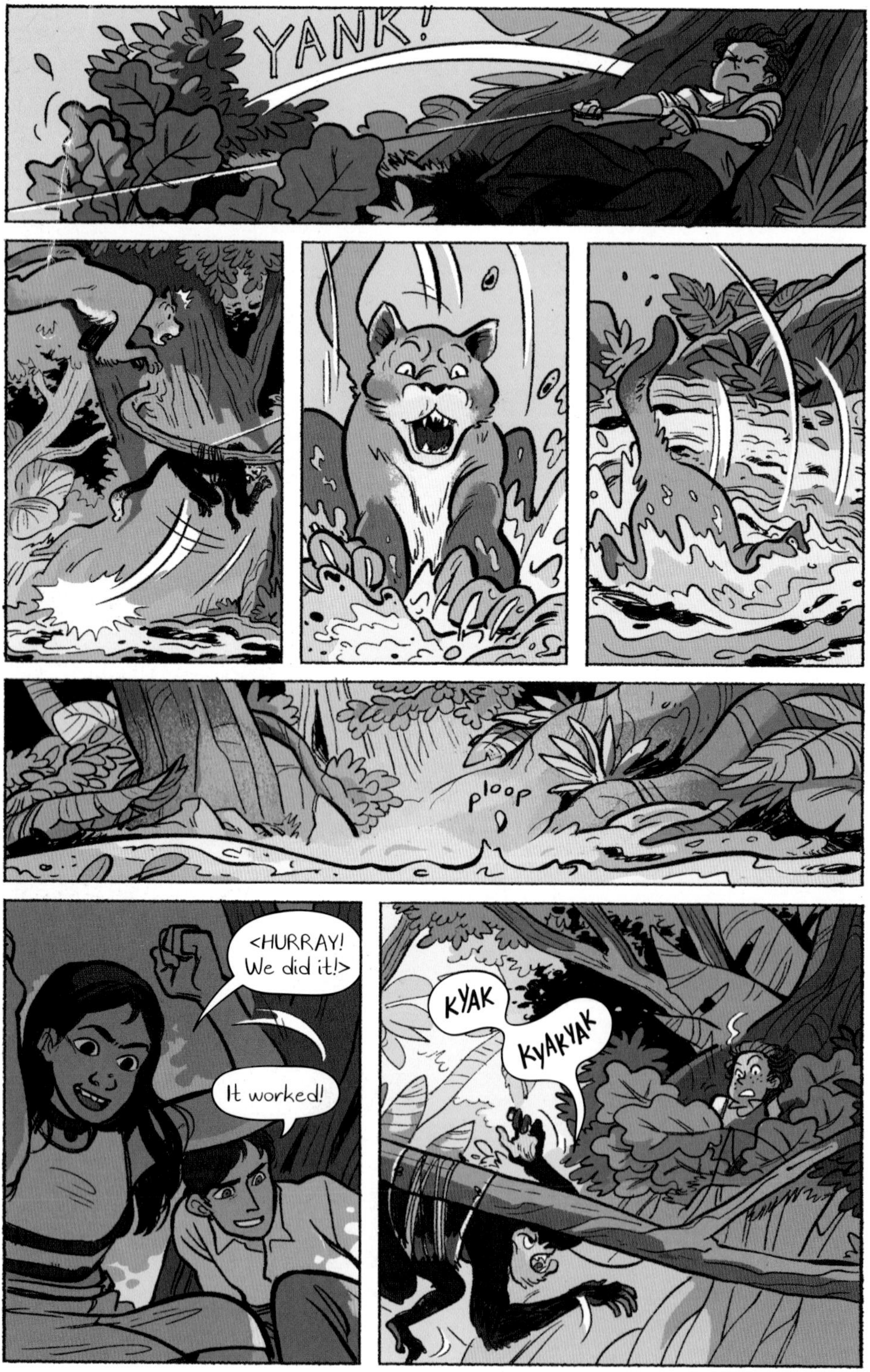
YANK!
ploop
<HURRAY! We did it!>
It worked!
KYAK
KYAKYAK

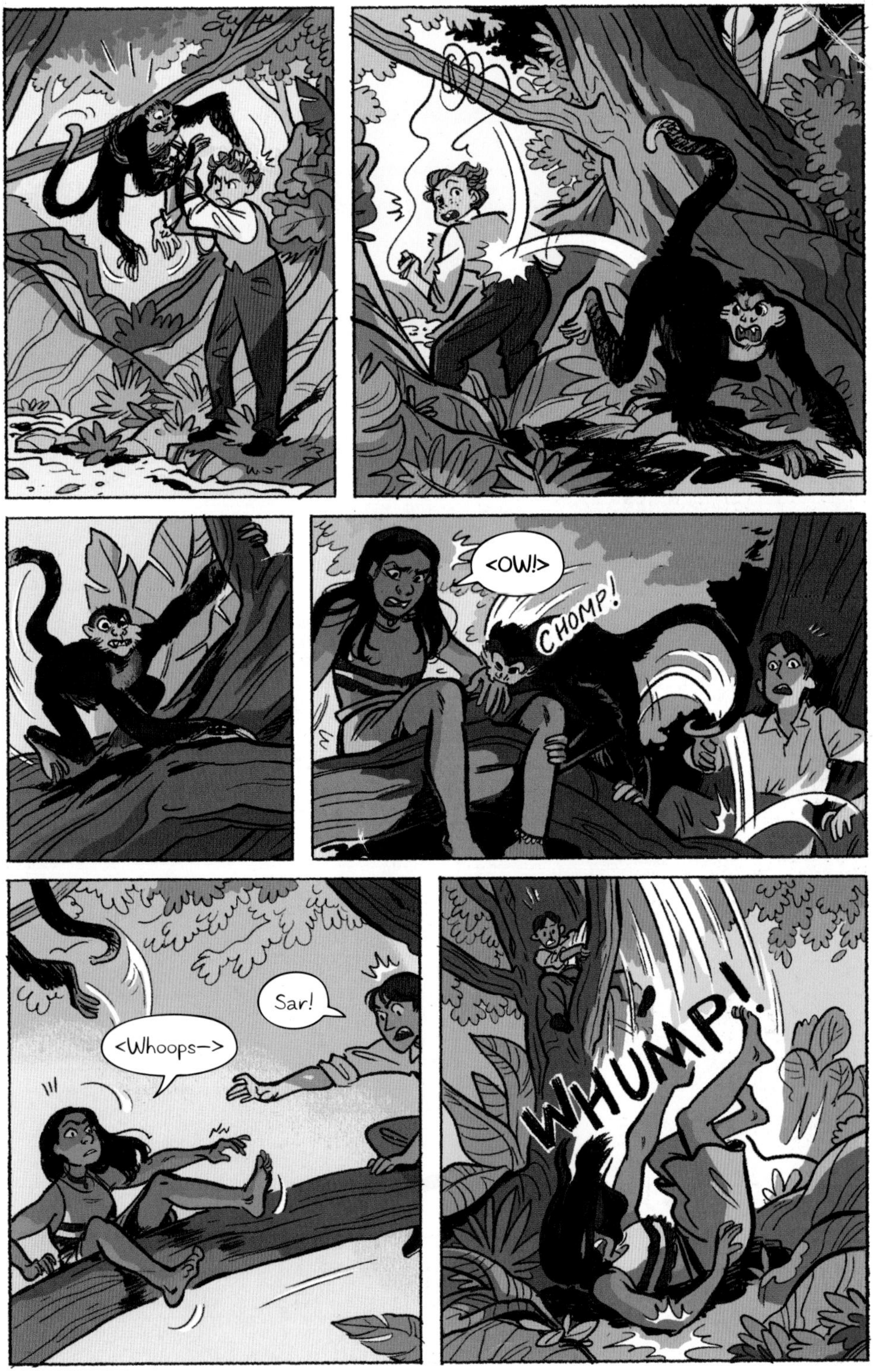

<OW!>
CHOMP!
Sar!
<Whoops—>
WHUMP!

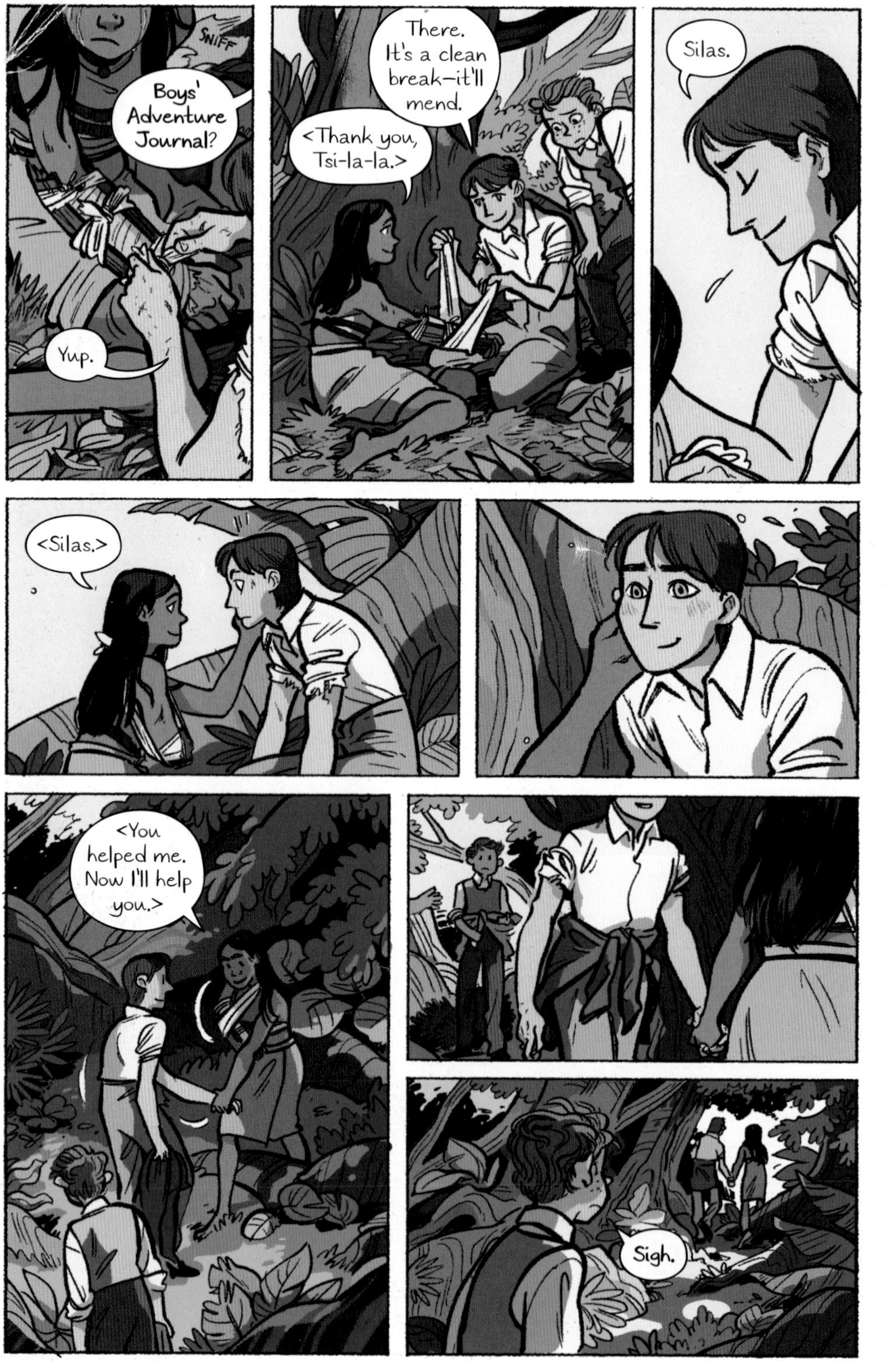
SNIFF
Boys' Adventure Journal?
Yup.
There. It's a clean break—it'll mend.
<Thank you, Tsi-la-la.>
Silas.
<Silas.>
<You helped me. Now I'll help you.>
Sigh.

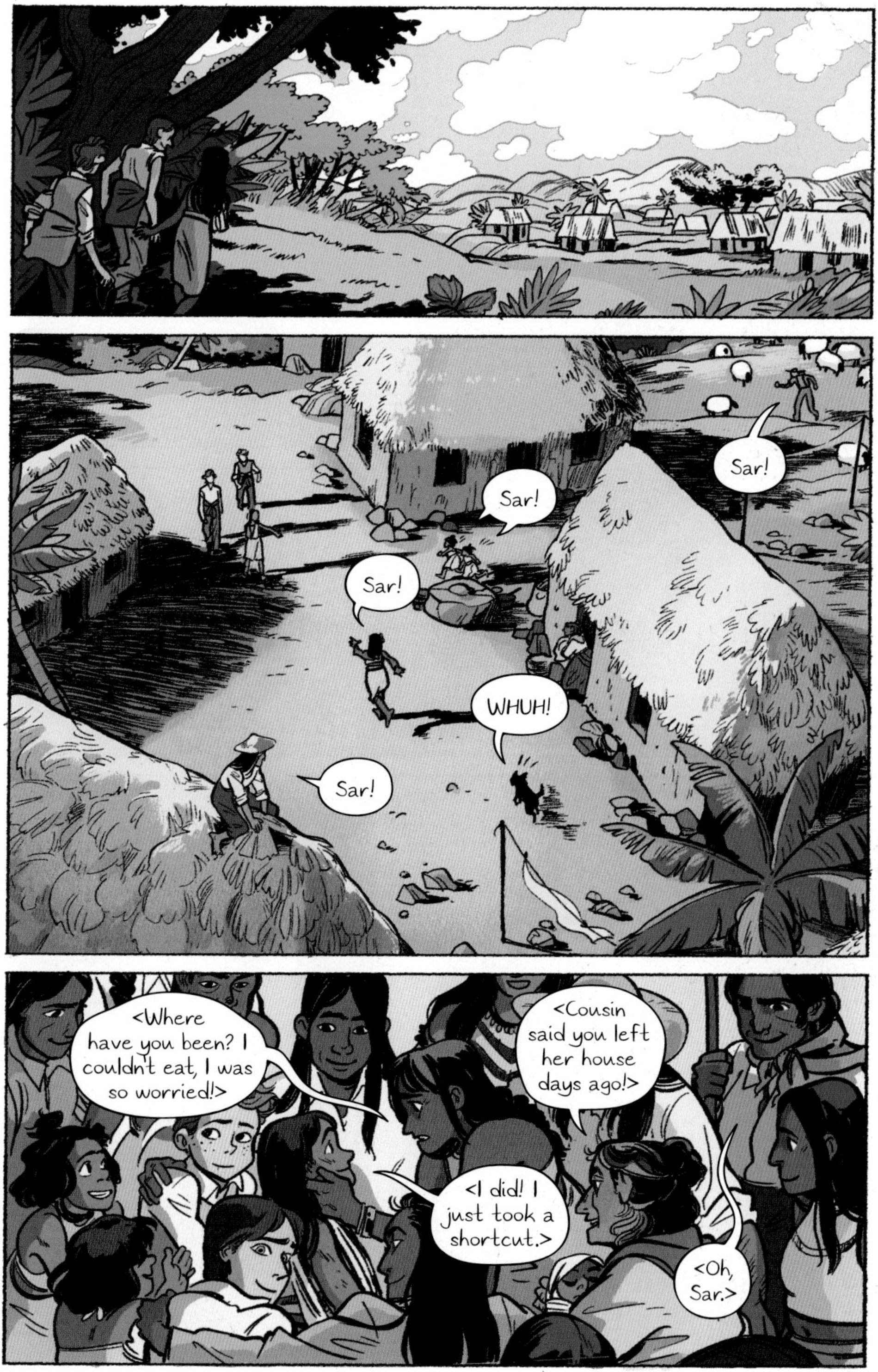
Sar!
Sar!
Sar!
WHUH!
Sar!
<Where have you been? I couldn't eat, I was so worried!>
<Cousin said you left her house days ago!>
<I did! I just took a shortcut.>
<Oh, Sar.>

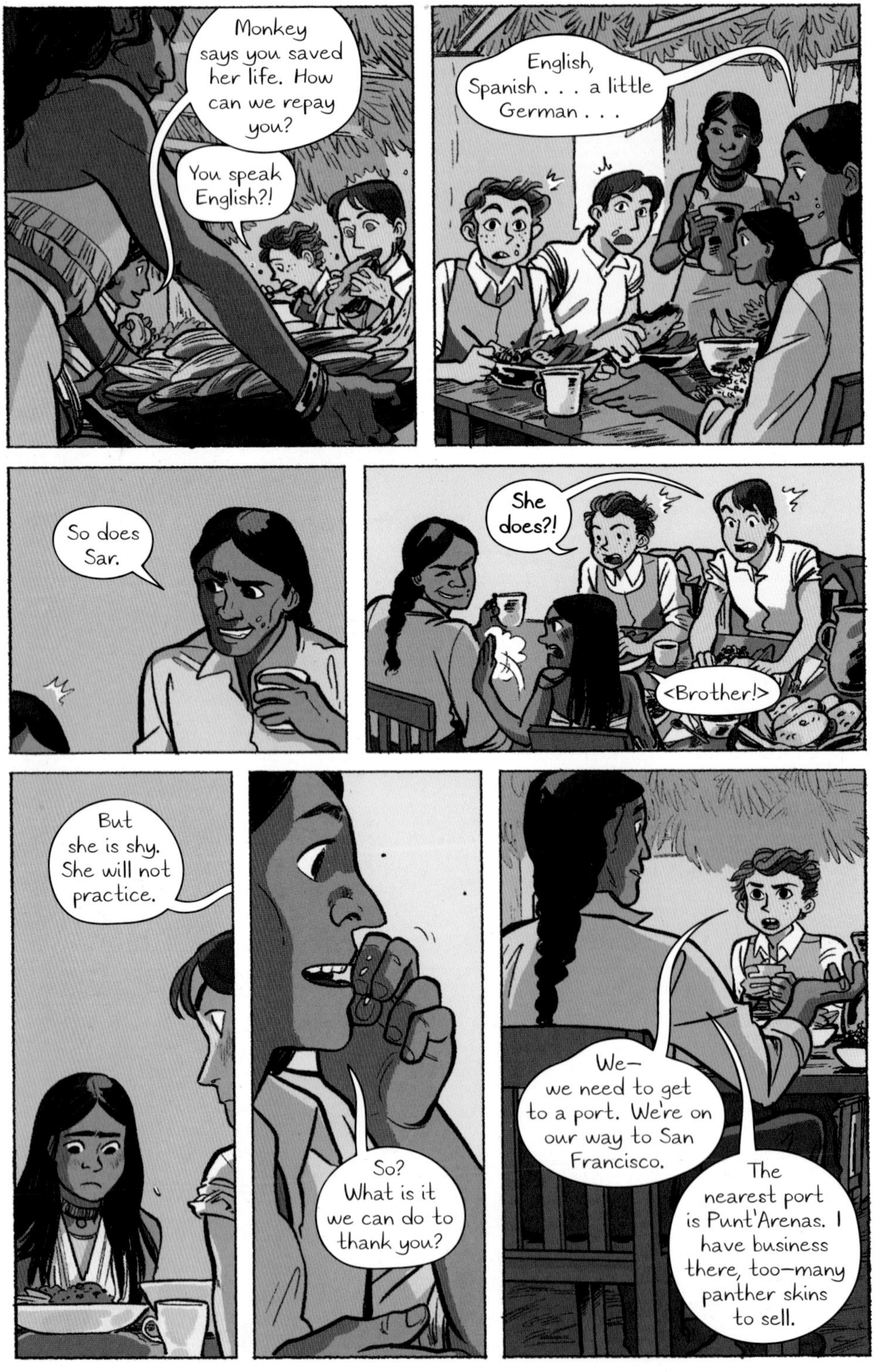
Monkey says you saved her life. How can we repay you?
You speak English?!
English, Spanish . . . a little German . . .
So does Sar.
She does?!
<Brother!>
But she is shy. She will not practice.
So? What is it we can do to thank you?
We— we need to get to a port. We're on our way to San Francisco.
The nearest port is Punt'Arenas. I have business there, too—many panther skins to sell.

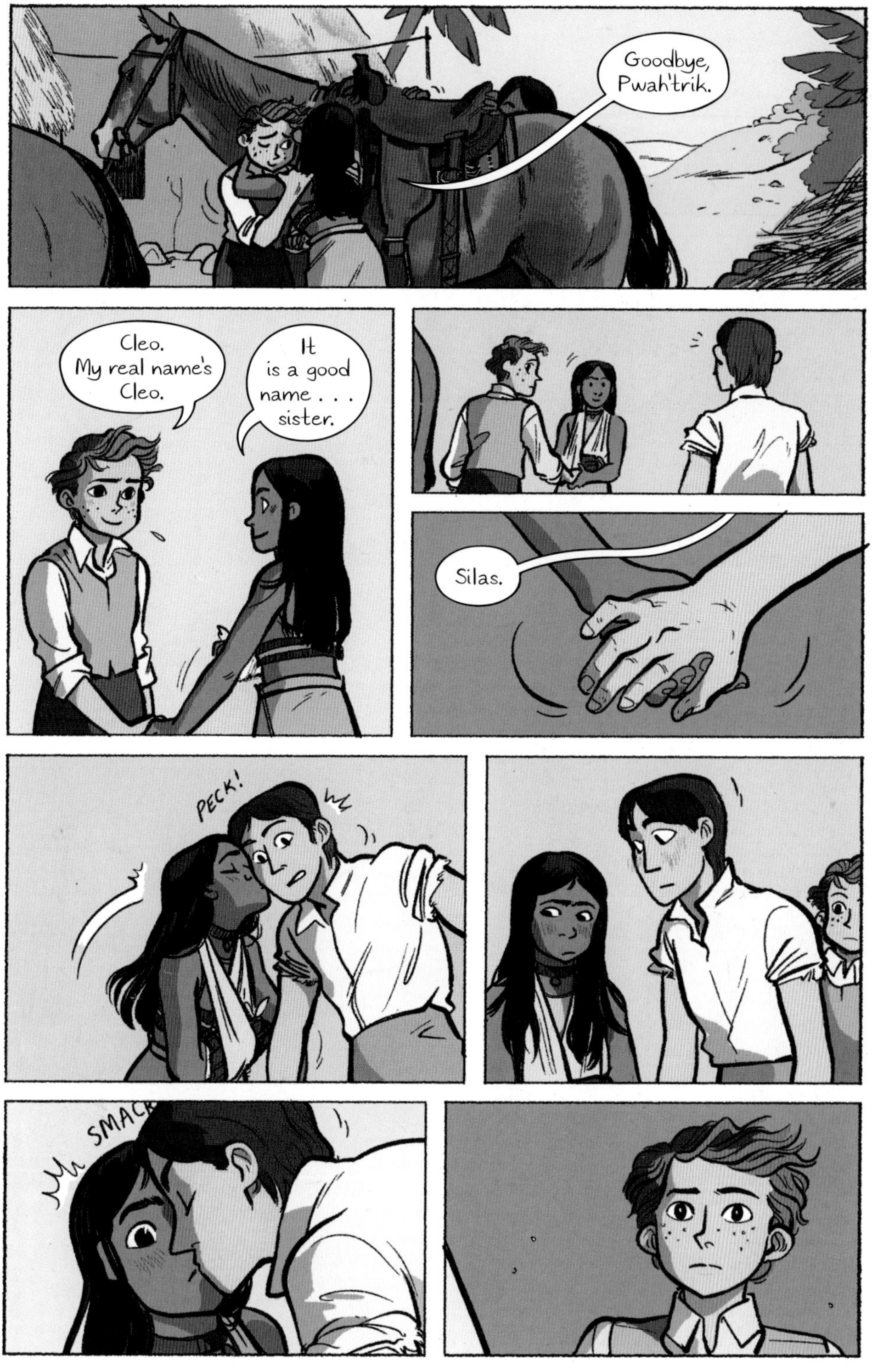
Goodbye, Pwah'trik.
Cleo. My real name's Cleo.
It is a good name . . . sister.
Silas.
PECK!
SMACK

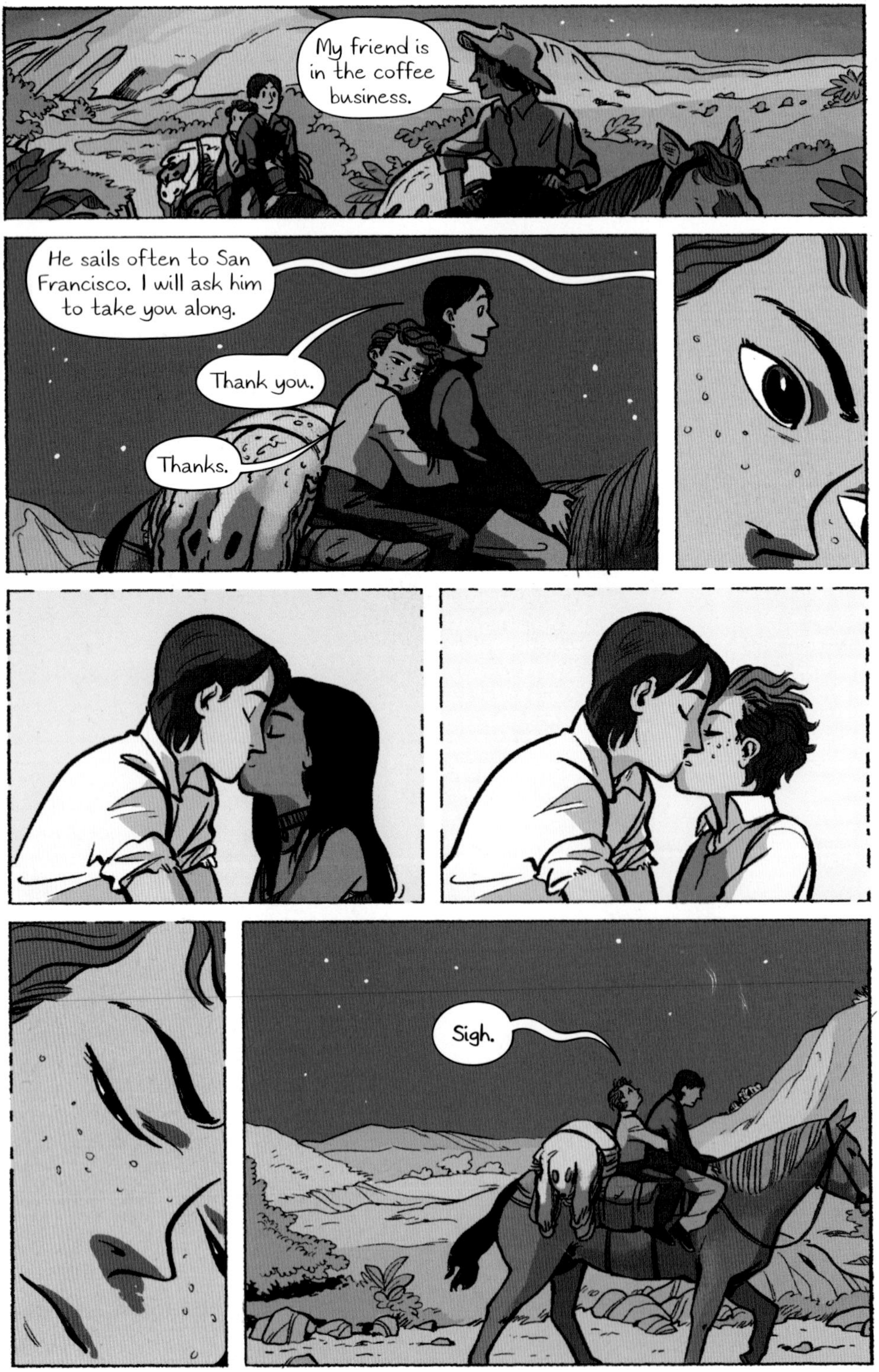
My friend is in the coffee business.
He sails often to San Francisco. I will ask him to take you along.
Thank you.
Thanks.
Sigh.

CHAPTER EIGHT
EL CALEUCHE

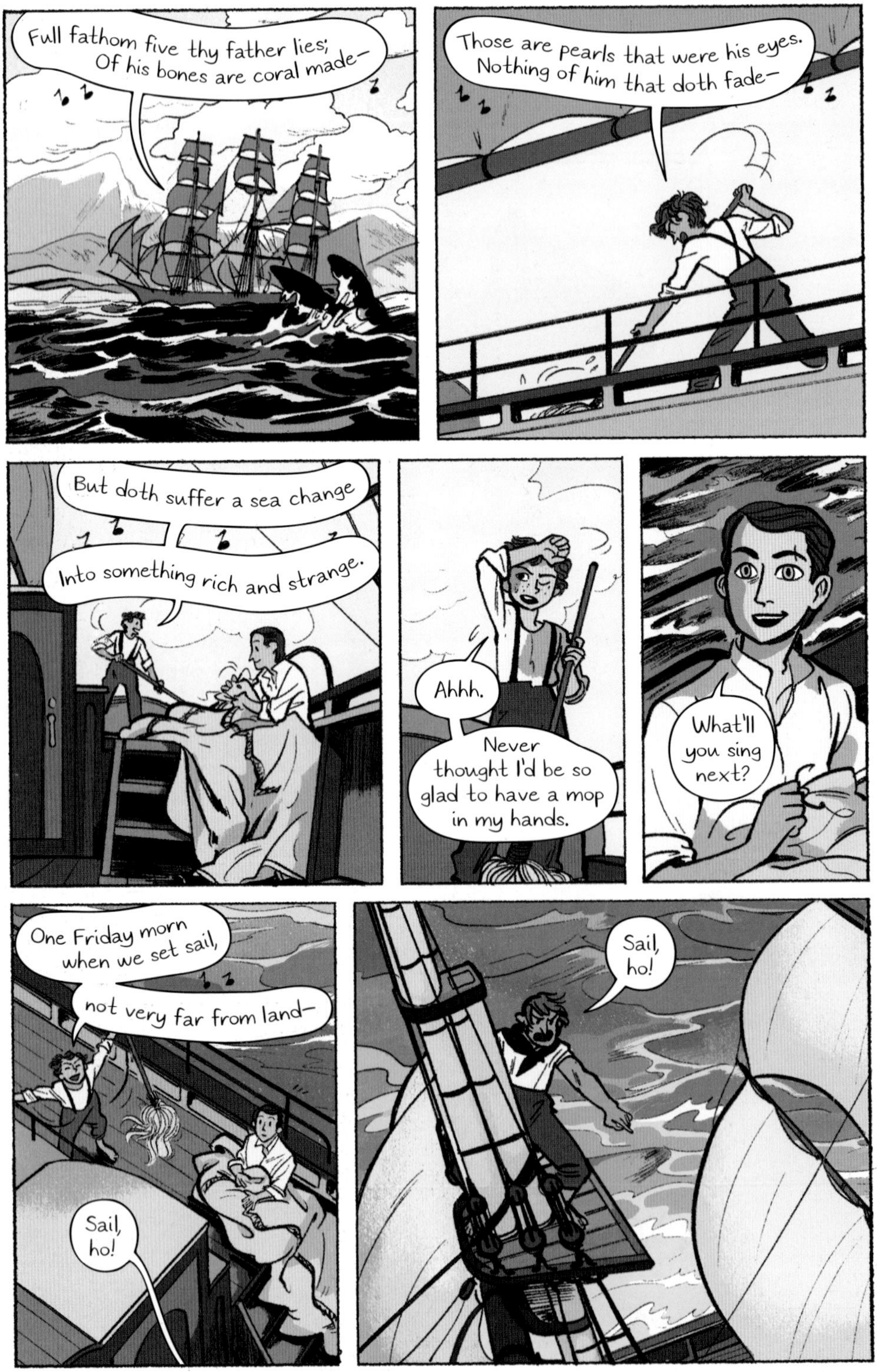

Full fathom five thy father lies;
Of his bones are coral made-
Those are pearls that were his eyes.
Nothing of him that doth fade-
But doth suffer a sea change
Into something rich and strange.
Ahhh.
Never thought I'd be so glad to have a mop in my hands.
What'll you sing next?
One Friday morn when we set sail,
not very far from land-
Sail, ho!
Sail, ho!

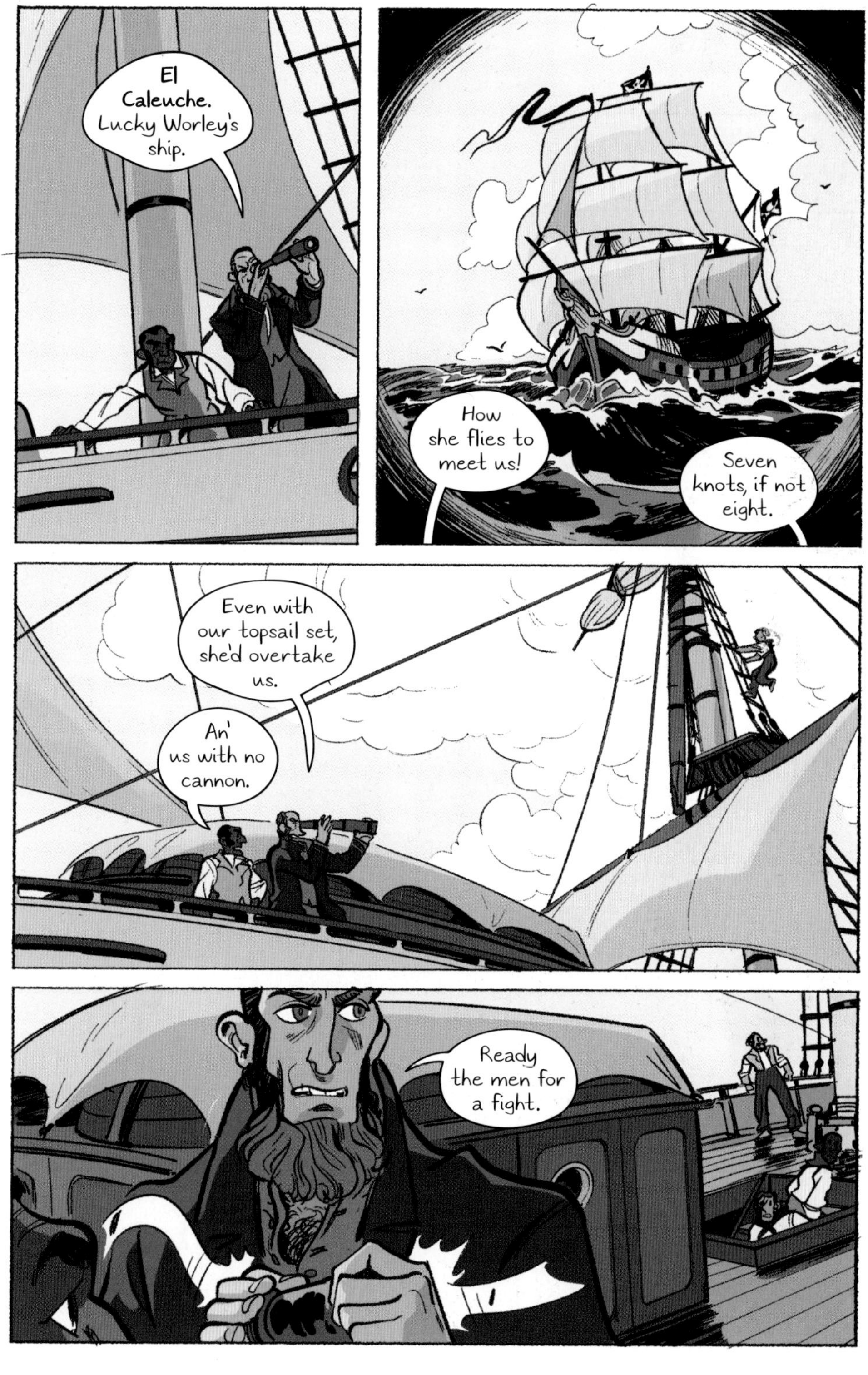
El Caleuche. Lucky Worley's ship.
How she flies to meet us!
Seven knots, if not eight.
Even with our topsail set, she'd overtake us.
An' us with no cannon.
Ready the men for a fight.

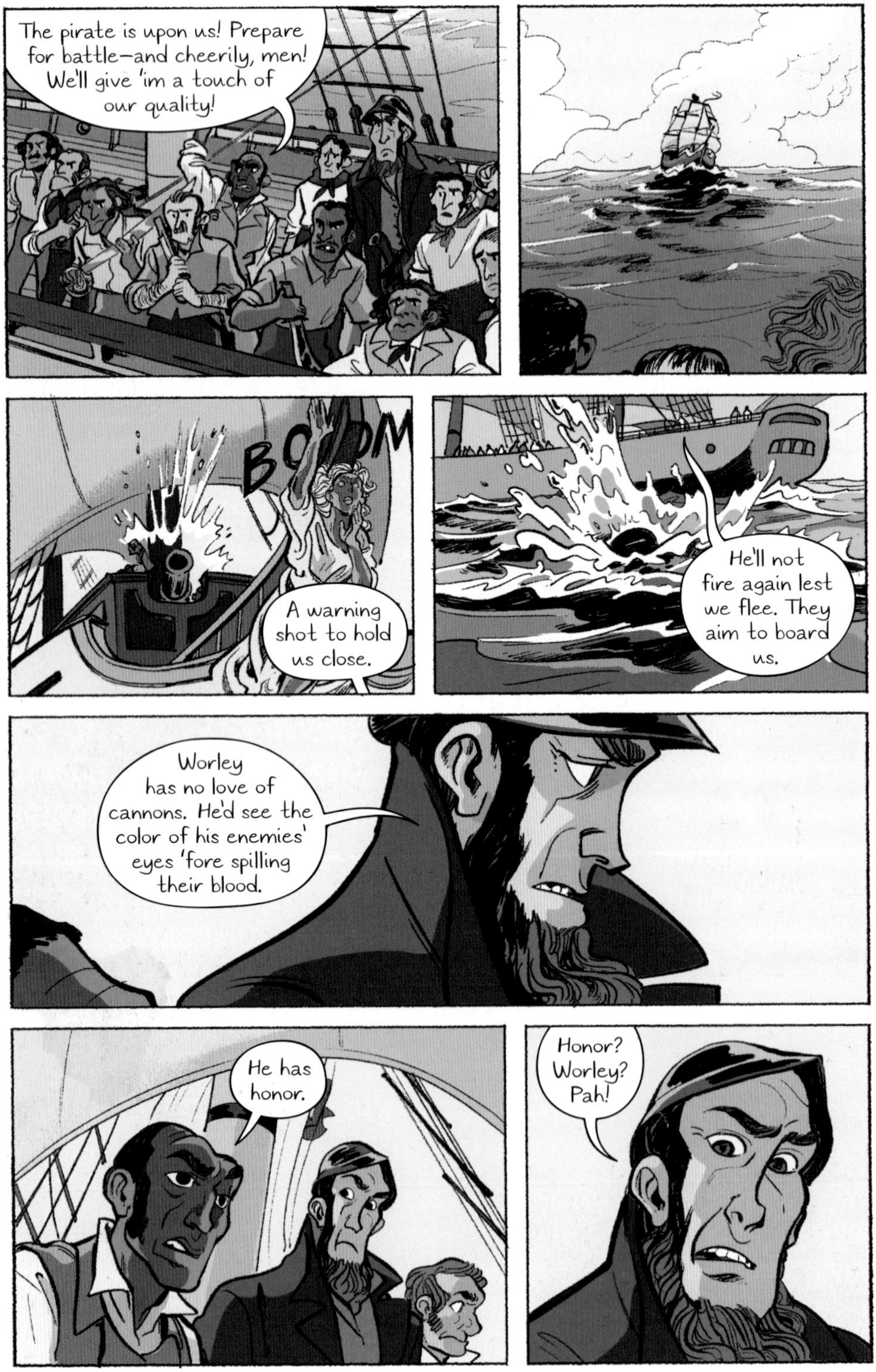
The pirate is upon us! Prepare for battle—and cheerily, men! We'll give 'im a touch of our quality!
BOOM
A warning shot to hold us close.
He'll not fire again lest we flee. They aim to board us.
Worley has no love of cannons. He'd see the color of his enemies' eyes 'fore spilling their blood.
He has honor.
Honor? Worley? Pah!

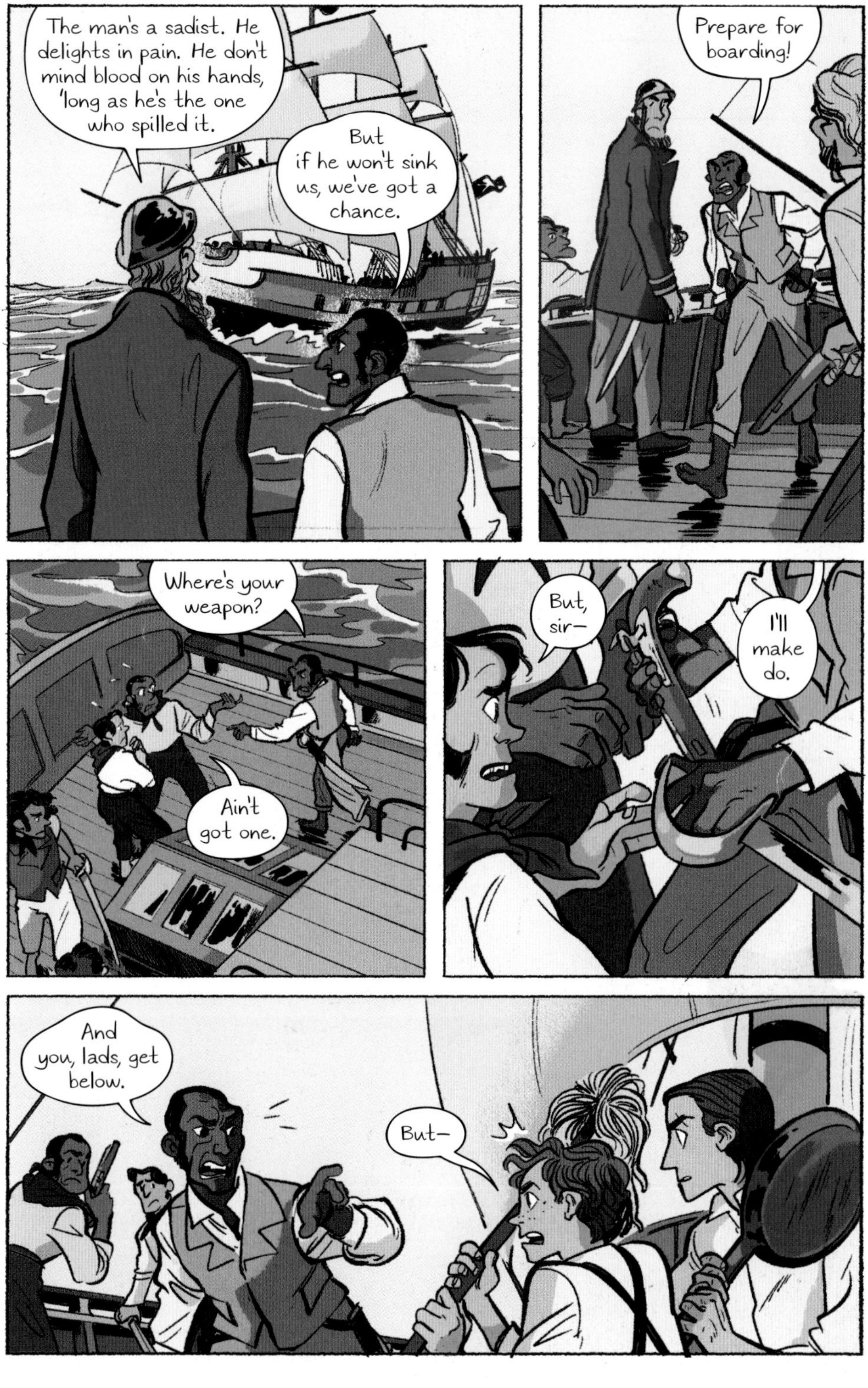

The man's a sadist. He delights in pain. He don't mind blood on his hands, 'long as he's the one who spilled it.
But if he won't sink us, we've got a chance.
Prepare for boarding!
Where's your weapon?
Ain't got one.
But, sir—
I'll make do.
And you, lads, get below.
But—

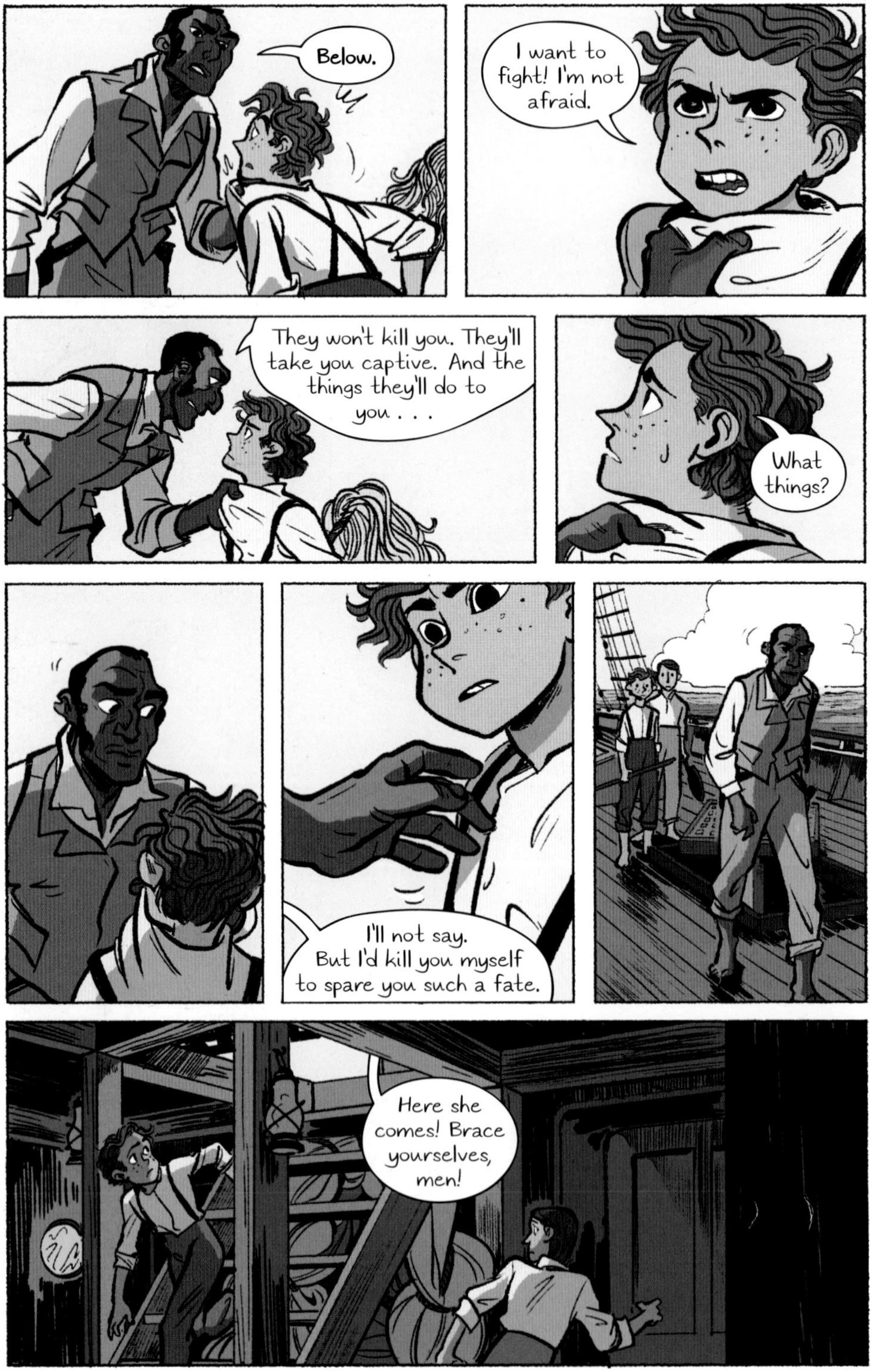
Below.
I want to fight! I'm not afraid.
They won't kill you. They'll take you captive. And the things they'll do to you . . .
What things?
I'll not say. But I'd kill you myself to spare you such a fate.
Here she comes! Brace yourselves, men!

Ready the irons!
Let fly!
SWSSSSH
Board, men! Board! Flesh your blades in their maggoty hearts!
CLANK!
Cut down the old dogs! Spare the bright eyes!

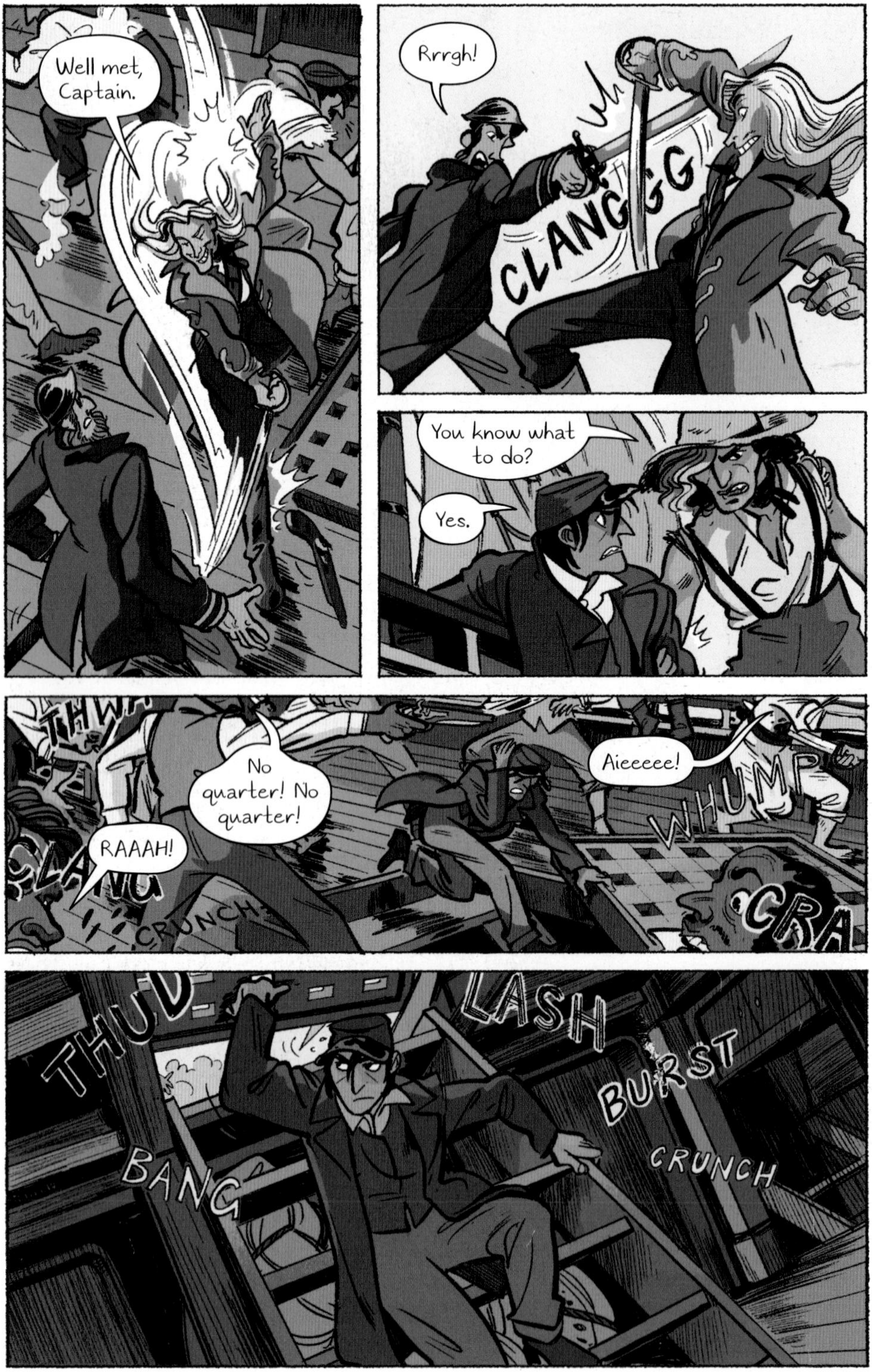
Well met, Captain.
Rrrgh!
CLANGGG
You know what to do?
Yes.
No quarter! No quarter!
RAAAH!
Aieeeee!
WHUMP
CRUNCH
CRA
THUD
LASH
BURST
BANG
CRUNCH

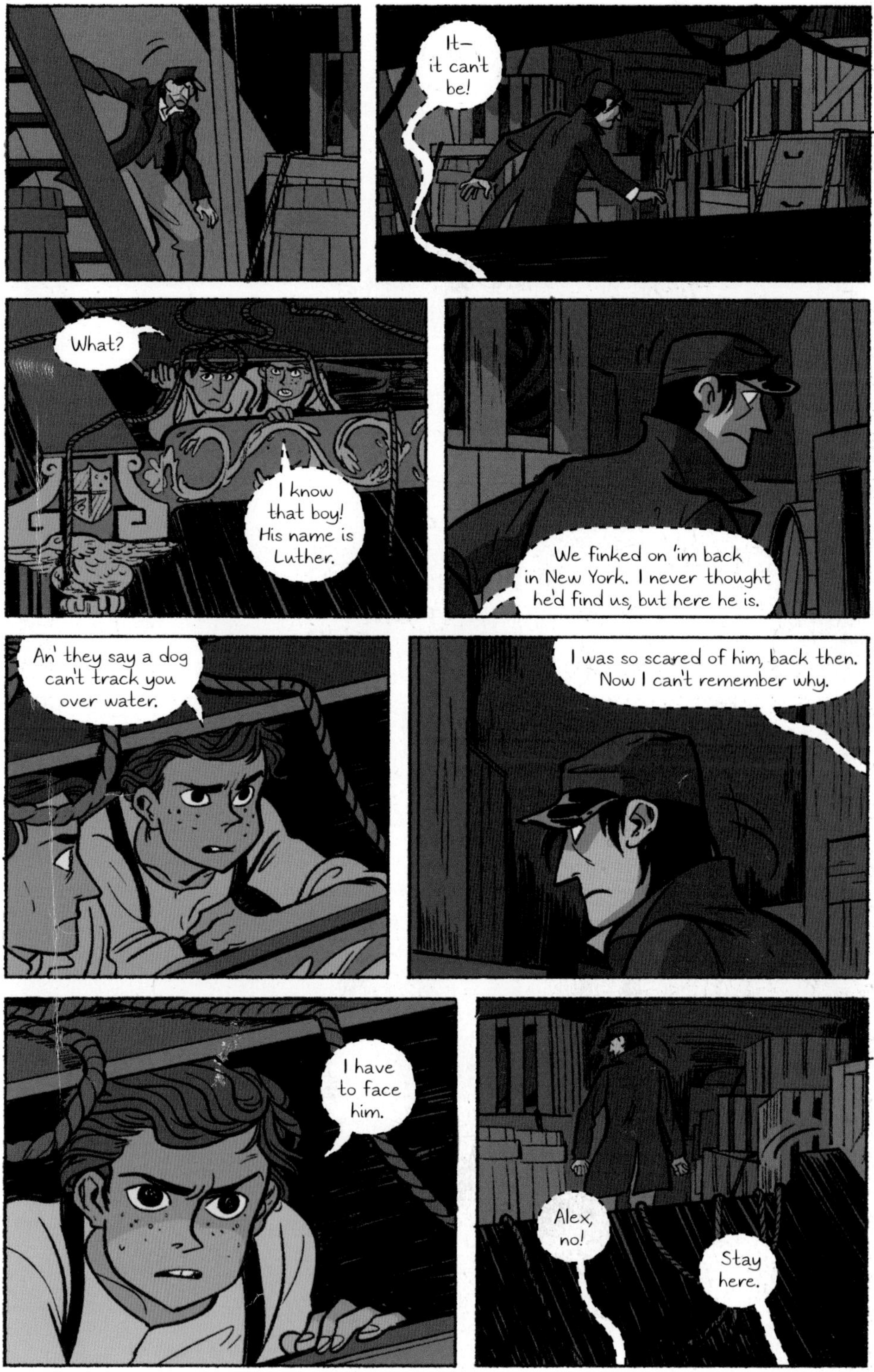
It—
it can't be!
What?
I know that boy! His name is Luther.
We finked on 'im back in New York. I never thought he'd find us, but here he is.
An' they say a dog can't track you over water.
I was so scared of him, back then. Now I can't remember why.
I have to face him.
Alex, no!
Stay here.

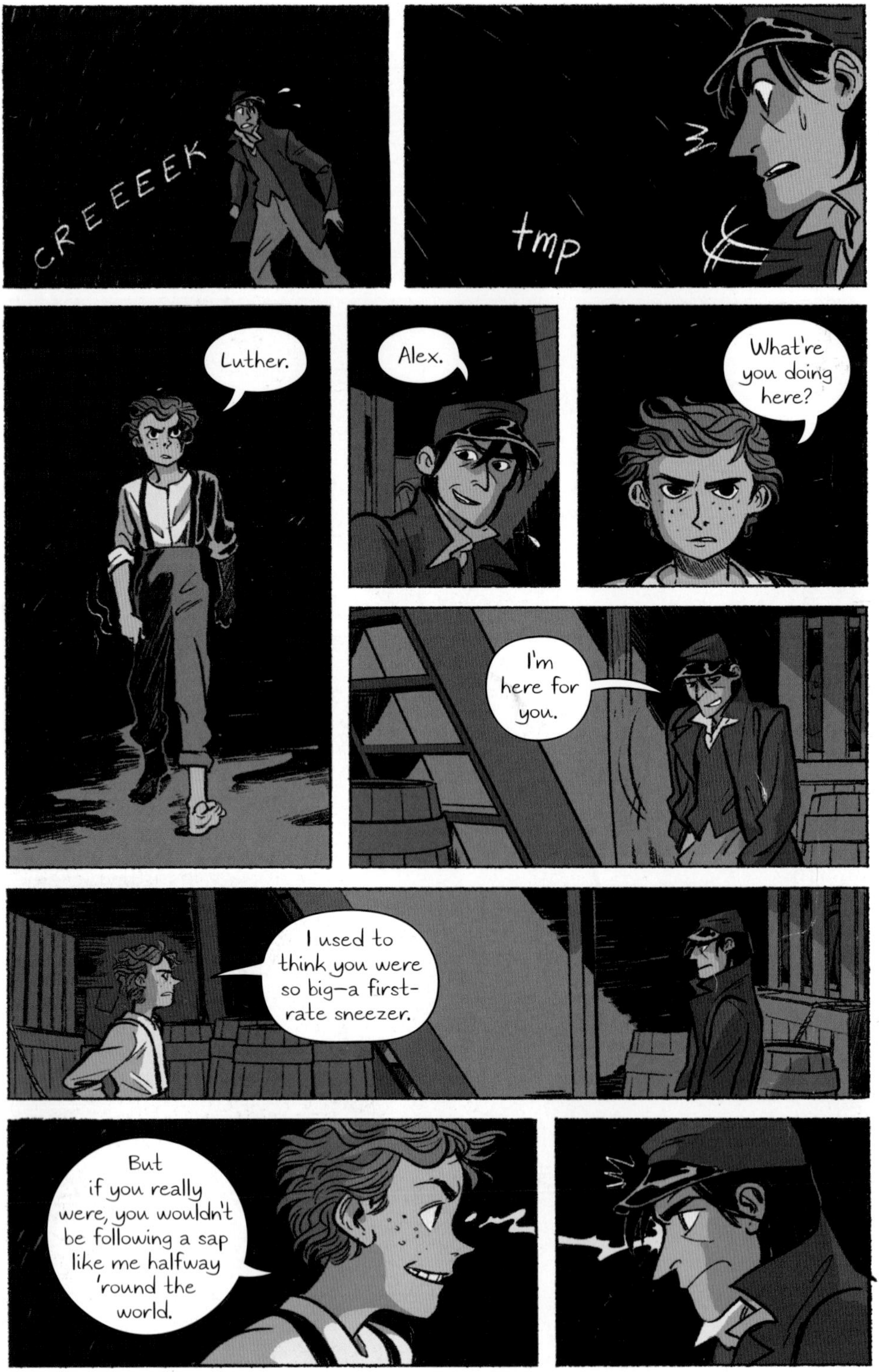
CREEEEK
tmp
Luther.
Alex.
What're you doing here?
I'm here for you.
I used to think you were so big—a first-rate sneezer.
But if you really were, you wouldn't be following a sap like me halfway 'round the world.

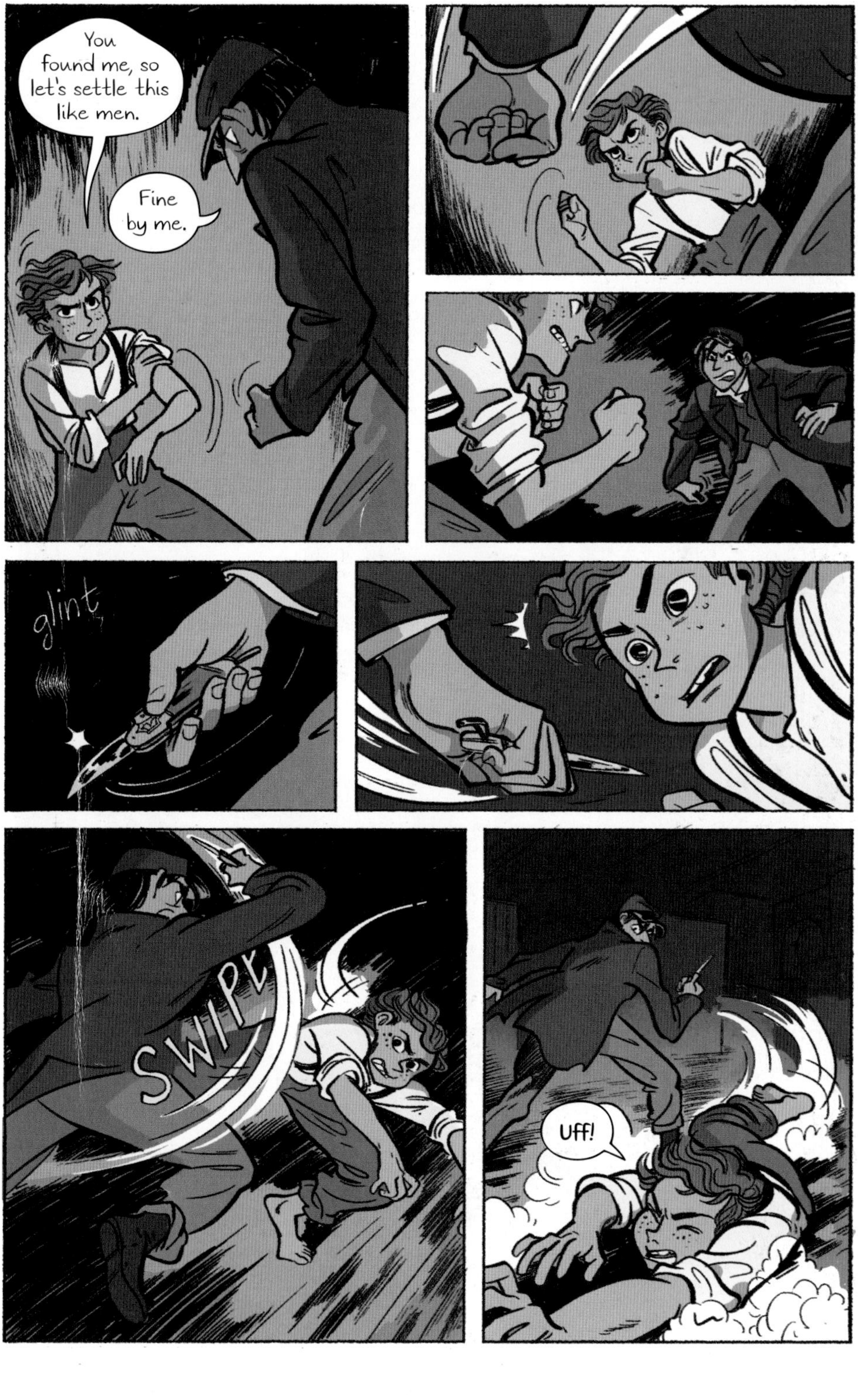
You found me, so let's settle this like men.
Fine by me.
glint
SWIPE
Uff!

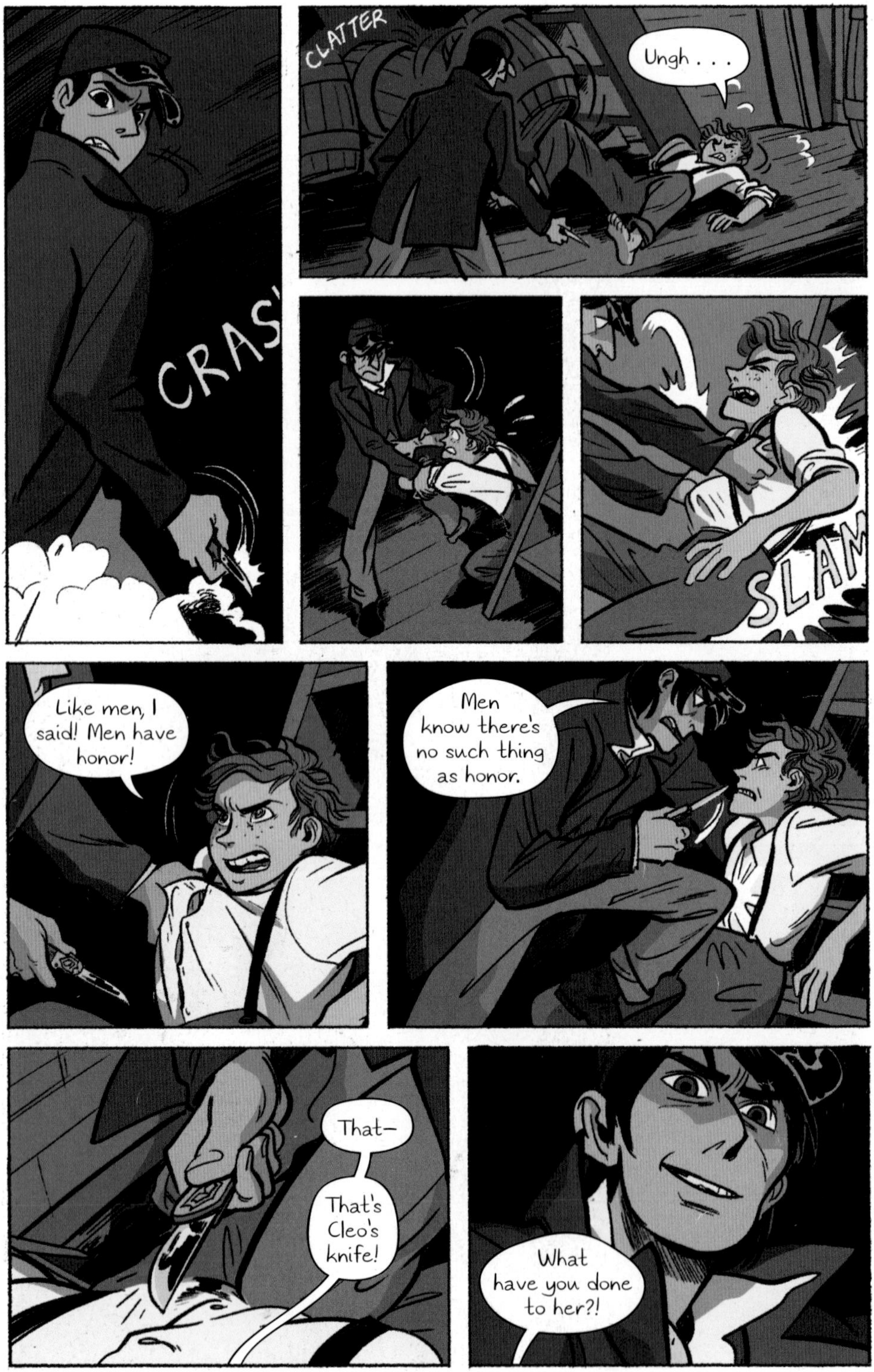
CRAS
CLATTER
Ungh . . .
SLAM
Like men, I said! Men have honor!
Men know there's no such thing as honor.
That—
That's Cleo's knife!
What have you done to her?!

What have you done?!

Nothing. She gave it up freely.

She gave **you** up.

Liar!

You're nothing to her. An inconvenience. Anyone would guess you're her kid brother, not her twin.

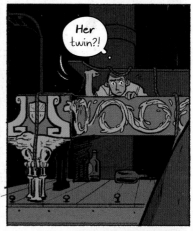

Her twin?!

She'd never give up the knife. You killed her!

NO!

I love her!

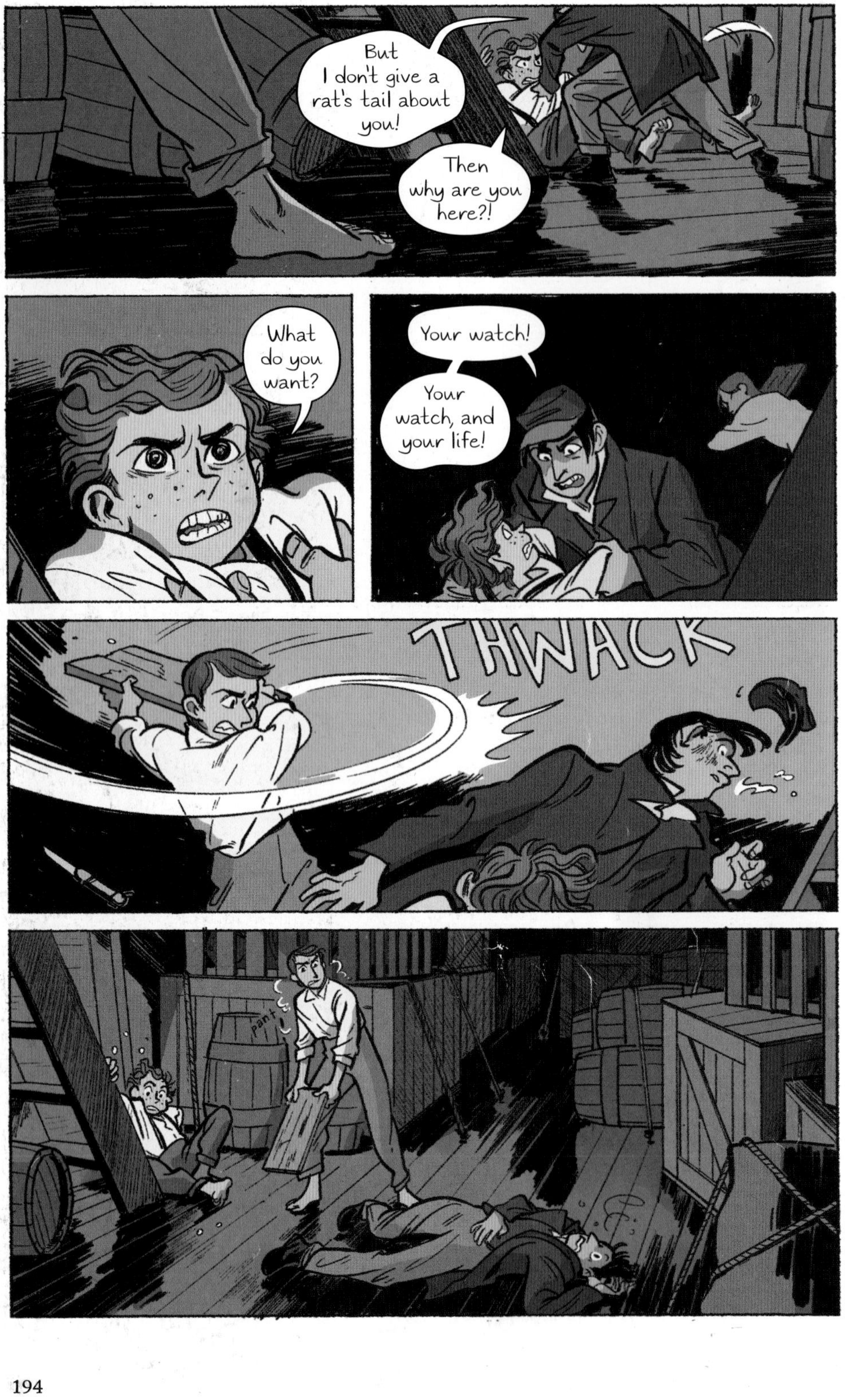
But I don't give a rat's tail about you!
Then why are you here?!
What do you want?
Your watch!
Your watch, and your life!
THWACK
pant

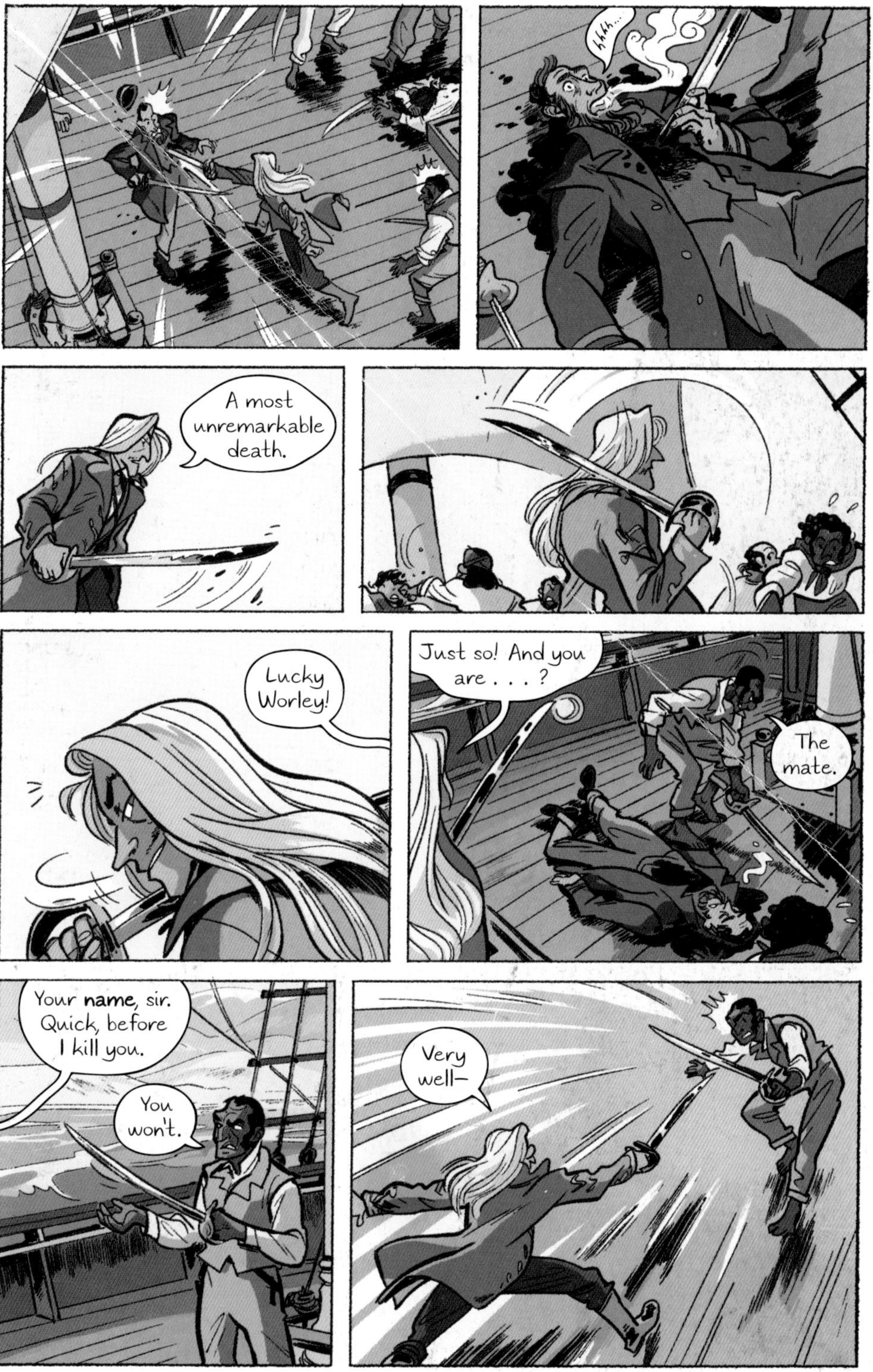
hhhh...
A most unremarkable death.
Lucky Worley!
Just so! And you are . . . ?
The mate.
Your name, sir. Quick, before I kill you.
You won't.
Very well—

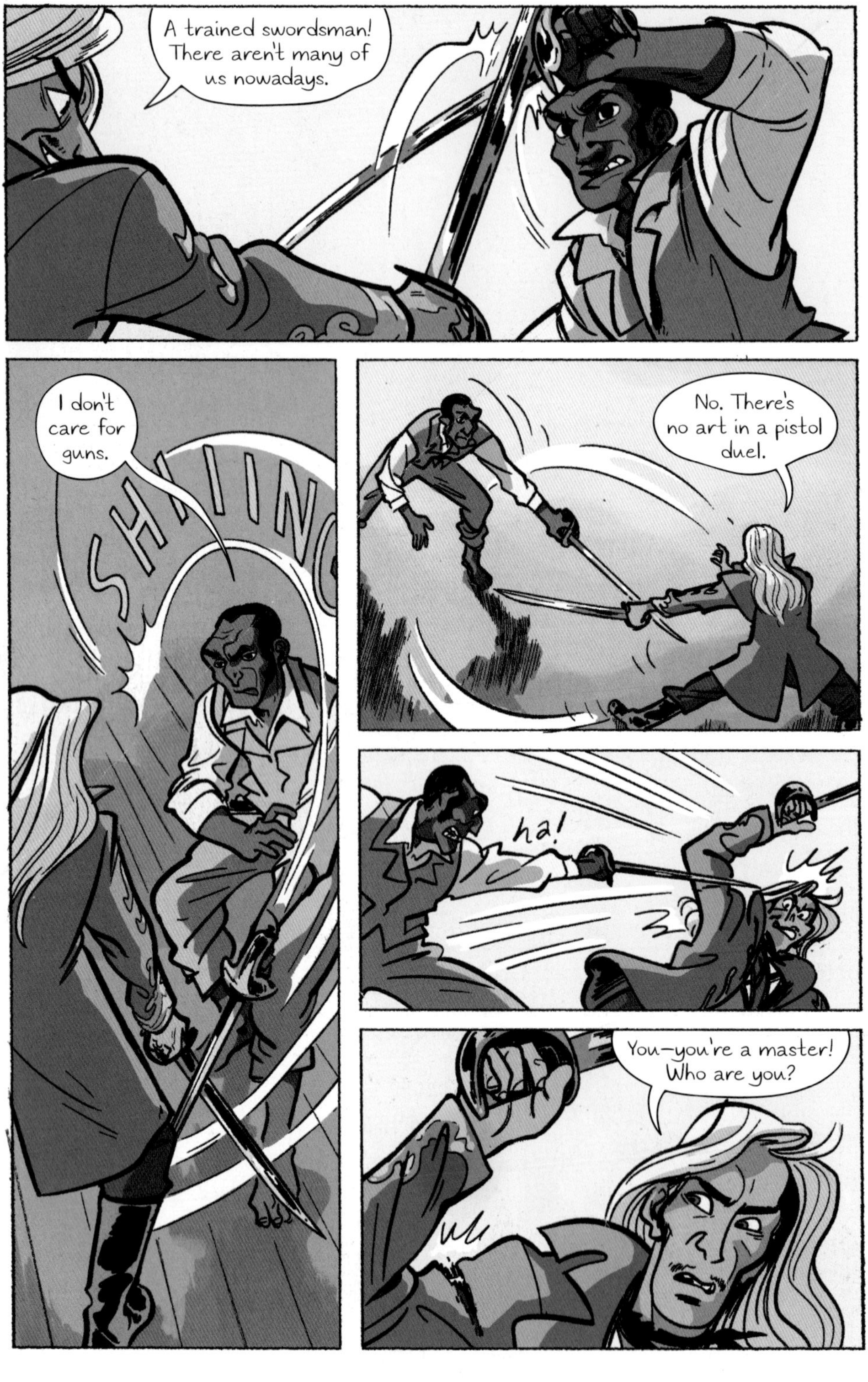
A trained swordsman! There aren't many of us nowadays.
I don't care for guns.
SHIIING
No. There's no art in a pistol duel.
ha!
You—you're a master! Who are you?

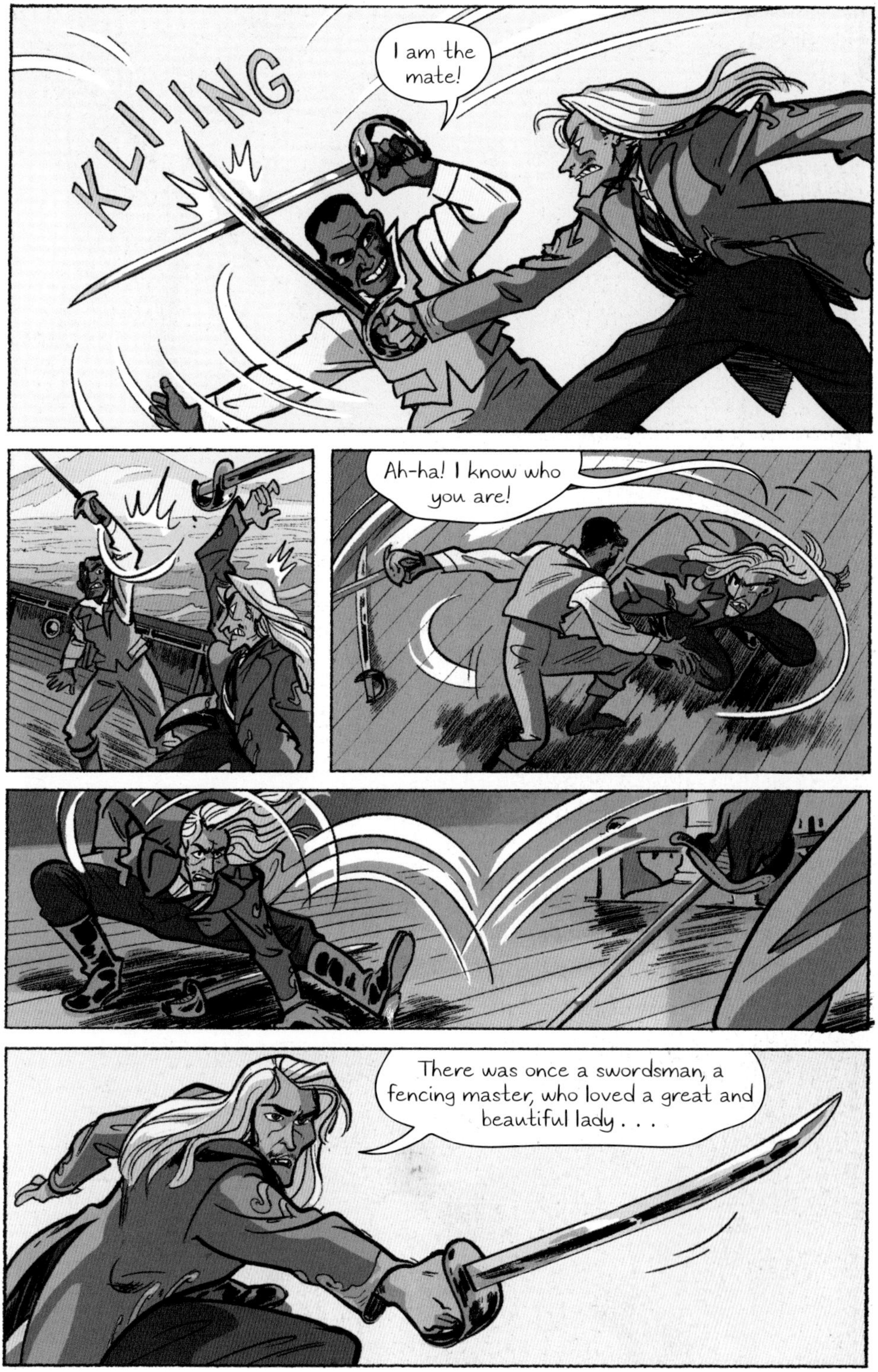
KLIIING
I am the mate!
Ah-ha! I know who you are!
There was once a swordsman, a fencing master, who loved a great and beautiful lady . . .

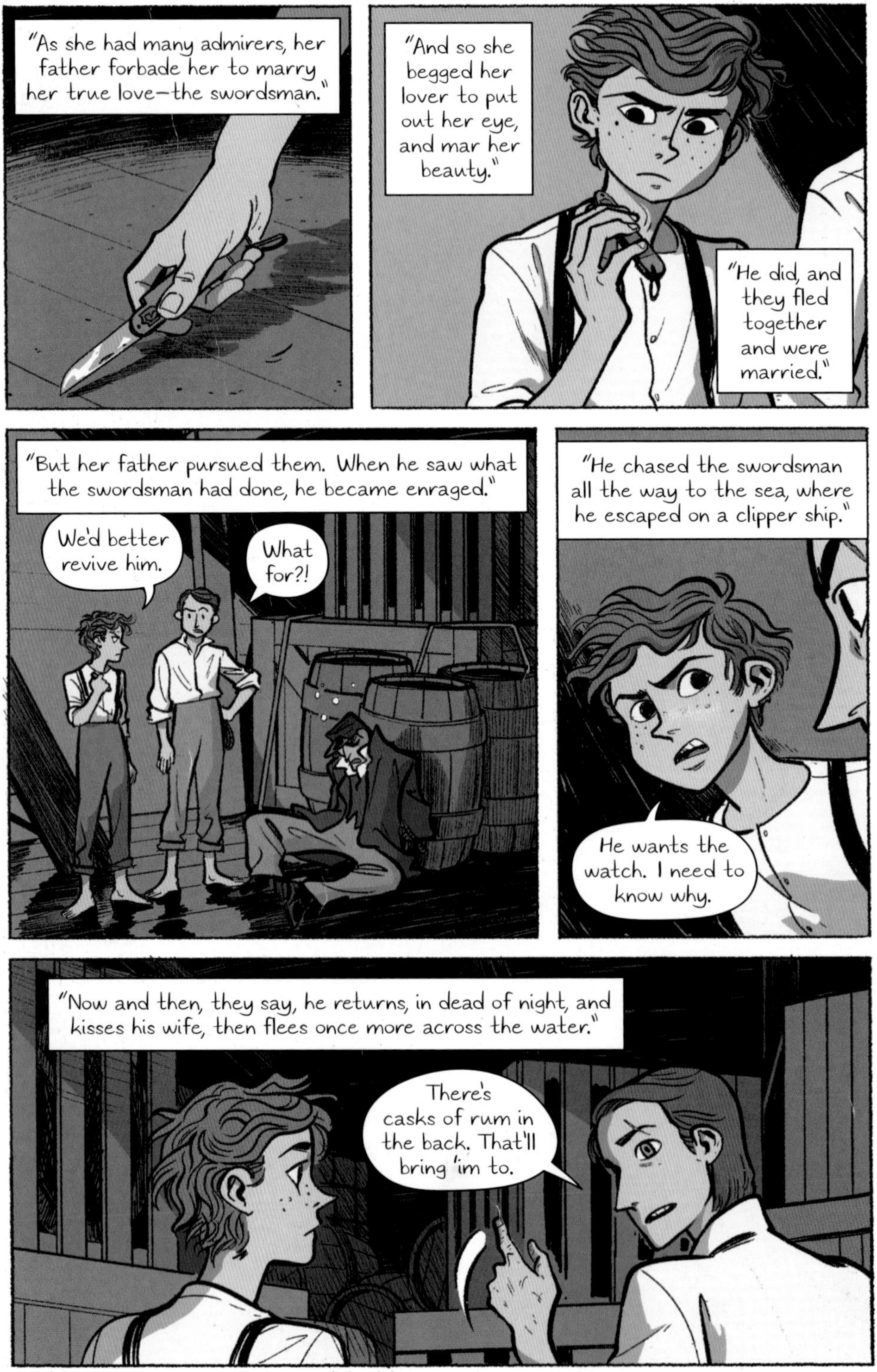
"As she had many admirers, her father forbade her to marry her true love—the swordsman."
"And so she begged her lover to put out her eye, and mar her beauty."
"He did, and they fled together and were married."
"But her father pursued them. When he saw what the swordsman had done, he became enraged."
We'd better revive him.
What for?!
"He chased the swordsman all the way to the sea, where he escaped on a clipper ship."
He wants the watch. I need to know why.
"Now and then, they say, he returns, in dead of night, and kisses his wife, then flees once more across the water."
There's casks of rum in the back. That'll bring 'im to.

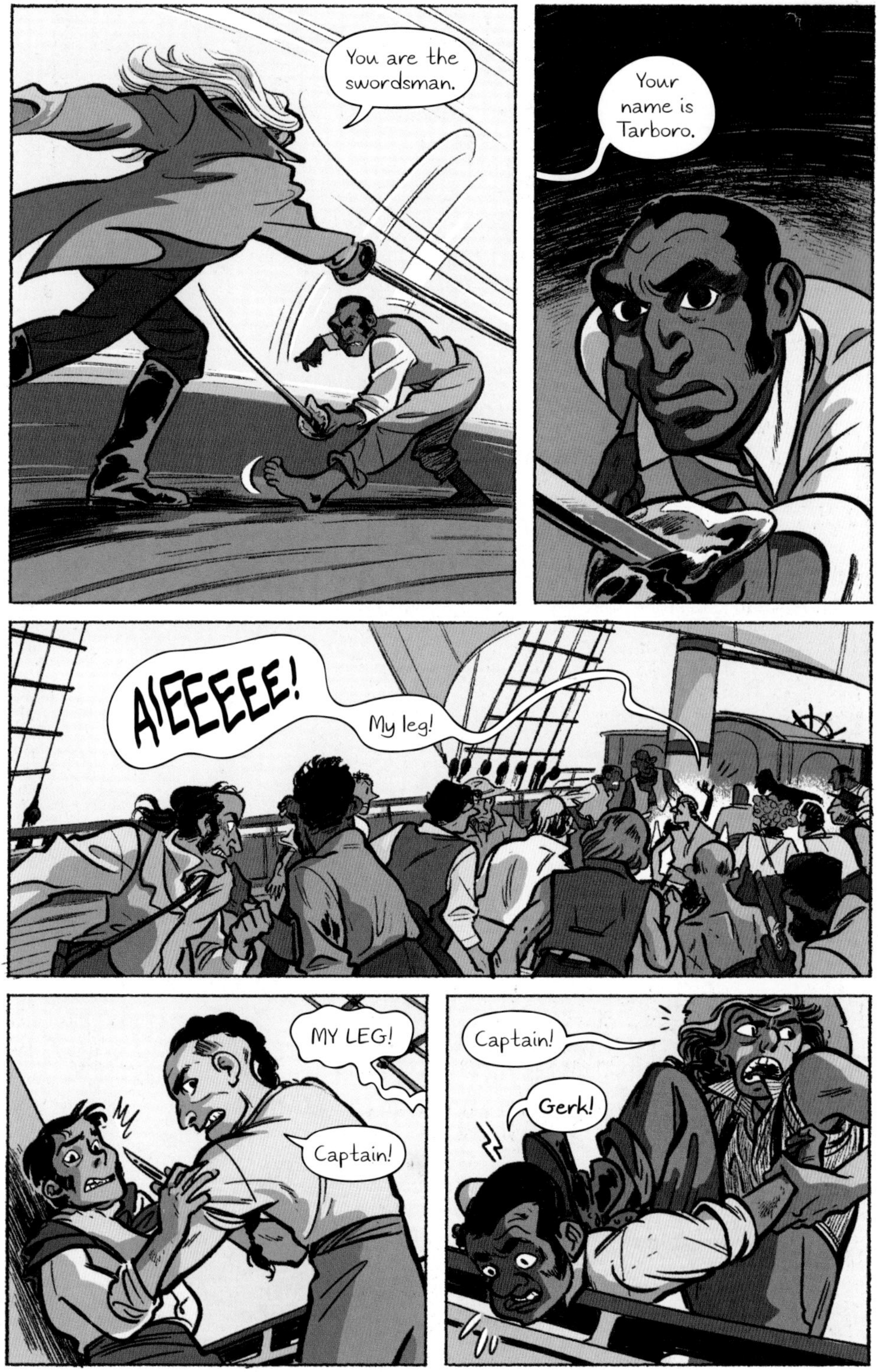
You are the swordsman.
Your name is Tarboro.
AIEEEEE!
My leg!
MY LEG!
Captain!
Captain!
Gerk!

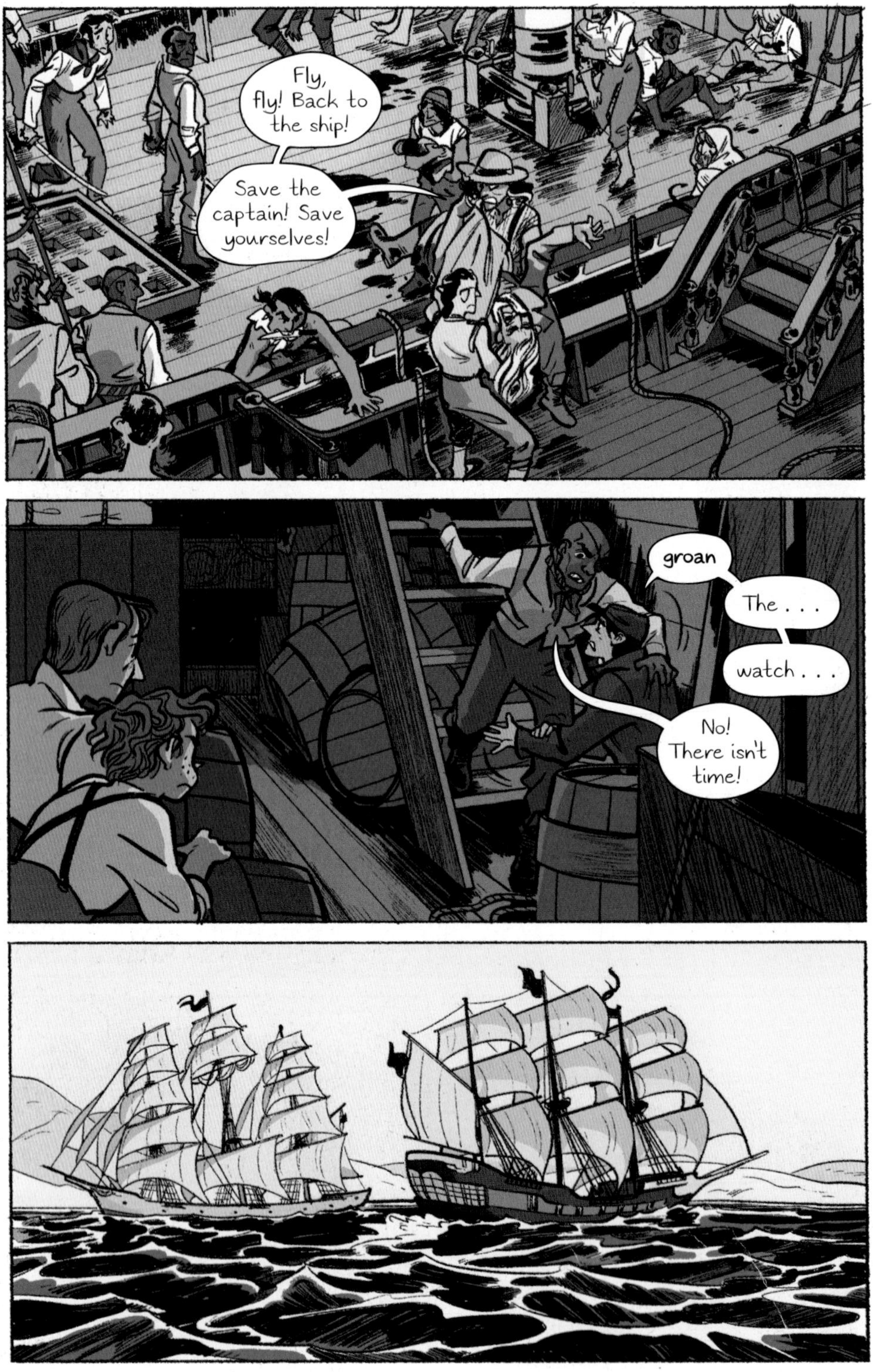
Fly, fly! Back to the ship!
Save the captain! Save yourselves!
groan
The . . .
watch . . .
No! There isn't time!

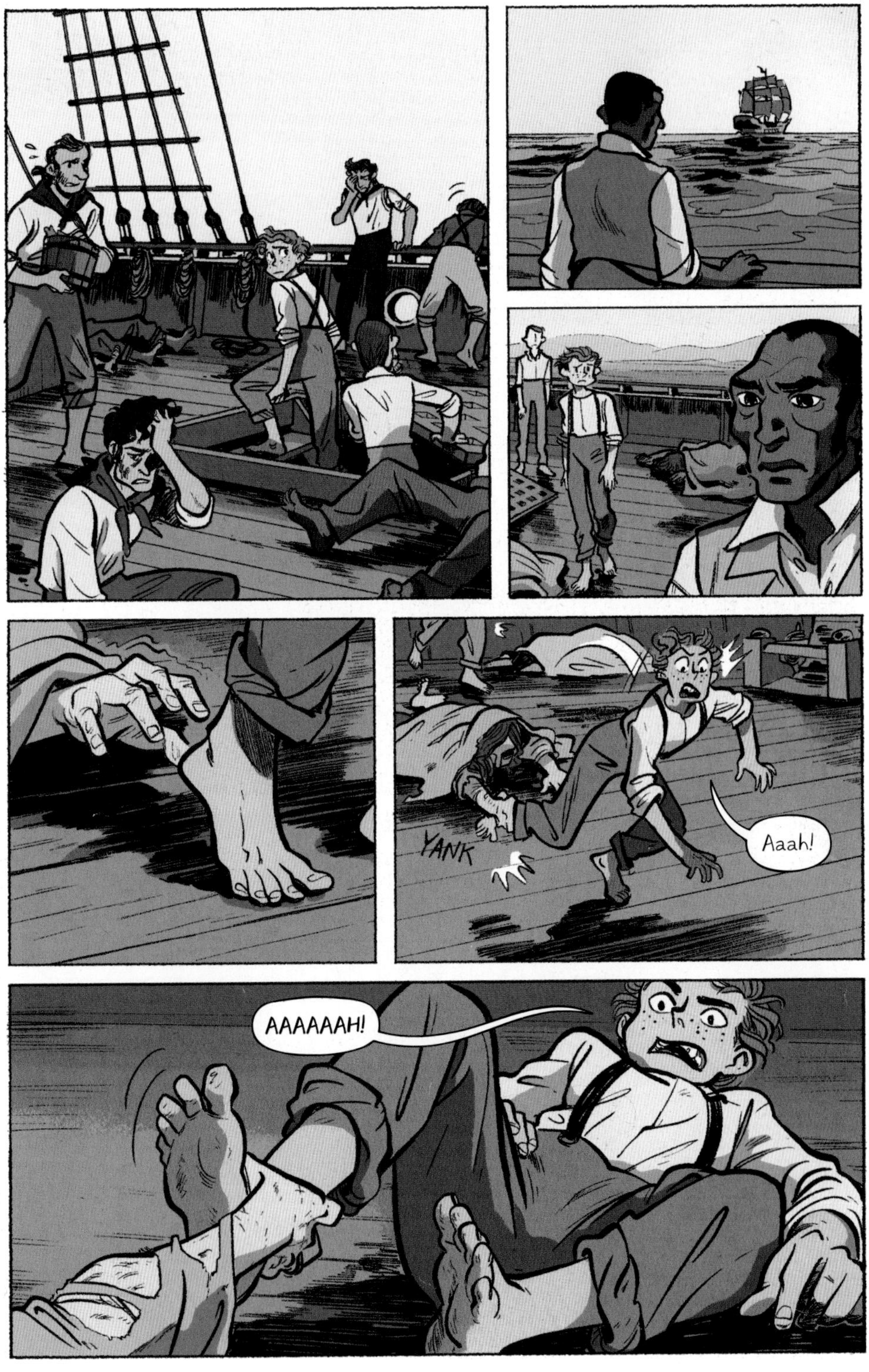
YANK
Aaah!
AAAAAAH!

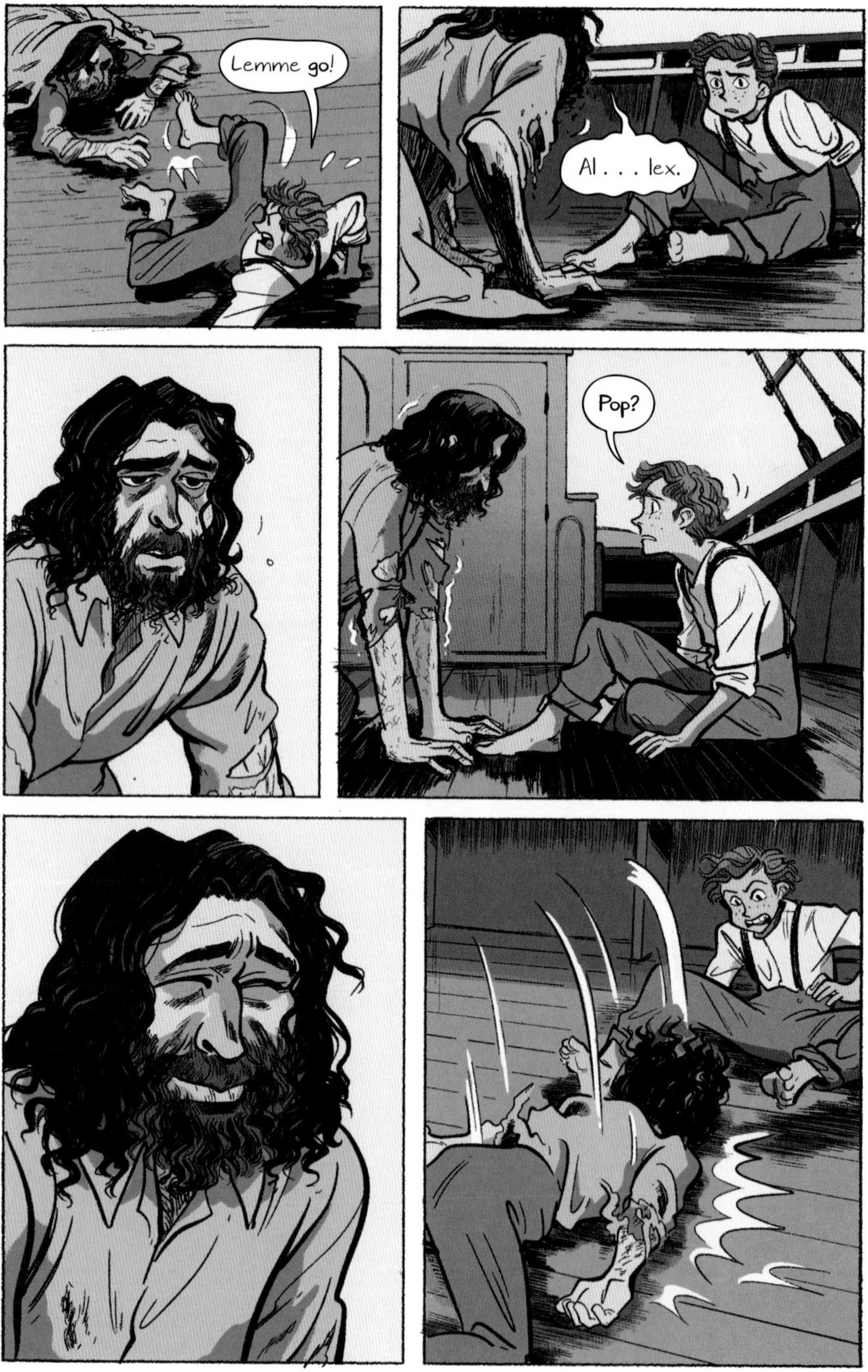
Lemme go!
Al . . . lex.
Pop?

CHAPTER NINE
CITY IN A CLOUD

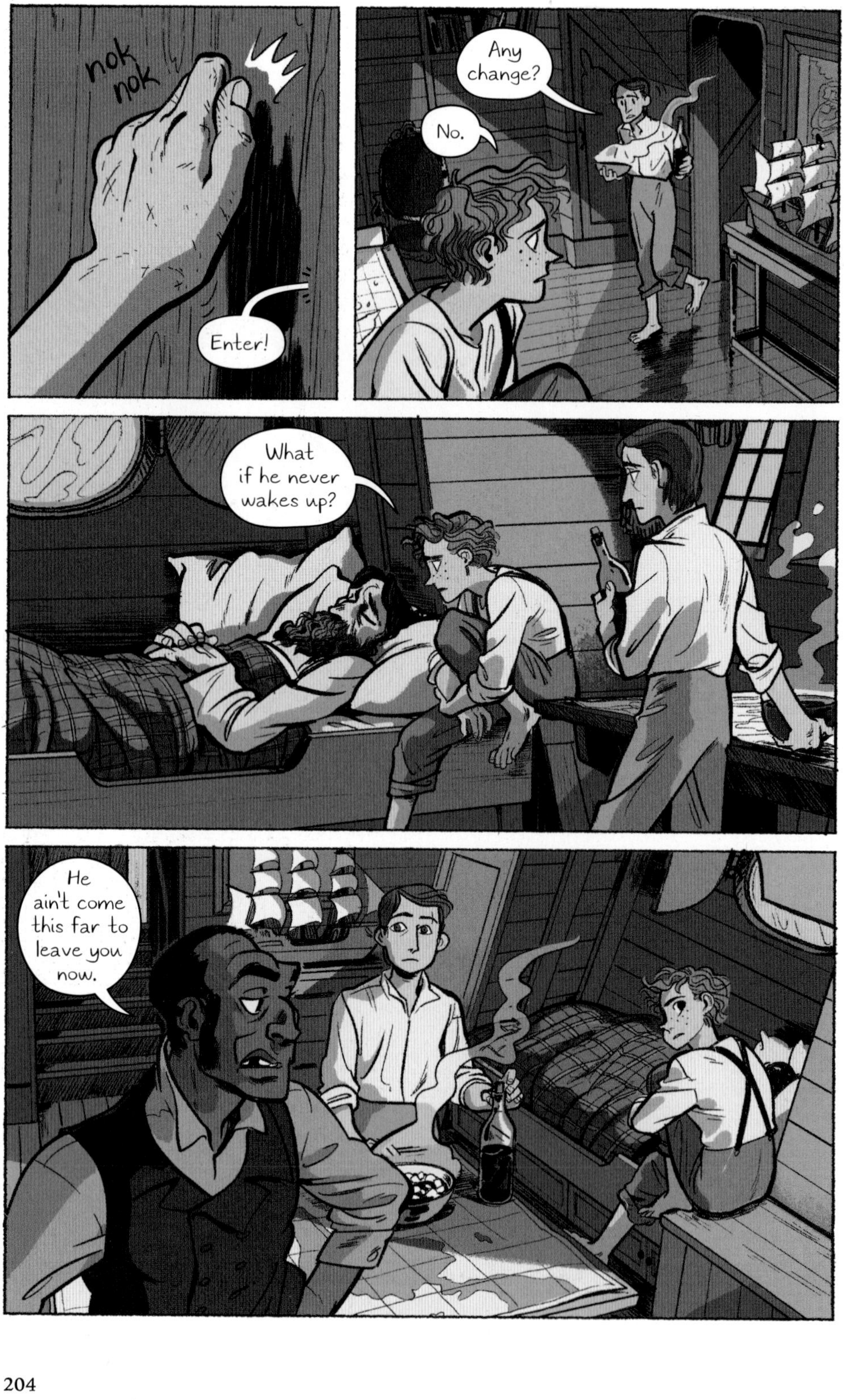
nok nok
Enter!
Any change?
No.
What if he never wakes up?
He ain't come this far to leave you now.

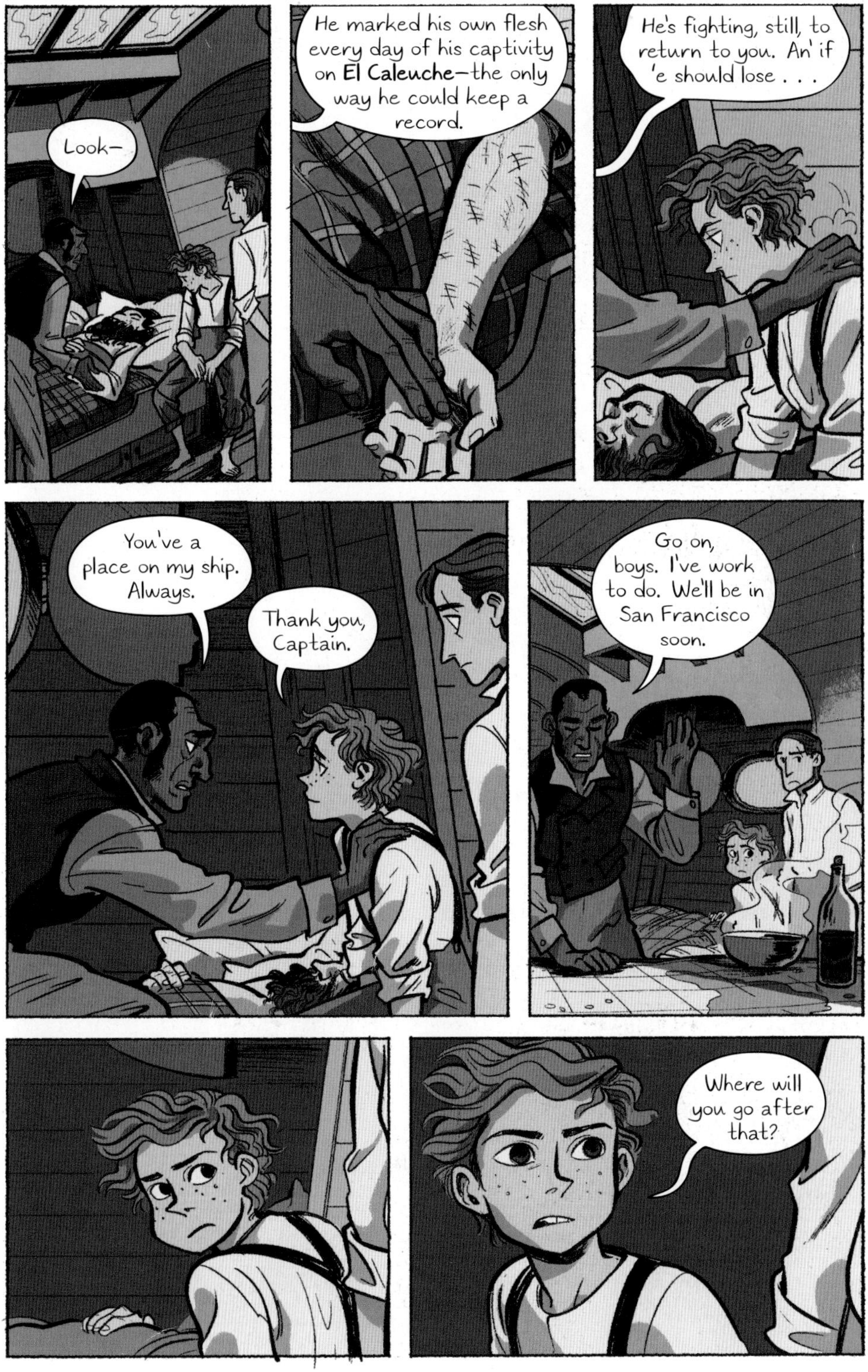

Look—
He marked his own flesh every day of his captivity on **El Caleuche**—the only way he could keep a record.
He's fighting, still, to return to you. An' if 'e should lose . . .
You've a place on my ship. Always.
Thank you, Captain.
Go on, boys. I've work to do. We'll be in San Francisco soon.
Where will you go after that?

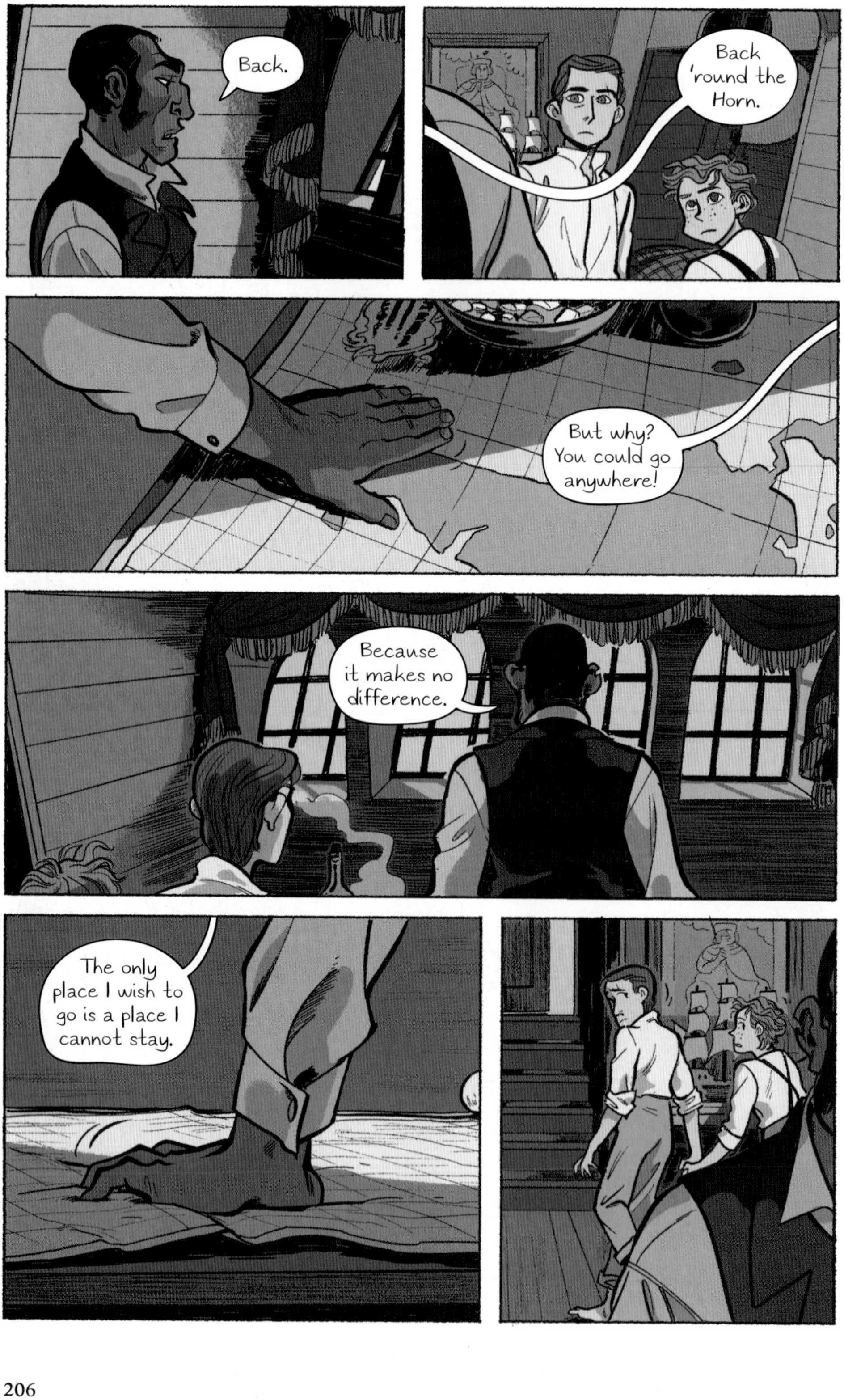
Back.
Back 'round the Horn.
But why? You could go anywhere!
Because it makes no difference.
The only place I wish to go is a place I cannot stay.

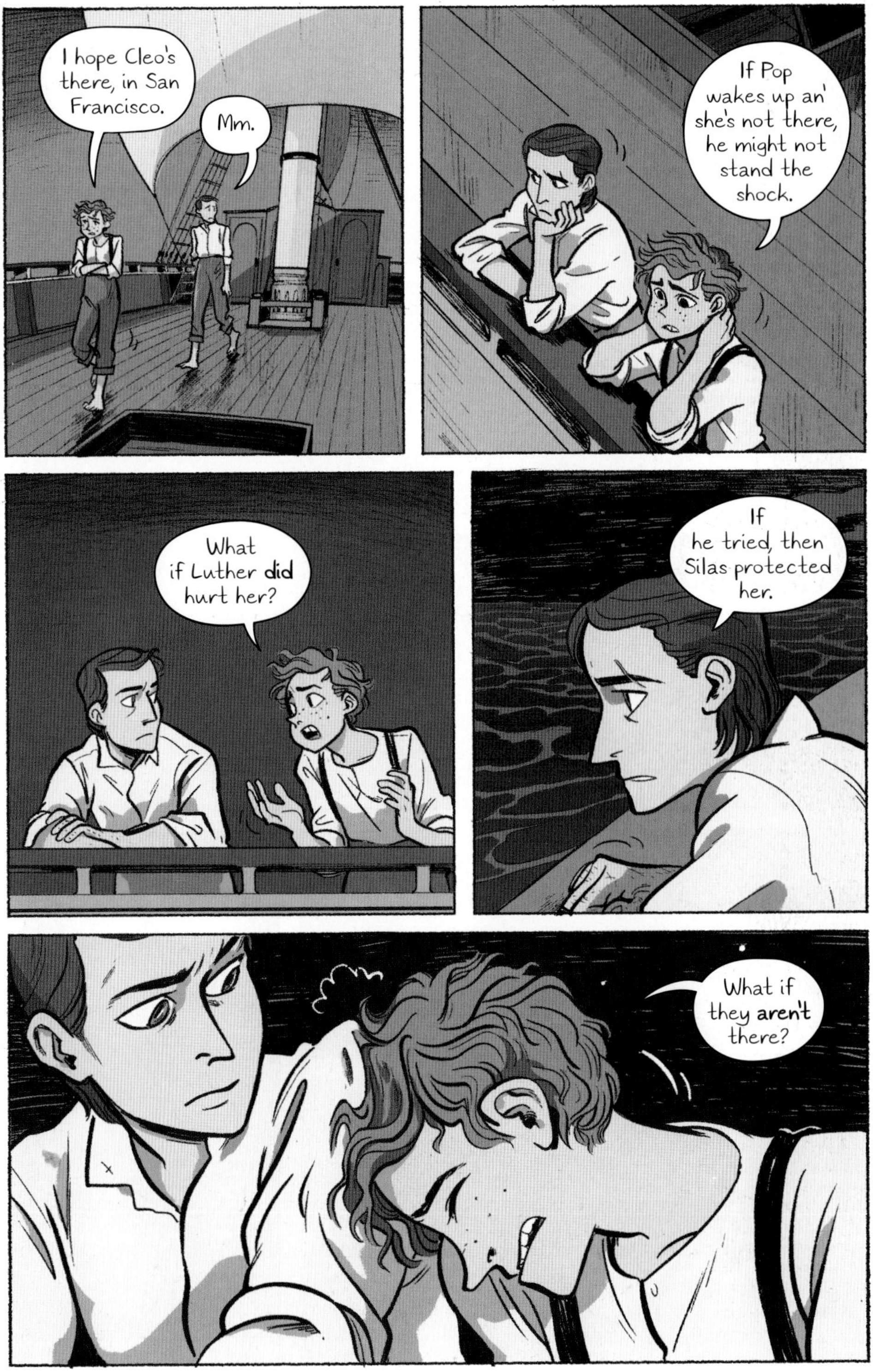
I hope Cleo's there, in San Francisco.
Mm.
If Pop wakes up an' she's not there, he might not stand the shock.
What if Luther **did** hurt her?
If he tried, then Silas protected her.
What if they **aren't** there?

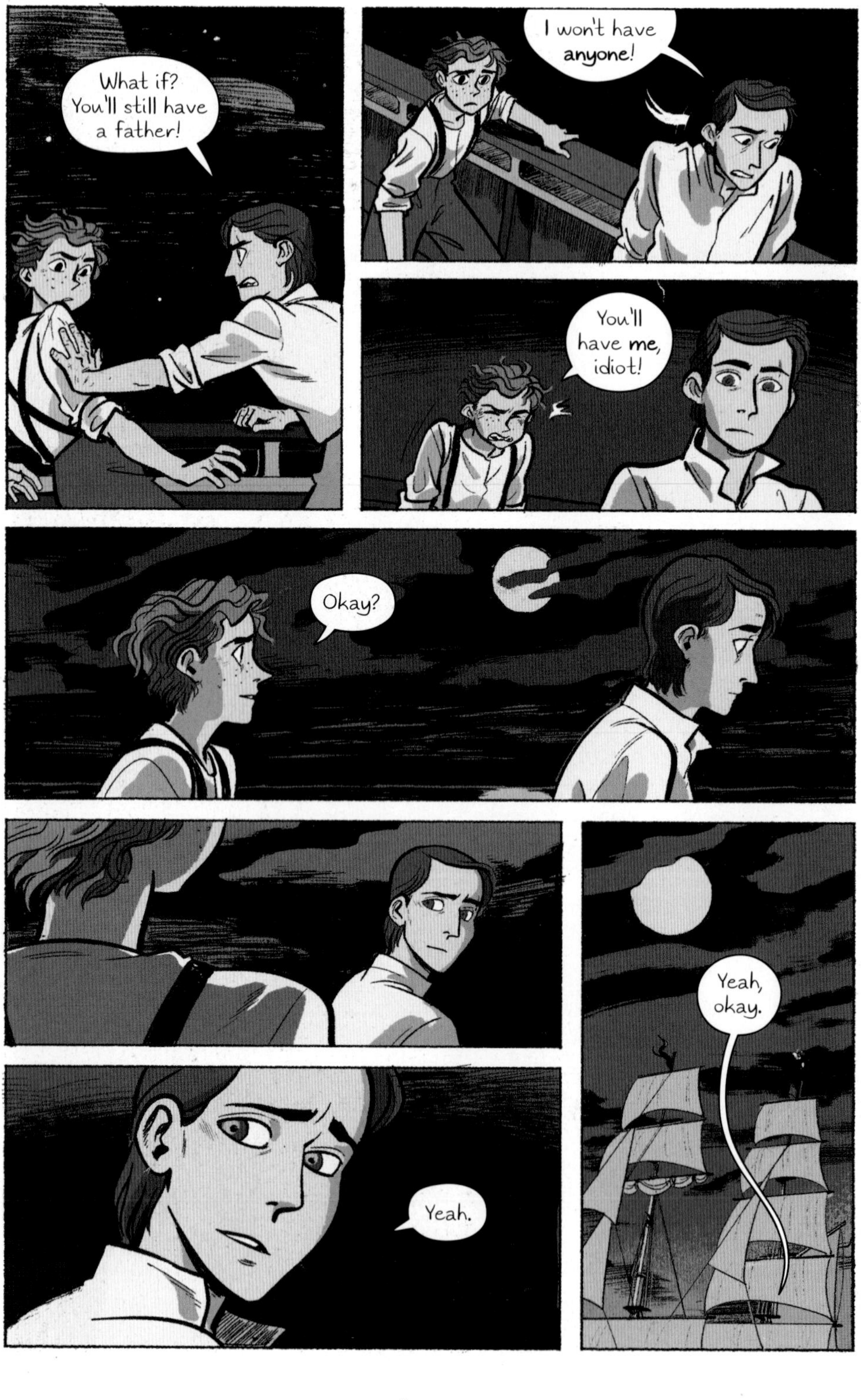
What if? You'll still have a father!
I won't have anyone!
You'll have me, idiot!
Okay?
Yeah, okay.
Yeah.

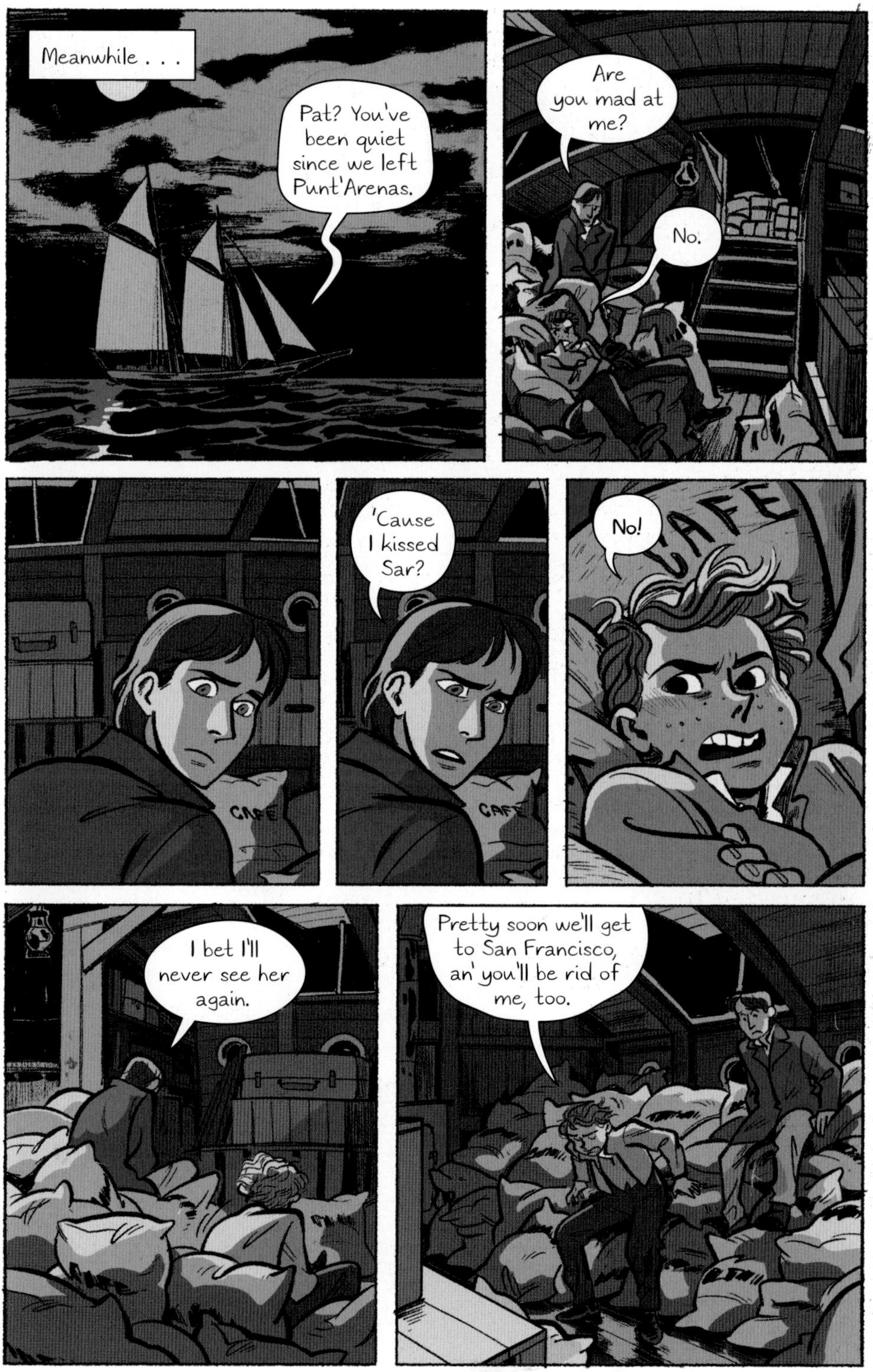
Meanwhile . . .
Pat? You've been quiet since we left Punt'Arenas.
Are you mad at me?
No.
'Cause I kissed Sar?
No!
I bet I'll never see her again.
Pretty soon we'll get to San Francisco, an' you'll be rid of me, too.

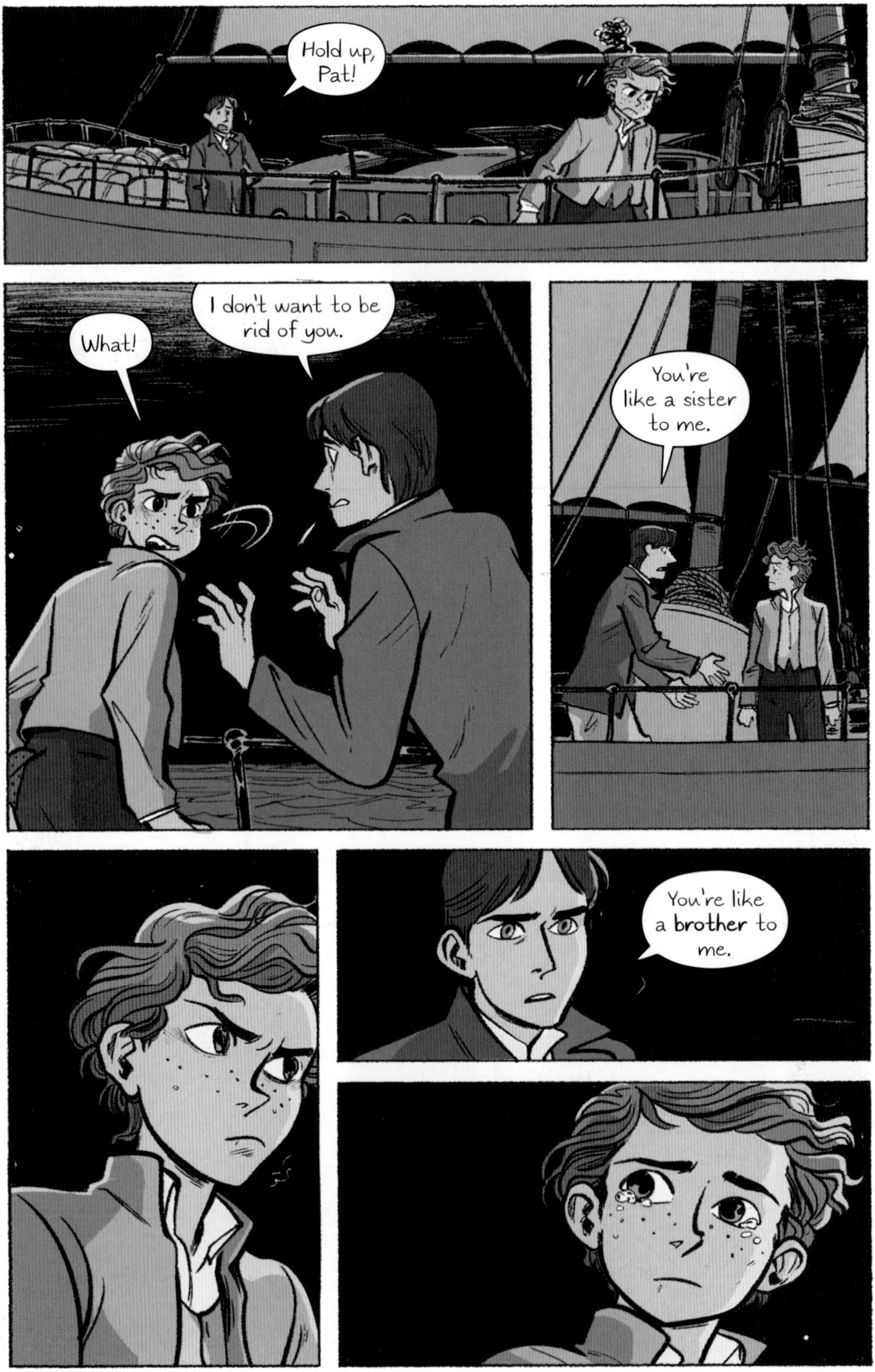
Hold up, Pat!
What!
I don't want to be rid of you.
You're like a sister to me.
You're like a **brother** to me.

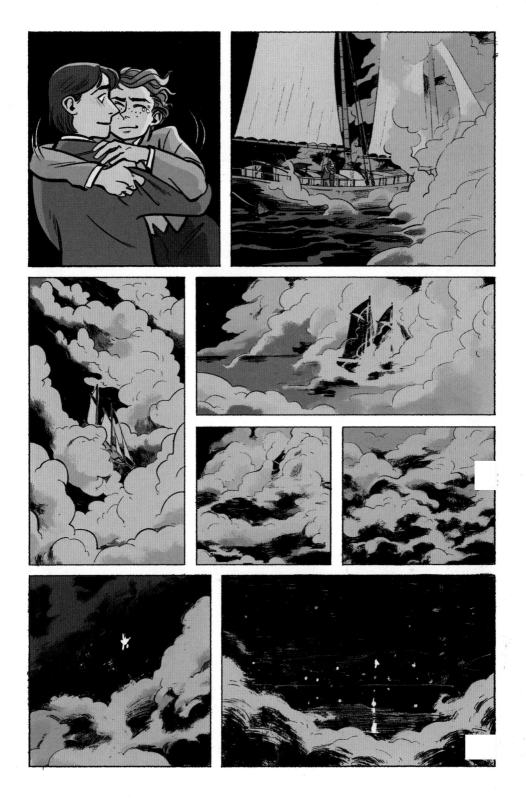

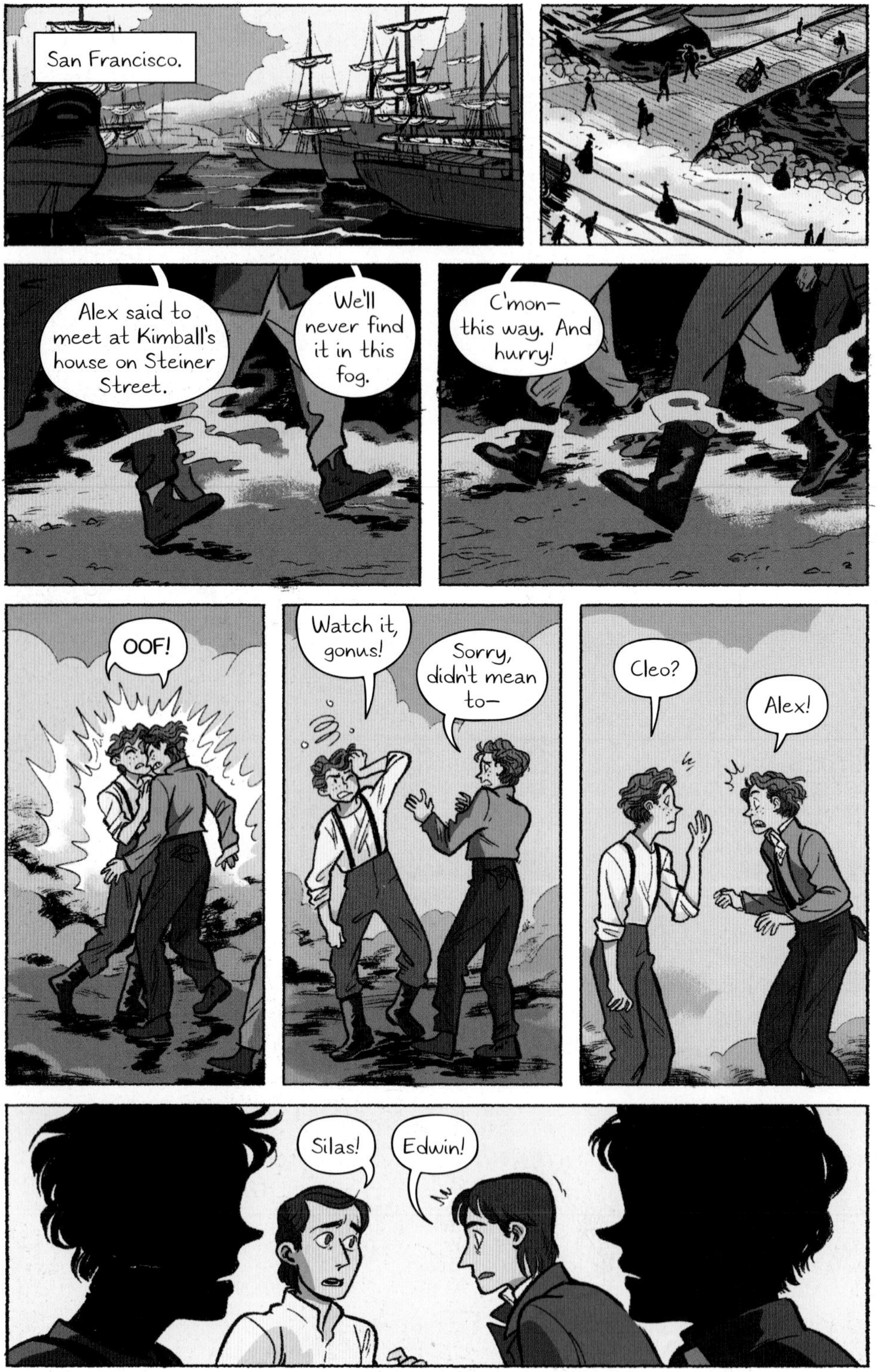
San Francisco.
Alex said to meet at Kimball's house on Steiner Street.
We'll never find it in this fog.
C'mon— this way. And hurry!
OOF!
Watch it, gonus!
Sorry, didn't mean to—
Cleo?
Alex!
Silas!
Edwin!

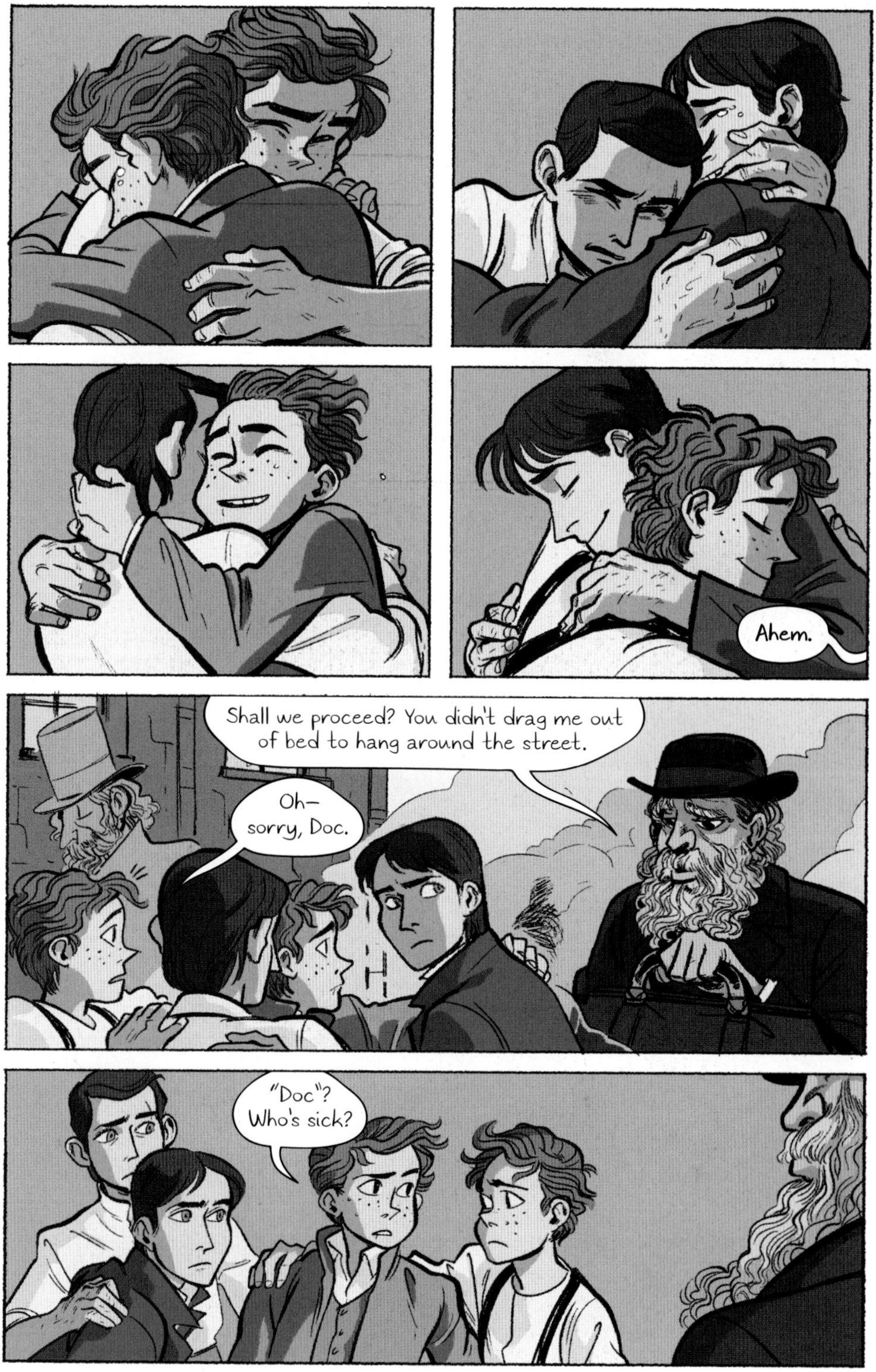
Ahem.
Shall we proceed? You didn't drag me out of bed to hang around the street.
Oh— sorry, Doc.
"Doc"? Who's sick?

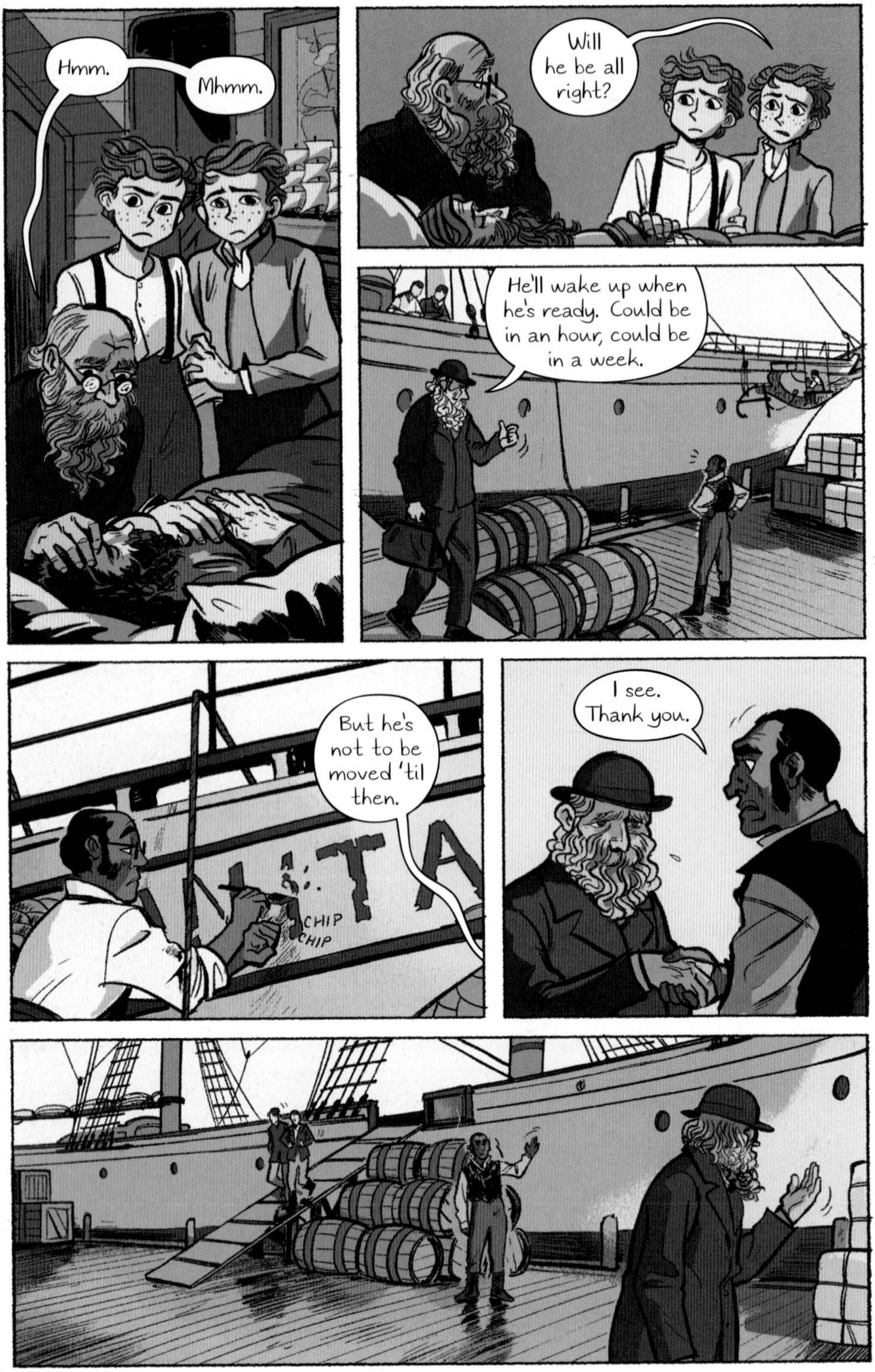
Hmm.
Mhmm.
Will he be all right?
He'll wake up when he's ready. Could be in an hour, could be in a week.
But he's not to be moved 'til then.
CHIP
CHIP
I see. Thank you.

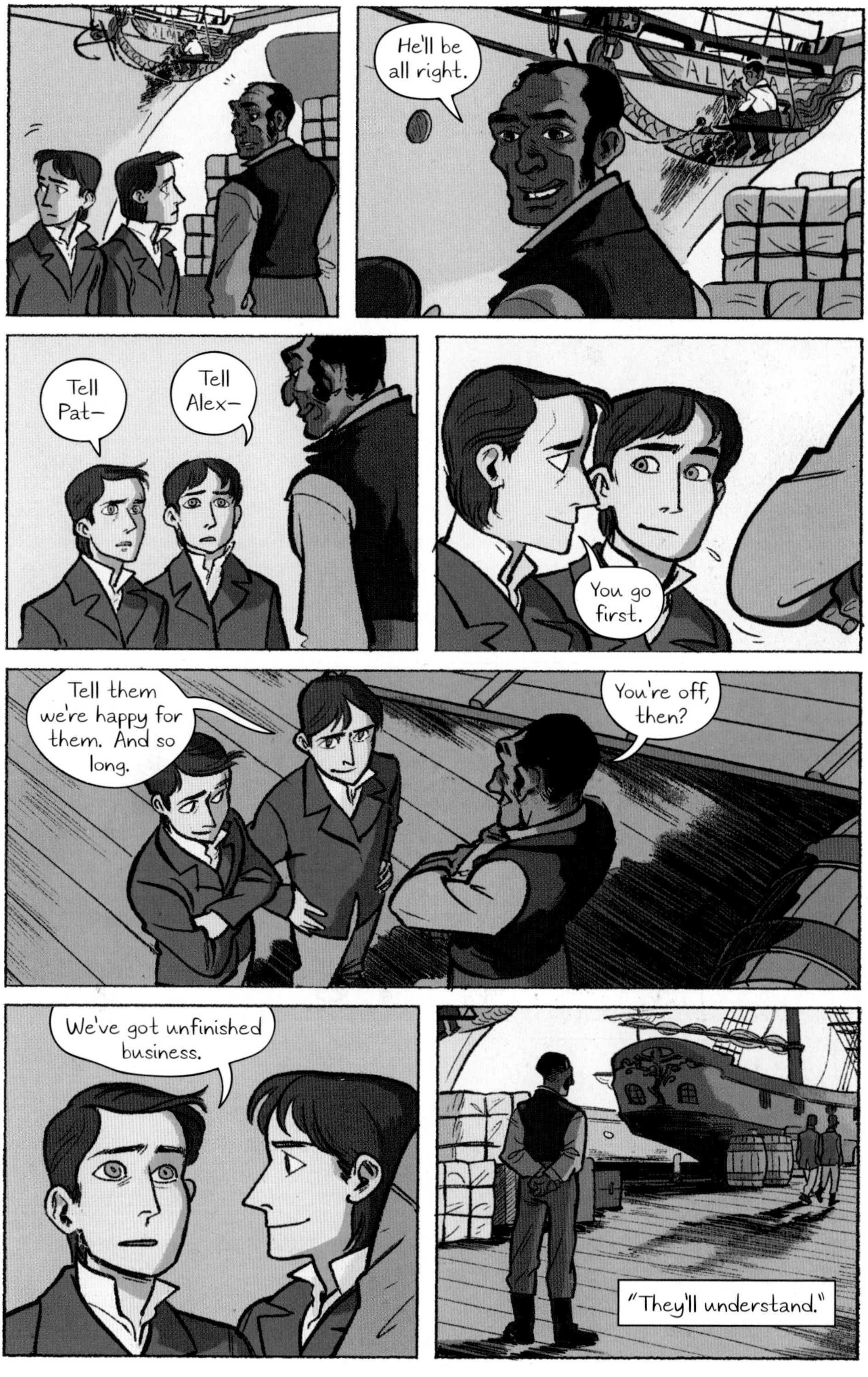
He'll be all right.
Tell Pat—
Tell Alex—
You go first.
Tell them we're happy for them. And so long.
You're off, then?
We've got unfinished business.
"They'll understand."

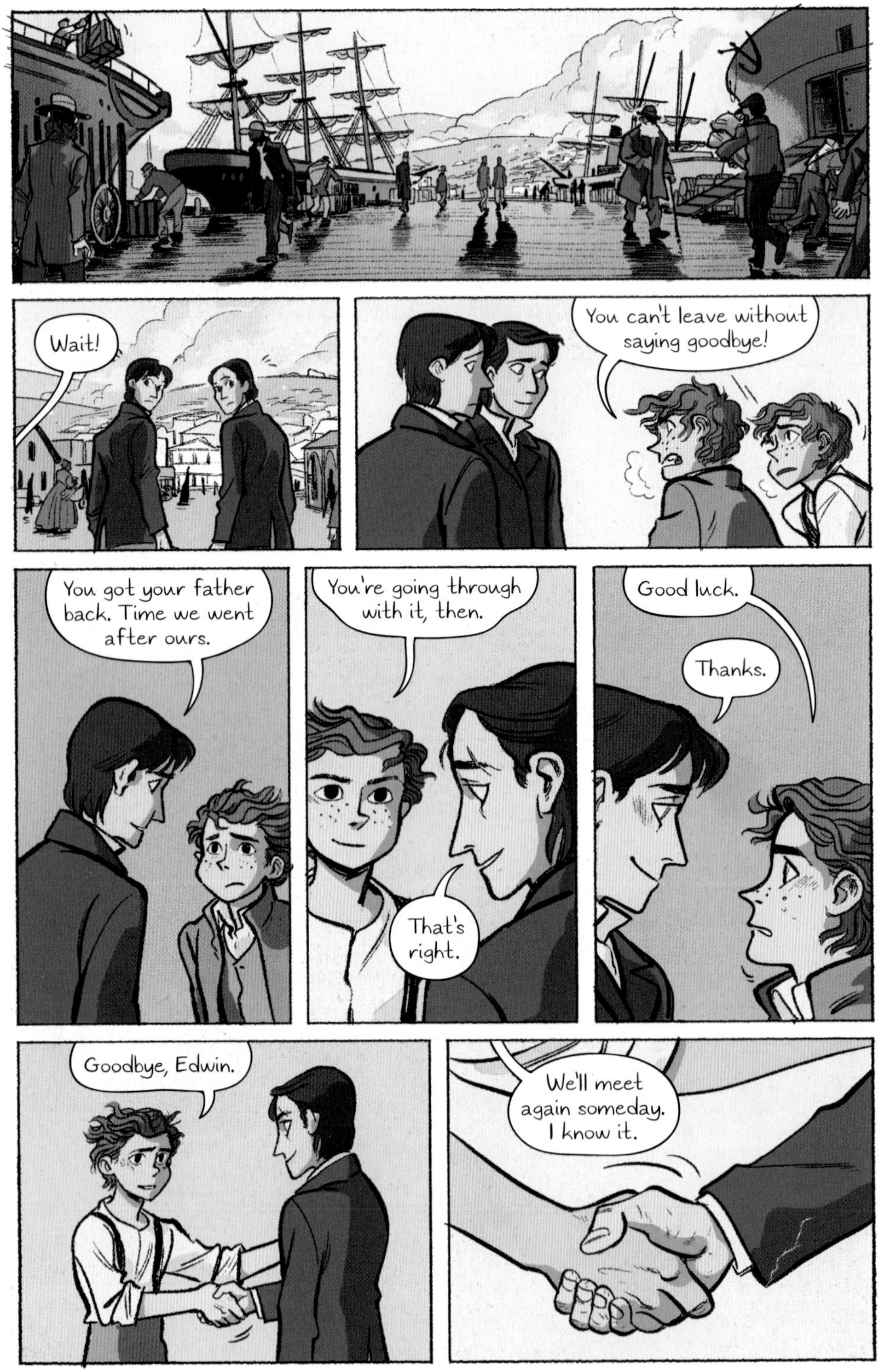

Wait!
You can't leave without saying goodbye!
You got your father back. Time we went after ours.
You're going through with it, then.
That's right.
Good luck.
Thanks.
Goodbye, Edwin.
We'll meet again someday. I know it.

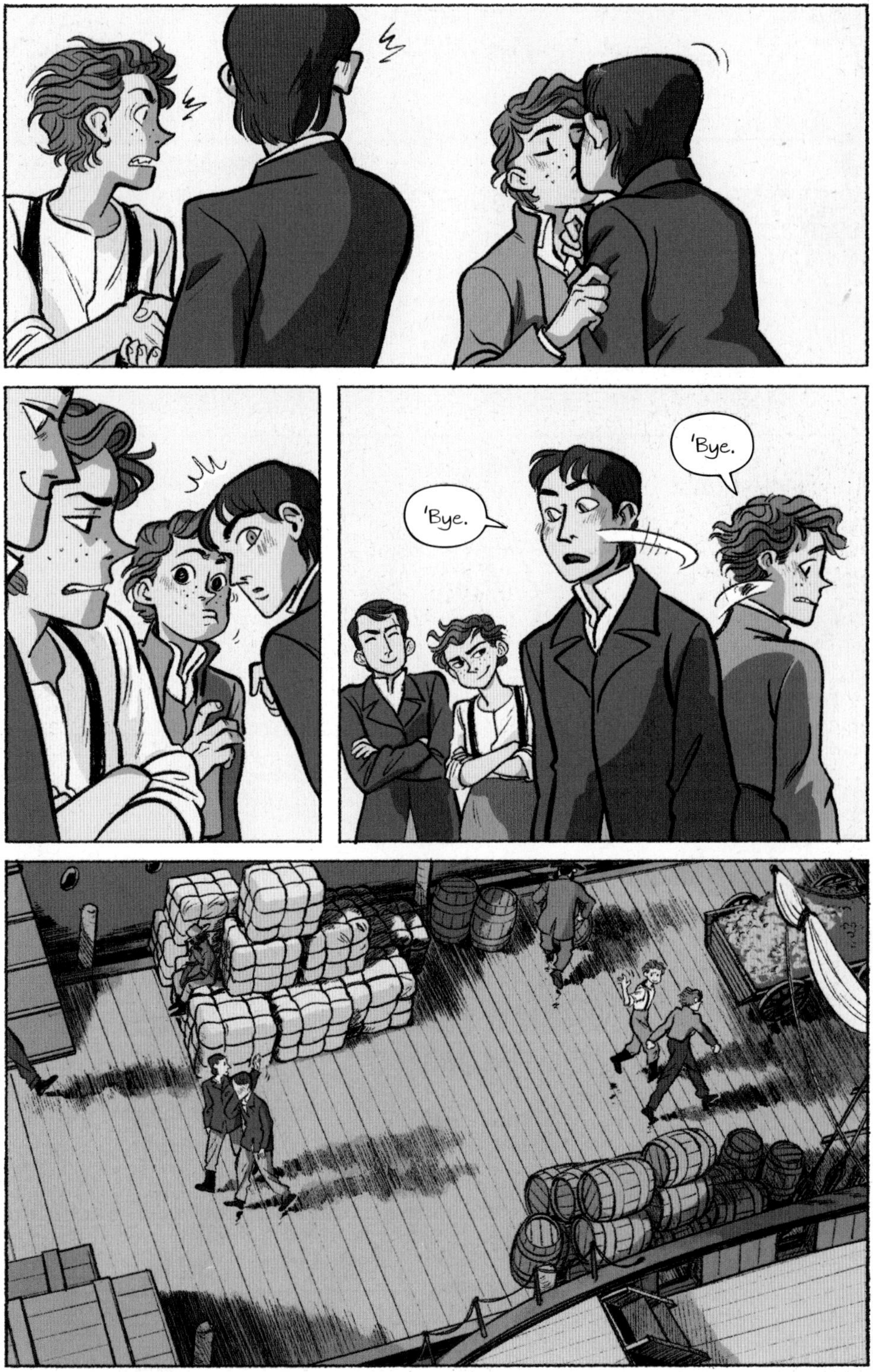
'Bye.
'Bye.

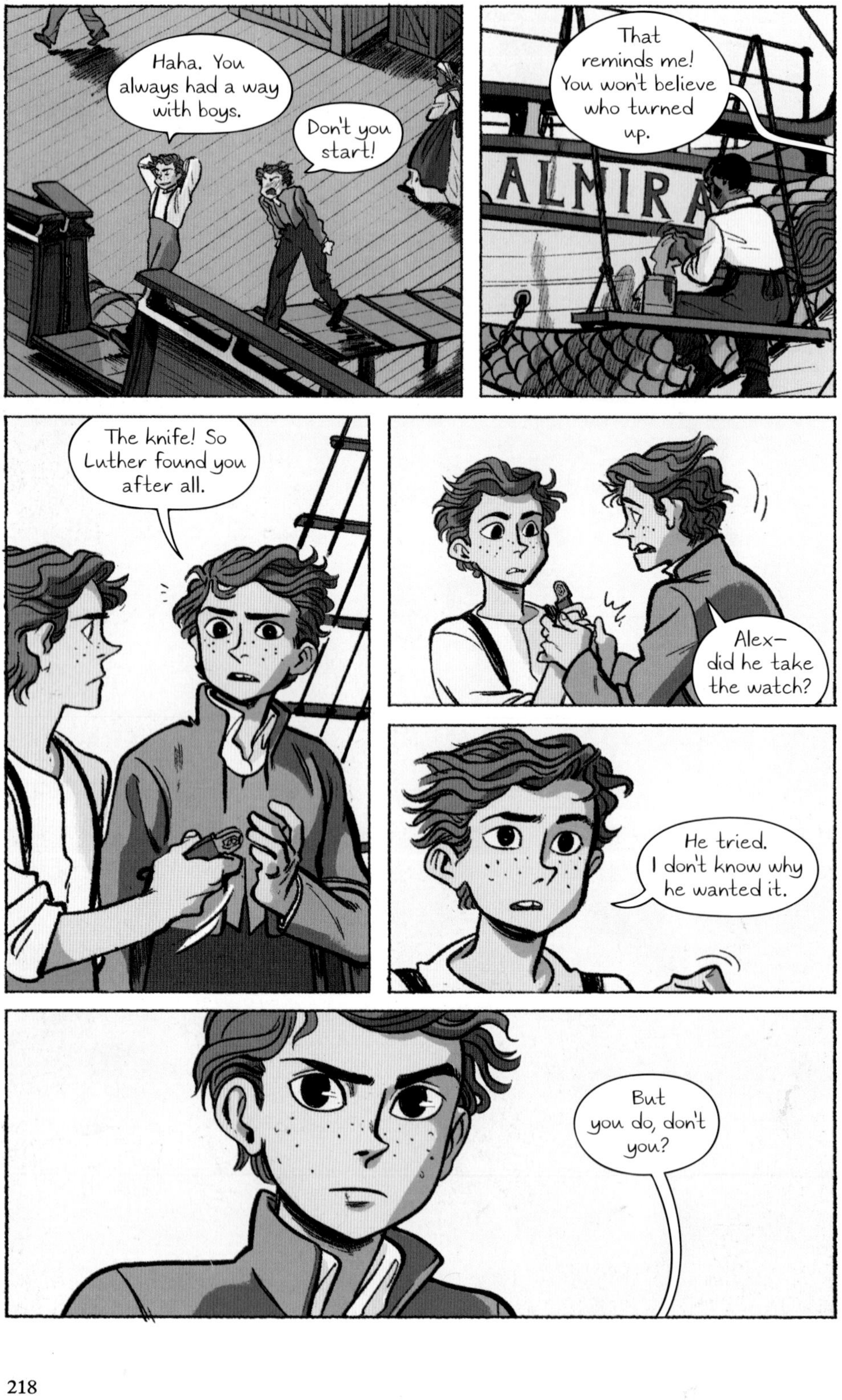
Haha. You always had a way with boys.
Don't you start!
That reminds me! You won't believe who turned up.
ALMIRA
The knife! So Luther found you after all.
Alex— did he take the watch?
He tried. I don't know why he wanted it.
But you do, don't you?

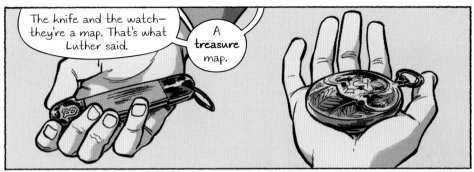

The knife and the watch— they're a map. That's what Luther said.

A treasure map.

We came all this way to seek our fortune when there was a fortune in our pockets all along.

But who cares about treasure when we've got Father back?

"I just want him to wake up."

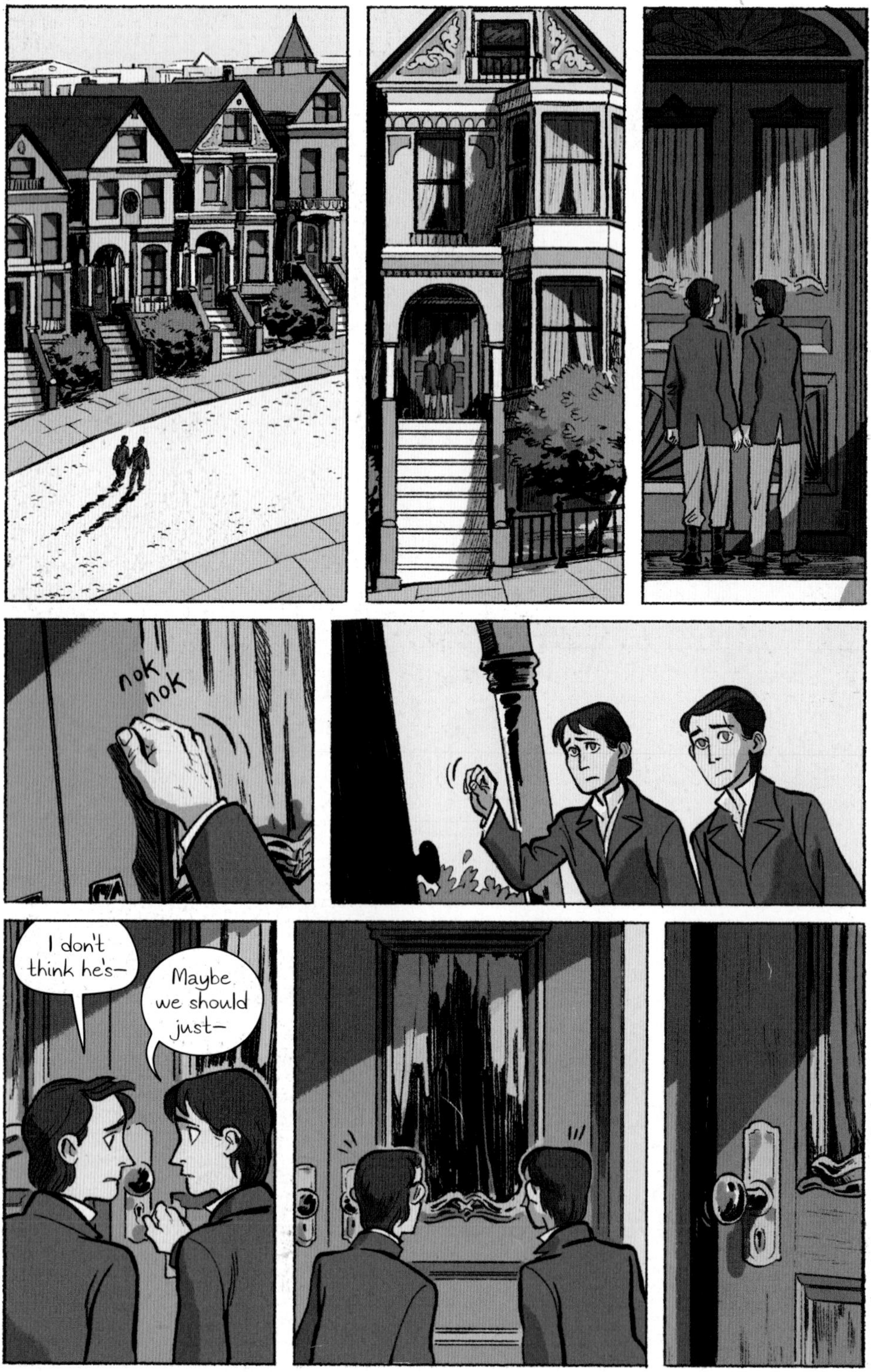
nok
nok
I don't think he's—
Maybe we should just—

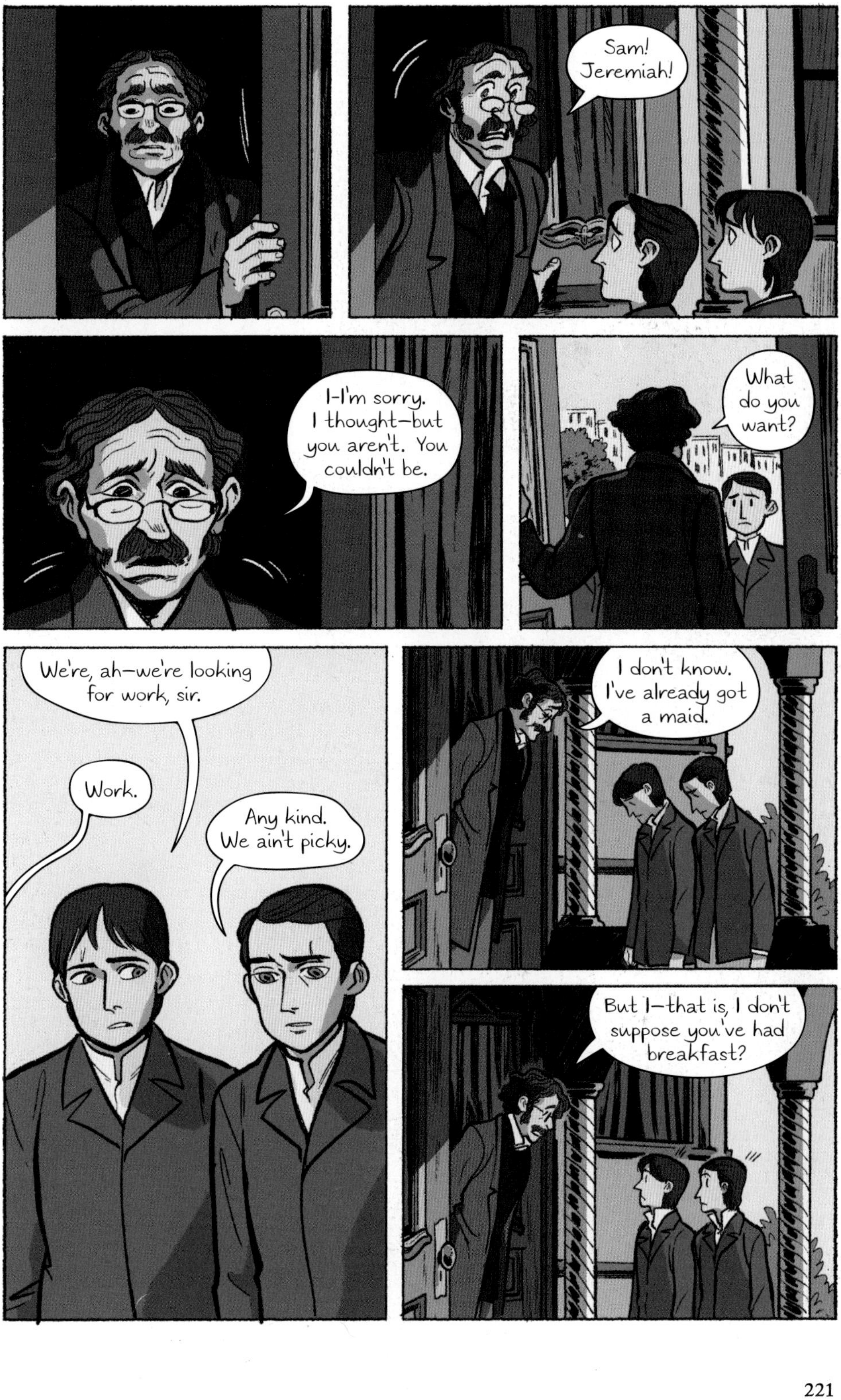
Sam! Jeremiah!
I-I'm sorry. I thought—but you aren't. You couldn't be.
What do you want?
We're, ah—we're looking for work, sir.
Work.
Any kind. We ain't picky.
I don't know. I've already got a maid.
But I—that is, I don't suppose you've had breakfast?

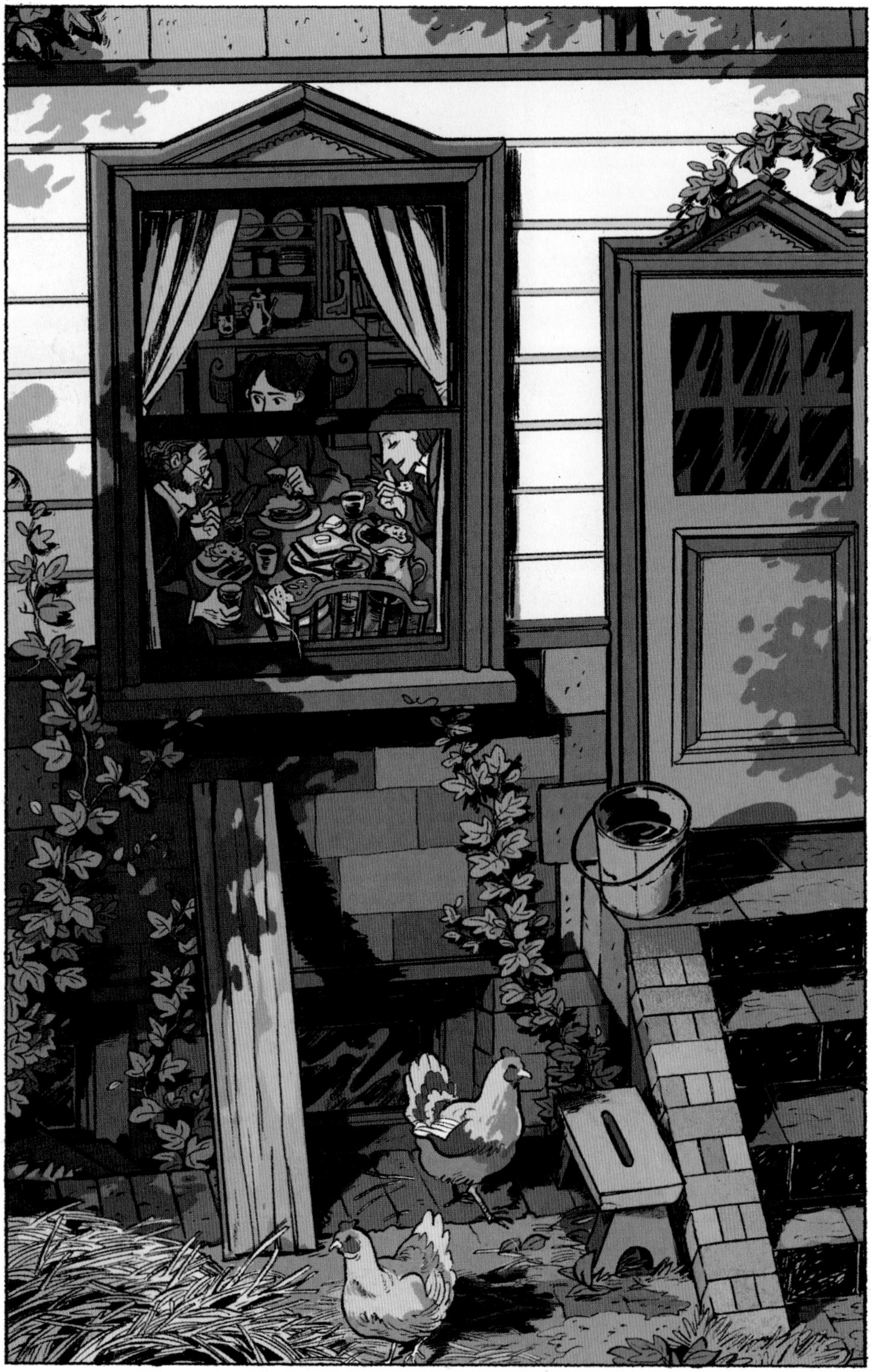

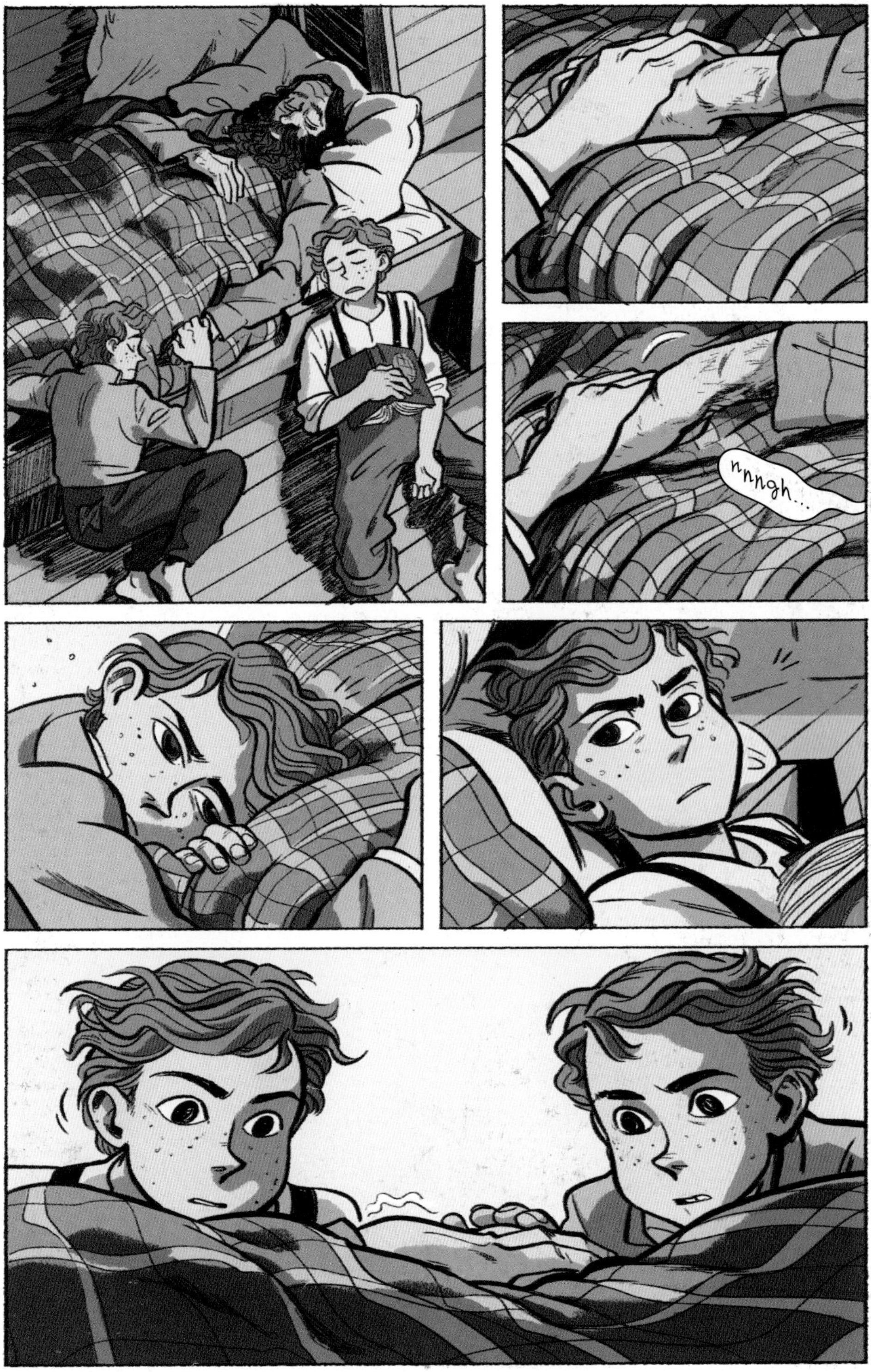
nnngh...

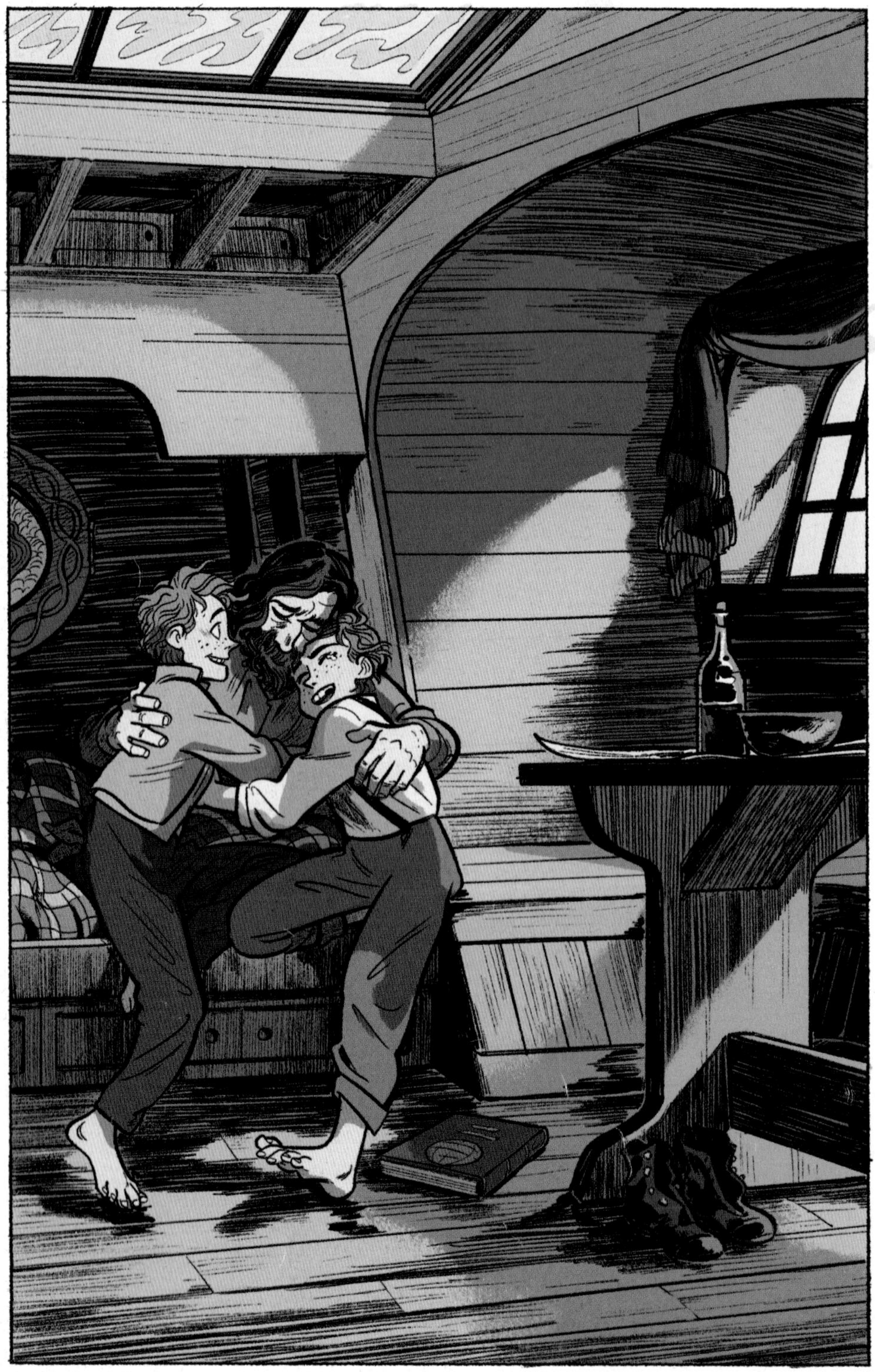